I0598248

LAST EXIT BEFORE TROLLS

Book 1

Swimming with Toasters

By

Nigel Cole

First published 2014 in Great Britain
by The Falston Gazette Press
www.falstongazette.co.uk
Copyright © Nigel Cole 2014

10 9 8 7 6 5 4 3 2 1

Cover Artwork and Toaster Shark logo copyright © N. Cole 2013

ISBN 978-0-9930624-2-1

For Lyn, without whom my life would be incomplete.

For Howard, without whom this book would have remained incomplete.

For Anchovies, without which all pizzas would be incomplete.

'Another?' It was more growl than question.

The shabby wretch at the bar looks up and nods. 'Don't s'pose there's any chance of a clean glass this time?'

The barman doesn't respond, but the wretch knows he isn't getting a clean glass. There isn't a clean glass in this place. There isn't a clean anything. The floorboards are thick with unidentifiable filth, the windows so heavily encrusted with grime that the orange-pink twilight only sneaks in where panes are smashed or missing. The front door clings gamely to the doorframe by one rusty hinge, though it's a singularly pointless gesture as the frame has parted company with the doorway and leans against the opposite wall, framing half a dartboard and a blackened plant pot topped with molten green plastic.

The refilled vessel slams down and the wretch tosses a handful of coins onto the bar. The hefty grin on the barman's face hints at an overpayment. The hefty cudgel at his side hints that there won't be any argument about it. The purveyor of ales takes up the requisite position of a man with a question, leaning forward and resting his sideboard of a chest on his folded arms. After lengthy scrutiny of his customer with the single large eye

5

in the middle of his forehead, the barman asks his question.

'So, you're the new king then?'

His name was Bladder.

Well it wasn't really, but Barry Ogleby had been called Bladder for as long as anybody could remember, and he was neither proud of it nor did he despair of it. He had no more opinion about his pseudonym than a dog or a cat had of the names chosen for them. In his youth he had been 'Barry Big Bladder', in keeping with the schoolboy's fondness for alliteration, but now it was just Bladder. Indeed, all but his closest friends were unaware that Barry *was* a Barry. Even the man himself was given to long pauses during introductions.

The origins of a nickname are often obscure, but not so with Barry. Barry Ogleby was called Bladder because of an organ now legendary in the locale for its capacity and the power of its output. Reliable witnesses claim to have seen Barry down in excess of thirty pints during a real ale festival at The Queen's Arms without once availing himself of the facilities. Only after eleven hours of uninterrupted drinking did he request, using hand signals and simple vowel sounds, that somebody assist him to the temporary amenities that Jack the landlord had hired for the day. Bladder was in there for over an hour, after which nobody else felt inclined to use it, all of the grass on the pub's back lawn yellowed and died, and Jack didn't get his deposit back on the Portaloo. Always one to look on the bright side, Jack was pleased to discover that his lawn was never again troubled by moles.

Bladder stumbled through Falston Wood, his capacious organ once again loaded to beyond the maximum fill level. This time his voidance was to be a premeditated act of sabotage. A useful urination. A piss with a purpose. Bladder was on a quest for vengeance, but more of that later.

Since 'the beer festival incident', Bladder's social status had been elevated to that of 'local character', joining the ranks of such singular types as Mad Ned, the village idiot, and Bobs, the three-legged dog, though this new standing in the village didn't afford Bladder the same grudging acceptance of public urination that was afforded Bobs. For the residents of Falston-on-Wold, bodily functions were like sex and falsifying tax returns. Such things were simply not discussed. Acceptable topics of conversation were the weather, the village fete, and the Christmas lights, but only after the second Tuesday in November. These were subjects that could be talked about openly because they were nice.

Everything in Falston-on-Wold was nice.

The sunsets were just a little pinker in Falston. Red squirrels and other native wildlife positively abounded in Falston Wood. The flowers were larger and more fragrant if they bloomed in Falston, and the bees that visited them seemed to hum happier tunes than other presumably less fortunate bees.

To complement all of this loveliness there was the River Wold, which for countless centuries had supplied the village with clean, slightly effervescent drinking water. Water that had been superior to any that Jack stocked at The Queen's Arms for the benefit of 'them that knew no better'. In the end he'd stopped ordering any of 'the posh stuff' and had taken to refilling the expensive designer bottles with river water during thrice-weekly 'black op' raids that tended to be short on stealth and long on clinking glass and vociferous cursing. Nobody in Falston drank the water that came out of their taps. That was only for bathing, washing, and the flushing of excrement into other people's water supply. Falston's *official* primary water source was Stoneley reservoir, which supplied the same chemically treated, possibly carcinogenic water that the rest of the country so enjoyed. Nobody was going to use that stuff to make their morning cuppa when there was Wold water available. For those involved, which was pretty much everybody, the daily bottle filling sessions at the riverbank had become an important community ritual. Then, overnight, everything had changed in Falston-on-Wold. The night of the 'accident in inverted commas'.

Those more knowledgeable in the ways of the world knew that things would eventually have to change in Falston. 'One of these days they're going to realize there's money in the Wold,' was how one of these knowledgeable types had put it. A sound statement, but one that was open to interpretation. Bladder's interpretation had been more literal than most, resulting in him bemoaning the demise of his metal detector to anybody prepared to listen. One of those who did listen was the sales rep from Whitworth's brewery, who was puzzling over shelves groaning with expensive bottled water when the invoices attached to his leatherette clipboard confirmed that The Queen's Arms hadn't ordered any for months. Bladder's confused tale of treasure seeking in the Wold had made the man from the brewery's eyes glaze over, and even the patrons on the other side of the lounge bar had heard that penny drop.

The very next morning the white van appeared. It had arrived just before dawn, and the only one to see it arriving was Mad Ned, who was often to be found in strange places at strange times. Ned had been hunched under Falston Bridge when the van pulled onto the riverbank, and by keeping to the deep shadows he was able to stay out of sight and watch the goings on. A man in a white coat got out of the van and made his way down to the river, where he filled a large plastic container with water. On his way back to the van the man had slipped on the muddy slope, the full container rolling over to Ned's hiding place, as these things are wont to do. Ned gathered up the heavy canteen and had made his way over to the procumbent water thief.

'Oh, goo-goo-good morning,' said the prone one, looking a touch muddy of the lapels.

'The most succulent cuts of cod in a light and crispy batter,' said Ned. Mad Ned, in case you needed reminding. Mad Ned, who was proper mad, and not just one of those colourful local characters whose 'madness' amounted to wearing a slightly odd hat.

The man in the white coat was quick to realize that Ned was in greater need of help than he, but the fellow seemed harmless enough. A muddy hand was extended in Ned's direction. 'Could you hel-hel-'

Ned backed away. 'Avoid contact with skin and eyes. If symptoms persist consult a physician.'

'All right, no-no-not to wo-worry. I'll ma-ma-manage.' The man in the coat struggled to his feet unaided, though at the expense of what little dignity he had left.

Ned handed over the water container. 'Call now for a no-obligation brochure and one of these lovely free gifts can be yours,' he said, inexplicably.

'In-indeed. Tha-thank you.' From force of habit, the man in the coat reached into a pocket and produced a business card, which rather undermined Ned's opinion that the man was up to no good. Generally speaking, skulduggerers don't hand out business cards whilst skulduggerying. Ned sniffed at the object. 'The only one with Aquaspheres?' he said as he reached out and took the innocuous little card that would be his return ticket to sanity. For the briefest of moments Ned's thumb had brushed against the hand holding the card. It was such a light collision that neither man felt it, but the aftershocks were going to shake the foundations of the world.

'Well goo-goo-goodbye then,' said the man in the coat before hurrying back to the van and driving away. At speed.

Mad Ned didn't move for a long time. The daily business of the village had begun, and it had continued around him while he'd stood there on the bank of the Wold. Nobody had approached him and nobody passed comment on his being there. He was Mad Ned, and that had been explanation enough.

The sun had been close to its zenith by the time Ned moved. He pushed the unexamined business card into the pocket of his trench coat and took a deep breath as he tried to come to terms with being part of a whole new world.

Because Mad Ned wasn't mad any more.

Well, not *as* mad.

One month later the regulars at The Queen's Arms found themselves staring en masse at an official looking document pinned to the dartboard. In ever more hushed tones the dreadful communiqué was digested, discussed, cogitated and dissected at such length that the extra takings at the bar easily qualified as the silver lining that Jack knew had to be there somewhere. So it was the next evening and again the one after that. Each night The Queen's Arms heaved with patrons eager to empty their spleens into Jack's till, but for all of the talking and heated debate, nobody really *said* anything. Then one night somebody did say something, and a most unexpected somebody it was too.

'They can't do that.' Mad Ned, with the first coherent statement he'd made in living memory, had distilled the debate down into its purest form.

'Ned's right, they can't do that!' All eyes turned to the new speaker, veterinary Phillip Morrison, generally referred to in the village as just Morrison, though he had no idea why. He had chosen the path of melodrama and was, unnecessarily for a man of six foot seven, standing on a chair. 'They just can't do it!' repeated Morrison before attention waned. There was muttered approval, and one cry of 'we should do sum'it 'bout it' from behind the bar. Jack had already calculated the potential fiscal gain to be had from geeing this lot up a bit, so for the next four hours gee them up he did, though he was glad when last orders approached as he was running short of both gusto and accents.

When 'twas time to ring time, the newly created Falston-on-Wold Action Committee took stock of their situation. President-elect Morrison addressed the assembled from his lofty perch, where he had remained all evening because his dodgy knee had seized and he couldn't get down. 'So, ladies and gentlemen, if I may sum up then, we the Falston-on-Wold Action Committee shall be taking all possible steps to prevent the creation of this so-called bottling plant ...' — so-called because that's what it was, but saying 'so-called' gave the place a nicely sinister overtone — '...which will be doing nothing short of raping our village, our countryside, and our river.'

'Hear! Hear!' came the enthusiastic response, with no prompting from Jack this time. The barman had lost interest in rabble rousing and was glancing nervously at his watch as he edged towards the front door. The local constabulary had little to do on their infrequent visits to Falston, so catching the entire population of the village engaged in after-hours drinking would have been a coup.

'Now,' continued Morrison 'I think it is time I passed a motion.' There was a pause whilst everybody waited for Bladder to comment, but even he thought that one was too easy. 'I believe that the heinous notice makes mention of a public forum at which all objections and grievances can be aired. Could somebody please confirm the exact date of said hearing so that we may plan our assault?'

It fell to Edna Peevey, eldest stateswoman of Falston, to provide the requested information. The ancient one hunted for her reading glasses, struggled to her feet, and then made her way slowly towards the dartboard. She scanned the notice, line-by-line, top to bottom, before giving a nod and removing her glasses from the tip of her beak nose.

'Yesterday,' she announced with some satisfaction, before adding a rather more considered 'Oh!'

'Bugger!' quoth the new president-elect as his legs went through the seat of the chair.

So ended the first and only meeting of the Falston-on-Wold Action Committee.

For Sale: Deluxe electric stair lift. Boxed, never used, complete with manuals, accessories and attachments. Unwanted competition prize. Contact Mrs. E. Peevey, Rose Bungalow, Falston-on-Wold.

The Falston Gazette Classifieds

Enthusiasm for a confrontation with the brewery had waned on discovery that they had already missed the fight. For an Action Committee they were an apathetic bunch, and it had been left to a distraught and limping vet to find out what had transpired at the public hearing that the public had neglected to attend.

In anticipation of a day of frantic phone calls, Morrison's surgery had remained closed on the morning following the meeting, leaving the small and furry of Falston to endure their suffering privately. It was a quiet day anyway. The only visitor to indulge in a spot of doorknob rattling was Edna Peevey with her cat Mister Snickles, and as that moth-eaten creature had received the delicate attentions of a taxidermist some twenty years previous there was little Morrison could have done for it. Bobs showed up as well, but his call was of a different nature.

Morrison did spend most of that day on the phone, and he lost count of the times he repeated the phrase 'yes, I know we should have been there', but the more calls he made the more apparent it became that things weren't as bad as he'd anticipated. True, the brewery had been granted planning permission for a 'discreet and ecologically sound' bottling plant, but no decision had been made regarding the brewery's plan to return the Wold to its 'original' course. That 'original' course was to the west of the village, and coincidentally exactly where the new bottling plant was to be situated, but sometime in the past the river had been redirected by a clever arrangement of huge stone steps. Nobody had come up with a definitive explanation of how it was done, but over the years lots of woolly men in bearded jumpers had come to Falston to have a go.

It had cheered Morrison greatly to discover that there might still be a fight to be fought. The brewery had won round one, but what point would there be to building a water bottling plant if there was no water to bottle? They could build elsewhere along the river, but elsewhere The Wold tasted like ditch water. Not unreasonable, given that The Wold was some water in a ditch. No, it was only here in Falston that the brewery could find what they wanted. With a hop in his step and a jaunty tune in his head, Morrison left the surgery to head for The Queen's Arms before there was further talk of bolting horses and stable doors. The day had been an unexpectedly good one.

'Bugger!' said he as he slipped in the deposit that Bobs had left on the doorstep.

Those who believe in little green men hidden in the Arizona desert will read much into the timing of the 'accident in inverted commas', but the patrons of The Queen's Arms saw nothing sinister about the six burly truck drivers who arrived just before closing and calmly announced that they had ''ad a bit of an accident'. The accident wasn't in inverted commas yet. They came later, as did an assortment of official types in suits who filed on to Falston Bridge to stare at where the river had been before six burly truck drivers had crashed six burly trucks of burly boulders. Those that had them wrote things on their clipboards with expensive looking gold pens. Those whose status didn't warrant suits or gold pens braved the mud and took samples of it in large test tubes. They had all worn the same emotionless expressions as they went about their work. Work that was being observed from the riverbank by The Falston-on-Wold Action Committee.

'I see this as an opportunity.' Kevin Flask, the village's only estate agent, was first to break the stunned silence.

'An opportunity to get covered in mud if you don't bloody shut up.' Taff the Bus was speaking for all those who would happily have lobbed Kevin into the Wold, even if it wasn't there. Why everybody in the village disliked him was a question that Kevin wrestled with every day, so it's a pity that he didn't spot that Taff's next statement was a concise and accurate answer to that question.

'You can be a right prat sometimes, Thermos.' Ieuan Williams, Taff the Bus to friend and enemy alike, was unique among the residents of Falston in that he had chosen his own nickname rather than have one thrust upon him. An ample Welshman, he had thought it best to pre-empt the whole nickname business with a choice that was more indicative of his national heritage than of his proportions. To make sure the name stuck, he modified his official Tulston and District Transport name badge using letters cut from The Falston Gazette. Everybody who saw the badge felt compelled to read it as they assumed it was some kind of ransom demand.

'Where's all the fish then?' Bladder had a point. There was not a single fish, living or otherwise, to be seen. There wasn't a single anything. There were no dry-docked ducks, no otters playing in that endearing manner that otters are wont to do, and no voles doing whatever voles did that was no doubt equally endearing though on a smaller scale. The river had gone, and its entire ecosystem had gone with it.

'No supermarket trolleys either.' Sara Hagget's observation was more startling than Bladder's, even allowing for the fact that Falston didn't have a supermarket. Sara Hagget was Falston's resident 'lady of easy virtue'. Spectacularly easy, if rumour and lavatory wall graffiti were to be believed. Sara was well aware of the existence of the rumours, mostly because she'd started them. She'd written the graffiti as well, though she had no idea what most if it meant as she'd copied it from a catalogue that Thermos had accidentally left in the pub. According to the cover, that innocuous looking catalogue had contained 'a huge range of exciting and stimulating toys'. Jack had flipped through it, as he was on the lookout for an educational gift for his nephew's fourth birthday. Jack got the education and his nephew got a card with a fiver in it. 'And where are the condoms?

Aren't there supposed to be condoms?' Randomly dropping condoms into conversation was one of Sara's preferred devices for reinforcing local opinion of her, but on this occasion the question was sincere. Sara Hagget had been depositing condoms filled with wallpaper paste into the slow moving waters of the Wold on an almost nightly basis for the better part of four years, and it seemed to her that there should be a few of them left down there somewhere.

Over the course of that day all of the residents of Falston had made an appearance at the riverbank, stood, and stared. For most of them, five minutes of standing and staring had sufficed; for others standing and staring for an hour or so had felt more appropriate. Only Bladder, Edna Peevey, Taff the Bus, Sara Hagget, and Morrison, had opted for the full day's standing and staring. Thermos had lasted until lunchtime before deciding it might be apposite to pop into his office and calculate how much damage this 'opportunity' had done to property prices. Jack had arrived just before opening time, hauling a barrow of empty water bottles. He'd stood, he'd stared, he'd added a 'bloody 'ell!' to the general discussion, and then he'd left. Everybody else had just come and gone with little or no comment. No, this hadn't been a day for long speeches and heated debate. It had most definitely been a day for standing and staring.

'Standing and staring is getting us nowhere. I'm going to see if any of that lot,' Morrison nodded in the direction of the officialdom on the bridge 'can tell us anything about this mess.' With that he strode off as purposefully as his limp would allow.

Pongo Smythe emerged from Falston Wood and smiled as he surveyed the Wold valley laid out below him. Pongo looked forward to these visits, as had his father before him. Making much use of his gnarled walking cane, he made his way down the gently sloping hillside and onto a narrow wooden footbridge that was being struck repeatedly by a strapping fellow with a large hammer. The man was either making repairs or he really didn't like bridges.

'How goes the day, John Bostwicke?' hailed Pongo as he stepped on to the rickety structure.

'Well bless my soul, 'tis Pongo Smythe. Has it been a month already?' The burly one pulled himself to his feet and extended the hand without the hammer in Pongo's direction.

Pongo took the hand and shook it vigorously. 'Indeed it has, John, indeed it has. As well you know, for your toil this day is surely for my benefit.'

The man laughed a booming laugh that echoed back from the hillsides. 'Aye, you have me there, Pongo Smythe, though if truth be known by next month there may be no need of a bridge here at all.'

Pongo frowned. 'For why, John Bostwicke?'

'Look for yourself, friend. The water dropped nigh on a foot this last night. Close to the same since dawn.'

Pongo did look for himself and was not best pleased. 'Oh dear me. This will not do. This will not do at all. Does Garthang know of this?'

John shook his head. 'Nay, I've not seen that one for many a day.'

'Then, John Bostwicke, I would ask that you seek him out and tell him of it. And once 'tis done I would also ask that you send a rider to Tulston and make the news known to The Guild.'

'The Guild?' John Bostwicke took up the frowning. 'Can you not inform them on your return?'

'No, John, I shall not be returning there for some time I suspect. I fear I have a very different journey to make before I see Tulston again. And I must leave directly.'

'So soon? Will you not take ale with me in The King's Arms?' John had been thinking of ale all morning, and Pongo Smythe was always generous with the contents of his purse.

'No John, not on this occasion, and nor should you delay. Heed my words, there is a great trouble brewing, and I must away. Good day to you, John Bostwicke.' Pongo turned on his heels and set off back across the bridge.

John Bostwicke suddenly felt very uneasy. His friend had looked worried, and Pongo Smythe wasn't a worrier.

Phillip Morrison wasn't a worrier, but he walked onto Falston Bridge as a lamb approaching hungry wolves. When it became apparent that he was heading in their direction, a small bespectacled man peeled away from the main group and moved to intercept. Staying with the wolf pack analogy, the specimen that strode purposefully towards Morrison was no Alpha male. More likely a sigma or a tau with delusions of kappaness. Beady eyes darted suspiciously around behind lenses originally designed by NASA to focus laser beams onto the moon.

'Can I help you, sir?' If the official was in any way intimidated by being a good eighteen inches shorter than Morrison there was no hint of it in his voice.

'Well I hope so. It's about our river you see-'

'*Your* river, sir?' The man smiled up at Morrison in a manner that put him at risk of getting his face caved in.

'The Wold. The *village's* river.'

'Ah, yes.' The short one pushed his spectacles firmly back onto the bridge of his nose, studied his clipboard, fiddled with the top of his gold pen, and then announced 'It's gone, sir.'

'I know it's gone! I meant what are you going to do about it?' Morrison couldn't help but wonder why the man had needed to check his clipboard to confirm the absence of the river.

'Me, sir? I'm not going to do anything about it. After all, I am but one man.' The official man's smile broadened, indicating that he had just made an official man's joke.

Morrison wasn't laughing. 'What are you, the *collective* you, going to do about it?'

'Us, sir? We're not going to do anything about it. Wrong department, you see.'

'Wrong department? There's a department specifically to deal with vanishing rivers?' Morrison was getting angry. Normally his conscience would have intervened, but his inner child had distracted it by throwing a Frisbee.

'Well, that's just it, sir. We're not entirely sure under whose remit this issue falls. We're from Fish and Game, and as you can see, well ... there isn't any.'

'Any what?'

'Any fish or game, sir.'

'Now you're taking the piss.'

'Not at all, sir.' That answered the question succinctly so the man from Fish and Game saw no reason to expand on it.

Morrison smiled, but it was a clever feint and he continued in the vein of a man who was more than a little peeved. 'I am going to ask you very nicely, and if you don't give me something positive that I can tell my friends over there I will not be held responsible for my actions. Now, what is to be done about our river, you supercilious gnome?' The supercilious gnome part probably didn't fit in with most people's definition of asking very nicely.

'I'm sorry sir. There's really nothing I can tell you at present. I'm sure somebody else will be along shortly who will be able to help you further. Now, what can I do so that you leave here satisfied?' The man decided to smile again. It wasn't one of the better decisions he'd made that day.

Phillip Morrison smiled back. 'Actually, there is one thing.'

After his short flight the man from Fish and Game hit the mud with a 'splat' that left Morrison feeling profoundly satisfied.

Later that evening came the first, and only, bottle-filling pilgrimage to the relocated Wold. The plan had been for each pilgrim to take a different path to the river and meet up in the pub afterwards to compare notes. As it turned out, identifying the best route to the river was a futile exercise because whichever way you went the water was equally undrinkable when you got there. You could boil it, filter it, or purify it with tablets, and it still tasted like you'd washed your smalls in it. Speaking of which, Edna Peevey had helpfully added that she wouldn't even wash her smalls in it because it made everything smell of burnt sausage. As the consensus was that nobody in their right mind was going to pay cash money for that stuff, no matter how quaint a bottle it came in, they had to wonder what the brewery was up to.

What indeed?

'Well?' Lord Gervais Mawlesby-Foresham, chief executive of Salsa Foods, the corporate behemoth of which Whitworth's Breweries was a minor subsidiary, sat at his huge mahogany desk and watched with disdain as a gaggle of scientist-johnnies milled about in his office. 'What's all this nonsense about then? Eh?'

The senior sycophant present made himself known. 'Well ... it's Fa-Falston, sir. Or Falston's wa-water, to be more precise. Sir.'

'What's with all the stammering?'

'Don't blame me, you chose him.'

'Yeah, trust you to pick somebody who talks with a limp.'

'Ah yes. Falston Water.' Lord Gervais allowed himself the tiniest of smiles at the thought of his salvation. For two hundred years Whitworth's Best Bitter and Whitworth's Light Ale had been the sturdiest of props, able to support any number of fool ideas the research division had decreed would be 'the next big thing'. But times were hard, and the props were creaking badly. Unless something was found to shore things up the whole bloody lot would come crashing down. Enter the now legendary Falston Water report. Low initial capital, low running costs and low recurring overheads coupled with a huge market demand equalled very big profits. Bloody marvellous reading that report had been. 'Now, Stephenson, you're not about to tell me there's a problem with this water thing, are you?'

Stephenson shuffled over and deposited two small beakers of clear liquid on the desk. The deed done he backed away as gingerly as a man in the presence of an unexploded bomb, which he was.

Lord Gervais Mawlesby-Foresham gazed down at these strange interlopers, imaginatively labelled as beaker 'A' and beaker 'B', and found himself wishing he'd stayed the extra week at his villa in Gstaad. 'Am I to assume that you want me to drink these?'

'Well ... if you woo-would ... just tuh-taste them. Sir.' Stephenson wanted the meeting over so that Lord Mawlesby-Foresham could jump on a plane and Stephenson could jump on Lady Mawlesby-Foresham, who'd never been terribly fond of either Switzerland or her husband.

As he raised beaker 'A' to his lips, Lord Gervais detected a faint odour that he couldn't quite place. Rose petals, perhaps? Certainly something of a floral quality to it. He took a sip. He took another. He drained the beaker. Falston Water. No mistaking it.

Now that he was aware of the contents of beaker 'A', Lord Gervais approached beaker 'B' more tentatively, as it was unlikely to be more of the same. It had a similar odour, but more earthy. Possibly even meaty. He took a sip and immediately wished he hadn't. After making the requisite disgusted face he spat the liquid back into the beaker.

'Good God man, that's ditch water! You could have run it through the purification process first!'

'We did ... erm ... sir. Twice. One beaker has ... wuh-water from the River Wold, as it is ... erm ... today, and the other has wuh-water extracted from the ... muh-mud samples we took from the o-o-old riverbed. Sir.'

'Mud samples? For heaven's sake man, why are you making me drink mud?'

'Go on, James. Thump him. Make the bastard bleed for us,' said an angry little voice in Stephenson's head.

Wisely Stephenson ignored the voice. 'The mud is in bee-beaker 'A', sir.'

'What!' A 'For Sale' sign appeared on the gates of Lord Gervais' villa.

James Stephenson couldn't help but smile. A sycophant he may have been, but he could do devious plotting with the best of them. Devious plotting that revolved around a beaker atop a cabinet in Stephenson's laboratory. Until somebody can produce evidence to the contrary we'll assume the beaker was labelled 'C'.

Mad Ned sat on Falston Bridge and emptied his pockets onto the wall. Ned was a smoker, so it's perfectly reasonable that he should have tobacco, cigarette papers and a box of matches. The business card we already know about, and given Ned's peculiarities there's nothing odd about the short length of string, the four sugar cubes wrapped in paper or the unpleasant looking hand-kerchief. The trillion cut emerald the size of a tennis ball might be trickier to explain, and Ned was thankful he'd never been called on to try. He stuffed all but the tobacco, matches and papers back into his pocket and rolled a cigarette as he waited for the Monday morning show to begin. It had been a weekly event for most of the six months since the 'accident in inverted commas', and Ned was always there to observe. These days it was a solitary vigil, interest in river-based shenanigans having dwindled since the news had come that the brewery had won. The Wold would remain in its new location indefinitely. The villagers weren't happy. The ecologists weren't happy. The brewery couldn't wipe the smile from its corporate facade.

This Monday morning they were late and Ned was puffing on his third butt by the time the tanker pulled up on the bridge. The men in the grubby blue overalls lowered the thick rubber hose into the mud as they always did, and as always the lowering was followed by the pumping and the muddy shlooshing and squelching.

'Why hasn't it all dried up down there then, Mister Talbot?' The two blue overalled ones leant on the bridge and stared down at the persistent bogginess below. 'And how come there's so much of it? We've had tons of the stuff away already.'

'That we 'ave, lad. That we 'ave.' Talbot, appointed leader of the blue overalled ones, removed his cap and scratched at his comb-over. His companion had a point. Back at the bottling plant there were a dozen ten-thousand gallon vats, all full to the brim with 'the stuff', but there seemed to be as much of it here now as there had been six months ago. Talbot glanced over at Ned, perhaps in the hope that he would proffer some opinion as to how a riverbed without a river could so stubbornly refuse to desiccate. Ned shuffled his cigarette from one side of his mouth to t'other but stayed silent.

With the tanker full and their surprisingly lucrative work for the day done, the two men climbed back into the cab and with a great belch of black smoke they were away. Away to the tune of miles three before Ned so much as blinked. After the blink he rolled himself a fresh cigarette and located a match. The match ignited spontaneously and Ned puffed the cigarette into life. The dead match was placed carefully on the wall and the rest of the matches arranged around it, Ned whispering all the while, the fingers of his left hand dancing as they traced out intricate symbols in the air. When he was done, Ned walked falteringly off Falston Bridge and didn't look back until he reached the boundary of the village. When he did allow himself a last view of Falston-on-Wold there was the hint of a smile on his face and a hint of a tear in his eye. Or was it sweat?

'Probably for the best,' he said to nobody in particular, and then he stumbled off the road and into Falston Wood.

As Ned vanished into the trees a pair of legs strode onto Falston Bridge. A pair of very long legs that poured down from a very short skirt into a very tall pair of patent stiletto thigh boots. The legs stopped at the point where Ned had been sitting, and beautifully long and manicured fingers tried to remove one of Ned's matches from the wall. It came as no surprise to the leg and finger owner that neither that match nor any of its neighbours would budge. Frankly there would have been more chance of moving the bridge, and she knew it.

'You daft sod, now why did you have to go and do that?' Sara Hagget raised her left hand and did a waving and whispering routine similar to the one Ned had performed. When she was done there was a flash of electric blue light, reducing Ned's legacy to a pile of smouldering ash that danced into nothingness on the breeze.

Now that we're all bang up to date, let's return to Bladder and his well-intentioned, but wholly symbolic, quest for vengeance. At that moment Bladder was as close as any man had come to experiencing the joy of childbirth and a joy it bloody well wasn't. He stumbled through the carpet of leaves and assorted biodegradable green bits, his obvious distress heightened by the knowledge that he could make the pain go away anytime he wanted. A quick unzip and the relaxation of a few choice muscles was all that stood between him and exquisite relief. But not yet. He couldn't capitulate when he was so close.

Bladder staggered out of the trees and onto the cobbled driveway of Edna Peevey's bungalow. Edna didn't own a car, yet she'd spent a fortune on that driveway so that her son and his family would have somewhere nice to park when they drove down from Nimlet, which they never did. Bladder allowed himself a moment's respite to muse on the clandestine joy of irrigating the old bag's front lawn. Then he groaned through tightly clenched teeth. If he was outside Rose Bungalow then he had just spent an agonising twenty minutes going the wrong sodding way.

Thirty minutes of loud profanity later, Bladder arrived at his destination. Ahead of him in the moonlight lay the 'accident in inverted commas' that had robbed Falston of its two greatest assets: the invigorating waters of the Wold, and the invigorating sight of Sara Hagget bending over to collect the invigorating waters of the Wold. The bottom line was that Bladder's life had been changed for the worse, and he wasn't standing for it. Not one to write letters or sign petitions, he needed some other means of giving his indignation an airing. He steadied himself and shuffled over to the water's edge, his trousers already at half-mast. This was to be a full evacuation and the increased pressure played havoc with his aim, so unzipping alone would have been too risky. Adjustments were made for wind strength and direction, angle of stance, conditions underfoot, and firmness of grip. Then Bladder let rip.

'My word! Excellent technique, sir.'

A startled Bladder spun around to face the direction whence the voice had come. Having gone well past the point of no return there was a degree of puddling as he stared in amazement at the thing that shouldn't have been there.

'My apologies for the untimely interruption, sir, but I was wondering if you could possibly furnish me with some information.' The thing that shouldn't have been there had a voice that was musical bliss, and as it spoke the moonlight broke through the trees, bathing the glade in an eerie luminescence. It was a breathtakingly picturesque scene, only marginally sullied by Bladder peeing all over it.

A cacophonous silence fell on the proceedings as Bladder stared at the thing that shouldn't have been there, and it stared back at Bladder. Then it lowered its elegant white neck, clipping at the new spring grass. Through a mouthful of greenery it said 'nice horn, by the way'.

For a moment the compliment was lost on poor Bladder. Then he looked down and beheld an erection that old Edna could have hung her washing on. Hallucination or no, Bladder was a tad embarrassed that such a creature as this should have to look upon a sight such as that. Still, a compliment was a compliment and Bladder knew his manners. 'Ta kindly. You an' all,' said he. Then he fainted.

The thing that shouldn't have been there tossed back its head, its mane billowing like smoke in the moonlight, a warm iridescent glow emanating from the spike protruding from its forehead.

'You know, I don't think I should be here,' said the unicorn.

For Sale: Forty-gallon water butt on custom-built trolley. Also small hand pump, length of rubber hose and ten demijohns with stoppers. Items in used but excellent condition. Slight smell of burnt sausage on all. Contact Mrs. E. Peevey, Rose Bungalow, Falston-on-Wold.
The Falston Gazette Classifieds

It was a Sunday. Rural communities treated Sundays with a deal more respect than Alec Gardener thought warranted; he'd once had a religious conviction, but had been acquitted through lack of evidence. On rural Sundays the roads were quiet. This rural Sunday was also warm. Warm enough to warrant driving with the roof down, which made it even more annoying for Alec that the roof of his ageing Triumph was jammed in the up position

Soft-top issues aside, Alec counted today as one of the good days. The sun was shining, he'd just found another pack of cigarettes in the glove box, and his most recent clash of heads with his 'significant other' was all but forgotten. Not that he and Claire argued much. They had long since realized that their problems could be avoided by not speaking to each other, and rarely being in the same place at the same time was an excellent way to facilitate that. This time Claire's 'place where Alec wasn't' was Daddy's new villa in Gstaad, acquired at a knockdown price from Lord somebody-or-other, and her absence had greatly simplified Alec's decision to take a new assignment for *Mystic*. *Mystic* was one of the modern breed of magazines that catered to would-be Wiccans, occultists, conspiracy theorists, and other assorted loonies. Alec had been a regular contributor since Claire had persuaded him to do an article about a group of her students who had formed a coven. For witches their philosophy was based more on smoking pot than steaming cauldron, but Alec had written the article anyway and *Mystic* duly published it. So it was that whenever some small town rag published a story about an alien abduction, a leopard sighting, or the occasional vanishing river, Alec Gardener was dispatched to interview the relevant inebriate. He wanted to believe this rubbish, but his natural cynicism kept getting in the way, and so far he hadn't seen anything to convince him that it wasn't a load of old codswallop. Still, these little trips got him out into the countryside and away from the idiots in the city. Not that the countryside didn't have idiots, but at least they were free-range idiots.

The silence that befell The Queen's Arms' lounge when Alec walked in was a fair indication that strangers had novelty value in these parts. He made a self-conscious dash for the bar, and as if by magic the barman appeared, wiping a perfectly dry pint glass with a grubby tea towel, as is a barman's wont. Alec took one look at Jack and knew instinctively that the impending conversation was going to be a toughy.

'Afternoon.' Alec put on his most cordial and non-threatening smile.

'Arf'noon,' replied Jack, practicing his West Country.

'I'd like a pint of your best bitter, and do you have any rooms available?' From experience Alec knew that the local pub was the best bet when it came to finding cheap accommodation in these backwaters, and it greatly simplified finding one's bed after a pint or six.

'Aye, that we do. 'Ow long yer'll be wanin tut stay tharn?' said Jack, laying it on a bit thick.

Once he'd deciphered it, Alec considered the question.

'Just tonight and tomorrow night should be enough.' It would be a rare story indeed to hold Alec's interest for more than a day.

Jack studied the stranger as he poured a pint of best and tried to remember where he'd last seen The Queen's Arms' guest book. Handy that he'd given the back room a decent going over with a duster not six months ago. Jack caught sight of Alec's car parked opposite the pub window. Definitely not from the brewery this one. Probably one of them international playboy types he'd read about. Jack's suspicions were confirmed when Alec handed him a twenty pound note.

'Sorry, I haven't anything smaller.' With that twenty gone Alec didn't have anything at all.

Jack smiled broadly as he opened the till and tried to remember where notes went. *Nothing smaller*. He'd often dreamt of having customers who said things like that. *Have one yourself, barkeep*. That was another good one. *Of course I'll do that for you, Jack darling* was his favourite, but that was an altogether different dream.

'Yer'll be wanin sum'it to eat arfer yer drive no dart.' Jack was regretting the accent, but had talked himself into a corner, so to speak.

'No, that's fine thanks. I'll just drink this and then I think I'll take a quick nap.' Alec knew better than to eat at a village pub until he'd witnessed somebody else doing so first, and the locals didn't count: over time they might have built up a tolerance, possibly even immunity.

Jack's disappointment ran deep; a man with nothing smaller than twenty pound notes and he didn't want to eat? Though there was some consolation to be found in the knowledge that they hadn't discussed the room rate yet. 'Yer gort ernie bags t'bring int den?' Jack's accent had departed the West Country and was heading in directions unknown.

'Just the one suitcase and a laptop, I'll bring them in myself.'

Jack nodded. He hadn't been suggesting otherwise.

'A lap what?' Taff the Bus was after a refill, and while he waited for Jack to do his sacred duty he felt it only polite to butt in on the conversation.

'A laptop,' Alec repeated for the benefit of the rotund Welshman.

'A laptop? What's one of those then?'

'It's a small computer.' A large gulp of Whitworth's Best Bitter went down Alec's throat as he was overcome by the need to finish his pint in a hurry.

'And it attaches to your lap then, does it?' Taff knew about computers. They had some in head office.

He'd never been to head office, him being just a lowly driver and all, but he'd seen pictures.

'Not exactly. It's more that you can-' Too late. Taff had formed an opinion and nothing Alec said now would change it.

'Well, there's clever. A computer that attaches to your lap. Comes on some kind of special belt, does it?'

'What's that?' Bladder had appeared alongside Taff, in the hope that somebody would take pity on his empty glass.

Alec stared mournfully into his beer, the chances of getting that nap disappearing faster than the head on his pint.

Oh, the horror! The horror! Alec Gardener lay sprawled on the bed, half awake and half dressed, staring up at the slowly rotating ceiling fan as he struggled to find a coherent thought. His head told him that he'd drunk too much. His grating breaths told him that he'd smoked too much. No doubt there would soon be a letter from his bank, voicing heartfelt disappointment that he'd spent too much. He hauled himself to his feet and completed the undressing process that he'd started eight hours earlier. Then he selected a new part-laundered ensemble and draped it over his aching frame before letting his thoughts turn to breakfast.

Three doors down from the pub was Sid's Café. Alec had oft wondered if being named Sid made a man more predisposed to running a cafe, and if so why could they never came up with original names for their establishments? In fairness to this particular Sid, he had fully intended to dub his eatery *The Call of the House of*

Rasher until he'd discovered that the bloke with the paintbrush charged by the letter. Following a short and penitent visit to the bank, Alec purchased a plate of warm cholesterol and read the brief for his assignment. Not that he needed to, as all of the stories he'd heard the previous evening had centred on just one subject—Whitworth's new water bottling plant. Colourful stories they'd been, with lots of effing and blinding, but for all of that colour the end result was rather dull. It was filler. The sort of story he was asked to do when there wasn't enough advertising booked for the next issue. The second page of the brief was usually reserved for the list of useful contacts, and for this assignment the short-list was as short as they get. Just the one name.

Some bloke called Stephenson.

Outside Sid's Cafe a crowd had gathered. As is the way of the crowd it had started with just the one person, that one person being Edna Peevey. She had been in an advanced state of agitation because, for the first time in living memory, she didn't have Mister Snickles tucked under her arm. She was joined by Thermos, who had witnessed her distress and gone to check if the distress was death related, and if so could he sell their house. Then Morrison, who had been limping to morning surgery, stopped to see if he could help with whatever it was that Edna and Thermos might need help with. Sid had popped out to see if anybody fancied a bacon sandwich, as he couldn't help but notice that nobody had any. Bladder, who'd been standing outside The Queen's Arms waiting for Jack to open up, caught the phrase 'bacon sandwich' drifting on the wind. He made his way over, just on the off chance that the word 'free' was drifting about as well. Jack had stuck his head round the door to see why Bladder wasn't there, and on spying the gathering outside the cafe he'd strolled over to see what all the fuss was.

Taff was the first to witness the chase, and he was so troubled by it that he opted to close his eyes and count to ten, just to confirm that he'd seen what he thought he'd seen. The Tulston and District omnibus had destroyed both the bus stop and a post box before Taff had reached five, at which point he opened his eyes and applied the brakes. He came to an abrupt stop, the front of the bus coming to rest in a space that had previously been occupied by the estate agent's front window. It was then that others became aware of the chase. Edna came over all peculiar and had to sit on the pavement. Thermos, who had previously shown no inclination towards being of a religious bent, crossed himself. Bladder did something he hadn't done since he was four years old. What happened to Jack's body chemistry at that moment is unclear, but he would later discover that his perspiration had dyed his string vest mauve. Morrison staggered back into the cafe doorway, reversing into Alec Gardener on his way out to see what all the banging and crashing was about.

'What's going on?' asked Alec.

' .' Morrison's mouth moved but no sound came out.

As no explanation had been forthcoming, Alec looked around to find one for himself, and he too became witness to the chase. 'The cat and the dog?'

Morrison stopped trying to make his mouth work and just bobbed his head up and down.

Alec knew that he was missing something. Cats and dogs were interesting enough, if you liked that sort of thing, but to his thinking not interesting enough to detract from a bus remodelling a high street. 'Erm ... what's the big deal, exactly?'

Sara Hagget, newly absorbed into the periphery of the expanding crowd, answered Alec's question. 'I think you'll find that everybody is a little freaked because the cat's a zombie and the dog has grown a new leg.'

Alec turned to face Sara and their eyes met. He kept his gaze locked there because it would have been impolite to look at any of the other places he wanted to. She was gorgeous. She was perfection. It was, as they say, a moment.

The moment ended as Mister Snickles and Bobs did another fly-by.

Stephenson hung up the phone on his huge mahogany desk and frowned. A deep frown it was too. He had hoped his first interview would have been with *The Financial Times* or *The Economist*. Hell, even *The Guardian* would have done. But *Mystic*? What was *Mystic*?

'They're snubbing you, James. I think you should make them pay for their short-sightedness,' said an angry little voice in Stephenson's head.

He had agreed to do the interview. He may never have heard of *Mystic*, but apparently it had a decent circulation, so lots of people would hear of his genius.

'You tell 'em, James. The world really needs to know how brilliant you are,' said voice number two.

Professor James Stephenson MSc PhD agreed. Was it not he who had discovered, albeit accidentally, that a single drop of the original Wold water, extracted from the conveniently self-replenishing mud of the riverbed, would purify more than fifty gallons of the foul liquid that was flowing into the plant's siphoning tanks? And was it not he, devious bastard that he was, who had withheld this pertinent information until there was an opening in the company worthy of his talents?

'Actually, that was my idea,' came voice number three.

An opening in the company *had* appeared. An opening created by the departure of the previous owner of Stephenson's impressive desk. He hadn't been appointed chief executive of Salsa Foods—there were other more devious bastards already higher up the ladder than he—but he had ascended several rungs in a single stride.

Stephenson leant forward and pressed the talk button on his intercom system. 'Miss Selby, would you come in when you have a moment?'

'*Told you I could fix his stammer,*' said voice number four.

Enter Stephenson's secretary (and Stephenson was planning to).

'*Oh, goody,*' said voice number five. '*Playtime.*'

Alec hung up the handset and the little screen on the payphone in The Queen's Arms helpfully displayed exactly how much change it wasn't going to give him. He would have called this Stephenson person on his mobile, but it didn't work in Falston. Probably a good thing, given that the mention of his laptop had resulted in Alec having to give a full account of its evolution from Charles Babbage onwards, and his knowledge of the life of Alexander Graham Bell was sketchy at best. It had taken several coins of the realm, and some serious telling of porkies regarding the magazine's circulation, but Alec had triumphed and Stephenson had agreed to the interview. Alec would be able to give *Mystic* their story of big business against the little people, but he was starting to suspect that the little people themselves made for a much better story.

The little people were all sat around in the lounge bar, treating their collective shock with medicinal pints of best and packets of pork scratchings. Jack had been so afflicted with an attack of the heebie-jeebies that he'd heard himself announce that drinks were on the house, and it had so exacerbated his condition that he'd gone for a lie down in the cellar.

Alec scanned the faces in the bar and was disappointed to discover that the pretty redhead he'd met outside was not availing herself of Jack's generosity with the ale and pig bits. It was probably for the best; things may have been at a low ebb with Claire, but it was a tad early for him to be assuming that the tide wouldn't come back in. Happily ever after and other such tosh. Of course if he'd known that he was never going to see Claire Thompson again then he'd have been all over Sara Hagget like a libidinous rash.

'Mind if I sit here?' Alec felt it was time to talk to the little people again, and to that end he selected the biggest little person in the room.

'Eh?' Morrison looked up from his barely touched pint and shrugged as Alec took the seat opposite him at the table.

Alec would have preferred a more verbose response. One involving words. 'Thanks. Could do with a drink myself, but it's a bit early in the day for me.'

'Oh.' This time Morrison did have a more verbose response, he just couldn't be bothered with it.

'You're the vet here in Falston, aren't you?'

'Aye.' Morrison sucked at a pork scratching and grimaced. He couldn't see the appeal of them, but Jack had drawn the line at free peanuts. 'You?'

Alec only needed an 'ee' from Morrison and he'd have the full set. 'Alec Gardener,' said Alec Gardener as he extended his hand for shaking purposes. 'I'm a journalist.'

Morrison gave Alec's hand a quizzical look. He knew he was supposed to do something with it, but he couldn't remember what.

'Do you mind if I ask you a few questions?' His years of journalistic experience had taught Alec that 'asking questions' was a good idea if he wanted to 'find things out'.

'Feel free. The name's Morrison. Phillip Morrison.' Morrison finally took and shook the hand that Alec had been wondering what to do with next.

'Very glad to meet you, Phillip Morrison.' Alec hoped he was glad, but so far he didn't have much to go on.

'You too. Sorry about that a moment ago, I was miles away.'

Lucky you, thought Alec. 'So what was all that about out there?'

Morrison decided now would be a good time to make inroads into his pint of best. Two sizeable gulps and a solid belch later, he spilt the metaphorical beans. 'Well, the thing of it is,' Morrison dropped his voice to a whisper 'that looked like Bobs and Mister Snickles out there.'

The big secret was out, and to Alec it meant both bugger and all.

'Sorry, that probably means bugger all to you, doesn't it? The point is that until this morning Bobs only had three legs, and Mister Snickles hasn't moved a muscle in twenty years.'

'Lazy?'

'Dead.'

'Oh.' Alec gave that some thought. 'I think I will have that drink now.'

There was no sign of Jack, so Alec went behind the bar and poured himself a pint and another for Morrison. On his way back he had to dodge Bladder and Taff, both speeding to the bar to partake of this new self-service policy.

Alec delivered his cargo and sat back down. 'So it was a cat and dog that looked like this Bobs and Snickles?'

'They call him *Mister* Snickles,' Edna Peevey interjected from the next table, proving that she could throw in a film reference with the best of them. Edna was on the sweet sherry—Sid had cottoned on to the relaxed serving regime and had furnished her with a bottle—'and in case anybody is interested,' the ancient one continued 'I put Mister Snickles in his basket when I went to bed last night, same as I always do, and when I got up this morning he was gone.'

Morrison ignored Edna and gave the bubbles in his pint some serious scrutiny before responding to Alec's question. 'I'm sure that must be it, of course. But I would have sworn it was our Bobs. After all, I'm the one who had to remove his leg.'

'And a shoddy job you must have done if the bleedin' thing's grown back.' It was Bladder's turn to add his tuppence worth as he returned to his table, lovingly clutching a tray laden with full pint glasses.

Before Alec had time to dwell on just how mad everybody was, Jack emerged through the trapdoor. 'Oi! Get out, ya bugger!' The landlord took two purposeful strides towards Taff, intent on evicting the interloper from the sacred ground that was the business side of the bar, but it went badly awry as his feet became entangled in a box of pork scratchings and he swan-dived back through the open trapdoor with an athletic grace that surprised all those who witnessed it. Less of a surprise was the tirade of obscenities that issued forth from the cellar once the ground had broken Jack's fall. At least the profanity was a fair indication that he hadn't done himself any serious injury. Probably.

Jack's departure did a grand job of lifting the dark cloud that had settled over the lounge bar, and the laughter didn't abate until the man himself re-emerged from the cellar and made a general announcement to all there assembled.

'My thanks for the concern. You're all barred, ya sods.'

Nobody in the pub on that Monday morning was paying any attention to the fact that it *was* a Monday morning, which also meant that yet again they weren't paying attention to the Monday morning ritual. For the first time in many months, not even Mad Ned was there to witness it.

Up pulled the tanker.

Down went the hose.

Slurp went the mud.

''Ere, what's that?' went Talbot, recurring leader of the blue overalled ones.

After Morrison had convinced Jack that it might not be prudent to bar all of his paying customers, even if they hadn't been paying, a calm had fallen over the lounge bar of The Queen's Arms. Of course, it *couldn't* have been Bobs and Mister Snickles. Now the very suggestion of it made them laugh.

Nervously.

The logical plan was locate the beasts in question and perform a positive identification, and it was a plan on which they were all agreed.

Well nearly all.

'No bloody fear,' was Bladder's sincere response. 'I've seen that *Pet Sematary*.'

The other absentee from the search party was Alec Gardener, who had his interview with Stephenson to prepare for. There had been some raising of eyebrows at the mention of the bottling plant, and Alec had retreated into a dark corner of the bar before any of the dirty looks could escalate into dirty comments.

Outside in the car park Morrison, Thermos, Taff the Bus, and Sid, had collectively suggested to Edna Peevey that she head home in case the cat turned up. As the new consensus was that the beast *wasn't* Mister Snickles there was no reason it should make for Rose Bungalow, but there were plenty of good reasons to send Edna there. With half a bottle of sweet sherry negotiating her antiquated plumbing, and the remainder stuffed under her coat, Edna was only too happy to accede to the request.

Inside the pub, Alec was staring at Bladder and Bladder was staring at an empty glass. Jack had confiscated the full ones and was back in the cellar, meditating on the problem of getting seven pints of best bitter back into the pressurized barrel from whence they had come.

'Another drink?' Alec directed the question at Bladder, as there was none other to direct it at.

'Thanks. I'll have a pint of best with a large rum chaser and a couple more packs of them pork things.' If people were going to ask stupid questions then Bladder saw it as nothing short of his duty to take the piss.

Alec wisely waited for Jack's return before ordering the drinks, and on seeing the barman's dishevelled condition at close quarters he felt compelled to add 'and have one yourself, landlord.' Jack was so happy he nearly cried.

Bladder downed his rum in one mouthful so that he could give the fresh pint his full attention.

Then Bladder and Alec Gardener had a little chat.

A very interesting chat it was too.

Eight hours earlier, and an indeterminate number of miles away from Falston-on-Wold, there was a traffic jam. Not a very big traffic jam yet as it was three in the a.m. on a Monday, but it was destined to become the biggest one in Britain's jam-packed history. Already there were blue flashing lights, yellow flashing lights, even a few orange flashing lights. Bathed in all of this diverse illumination were almost as many police as there were traffic cones, which was a lot.

'What, both of them?' Mike Carter stared an incredulous stare at the damp traffic policeman whose face was at his passenger door, his peaked cap directing a stream of rainwater through the open window and into the car's ashtray.

'I'm afraid so, sir. You could be stuck here a while.'

Mike didn't doubt it. Dartford Tunnel and Dartford Bridge closed. Either one was bad enough, but *both* of them! In a traffic jam was not somewhere Mike wanted to be. The somewhere Mike did want to be was on the other side of the Thames, and now he could go neither under nor over it. 'Why?' It was a truly heartfelt question.

'I'm afraid we don't have all of the details yet sir. At the moment all we know is that both the bridge and the tunnel will have to remain closed until further notice.'

Until further notice. The words were pointy daggers thrusting into Mike's brain. 'Until further notice' meant he was stuck here until somebody else arbitrarily decided he didn't have to be stuck here any more. 'Until further notice' was better than 'indefinitely', but worse than 'soon'. Mike hated it when somebody else was in control of his destiny; it made him angry, and you wouldn't like Michael Carter when he was angry. Or so he liked to think.

'Oh c'mon, you must have *some* idea when we'll be moving again?' Mike put on his most authoritative and subtly persuasive voice—he hadn't sold more Zuz-Zuz water softeners than anybody else in the eastern region for nothing—but the soggy gendarme had already moved on.

Mike slumped back in his seat. As he watched black gunge dribble from the passenger ashtray, he knew what he had to do. Sitting doing nothing wasn't the Mike Carter way. Sitting doing nothing wasn't Mike Carter being all that he could be, because Michael Carter was a man above other men. One of the elite.

Yes, Michael Carter was a paintballer.

Builds character does paintballing. Some very odd characters.

Ten minutes later Mike Carter was crouching beside his nearside front wheel, being all he could be. He was being it in his best camouflage combat fatigues and a black woollen balaclava, clutching his corrosion resistant aerospace-grade aluminium with wear-resistant-Teflon-finish-on-all-internal-parts paintball gun. Perched on his forehead were a pair of Russian military night vision goggles, with the built in infrared illuminator and the comfortable padded head straps. Mike negotiated the stationary traffic with some fine examples of bobbing, weaving, and dashing, and as he approached the tollbooths at the entrance to the tunnel he did a diving roll into some convenient shrubbery. Mike had used the Dartford Crossing every day for seven years, but he'd never seen it looking like this. All of the lights on the approaches were out, and both the bridge and tunnel were in almost total darkness. There were lots of police cars, and consequently lots of police, but luckily for Mike they were all milling around near the tollbooths. As far as he could tell there was nobody on the approach road or at the tunnel entrance. I think that should have told him something.

With more surreptitious bobbing and weaving, Mike skirted around the edge of the last booth and made for the slope down into the tunnel. At one point he passed only three feet from a pair of armed officers, but they were doing little more than getting wet and they failed to notice as Mike slipped by. For his part, Mike completely failed to notice the armoured car and the military types with the rocket-propelled grenade launchers. All in all, Mike's was the bigger failing. In his position I'd have been asking the Russian army for a refund on the goggles.

The tunnel lights were out, and with their limited range even his battery-powered eyewear was having difficulty piercing the very blackest bits of the blackness. The tunnel was full of dark. It was also full of smell; it stank something rotten, and twenty feet further into his intrepid venture Mike found part of why. A sort of arm part. The arm part was followed in quick succession by three leg parts, another arm part, a torso part, two head parts, and then by a gore splattered guitar. As the aforementioned body parts looked to be unrelated, Mike ruled out the possibility that a three-legged, two-headed busker had exploded in the tunnel. Mike had a strong stomach, and because it was strong it could throw a lot of sick a long way. I think it best not to dwell on that as Mike's balaclava only has eyeholes. The sounds of muffled retching echoed back from the depths of the tunnel, and with them came a sort of shuffling sound. Mike stared out into the darkness and watched in horror as the sort of shuffling sound became a sort of shuffling shape. Everything looked grey-green through Mike's night vision goggles, but it so happened that the shuffling shape actually was grey-green. And naked. And huge. So huge that it had to stoop to negotiate the tunnel. It was basically a man in that it had legs and arms and a head, as well as other prerequisite man parts, but then there were hairy bits, warty bits, dangly bits, and bits that Mike couldn't think of suitable adjectives for. And there was the stick. More of a club really. Sort of a big cudgel. Actually it was a tree. The branches had been torn off and it had been subjected to some rudimentary tapering to make it more club-ish, but it was a tree nonetheless.

'Grrrr!' went the huge grey-green thing. What it lacked in enunciation it made up for in volume.

The sound galvanized Mike into action, his well-honed survival instincts taking over as he dropped to one knee and got off five shots in rapid succession, all of them hitting the target precisely where Mike had intended. He'd been certain that there was no chance of bringing the creature down, so he'd gone for the arm holding the club—if he couldn't drop the beast then perhaps he could make the beast drop its weapon. Five staccato spluts produced five yellow blotches on a bicep the size of a Volkswagen Beetle. Very pretty, and nice grouping too.

'Yes!' exulted Mike as he congratulated himself on his marksmanship.

'Grrrr!' went the beastie.

'Oh bum!' went Mike as it finally struck him just how ineffectual his paintball gun was always going to be against this thing. Just after that struck him so did the thick end of a tree.

And so Michael Carter departs our story. The man who had single-handedly revived the fortunes of the Zuz-Zuz Water Softener Company had always seen himself as a man of substance, and now others would see him as a man of substance as well.

That substance being pâté.

*Reward: offered for safe return of missing semi-antique
ginger tomcat. Last seen Falston high street. Stitching
coming apart in places and tail held in place with a safety
pin. Answers to the name of Mister Snickles. Contact
Mrs. E. Peevey, Rose Bungalow, Falston-on-Wold.*
The Falston Gazette Classifieds

Professor James Stephenson watched Alec's arrival on
one of the many small monitors built into his office wall.
He watched the red Triumph pull up at the main gates.
He watched Alec park beside a pristine white 1973
Corvette Coupe, identical to the one that Bill Bixby used
to drive in *The Magician.* He watched him walk into
reception. He watched him talking to the receptionist. He
watched him get into the lift. He watched him in the lift.
He watched him get out of the lift. He watched him walk
across to Miss Selby's desk. He watched him talking to
Miss Selby. He watched him trying not to stare at Miss
Selby's ample cleavage. He watched Miss Selby press a
button.

The intercom box on Stephenson's desk crackled
into life. 'There's a Mister Alec Gardener here to see you,
Professor Stephenson.'

'Show him in please, Miss Selby.' Ah, let the games begin.

Miss Selby escorted Alec into Stephenson's office. There were introductions and handshakes.

'He's touching us! We on the move again?'

'Not this time, I like it here.'

'Yes, let's stay put. I think we can have some fun in here.'

Another round of assorted platitudes concluded with Alec seated at Stephenson's impressive looking desk, and a pot of coffee being delivered by Stephenson's impressive looking secretary.

'And some chocolate biscuits. I just fancy a chocky bicky,' said another new voice in Stephenson's head.

'And some chocolate biscuits, Miss Selby.' Stephenson had learnt that it was best to go with the flow as far as his voices were concerned. So far the rewards for doing exactly what they wanted had been substantial.

'Stop thinking about food, we've got things to do.'

'I'd like to do Miss Selby some more.'

'Do you mind if I record this?'

It took Stephenson a few seconds to realize that the last voice wasn't inside his head. 'Sorry?'

'I said do you mind if I record this?' Alec waved a small tape recorder around in a 'with this' sort of way.

'Oh, yes, of course. Feel free.'

'That's nice; why don't we have one of those?' It was a seventh voice. Much as Stephenson appreciated all that his voices had done for him, he was beginning to wonder how much more of this he could take before his head exploded.

'Thanks. Wouldn't want to misquote you later.'

'We'll make him pay if he does.'

'Yeah, we'll really cook his goose.'

'If the plural of goose is geese, why isn't the plural of moose meese?'

'Oh, shut up.'

'If you could just tell me a bit about what you do here, Professor Stephenson ...' Alec paused for Stephenson to say 'call me James', which he didn't '... and then I'll ask a few of the more specific questions that I have jotted down here.'

The highlight of the next forty minutes of Alec's life was the return of Miss Selby with the coffee and biscuits. Not that Alec got a look in with the biscuits. Stephenson just kept on shovelling them into his mouth, in those rare moments when he wasn't spouting the gospel according to Whitworth's Breweries. He wasn't forthcoming with a single titbit of information that Alec couldn't have read in one of the glossy corporate publicity brochures in the outer office. Alec would normally have picked a few up, for appearances' sake, but there had been cleavage.

'... which pretty much brings us up to date vis-à-vis this grand building in which we now sit. Right, that's my sermon done. I believe you said that you have some questions for me?'

Alec turned from the blank page he hadn't written on during the interview to the equally blank page where he didn't have any prepared questions. 'Thank you, yes. Tell me, Professor, what would you say to the people who are dubious about just how accidental the accident that redirected the River Wold to this plant was?' Alec hadn't intended to be so blunt, but never mind. It would be interesting to see what sort of reaction he got.

'Let me twat him one!'

'No, go on, James. Tell him! Tell him of your genius!'

'A fair question, Mister Gardener. The only answer I can give you is that while it is true to say that the accident did prove to be a fortunate one for Whitworth's, the brewery deeply sympathizes with the people of Falston and fully understands their objections. However, the bottom line here is that it *was* an accident, and the official inquiry's findings were without reservation. Happy accidents do happen.'

'And when do you expect Falston Water to be available to the public?'

'Well there's no definite date set, but we're hoping for a full product launch within the next three to five months.'

'Excellent. I look forward to it,' lied Alec.

'I'll make sure you get an invite to the press shindig,' lied Stephenson.

'Your next appointment is here, Professor Stephenson,' lied Miss Selby, who'd been given instructions to interrupt the interview precisely thirty-seven minutes after it had started.

More platitudes and more shaking of hands.

James Stephenson returned to his bank of monitors and watched Alec leave.

'Nicely done, Jimmy boy.'

The intercom crackled into life again. 'I have Mister Talbot from logistics on line three, Professor. He says they've found something.'

As tree stumps went, this one was perfect for sitting on and eating packed lunches, so John Bostwicke sat on it and dribbled egg yolk down the front of his tunic. He did it at the same time as Alec was sitting in Stephenson's office, though John knew nothing of that. Apparently he knew nothing about hard-boiling eggs either as biting into his second one sent yolk squirting up his left nostril.

John looked around and tried to improve his humour by absorbing some of the glory of the day. The sun was shining brightly, the azure sky was dotted with fluffy white cotton-wool clouds, and the perfect birds in the perfect trees were joyously singing their sweet songs in especially complex multi-part harmonies. Yet even surrounded by all of this natural splendour, John Bostwicke didn't look to be a happy man. He hadn't looked to be a happy man even before he'd had egg dripping from his nose. No expression in the same ballpark as happiness had been seen on John Bostwicke's face for six months. The very same six months since Pongo Smythe's uncharacteristically brief visit to Falston-on-Wold. It was not a six months that John Bostwicke would remember with fondness. Pongo had tasked John with two simple, if unpalatable, errands. John had begun the first of them on the afternoon of Pongo's visit. After three days in Falston Wood, with neither food nor sleep, he had found Garthang and delivered the news of the sudden change in the level of the Wold. Garthang's reaction had been to excuse himself and depart in much the same way Pongo had, though Garthang had looked more picturesque doing it.

The second of the two errands had been even more distasteful. Send a rider to The Guild in Tulston, Pongo had said. Send a rider? Presumably that had been Pongo's attempt at wit. They both knew that no man in the village would undertake a visit to The Guild. No man but John himself.

It had taken a good many ales at Tulston's largest inn before John had felt able to ride beneath the great stone arch marking the entrance to Malecot.

Malecot: the grand name for the not at all grand corner of Tulston that The Guild had forcibly annexed when they had eschewed tradition and stopped living in tents. For centuries The Guild had lived the semi-nomadic lifestyle of their Druidic ancestors, until it struck them that wearing soggy robes and sleeping in cold mud was really rather silly when the people they considered themselves to be infinitely cleverer than were living in nice dry houses.

John dismounted in the centre of the courtyard as a tall man in heavy blue robes approached.

'Good day, John Bostwicke.' The man's voice was quiet, self-assured, and with the subtle undertone of arrogance that came with the robes.

'Good day to you, sir. Have we met before?' John had met a few who called Malecot their home, but there was nothing familiar about this one. He would certainly have remembered a man with a false eye.

'No, we have not met, John Bostwicke. Not yet.' Saying things like that did nothing to endear The Guild to those that were forced to have dealings with them. John was sure they only did it to upset people.

'Yet you know my name. How is that?' John was trying hard not to look at the man's eye, but it kept drawing his gaze.

'There is much that is known to us, John Bostwicke.'

John glanced across at the quarterstaff bound to the rear of his saddle. The glass-eyed man in the robes was only going to get away with so much of this inscrutability lark before he got a demonstration of John's skill with the big stick. 'Then you must also already know of the message I bring from Pongo Smythe'

'Message? Ah, yes, of course. Your message.' The man smiled knowingly, but he was fooling no one.

'And if you know of my message then there is no purpose to my repeating it, so I shall bid you good day and be on my way.'

'Wait, wait, John. We would still prefer to hear your news of Pongo from your own lips.' The flustered acolyte took hold of the reins of John's steed and whispered something into the horse's ear. The creature nodded once and then walked off, disappearing from sight down an alleyway at the edge of the courtyard.

'Your beast will wait at our stables until you are done here.' The haughty air had returned, probably because John's quarterstaff had left with his horse. John had heard tales of The Guild's skill with animals, but this was the first time he had witnessed it. 'Now, if you would be good enough to follow me.'

John followed.

The building they entered looked simple from the outside, but inside it was anything but. Once through the heavy oak door they entered a vast hall with high vaulted ceilings that arched over row upon row of polished bench tables. Huge tapestries hung on the walls and huge crystal chandeliers dripped from the ceiling. Golden statuettes peeked from alcoves and massive onyx busts were raised high on marble pillars. There was even an elegant multi-tiered fountain bedecked with golden cherubs. It was opulence at a level that John hadn't known existed, and so impressed was he that he didn't dwell on the fact that the hall was much too big to fit into the building.

'Wait here a moment,' said the acolyte as he glided off in that way that only people wearing really long robes can.

John waited. It was a particularly good room for waiting in.

In the middle of a dusty room there sat a dusty man. He wore robes similar to those that all in Malecot wore, but his robes were bigger, heavier and redder. His robes were bigger, heavier and redder than everybody else's because he was more important than everybody else. Given his obviously advanced years, the man under all the dust was displaying admirable flexibility by sitting in the lotus position.

Brother Thelonius Wisp looked up from his meditations as the acolyte entered, his well-practiced gliding throwing up dusty clouds in his wake. 'Well? Is he here, Acolyte Tauper?

'He is here, Brother Wisp.'

'And?' Wisp threw back his hood in the dramatic fashion that was his wont.

'He is strong, of low to medium intellect, with good impulse control and a pure heart.' Tauper was glad of the impulse control; he had known full well where John had wanted to shove his quarterstaff.

'Promising. And is he brave?'

'I sense it took great courage for him to come to us.' Acolyte Tauper was struggling with the tingle in his nostrils that was trying to evolve into a sneeze.

'You sense that, do you? And what else do you *sense*, Acolyte Tauper?' There was disdain in Wisp's voice. How dare a novice suggest that his abilities had reached such a level.

'I sense nothing more from him.' Tauper knew his place. He didn't like Wisp, but he wouldn't be doing himself any favours by getting on his bad side. Not that Wisp had a good side.

'Good. Then from what you say I think he will serve our purpose. Does he have a name?'

'John Bostwicke, I believe. That is the name he gave when he took a room at the inn.' John would have been disappointed to learn that Tauper's insight had been nothing more paranormal than a bit of eavesdropping at the inn.

'John Bostwicke?' Wisp nodded. 'Interesting choice.' He didn't find it interesting at all, but Wisp had his own air of inscrutability to maintain.

'I hesitate to touch on this, Brother Wisp, but there is one slight problem with our man.' Tauper shuffled his feet nervously, sending a cloud up inside his robe that wasn't going to help his dust allergy much.

'Problem? What problem?' Wisp didn't like problems.

'This is not our man, Brother Wisp. John Bostwicke is here on his own business, not ours.'

'His own business? And what business is that?'

'He claims to bear a message from Pongo Smythe.'

'A message from Smythe? Then this John Bostwicke is an acquaintance of Pongo's?'

'A close acquaintance, I suspect.'

'Now that is a problem. We can hardly ask him to kill a friend, now can we? Perhaps I had best meet this John Bostwicke and hear his news.' Wisp was fighting hard to maintain his sombre demeanour in the face of such an incredible stroke of luck. A friend of Pongo's was here now? Amazing. Truly amazing. So amazing that it was a real pity that he couldn't let on just how amazing it was. Or even *think* about how amazing it was because there were those in Malecot who could sense such things. Those like Acolyte Tauper.

'Indeed, Brother Wisp. He is waiting in the main hall now.' Tauper sounded nervous, mostly because he was. He always felt nervous around Wisp these days because he could sense great duplicity in the man. Possibly even triplicity. There were plans lurking within plans and even smaller plans lurking within those plans. A Russian doll analogy would work nicely, but Tauper knew nothing of such things.

Wisp smiled. 'Excellent. I shall see him alone. Go to the dining hall and assemble The Guild.'

'Everybody, Brother Wisp?' Tauper didn't hide his surprise. Full meetings were rare these days because putting so many serene and enlightened types in a room together usually led to a lot of childish bickering.

'Everybody, Acolyte Tauper.'

'Yes, Brother Wisp.' Acolyte Tauper turned to leave, the urge to sneeze becoming all-consuming.

'Oh, and before you go, there is a great service you can perform for me.'

'Yes, Brother Wisp?'

'Uncross my legs, would you? I appear to be stuck.'

That was six months ago. Nice of John to remember it for us in such detail, particularly those bits when he wasn't even there.

John reached into his holdall—it's a potato sack, but as John uses it to hold everything we'll go with holdall—and rummaged around for his last slice of rabbit pie. As he did so his fingers brushed against the glyphweave. Still in an accommodating mood, John removed the object from the sack and examined it. Examined it as he had done hundreds of times since Brother Thelonius Wisp had handed it to him. It was obviously a thing of some value, and not only to The Guild; why else would they have secreted it secretly in a secret compartment in the base of their fountain? Slightly bigger than John's clenched fist, the glyphweave was a round metal basket of the most intricate construction. A perfectly spherical and hollow web of etched brass, the outside decorated with runic symbols and the inside a mass of tiny inward facing spikes. It had a small hinge on its equator so that the device could be opened, presumably so that something could be put inside. John had tried to open it, but there was obviously some special knack required to open the catch, and John had never been one for acquiring special knacks. Both delicate and strong, the material looked like brass but it didn't feel cold to the touch, even in the depths of winter. John had never been this close to magic before, and he had asked many questions of Brother Wisp, who had evaded all of them. All he had said was that it was called a glyphweave, and that Pongo would know what should be done with it. John's only concern was to deliver it safely, which brings us to John's problem: Pongo Smythe was missing, as was Garthang. Neither of them had been seen since last autumn. Pongo had stopped coming on his monthly visits, and John had managed five days and nights in Falston Wood without food or sleep, yet Garthang had not appeared to him. It was bothersome. John was a simple man who led a simple life, and all of these complications were getting right up where his last egg yolk had gone.

John returned the glyphweave to his holdall and his thoughts returned to rabbit pie. As he took a bite something caught his eye. It caught his ear first, and then his eye. A distant drone, like constant thunder, coming from everywhere and nowhere. It was enough to make John put down his pie and look skywards, shielding his eyes from the midday sun with his hand. That's when he saw them. Two long white clouds, like cart tracks across the sky, a dark and indistinct shape at their head. It was as if the finger of God was writing His Word on the heavens. Apparently The Word of God was 'll'.

Luton air traffic control were a very confused bunch. All of the computers and the electronic gizmos seemed to be working as they should, yet they had still managed to mislay flight 2202 inbound from Madrid. Mind you, their confusion was nothing compared to the confusion of the flight crew on 2202. Luton had only lost one plane; those guys had lost an entire airport.

'You never know,' said Taff, but his words lacked conviction.

'I bloody do know,' said Thermos, with bucketloads of conviction, 'and I'm not bloody going.'

Taff sighed. He really should have objected when the search party had split into pairs and he'd been landed with Thermos. 'I'm telling you there's something out there.'

'Well I'm still not going. I can't see anything anyway.' Thermos was fibbing.

'It's only mud boy, what's the problem?'

'If it's only mud then you go. I'm not getting filthy just 'cos you thought you saw something. This is my best tank top.' And it was too.

'You're lighter than me.'

'Falston Bridge is lighter than you.'

'Can you see a stick or something then so we can reach out to it?' If Thermos wasn't going to wade out into the mud then Taff would have to come up with a plan that didn't involve having to do it himself.

'A stick? Where are we going to get a stick that long?'

'Well perhaps we can tie them together.'

'Tie what together?'

'The two short planks that you're as thick as.' Taff had been saving that one for the right moment. Apparently, that had been it.

'Well at least I'm not a pudgy Welsh short-arse.' Thermos was running low on ammunition, and it showed.

'Twat.' Taff's supply of witty comebacks was also being drawn from a decidedly shallow well.

The scintillating repartee was cut short by the arrival of a truck. A big truck. With some big men in it. And a tent. The big men got out of the big truck and unloaded some long planks. And a tent. The big men put on some long waders and squelched out into the deep mud. Some more big men handed the first big men some long poles that got pushed down into the deep mud. The long planks were laid onto the long poles and secured with long nails. You've probably guessed that the long nails were hammered in with big hammers. The end result of these strange goings on was a makeshift causeway over the deep mud. With a tent at the end.

'I think we should tell the others about this.' Thermos was keen to be gone. Those were big men, and big men could cause big hurt.

Taff nodded his chins. 'I think you're right. Let's go.'

And go they went, post-haste.

The great white hunters had spotted their quarry disappearing under Ned's caravan, and Morrison had gone into predator mode. He'd come at the caravan from downwind, like a real predator. He'd walked slowly and lightly, like a real predator. Sid had started whistling the theme from *Mission Impossible*, like a real idiot. A ginger tomcat, still looking disturbingly like the late Mister Snickles, had bolted from under the caravan and into a thicket, but it hadn't emerged from the other side. There would have to be sneaking. As thickets went, this one wasn't terribly conducive to sneaking, all brambles and nettles that helpfully placed themselves under Morrison's hands as he shuffled forward on all fours.

'Oh bugger this!' As Morrison tried to stand, two large thorns bit into his neck and a feline missile struck him hard in the groinal region, all fur and claws and hissing and spitting. Morrison tumbled backwards as he grabbed the enraged beast by the throat, landing heavily on the grass as he struggled to defend his favourite body parts. It took him a full thirty seconds to notice that his attacker had stopped attacking.

'You alright, Doc?' Sid's face loomed into view, blocking out the sky.

'I think so, Sid.' Lying on his back on the grass Morrison did a quick systems check. His neck stung like billio, but early indications were that his genitals were still intact. It didn't seem like an appropriate moment to confirm that with a touch test. 'Sid?'

'Yes, Doc?'

'What am I holding in my right hand?'

'The cat, Doc.' Sid lacked Phillip's veterinary training, but he could be trusted with basic species identification.

'And what am I holding in my left hand?'

'The cat, Doc.'

Morrison's hands were a good three feet apart, which didn't bode well for the aforementioned cat. He levered himself up into a sitting position and examined the items for himself. From his left hand a pair of glass eyes stared up at him from long dead sockets. In his right hand was a stitched mess of ginger fur with clumps of blue-green stuffing material tumbling from the gaping neck hole. A few feet away, caught in the brambles, was the beast's tail, complete with safety pin retainer.

'Oh shit, it *is* Mister Snickles!' Phillip Morrison sat dejectedly in the grass and hunted for a feasible explanation for what had just happened. Every time he tried he ended up back at the only explanation that fitted the facts, and down that road madness lay. Not very far down it either.

'I think Jack's got some superglue back at the pub' said Sid, whose own approach to rationalising the event relied heavily on missing the point completely.

Alec Gardener wanted to be on the other side of Falston Bridge. On the other side of Falston Bridge there were good things like fish suppers, beer, and an unfinished conversation with that Bladder chap. In the way of Alec getting to the other side of Falston Bridge was a big truck. Alec glared at the obstacle through the layer of brown filth that was accumulating on his windscreen and considered honking the horn. Honking the horn would have been rude. Honking the horn would have displayed a lack of patience born of weakness of character. Even though he was feeling hot and bothered and the roof was stuck and he was out of cigarettes and he needed a pee and was getting a headache and his relationship with Claire was falling apart and there was a pointy stone in his shoe and he hadn't won the lottery yet and he had a shitty life and he wanted over this damn bridge, Alec didn't honk the horn. Because it didn't work. He hauled himself out of the car and slammed the door loudly, announcing his intention to get good and pissed off at somebody, and pity the fool who got in his way.

'Excuse me, hope you don't mind me asking, but are you going to be moving soon? Not to worry if you're not though. No rush,' said Alec, ever so politely, to the sizeable fool in his way.

'Just leavin' mate,' said the overalled colossus, his sleeves bulging like sacks of coconuts.

The truck pulled away behind a pungent black smokescreen, and Alec finally noticed why it was parked there in the first place. A planked walkway had appeared on the upstream side of the bridge, extending out into the mud of the Wold and looping around one of those small red and white striped tents popular in pratfall gags. Where the planks met the bank there sat two deckchairs, and in the two deckchairs there sat two men. Two men of similar build to the one Alec had just met, which made for very strained deckchairs.

Alec thought it might be best to go tell the others about this, so go he went, post-haste.

Had he not been in such a hurry, Alec might have glanced in his rear-view mirror and seen another car pull onto the bridge behind him and stop. A white 1973 Corvette Coupe, identical to the one that Bill Bixby used to drive in *The Magician*.

To call Mad Ned's home a caravan was to do it a mighty injustice. No prefabricated machine-built tin box this. Doyens of the roving abode would have called it a

Reading Wagon; a horse-drawn wooden cottage on wheels, gaily painted in reds and yellows, with a raised skylight roof and shuttered windows. Reading Wagons of any quality were in museums now, and Ned's was as fine an example as you were ever likely to see. They had once been the epitome of luxurious mobile living, and it was amazing what you could fit in one.

'It's amazing what you can fit in one of these,' said Taff as he and Thermos climbed the wooden steps up to the door.

Amazingly well fitted into this particular wagon were Phillip Morrison and Sidney Aluitious Poe. A very happy Phillip Morrison and Sidney Aluitious Poe, the two bottles of finest brandy they had found in one of Ned's cupboards having cheered them up no end.

'What are you two doing in here, then?' asked the surprised chauffeur of omnibuses.

'Could ask you two the same,' replied Sid, with barely a hint of slurring.

'Looking for you,' said Thermos, eyeing up the unfinished bottle on the table.

'Well done, you've found us. Does that mean it's your turn to hide?' Morrison snorted and brandy came out of his nose.

'You're drunk!' cried Thermos, more out of envy than reproach.

'Yep.' Morrison smiled the smile of a happy inebriate.

'So while we've been chasing all over the village looking for that sodding cat, you've been in here having a party?' Taff was embellishing the gentle stroll he and

Thermos had taken down to Falston Bridge, but other people had brandy and he didn't.

'Not exactly. We found that in the bushes.' Sid did some dramatic pointing.

Thermos followed the point. 'A stove?'

Sid squinted for a moment and then adjusted his angle of point by ninety degrees.

'Bloody hell!' Taff and Thermos produced a lovely two-part harmony as they spied the various remains of Mister Snickles perched on the shelf behind Morrison.

'And then we came in here and found this.' Morrison thrust a sheet of paper at Taff.

Taff read the note and handed it to Thermos. Thermos, for no good reason given that everybody else present was aware of its contents, read it aloud.

> Triumphant stranger,
>
> My apologies for not being here to greet you. In my absence, please accept the hospitality of my vardo. You will be safe here.
>
> God be with you.
>
> Your servant
>
> Robin
>
> PS Take care of Bobs for me. He likes Munchipals, the nutritionally complete dry dog food fortified with vitamins and iron for bright eyes and a healthy coat.
>
> PPS Help yourself to the brandy.

'So what we dealing with then?' Taff was still staring at the dismantled feline as he voiced the question on everybody's mind.

'Well I think it's safe to say that we're into the realms of the supernatural.' Morrison wished that he hadn't heard himself say that.

'Supernatural? That's just daft.' Sid saw himself as the voice of reason, and too grounded in reality for any of this supernatural rubbish. But he crossed himself anyway, just in case.

'Daft, Sidney? Right now I wouldn't think it was daft if you told me that we were dealing with The Prince of Darkness himself.'

'You mean-,' began Thermos

'Yes, I do.' Morrison's voice was pitched to convey the full gravity of what he was saying.

'Count Dracula!' finished Thermos, followed by 'Ouch!' when Taff did the necessary. 'What did you do that for? The Doc does have those bite marks on his neck.' Thermos rubbed the back of his head and felt decidedly picked upon.

'They're not bite marks, Kevin. I caught myself on some thorns.'

'That's what his victims always say. It's always thorns or brooch pins or ... ouch! Cut that out Taff! So who is this stranger then? And who's Robin?'

'Robin is Ned, Thermos.' Morrison despaired of Thermos. Often.

'And the stranger?'

'I have no idea,' Sid's statement surprised nobody 'but how about we adjourn to The Queen's Arms and think about it.' No surprises there either. He waved an empty brandy bottle to lend weight to the suggestion.

There was general nodded agreement so they all stood and made unsteadily for the door. As they negotiated the now perilous steps of the caravan, Alec arrived.

'Why are you all looking at me like that?' asked Alec the stranger as he got out of his Triumph.

Professor James Stephenson gazed down his nose at the man in the muddy blue overalls. 'And you're sure that's what it is?'

'Oh yes, sir. No doubt 'bout it. 'Ow do you think it got there?' The man in the blue overalls was feeling uncomfortable, and not just because his boots were full of mud.

'It must have been out there for years, stuck in the mud.' Stephenson was voicing his thoughts aloud. Just his own. The alien thoughts he was keeping private for now.

'Right you are, sir. Now if you don't mind I'll be off.' Talbot didn't wait for a response before scurrying away.

'Has he found what I think he's found?'

'I don't know, but it looks promising.'

'So that's why old Madden came here!'

'He can't have known about it, can he? Surely if he knew, we would have known.'

'Not necessarily. He managed to keep us out of most of the interesting bits of his mind.'

'True, but whether he knew or not, it looks like it's here.'

'Well that's a bit of a bonus.'

7

Thelonius Wisp knew the guard was only an illusion, but it still gave him the collywobbles. Being so deep within the bowels of Malecot always unsettled him. Shit happened in bowels. Shit that only he knew about. Shit like this huge muscle-bound, loincloth-clad guard that was blocking his way. Big and strong were clearly prerequisites for good guarding, but Wisp was less clear on the benefits of being semi-naked and lightly oiled.

'Stand aside,' commanded Wisp in his most authoritative voice.

No response. Not so much as a flicker.

'Stand aside. Please?'

Nope. Nothing. Not even the deep, resonating 'none shall pass' that the moment called for.

Wisp took a step forward. The illusionary guard raised its illusionary sword, and the tip of the blade struck the wall and made real, non-illusionary, sparks. There was a growl, a glint of steel, and a big swooshing noise. Somewhere between glint and swoosh, Wisp closed his eyes in preparation for the inevitable.

'Now, now, Caleb. Play nice.' It was a powerful voice. A voice that demanded obedience. A woman's voice.

Wisp opened his eyes and was pleased to discover that he wasn't dead. Inevitability is funny like that. The guard was motionless, the business edge of its weapon less than an inch from Wisp's throat.

'Stand aside, Caleb. Let our guest pass.'

The sentinel complied, lifting its sword from Wisp's neck and stepping away from the door.

'Do we have to go through this ridiculous charade every time I come down here?' Wisp's voice was steady and controlled, belying the fact that he had almost soiled his robe. Lady Gaynor Elfam scared him, but he would never give her the satisfaction of seeing it. Weakness wasn't in Brother Wisp's vocabulary. Neither was anagram, and that would prove to be the more significant omission.

'Oh Thelonius, don't get all uppity again. You really need to relax more.' A figure in a black robe stepped through the portal and rested a gloved hand on the guard's Popeyean forearm. 'Now come, tell me your good news. You do have good news for me, don't you?'

Yes and no, thought Wisp. 'Yes,' said Wisp, following the robed silhouette through the doorway.

The room was well lit, but the silhouette stubbornly remained a silhouette. Gaynor's black robe sucked in the light, and the deep cowl hid her features behind heavy curtains of shadow. Wisp had never seen The Lady Gaynor's face, and with each meeting he became more convinced that he didn't want to—the ugliness within was sure to be echoed in her visage. Her choice of domicile didn't suggest that the lady was much of a Lady either. As caverns went this one was particularly cavernous, and the decor was straight from the 'Hell and Damnation' collection. Black candles aplenty. Huge stone gargoyles of the most hideous order. Instruments of pain. Instruments of perverse pleasure. Instruments that promised both at the same time. In size and scope, this room was the mirror of The Guild's great hall far above them, and at the same time it was its complete antithesis. There were tapestries here too, but here they depicted garish images of the most foul and debauched carnal acts. Were they images of reality, or creations of a lunatic mind? Were they echoes of the past, or portents of the future? Were they for sale?

'Now, your news, Thelonius. Tell me your news.' Gaynor sounded impatient.

'We have an unexpected development, milady.' Wisp knew she rather liked it when he called her that. He was no sycophant—she would have seen right through any obsequious flattery anyway—but it served his purpose to stay in her favour. For now.

'Unexpected? Surely nothing that transpires can be unexpected in the all-seeing eyes of The Venerable Guild of Magi.'

Wisp cringed on hearing The Guild addressed by its full title. The name had meant something once, but she was using it to mock him. 'Indeed, milady.' Wisp smiled. For all her arrogance and taunting, Gaynor still needed The Guild. She mocked them for their poor sight, but in comparison she was blind, her powers too weak to see far beyond the confines of this cave. 'We have the long-awaited report from our agents in Gallowtree.'

'And?'

'And they've found it, milady.'

Pongo Smythe had been here many times before, but the place never looked any less wrong. The buildings were wrong. The bridge was wrong. The roads were wrong. The air was *very* wrong. Now the river was wrong too. That had always been right, but now it wasn't where it was supposed to be, which made it wrong. Nevertheless, for all its wrongness, it was still Falston, which made Pongo responsible for it.

'Salutations, Pongo Smythe.' Garthang emerged from the trees and joined Pongo in his gazing. 'Different, is it not?'

'Very different. But somehow very the same.' Pongo turned to face his unexpected companion and did some eyebrow manipulation that plunged his demeanour into the depths of grave and serious. Pongo had exceptionally expressive eyebrows. 'I think we have much to discuss, my friend.'

The unicorn nodded his agreement, blessing Pongo with a faceful of golden mane in the process. 'Indeed we do. And I think we should begin with how you came to find me.'

'Find you? I didn't know you were lost.'

'You didn't? But surely John Bostwicke has told you of my absence?'

'Absence? How long have you been here, Garthang?' Pongo's eyebrows tried to do worried, but as they were already doing grave and serious they just made an untidy mess on his forehead.

'It's difficult to be exact as my kind does not place the same value on the passage of time, but I would estimate one hundred and eighty two days, twenty-two hours, six minutes and thirty-seven seconds. Roughly.'

'Good grief!' Both eyebrows did the upward leap of stunned amazement.

'Thirty-nine seconds now. Can grief ever really be good?'

Pongo thought it best to ignore the question as philosophical debates with unicorns tended to go on a bit and often led to self-harming. 'What happened?'

'In truth there's little to tell. It was on the day John Bostwicke sought me out to deliver a message from your good self. The nature of that message suggested to me that it might be prudent to pass the information on to Draknoor, if only as a precaution, yet when I tried to leave the wood I found myself here. It appears that I am confined to this Falston, and the situation has me sorely vexed.'

Pongo nodded. 'I can see that it would,' he said, not terribly helpfully.

Garthang looked thoughtful, making it a red-letter day for his species. 'So what brings you to this place, if not to find me?'

'Unlike you, I am here of my own accord. I received a runecall. Or rather, an ancestor of mine, Tobo Smythe, got one. He was Falston's Guild Monitor many years ago, and as he's long been at rest the call was redirected to me.'

'A runecall? I've not heard of one of those being used in some considerable time.'

'Indeed not. Moreover, this one was unusually brief. I think it got disconnected.'

'Who sent it?'

'I don't know. Either it was unsigned or it was stopped before the signature reached me.' Pongo suspected the latter.

'And when did you receive this call?' Garthang tried to sound interested, but his attention came with minimal span when he was hungry.

'A little over a week ago. I was in The Grand Library at the time, and they were none too pleased that I got a call whilst I was in there.' Pongo frowned; there had been shushing. 'I've been doing research there for close on six months, which is why I wasn't aware of your absence. This is bad, Garthang. Oh dear me, yes, this is very bad.' Pongo's eyebrows concurred. 'Tell me, my friend, has anybody seen you here?'

'Well, actually, yes.' Garthang shifted on his hooves, embarrassed by the admission that he had allowed himself to be seen. 'A pleasant enough fellow. We had a brief chat and then he fainted.'

'I take it he was inebriated then?'

'Very. I could smell it in his urine.'

'Should I ask?'

'I would say not, though you may take it from me that he'd had an evening on the ale.'

Pongo nodded. That made sense. The only way to see a unicorn was to take the mind to a place that was normally beyond its reach. Some, including Pongo himself, could do it by force of will. John Bostwicke did it by fasting and denying himself sleep. Most people did it inadvertently by getting stupendously drunk. Hallucinogenic drugs don't do it, so those of you that see unicorns whilst tripping the light fantastic are just being delusional.

'So what is to be done, Pongo?'

'A good question. It would appear that unseen hands are manipulating these events, and those hands have some considerable knowledge behind them. I suspect that you were sent here to prevent you from reaching Draknoor.' Pongo frowned again, turning the frown he was already frowning into a deep trench in his forehead. Adding a third frown at this point would require surgery. This was a puzzle, and his mind raced as he tried to orientate the disparate pieces of it and nudge them into place to form a uniform whole. A bit like *Tetris*, but only a bit. 'But now that I am here I can guide you back to Draknoor. Surely they would have known that and prevented me from finding you? Ah, but my visit to the library was unexpected, and may have hidden me from their view. Now that I am here I will be easy to locate and ...' Pongo paused.

'And?' prompted Garthang.

'And dispose of. Oh dear.' Pongo sat down. Discovering that there were people who might want him dead required a little sit down.

'Would it not have been simpler to just kill me?'

'Kill a unicorn? Hardly a wise choice.'

'True, I always forget about that. So what do we do next, Pongo Smythe?' Unicorns preferred not to act without a plan, and they normally preferred somebody else to come up with it so they couldn't be blamed for any gargantuan cock-ups that might happen along.

What next indeed? Pongo was going to have to think on that one. It would help if he knew what had become of John Bostwicke. He also needed to know if there really was an assassin tracking him. Both were vital questions, but for the moment Pongo could see no way of getting answers to them.

By the clever and expedient act of doing nothing, Pongo got the answers to both questions.

'Good afr'noon, Pongo Smythe,' hailed John Bostwicke as he emerged from the trees, dragging the assassin by his boot. 'Found this fellow hiding behind a tree and pointing this here crossbow in your direction, so I thinks to myself, John Bostwicke, that fellow is trying to harm your friend Pongo, so I hit him with a rock.'

'John, I'm exceedingly glad to see you! However did you get here?' Pongo's simultaneous relief and joy found expression as an inane grin.

'Get here? Whatever can you mean Pongo Smythe? I live here.'

'He doesn't realize where he is,' said Garthang. Quick of mind, your average unicorn.

Pongo nodded. 'So I see. Well I shall have to tell him.'

'Is that wise?' Garthang was beginning to wonder just how many people could know a secret before it qualified as being common knowledge.

John Bostwicke was confused. 'Are you all right, Pongo? Or did someone hit you in the head an' all?'

'My apologies, John. I was speaking to Garthang.' Pongo could see a certain amount of whimsical confusion looming on the horizon.

'Garthang is here?' John looked around for the unicorn. The invisible unicorn that John couldn't see. So he didn't see him.

'I'm here beside you, John Bostwicke' said the invisible, inaudible, inane unicorn.

'Nor can he hear you, Garthang.' Pongo had never credited unicorns with much in the way of mental acuity, and Garthang was doing little to change his opinion. He reached into one of his jacket pockets and produced a small vial of clear liquid. 'John, would you be so good as to drink this? It may assist with this rather complex situation'

John took the vial and downed the contents in one. Then he did quite a lot of blinking, some coughing, a bit of staggering and finally some sitting down. 'My Lord, they don't serve anything like that in The King's Arms. Oh, hello Garthang, there you are.'

Garthang thought the statement superfluous, as he was perfectly aware that there was where he was. 'Hello, John Bostwicke. Do you know where you are?'

John laughed heartily, for he knew no other way. 'The drink wasn't that strong, you daft horse! I'm in Falston Wood, of course.'

'Indeed you are.' Pongo thought it best to take over at this point. 'Now, prepare yourself for a shock, John.'

John nodded, but he had no idea how to prepare himself for a shock.

'Take a look down into the valley,' said Pongo, 'and tell me what you see.'

John laughed and shook his head. 'Are you jesting with me, Pongo? It's Falston.'

'Yes, it is Falston. But look hard, John. Look, and see.' Pongo made a few of those complicated finger movements that had become popular in the locale of late.

John looked. John looked and saw. John passed out. See John fall backwards off his tree stump.

Somewhere off the Florida coast, Carcharodon carcharias was going about its daily business. The daily business of being a great white shark. Today's daily business was swimming and eating. Sometimes the daily business involved making little sharks as well, but not this day. This was a swimming and eating day. With lots of swimming under his belt already, it was time to eat, and today's house special is *l'enfant sur un gonflable*. Everything was unfolding pretty much as you'd expect. Small child on inflatable rubber raft. Lots of leg thrashing. Nature's greatest predator thundering its torpedo shaped body through the water, all menacing grace and an unfeasibly large number of teeth. The shark rises, slowly at first, gaining speed as the signals from the child's thrashing grow stronger. It comes from beneath, rising almost vertically, impelled to attack. There is one final sweep of that massive, powerful tail. The mouth opens. The black eyes roll back.

I'll give you one guess what happens next.

But I guarantee you'll guess wrong.

His name was George.

It really was, but then why shouldn't it be? George was a perfectly ordinary name. A name that had drawn little attention in its owner's formative years, allowing him to negotiate his mediocre education without significant name-based ridicule. It was only when he began to progress in his chosen vocation that his name lead to bouts of tittering.

No, a policeman's lot was not a happy one for Detective Inspector George Guv.

'So, what's the story on this one, guv?' Detective Sergeant Nigel Sillcott had a grudging respect for his superior, but that wasn't going to stop him from taking the mickey whenever the opportunity presented.

George had long since stopped asking his subordinates not to call him guv. Every other officer of his rank was referred to as guv, so to make an issue of it was to draw attention and just make things worse.

'Terrorists.' George was a man of few words and he liked to make each of them count.

'Terrorists? In Dartford Tunnel? They said it was ground subsidence on the news.'

'Believe everything you hear on the news, do you, Sillcott?'

'Normally, yes I do. Guv.' Sillcott particularly enjoyed leaving a pause before the 'guv', just to tease George into thinking it wasn't coming.

'Well perhaps that's why you're still a sergeant, sergeant.' George flicked away his cigarette in enigmatic fashion. It was nowhere near finished, but that had seemed to be the right moment to flick it. He'd also managed to emphasize his colleague's subordinate rank twice in succession, and that kind of thing always lifted his spirits.

Deception it may have been, but subsidence was a plausible reason for both the bridge and the tunnel to be out of action. The motorway and all other approaches were closed for three miles in all directions, ostensibly for safety reasons, and not at all because it would be a dead giveaway if anybody saw that the 'construction workers' dealing with the 'subsidence' were heavily armed and kept saluting each other.

'Not really our sort of thing this, is it, guv? One for the anti-terrorist boys, don't you think?'

Anti-terrorist boys? Yes, they were already there. George Guv had been a professional and played the game, liaising with the senior officer when he'd arrived at the scene. Equally professionally, he had offered them his services, emphasising his local knowledge and drawing particular attention to the one-day seminar he'd attended on hostage negotiation (leaving out the part about missing the afternoon session because he had a migraine). After due consideration of George's offer they had told him to piss off.

'Looks like something's happening down there. Guv.' Sillcott was watching the tunnel through expensive binoculars. His own personal expensive binoculars, purchased so that he'd have a pair available should he need to look at things that were far away. George didn't have any expensive binoculars, and he knew that if he wanted to borrow Sillcott's then he would have to ask nicely. George wasn't good at asking nicely, so things that were far away stayed very small.

Something *was* happening. From their elevated vantage point, George and his long-suffering sergeant saw a big metal happening trundle slowly towards the tunnel entrance. The heavy armour and big gun suggested that this wasn't a vehicle of quiet negotiation.

'Somebody means to dish out an arse-kicking on this one, guv.'

Lucky buggers, thought George. Modern policing was more about paperwork these days. Not once had George had to drag a villain out of his Jag by his barnet and kick him into a right two and eight to get him to grass on where the blag was going down.

George lit another cigarette. Whatever happened he was going to need one to flick away when the time came to deliver his punchy one-liner. Hopefully it wouldn't be over too quickly as he needed time to think up a goodly selection of pithy remarks.

The impressively armoured and beweaponed vehicle trundled from sight into the unfathomable blackness. For a few moments there was only the deep rumble of its engine to be heard, amplified by the great concrete organ pipe that was the Dartford Tunnel. Then there was a crash. Then several more. Some shouting.

Panicked shouting. Then the rapid *whump-whump* of the machine gun. The boom of a stun grenade. Grinding metal. An explosion. More shouting. Then silence. Then more silence. Then four figures came running out of the tunnel at speed, closely followed by their armoured car. It sailed over the heads of its crew, bouncing and rolling along the road until it crashed into the tollbooths. For a few seconds it kept everybody in suspense about what it was going to do next. Then it exploded. In the light of the explosion, the gathered throng got their first look at the 'terrorists' who had just lobbed several tons of armoured car like it was a tennis ball. There were two of them, both close to twenty-foot tall, grey-green in colour, naked, and ugly as sin.

'Grrr!' roared one of the creatures, and everybody knew exactly what it meant.

As the monsters retreated into the tunnel, everybody else retreated to anywhere they could because the ammunition in the burning armoured car had started going off in a decidedly random fashion. A stray bullet struck the ground just in front of Detective Inspector Guv and ploughed a little furrow in the earth between his shoes.

'Looks like we've got ourselves some trolls,' said George as his cigarette sailed away.

Bladder was content. Sitting alone in the lounge bar of The Queen's Arms, lovingly clutching a pint of best to his bosom, he was as content as mortal man could ever be. His only concern at that moment was what to do with the glass he was holding, as there were already too many on the table for him to put it down. He would have to have a word with the landlord about the timely collection of empties. Alternatively, he could change tables. A more prudent choice perhaps, as the landlord was not currently in the best of humours. That Alec bloke had put twenty quid behind the bar to fund Bladder's imbibing and keep him in situ, so Jack had gone for another little lie down. It seemed to Bladder that Jack's much vaunted ability to find the good in all situations had deserted him since the stranger with the flashy car had arrived in the village.

Not one to waste a quality cue like that, Alec Gardener made his entrance to the bar. With him came Morrison, Sid, Taff and Thermos.

Bladder was overjoyed to see all of his friends return safely. The twenty quid had run out.

When John Bostwicke awoke, it was with a head he'd happily have traded for a turnip. He couldn't remember why he was flat on his back so he sat up, immediately acquiring a profound new appreciation for the joys of lying down. Above him there was a big blue blur dotted with little white blurs, and he was surrounded by a variety of green and brown blurs.

'It is called kribble. An ale of singular potency, I'm sure you'll agree,' said a Pongo shaped blur. 'I discovered the secret of its fermentation many years ago, and I make use of it regularly.' Pongo though it best not to mention what it was fermented from, or that his regular use of it was to dissolve hardened grease off cart axles. 'While you slept I was able to assist Garthang in returning to the world in which he, and you, more properly belong. At my request he shall seek you out when you also return there, for you have a task to perform together.'

'Slept?' John looked around in the big blue blur for the bright yellow blur. It was indeed much closer to the big green blur than it had been the last time he'd seen it. 'I would appreciate an explanation of all this, Pongo, for I am sorely vexed.' Garthang had said the same. Causes nasty sores, this vexing.

Pongo explained. John nodded and shook his head in equal measure. He asked questions. He got answers. He didn't understand everything that Pongo Smythe said, but in truth that was often the case, and he understood enough to know that his friend needed his help. 'So who is this fellow then?' John kicked the prostrate assassin hard on the shin.

'He's the man sent to kill me.' Pongo wasn't one to bear a grudge, but then he wasn't the one who was dead.

'Kill you? Are you certain of it?'

'I'm certain, John. While you slept I searched his pockets; apart from his weapon he carried only these.' Pongo emptied a small bag onto the ground beside him. There were a dozen crossbow bolts, an equal number of gold coins, a paper-wrapped package of something that resembled blackberry jam, a scrap of parchment with writing on it, and a dead toad. 'The foul smelling stuff in the paper is spiderbite, a very nasty and very ancient poison. The parchment gives a detailed description of my appearance and habits, and the gold is a measure of the value of my life. I should take some comfort from the amount; this fellow didn't come cheap.'

'And the dead toad?'

'His lunch. Regularly ingesting certain toads gifts immunity to spiderbite poisoning, though thankfully it doesn't seem to gift immunity to being hit in the head with a sharp rock.'

'He's dead then?'

Pongo nodded. 'I don't believe anybody could look that calm and still live.'

'Oh.' John frowned. 'Sorry.'

'No apology necessary, old friend. Better his death than mine.' Pongo was being truthful, though it was a pity that John's enthusiasm had made questioning the assassin a trifle difficult.

John shook his head. 'I was apologising to him.'

'I don't think he'd be disposed to accept your apology at this point, John.'

'What if he had a wife? A family, perhaps. There might be children who will have empty bellies because of what I've done.'

'The likes of him don't have families, John. It's not their way. The Servants of Maurisamern may be a distant memory, but there are those who would try and keep that memory alive. Think no more about this man, and know that you did a great service by ending a wretched life. Now, tell me of your visit to The Guild.'

John told what he had to tell. Most of it was a message from Thelonius Wisp that John had been charged with delivering to Pongo. The message made much of 'sworn duty' and 'challenging times ahead', and in John's opinion seemed to be using a deal too many words and saying very little. When he was done, he reached into his holdall and retrieved the glyphweave. Pongo studied it in great detail. He examined the exquisitely engraved runes on the outer surface of the brass web. He tinkered with the intricate and cunning locking mechanism. He rolled it around on the grass. He tossed it in the air. He tapped it with his cane. He put it on the ground and worried at it. He studied the runes once more. Then he studied them again. Finally, Pongo gave his very considered opinion on the device.

'Oh dear me. Oh dear, dear me.'

'Shit fuck wank bollocks!' Alec Gardener wasn't the 'oh dear me' type. He was lying on the surprisingly comfortable bed in Mad Ned's surprisingly spacious caravan and was, not surprisingly, wondering why he was there. Alec had read Mad Ned's note, and whilst he could see where the rest of them were coming from, it still struck him as ridiculous. Yes, he was a stranger, though it had taken a pint of Jack's best for Alec to concede even that much. Two more and he grudgingly accepted that arriving in a Triumph might make him triumphant. Another three pints and a burp of resignation later, Alec had capitulated and accepted Mad Ned's in absentia offer of the hospitality of his vardo (once Morrison had looked up 'vardo' in his *Children's Big Encyclopaedia of Knowledge*). Alec's only proviso had been the immediate and unconditional removal of Mister Snickles.

Alec decided not to dwell on the evening's events and returned his attention to the items he'd just found under the bed. There was a portable television, a video recorder, and two large stacks of videos. He was surprised to discover that both the telly and the VCR worked even though they had no discernible power supply, but then what did he know about modern caravanning equipment? He knew all about under-the-bed videos though, and as he was feeling in the mood he popped one of the cassettes into the VCR, hit play, and waited for everybody to get naked. Forty seconds later he was thankful that nobody in the advertisement for denture fixative he was watching had felt the need to get naked. He hit fast-forward in the hope of finding something more erotic. Advertisements for breakfast cereal and toilet cleanser weren't *less* erotic, but that wasn't really the point. A swift and frustrating perusal of Ned's under-bed collection revealed that all seventeen tapes—totalling fifty-one hours of quality viewing—were comprised of nothing but television commercials. As frustration hadn't completely killed his mood, Alec lay back and let his mind drift away on a sea of fancy until it made landfall, and the island it found was named Sara Hagget. Rather than keep thinking of her as 'that bird with the long legs', Alec had made certain discreet inquiries. He had asked Jack for the name of 'that bird with the long legs'. As Jack was in whimsical mood he had run through a list including ostrich, emu, cardinal, stork, flamingo and roseate spoonbill, before deciding that the joke had run out of steam, which was a good ten minutes after everybody else had. Then Thermos started a new ball rolling by adding pheasant and partridge to Jack's list because she of the long legs was also a game bird. Eventually Jack had obliged Alec with Sara Hagget's name, and directions to the best public lavatory walls to peruse for further information. Alec unzipped his trousers. He had something he needed to do.

But it wasn't *that*.

For all of the caravan's conspicuous luxury it had no toilet facilities. Mad Ned, quite literally, had no pot to piss in. The great outdoors would suffice for Alec's immediate requirement; more solid issues could be dealt with later. Ned probably had some sort of 'hole-in-the-ground' based amenity in the bushes somewhere, but Alec didn't feel inclined to go looking for it in the dark. He only made it as far as the bottom of the caravan steps before Mister Tinkle came a calling, and this man did what he had to do, and he sang a happy song whilst he did it. Alec's moving rendition of the theme to *Postman Pat* was interrupted by a figure emerging from the bushes and striding towards him.

'Aarrghhh!' screamed Alec.

'Aarrghhh!' responded the figure, always open to new styles of formal greeting.

Alec panicked. There was only one thing for it. Actually there were several things for it, but Alec could only think of one. Clearing the caravan steps in a single bound, he was about to turn and slam the door shut when a hand took hold of his ankle and he pitched forward onto the caravan floor. He rolled onto his back and tried to kick out with his free leg, but his foot shot out harmlessly into thin air as his opponent anticipated the blow and somersaulted upwards, sailing through the caravan doorway to land knees-first on Alec's chest. In the glow of the caravan's oil lamp, Alec got his first look at the great warrior who had pinned him to the floor. The man was short, balding, a little soft around the midriff, and dressed in what appeared to be a pea-green velvet three-piece suit. In one hand he was holding a gnarled walking stick, and in the other a small woven sack, which had Alec wondering what the strange little man had used to grab his ankle.

'Hello there,' said the new arrival with a cheery grin that really wasn't in keeping with the circumstances. 'The name's Smythe. Pongo Smythe.'

The Sean Connery impersonation didn't seem entirely appropriate either.

'Want a bite?' Thermos shoved a half-eaten bacon sandwich under Taff's nose.

'No, thanks. I'm watching my figure.'

'Aren't we all? Can't see anything else when you're around.' It gave Thermos deep satisfaction to get the first one in.

'Give it a rest, would you? We've got better things to do this morning.'

'Sorry,' said Thermos, spraying bits of soggy bread over the side of Falston Bridge.

The better things were Morrison's idea, formulated after that journalist bloke had left The Queen's Arms on the previous evening. The specifics of the plan had melted away with the morning mist, but both Taff and Thermos had remembered enough to make their way down to Falston Bridge just before dawn. Then at dawn it had dawned on them just how bloody early it was. After a couple of hours of general complaining about the earliness of it, Thermos had gone in search of sustenance and Taff had himself a revelation. 'I remember what we're supposed to be doing,' he announced when Thermos had returned bearing armfuls of newspapers, warm beverages and bacon sarnies.

''Bout bloody time. So why are we here then?'

'We're supposed to go and take a shufti in that tent thing.'

'So what about those blokes on the deckchairs?' Thermos nodded in the direction of two very large men in very black suits. It's highly probable that Thermos would be amused to discover that the very large men were called Bill and Ben. It's equally probable that Bill and Ben did physical damage to those who found their names amusing. 'How we supposed to get past them?'

'Good question. Perhaps they'll go for a walk or something later, we'll just have to stay here and watch them until they do.' Taff clearly had his own personal definition of the word 'guard'.

'What, all day?'

'If need be.'

'Flippin' 'eck.'

'Can't be helped. Morrison is at the surgery today, Sid's got the cafe to run and Bladder won't be awake until tomorrow at the earliest. You and me, we have the day off see.'

'You only have the day off 'cos you wrecked your bus, and I only have the day off 'cos you wrecked your bus in my office.' Thermos took a contemplative munch on his sandwich. 'This all sounds dodgy to me, and I still don't see why we have to do it.'

'Because we're 'ere lad, and nobody else. Just us.' Taff hummed a few bars of 'Men of Harlech' to help Thermos get the reference, but to no avail.

And so, because they were there and nobody else, just them, Taff and Thermos waited. Thermos ate sandwiches, drank tea, and then went off to get more of the same. Taff ate sandwiches, drank tea, and made up words that fitted the newspaper crossword. 'Cormac-funge' was about his best for the day. The men in black suits just watched in that impassive way that men in black suits do. Went with the territory.

It was shortly after Thermos' third visit to the café that developments developed.

'Hold up, we have some movement,' said Taff, nodding discreetly in the direction of the deckchairs.

'We have?' said Thermos, turning to face in the direction that Taff had hoped he wouldn't and staring in the way Taff would have preferred him not to.

One of the two guardians of the causeway was on his feet and striding towards them.

'What's our cover story?' hissed Thermos through the side of his mouth.

'Cover story? I know, I'll tell him I'm a mental health worker and you're part of my care in the community programme.'

They needn't have worried. The dark suited one strode past them without so much as a nod, but the sideways glance he gave Thermos' sandwich hinted at the guard's quest.

'What now?' Thermos' grasp of the plan was not that secure.

'Well there's not much we can do with one of them still there.' Taff returned his attention to guard number two, still entrenched on his deckchair. 'Oh, now what's *she* doing here?'

Taff and Thermos watched, transfixed, as Sara Hagget glided out of Falston Wood and over to the remaining guard, bending over ever so slowly and deliberately to whisper in his ear. He shook his head. She repeated the manoeuvre, and this time she pointed up at Falston Wood as she did it. Ben glanced around and nodded vigorously. Then Sara Hagget took big strong Ben by his big strong hand and led him away into big old Falston Wood.

The two men on the bridge gazed longingly at the place where Sara and her new 'friend' vanished into the trees. Suddenly Sara reappeared. She pointed at them. Then she pointed at the tent. Then she pointed at them again. Then she pointed at the tent again. Then she repeated the whole display with extra urgency. Then she shook her head and threw her arms up in despair. Then she was gone.

Both men pondered on what Sara was up to. Taff got out of the pond first. 'She's distracting him so we can get to the tent!'

'Jammy bastard!' said Thermos. 'Could do with some of that distracting myself.'

'Come on, let's get a move on.'

They got a move on.

The causeway was a surprisingly rigid structure, and Thermos and Taff made their way down it and into the tent as surreptitiously as they could, which wasn't very.

'Bloody Hell!' said Thermos.

'What?' said Taff.

'Look,' said Thermos

'Where?' said Taff

'There,' said Thermos.

'Oh,' said Taff.'

'It's a flippin' sword,' said Thermos, using syllables like there was no tomorrow.

And a sword it was. Probably. As only the top half was visible it could potentially have been an ornate shovel, but a sword seemed more likely. It was protruding from the centre of an inverted plastic cone affair that had been pushed down into the mud, and it couldn't have been there long because even in the dim light inside the tent the metal shone like burnished silver, and the black leather binding on the hilt showed no sign of wear or decay.

'Myn uffern i!' said Taff, a spanner firmly wedged in his translation engine.

Bill placed a brown paper bag onto his deckchair, where a nasty looking grease stain began to spread across the gaily-striped fabric. His quest for coffee and Danish had led him to Sid, who had translated the petition and supplied two cups of tea and two bacon sarnies. Bill frowned; it wasn't like Ben to leave his post. They'd been a team for years, and Bill had once seen his stalwart partner soil himself rather than neglect his sworn duty. Then Bill spotted that the tent flap wasn't in precisely the same position it had been when he'd left; it was off by at least two degrees to the vertical, and pushed further out by eleven eighteenths of an inch. Ben must have gone to the tent for some reason, so Bill set off to fetch him before their breakfast congealed into one solid lump of pork product

'He's coming!' said Thermos with some urgency.

'How can you tell from here, they're right up in the trees?'

'Not *that* one, the *other* one.'

'The *other* one? Shit! Well don't panic,' said Taff, panicking. 'There's two of us and only one of him, and at least he hasn't got a gun.'

'Taff ...' said Thermos

'What?' asked Taff.

'He's got a gun,' said Thermos.

'Really?' asked Taff.

'Really,' said Thermos.

'A big gun?' asked Taff.

'A very big gun,' said Thermos.

'Okay, now you can panic,' said Taff.

'Will do,' said Thermos, and he did.

Bill had already drawn his .44 Magnum (seriously though, what else could it have been?) from its discreet but chaffing shoulder holster, and the weight of his chrome-plated cliché gave him the sort of reassurance that only a huge handgun can. It may no longer have been the most powerful handgun in the world, but it still had oodles of cachet. As the British government hadn't yet seen the benefits of placing lethal weapons in the hands of the likes of Bill, he had to make do with a gas-powered replica that fired small plastic pellets. Lethal it was not, but his mother was probably right; he *could* have someone's eye out with it. Stung like buggery at close range as well, and the lead weights he'd placed inside the grip gave it a more appropriate heft, though they spoiled the balance a tad and the man at the toy shop said they probably invalidated the warranty.

Thermos backed away from his peephole and reversed into Taff, who in turn fell over backwards. The corpulent Welshman instinctively made a grab for something to steady himself, and his hands came to rest on the sword, one set of chubby digits wrapping around each side of the cross guard.

'Help,' said Taff. He said it very quietly so as not to excite the man with the gun who was just outside.

Thermos grabbed Taff's belt with both hands and pulled. Most of the effort was absorbed by Taff's belt sinking into his midriff, but some of it got to Taff's hands in the form of a gentle tug on the sword.

From the commotion inside the tent, Bill could tell that it wasn't just his missing partner in there. Subversives! Subversives were bad. Bill's 'How to be a Heavy' self-paced home-study course had been very clear in that regard. It had also included some excellent descriptions of how to roll through doorways and come up shooting. There had been numbered diagrams and a foot placement chart and everything. Bill rolled through the tent flap and came up shooting. Perfect posture. Down on one knee, both hands on his weapon, arms extended, elbows slightly bent.

'Freeze!' he yelled. Went with the territory.

Those who understand Bill's love of his chosen vocation should be feeling very sorry for him at this moment. He'd been waiting a very long time for the chance to make use of his training. Not to mention all of the years of sacrifice that had been required to hone him into the man he was today. But when the time had come to show the mettle of the man inside the suit, there had been nobody there to see it. The tent was empty.

As for Ben, I don't think we should be feeling anything but contempt for his behaviour. So easily lured away from his post by promises of hanky panky in the woods. So easily parted from his clothes. 'Strip off and close your eyes, big boy,' she'd said. Stripping and eye closing by big boy had taken place at the double. After five minutes, Ben succumbed to his increasing unease and slowly opened one eye. There was no sign of either the stunning redhead or his clothes.

'Fuck me!' said Ben as it dawned on him that the redhead had never intended to.

Professor James Stephenson was a man going through changes. Big changes. He was fitter and stronger than he had ever been, and it showed. So impressive was his new physique that none of his clothes would fit over it. Initially he'd wondered about these sudden improvements, but his voices had told him not to worry, so as Stephenson undressed and admired his new body in the boardroom mirror he thought no more about it. If he had thought about it then he might have realized that all of this tinkering with his metabolism and body chemistry would have consequences. He may have looked a million dollars, but Stephenson's major organs wouldn't have fetched tuppence-halfpenny and a bag of marbles.

'Good God, man. What do you think you're playing at? You're naked!' The Right Hon. Edward Dowdeswell, Member of Parliament for Skipthorpe East, was Salsa Food's big gun, and he could feel a firing coming on.

'And your point is, Ted?'

'I'll thank you not to call me Ted, Professor Stephenson. My point is that you have, as we've suspected for some time, gone completely insane. I just needed to see it for myself, and now that I have seen it I'm satisfied that you're bonkers. Loopy. Doolally tap.' With that assessment, the Right Hon. was right on.

'Mad? Oh, now why would you say such a thing, Teddy boy?'

'Why? This new project of yours, that's why.' Dowdeswell waved his cigar around as he spoke and unintentionally spelt out 'cleft' in smoke. 'Until now we've been prepared to overlook your bizarre eccentricities because your purification process saved us from a potentially embarrassing situation. That, plus your father, of course. He was a great man, your father, and he did sterling work for Salsa's perfume division during the Cologne Wars. But this sword business? That's a step too far, laddy. And for God's sake put some clothes on.'

'Too far? Really? How so?' Stephenson retrieved his underwear from the boardroom table and did a standing jump into them, just because he could.

'Excalibur? You really expect anybody to believe that you've found Excalibur? *The* Excalibur? The *legendary* sword of King Arthur? King Arthur, for Heaven's sake. The round table and all that twaddle?'

'And all that twaddle, yes.'

'Well I don't believe a word of it. I don't know what you're up to Stephenson, but I'm going to make sure you don't get away with it.'

'Finished?' Stephenson skipped around the table until he was directly opposite the enraged Dowdeswell.

'I'm most certainly not, but you are, Stephenson. Finished. I'm having you replaced, do you hear me?'

'Oh, we hear you.'

'We? And who is 'we' exact-'

Making full use of his new agility and brute strength, Stephenson leapt the table, clamped his hands firmly either side of Dowdeswell's head and give sharp twist. The Right Hon. Edward Dowdeswell MP slumped forward, his head thudding hard against the polished wood. The *back* of his head. With little more than a flick of his wrists, Stephenson had taken a life and given birth to a by-election. He plucked the still smoking cigar out from between lifeless lips and took a long, satisfying puff.

'*Well, did you enjoy that, Jimmy Boy?*'

'I did. I really did.' He really had.

Stephenson bounded half the length of the room and pressed the intercom button. 'Miss Selby, hold all my calls for the next two hours, I'm going to be lunching with Edward Dowdeswell in the boardroom.' Stephenson looked down at the corpse slumped at the table. Dowdeswell had been a big man. 'On second thoughts, Miss Selby, take the rest of the day off. Edward and I will be dining for some time I suspect.'

'*Hey, look what I've found buried back here. There's some guilt, some compassion, and a bit that looks like mercy. What should I do with them?*'

'*Ditch them, we don't need them.*'

'*Okey-dokey. Save me an eyeball.*'

Professor James Stephenson was a man going through changes.

Seemingly they weren't for the better.

Alec Gardener woke with a start. A really bad start. He sat up and fumbled around for his cigarettes, lighting one as he swung his legs over the side of the bed and fought to remember why his ribs and ankle hurt.

'Smythe. Pongo Smythe. We met last night.'

There was a thud and a slight rocking of the caravan as Alec bounced off the roof.

'Sorry, did I startle you?' asked Pongo, unnecessarily.

'Urrphh,' said Alec, spitting out a cigarette filter. 'I thought I'd dreamt you.'

'I get that a lot.' Pongo smiled a thoroughly disarming smile.

There were a lot of questions that suddenly needed to be asked. Alec selected the most important of them. 'You're not planning to hurt me again anytime soon, are you?'

Pongo's smile broadened and his eyebrows did cheerful things. 'Me? Heavens no. I'm a perfectly harmless old thing, I assure you.'

Alec dejectedly rubbed the sore spot on top of his head and wondered how a day only one minute old had become so complicated. 'You know, I was told I'd be safe in this bloody caravan, but so far I've had my ankle twisted, my chest crushed and my head nearly split open.'

'You were told? By whom, pray tell?'

'Any good reason I should trust you?'

'At this point I would have to concede that you have none, but if I really intended you harm I would have had ample opportunity after you passed out last evening, would I not?'

There was no arguing with that, so Alec didn't try. When all was said and done, at the end of the day, and all that malarkey, he had no choice but to play along. He'd seen enough to know that he wasn't going to beat Pongo in a straight fight. He didn't rate his chances of beating him in a bent fight either, where he had a polo mallet and Pongo didn't. With a feeling of abject resignation, Alec reached into his back pocket and produced Mad Ned's note. As he handed it to Pongo he noticed that the odd little man was wearing a pale yellow suit. Hadn't he been wearing a green one last night?

Pongo unfolded the note and read it. Then he laughed.

'What?' Alec couldn't recall anything on the note that had constituted a rib-tickler.

'This Robin, did he go by any other names?'

'I think everybody around here calls him Mad Ned, and apparently he has a thing for television commercials.'

Pongo grinned. 'Mad Ned! The man's audacity knows no bounds!'

'You know him then?'

'I can't say that I know him, but I certainly know *of* him. Though not as Mad Ned. His name is Madden. Robin Madden. Oft referred to as The Thieving Magpie.

Or he was, a long time ago.' Pongo came over all troubled. 'A very long time ago. In truth, he should be dead by now.'

Alec made with the big frowning. 'Tell me if I'm holding the wrong end of the stick here, but are you saying he's a thief?'

'No, not at all.'

'Oh good.' That was a relief. Associating with the criminal element was on Alec's list of things best avoided. It was even underlined.

'I mean no, you aren't holding the wrong end of my stick. Robin Madden is indeed a thief. A most renowned thief, as a matter of fact. There can be few people in England who haven't heard tales of The Thieving Magpie.'

'Well, I haven't.'

'Which is as it should be. Nobody here would know of him.'

'Didn't you just say that there were few in England who *hadn't* heard of him?' Alec could feel a confusion coming on.

'I did, but then I was speaking of my England, not yours.'

'*Your* England? Where is that, exactly?'

'Right here.'

'And *my* England?'

'That is right here also.'

'But they're not the *same* England?'

'No.'

'But they're both here?'

'Yes.'

'And are they both here now?'

Pongo gave that one some thought before giving a less than committed answer. 'Not really.'

'I think I'd prefer it if you weren't really here either,' said Alec. He tried to inject a menacing undertone into his voice, but not so menacing that Pongo would feel the need to hurt him.

'But there is something I need to-'

'Please go away.'

'I really believe you should-'

'Fuck off!' hinted Alec.

Pongo sighed. He'd anticipated this moment, but knowing it would come made it no less irksome. 'As you wish. It would be froward of me not to do as you ask.' Pongo reached for his cane and made to stand, winced and sat down again. He stretched out a hand towards Alec. 'Perhaps you could assist me in getting down the steps; it would appear that last evening's exertions followed by a night in this chair have left me rather stiff.'

'Of course.' Alec got to his feet, ignoring an assortment of genuine aches and pains in order to help Pongo Smythe overcome some fictitious ones. If Alec hadn't been trying to remember if 'froward' was an actual word, he might have noticed that Pongo had his eyes closed and was whispering something. The walls shimmered and seemed to expand outwards by several feet and then collapse back, as if the vardo itself had taken a deep breath. Alec stopped, as you would.

'Did you see that?' Alec needed to hear Pongo say yes.

Pongo said nothing. He hadn't seen it, but he'd felt it. It had run through his brain and down his spine like an electric shock, and if Pongo hadn't had the skill to defend himself then it might have killed him. It seemed that The Magpie knew a trick or two.

'I said-' Alec Gardener didn't get to finish his sentence as Pongo leant forward and their fingertips touched, and from that moment on Alec Gardener's plans for the rest of his life were scuppered, shagged, and right royally screwed. There was a flash of blue light that filled Alec's nostrils with the acrid smell of ozone, and he was thrown backwards to land as an undignified heap on the bed.

Pongo got to his feet and walked over to examine Alec's prone body. Both men were dripping with perspiration, but only Alec had wisps of purple smoke drifting out of his nostrils. Pongo lifted an eyelid and stared into an unconscious eye, took the pulse from a very limp wrist, and put his ear to a chest that wasn't showing any outward signs of inner activity.

'That's good,' said a relieved Pongo. 'It would appear that I didn't kill you. Or me, for that matter. The seed is planted, so let us see what grows, shall we?' Pongo Smythe returned to his seat and sat down to wait. While he waited, he hummed the catchy little ditty he'd overheard the night before. 'Dumdum tum, dumdum tum, dumdum tum and his dum ti tum cat ...'

The gusting wind lashes the rain against the stumbling figure in the long grey robes. As he crests the hill he gazes down into the valley below, a thin smile appearing on lips almost completely lost behind a heavy white beard. The Heavens must have glimpsed that smile as they roar their disapproval, darkening the sky and spearing the rain down harder yet.

Undeterred the man in the robes struggles on. The midday sky is as black as midnight, and the rain turns to stinging hail.

'Do your worst, I fear you not,' the traveller yells up at the laden clouds. A bolt of lightning strikes the ground close enough for him to feel the heat of it. 'Missed me,' he cries, but there is a tremble in the voice now, and the defiance sounds hollow.

The hail makes the mud on the riverbank bubble as though on the boil, and the river itself is alive. Alive and afraid. Fish leap from the turbulent waters, their tails flapping out a funeral march in the mud as they mouth silent curses at the robed figure. That figure raises his arms wide and screams strange words that are whipped away by the wind almost before they have left his lips. The ground at his feet trembles, gently at first but with growing intensity, until the man can barely keep his feet. The earth rips apart, a trench opening in the ground like a muddy wound that stretches away to the horizon. Still chanting, the figure steps down into that wound and draws his most precious cargo from the folds of his robe. He unwinds cloth coverings and holds the contents aloft so that the enraged heavens can witness his act of defiance.

'You must not do this.' It is the voice of a woman, and she is standing before him in the ditch, her white dress no more than sheen on her skin in the rain. We can only see her from behind. She is beautiful.

'I must do this. You know that.' The man can see her face when we cannot. He recognizes her. She is beautiful.

'I do not know,' she says. The man shouts to be heard over the gale. She does not. She speaks quietly, yet her voice is clear and reaches out to him, unhindered. Her voice is beautiful.

'You must know. You must understand. It is the only way.'

'It is not. Return the sword to me now. It was not created for this.' The voice is still soft but the power of the command thunders louder than the storm. The wind tosses her hair like burnished flame. She is beautiful.

'I cannot. I will not. This has to be.' He raises the sword high above his head. 'You know what will become of us if I do not.'

'I do. I know what is to come. I do not fear it. I fear what will become of us if you do this thing.'

'What we stand for must survive. It cannot be allowed to fade. Do you not see that?' The man is pleading, but he knows that his plea will count for naught this day.

'We have lived long enough. Our time is over.'

'No. I cannot accept that. I will do this. I must do this.' The man shields his face from the lashing wind.

'Then what you do here today will be undone.'

'That cannot be. The bloodline will be severed.'

The woman shakes her head slowly. 'No. The bloodline will continue. And it shall continue under my protection.'

'So be it. My will be done.' Lightning strikes the blade. Metal and flesh glow like blue fire. The blade is plunged into the sodden earth. The heavens scream in sympathy.

The woman is gone. She was beautiful. The scene rips and there are two rivers and two trenches occupying two valleys. The same yet different. They drift apart, these flickering photographs of the same scene. Then there is only one.

The robed figure falls to his knees, exhausted. Drained. He crawls from the trench and sits in the mud. The storm abates. The howling gale softens to a whisper in the trees. The hail becomes rain; the rain becomes mist; the mist clears. The clouds break and the sun returns once more. The man closes his eyes and raises his hands, only his fatigue fighting against him now. The ground shakes again as huge slabs of rock push up from beneath the river. Granite steps spew out of the mud and silt, damming the old watercourse, forcing the river into the new channel. The sword is lost beneath a torrent of white foam and muddy brown water.

The man is done. The heavens are not. A bolt of lightning snakes across the blue sky like a hissing cobra, striking the old man in the chest.

'Bloody weather!' he says as he slumps back onto a bed of dying fish.

Alec was flapping around on the bed like a dying fish. The seed Pongo had planted had germinated successfully, though that wasn't quite how Alec saw it. From his point of view it was a widescreen Technicolor surround-sound high definition bloody nightmare. As for Pongo, he was having a few mental flashes of his own. A touch of cerebral feedback from this Alec Gardener. Alec Gardener? Oh, so that was his name. Pongo had introduced himself twice, but Alec hadn't taken either opportunity to reciprocate. As there had been direct and intimate contact between their two minds it was fair to say that they were beyond polite handshakes and formal introductions now.

Mad Ned. Pongo mulled the name over. The Magpie. Mad Ned. Television commercials. Pongo suspected there *was* a link, and there was a simple way to confirm that suspicion. He reached into his sack and produced the glyphweave, placing it in the centre of the table. Nothing happened. Nothing happened some more. Then it wobbled. The wobble became a shake. The shake became a spin. Then it stopped spinning, rolled around for a few seconds, made an assortment of mechanical clicking noises, and then became still.

'Oh dear me,' said Pongo because he hadn't said it for a while.

Detective Inspector George Guv sat in his superior's office and tried not to dwell on the reasons for his being there. He wasn't well liked amongst the hierarchy, George knew that. He'd had always made his superiors uneasy with his interest in things 'not of this world', and he'd gained a reputation for always seeking the bizarre explanation, for suggesting the outlandish motive, for writing unfathomable reports. George Guv was not a man who shaved with Occam's razor.

By the time his immediate superior, Detective Chief Inspector Grant, and his superior's immediate superior, Detective Superintendent Sumner, arrived in the office, George had his resignation speech all set to go. He was sure he was about to be dismissed, demoted, or at least decried, for his unsanctioned interference at Dartford Tunnel. Incredibly, only two of those present at the 'Dartford incident' had suffered anything more than cuts and bruises. Joining the unfortunate Mike Carter on the official casualty role is Detective Sergeant Nigel Sillcott, who required treatment for second-degree burns to his left leg after George's cigarette landed in his turn-up and set his trousers alight. The official casualty role was, of course, officially wrong because nobody sufficiently officious to update official lists knew about the assorted body parts liberally strewn around inside the tunnel. Officially.

'George,' said Detective Chief Inspector Grant.

'Yes, guv?' said George Guv. There was no fighting with tradition in these matters.

'We'd like to have a little chat with you about what happened at Dartford yesterday.'

A little chat? That sort of thing really disappointed George. Where were the shouting and screaming and the thumping of desks? Where was the 'give me your badge and gun now you insubordinate bastard'? George poured all of his angst and frustration into his 'righto, guv', but nobody seemed to notice.

'Now, George,' it was Det. Supt. Sumner who presumed to be on a first name basis this time 'I believe that you identified the creatures in Dartford Tunnel to your Sergeant as ... ogres, was it?'

'No, sir. Trolls, sir.' Tradition dictated that George refer to his superior's superior as 'sir'. Only his superior could call his superior's superior 'guv'.

'Ah, yes, that was it. Trolls. Tell us, George, what do you know about trolls?'

'Only what I've read in books, sir. It's a hobby of mine.' This meeting wasn't going at all how George had expected.

'Excellent. In which case we may have a job for you, George.'

'A job, sir?'

'Please, call me guv.'

Forty-Five minutes later George Guv left the office with a large manila folder under his arm and a Cheshire cat grin on his face. A grin not unlike those that Det. Supt. Sumner and D.C.I. Grant were sporting as they watched George go.

'Trolls indeed! Still, that little lot should keep the irritating wanker out of everybody's hair for a while. The problem, Grant, is that Guv's not a team player. I don't want somebody on my team who isn't a team player, and I especially don't want somebody on my team who isn't a team player and can't spot a terrorist when he sees one, just because of some clever animatronic costume gizmo, now do I?'

Grant nodded. 'Too true, guv.'

'For Heaven's sake man, call me sir.'

Jack gazed in silent dismay at his one and only customer. Bladder gazed back equally silently at his one and only barman. The landlord of The Queen's Arms had an extensive range of well-rehearsed patois, but Bladder had heard it all more than once. Jack opted to go with something new. It was a risky tactic. Over the years, Bladder had become a dab hand at shooting down even the most impressive Jack fact, twisting the soundest logic into an oxymoronic collection of non-sequiturs. Every night Jack would try to impress his inebriate sparring partner, and every night he would fail spectacularly. Tonight's titbit was a good one, but the increasingly querulous landlord wasn't holding out much hope for it. He'd long since come to realize that, contrary to popular opinion, Bladder was a man who understood that erudite wasn't a type of glue.

"Ere, Bladder, did you know that you're two hundred times more likely to be killed by a faulty toaster than by a shark?'

Bladder cogitated, deliberated, and then responded. 'Wot, when you're swimmin'?'

'I don't think so.'

'When you're makin' toast then?'

'S'pose so.'

'Makes sense then, don't it? Not very likely to be killed by a shark when you're makin' toast.'

'S'pose not.' Jack sighed and returned to breaking a goodly number of health and safety rules. With the battle already lost, he saved his fact about the anomalous chromosome structure of the common okapi for another time, returning instead to an old favourite: Bladder's job, or apparent lack thereof. Little was known about Bladder, beyond the usual village gossip and idle speculation, though it was known that he had once played trombone in a band. A very good band, by all accounts, who played an innovative blend of jazz, funk, and mellow soul, and who would probably have made it big if they'd not chosen to call themselves *Satan's Motherfuckers*.

'So 'ow's business, Barry? Got any big jobbies in the pipeline?' In his eagerness Jack had delivered a critical phrasing error that had him sounding like a closet coprophiliac. He added a sullen 'never mind' and waited for Bladder to select a new topic. Any topic. Any topic at all.

'Ow's the wife, Jack?' grinned Bladder.

Any topic but that one.

'She's grand thanks, Barry.' That was the only answer Jack ever gave when any of the regulars asked after his old lady. The ever-absent Mrs. Jack had become a creature of legend. Many believed in her existence, but none alive could claim to have seen her. Recently. Certainly not since Jack had built the new patio for the beer garden, though she was often to be seen moving around in the bedroom of the flat above the pub, the previously waif-like Mrs. Jack having gained in both weight and height so that she now strongly resembled her husband in drag. It was fertile ground for gossip, but there were no rumours, no idle speculation, and no tongues wagged. Nobody speculated about the whereabouts of the agoraphobic Mrs. Jack, because everybody in the village knew she had moved to Brighton with an accredited gas service engineer called Derek. It was just that they all cared too much about Jack to *admit* that they knew, and they thought it was rather sweet of him to go to all this bother to convince them that he'd done away with his spouse. Jack was thoughtful like that.

'That reporter bloke up in Ned's caravan now then?' Jack had seen it happen and didn't need the confirmation, but with Bladder the safest questions to ask were the ones you already knew the answer to.

'Aye. Don't reckon we'll be seein' any more of him.'

'No? How so?' Jack was feeling troubled by how easily Alec Gardener's expense account had escaped.

'Things gettin' just a bit too odd 'round here for him I'd say. He's one of them city fellas, likes everythin' just so. Can't be doin' with the likes of us, Jack Woodall.' Even when he was full to the eyebrows, Bladder was a very perceptive man. He'd known Alec wanted to leave before Alec did.

'Pity, 'e 'ad a nice wallet. Real leather. Quality stitching. Spaces for more than one of 'em credit card things. I'll sorely miss it.' Jack's expression became all dreamy and distant.

'Me an' all. But we've seen the last of it I fear.'

There could have been no better cue than that for Alec to walk into the lounge bar of The Queen's Arms. It was so good that both Jack and Bladder cast an anticipatory eye towards the bar door. They were still greatly surprised when Alec Gardener walked through it. He wasn't alone either.

'Well hello Pete. Not seen you in these parts for a while.' It was an ebullient greeting by Jack standards, and it took Alec a few moments to realize that it was directed at Pongo.

'Hello to you, Jack. Yes, it has been a long old time,' replied Pongo in that cheery fashion that Alec was starting to find really annoying.

'The usuals, gentlemen?' Jack's smile was full of fiscal anticipation.

'If you'd be so good, Jack. And a packet of peanuts.' Pongo was partial to a peanut now and then. He was having some now because he hadn't been able to get any then.

Alec just nodded and supplied money. His 'usual' was a pint of best. In The Queen's Arms everybody's 'usual' was a pint of best, regardless of what they might usually choose to order.

Pongo grabbed the drinks and hastily ushered Alec over to the most distant table, leaving Jack clutching the change from a tenner and nobody to relieve him of it. He stored it in the till for safekeeping.

Alec sat down beside a large plastic yucca plant in need of dusting and stared across the table at Pongo. On the walk from Ned's caravan the strange little man had somehow managed to change his suit and was now sporting a natty blue pinstripe. 'Pete?'

'Jack and the others in Falston I've had contact with over the years know me as Pete Smith, a sales representative for a women's lingerie manufacturer. It has proved to be a useful device for initiating conversations,' said Pongo between mouthfuls of protein-packed salted nibbles.

Alec nodded. He could see how being big in ladies knickers might be an ice-breaker. Now that he had beer Alec felt better equipped to tackle the intricacies of the day, more specifically the details of what had happened in Ned's caravan. Pongo Smythe had done something to him, and Alec wanted to know what. He initiated his clever plan for finding out. 'What did you do to me?'

Pongo thought. Then he drank. Then he thought some more. Then he drank and thought at the same time. Then he reached a decision, and for the second day running he gave up the secret that his family had kept for more generations than he cared to think about. 'What I did, Alec Gardener, was give you a glimpse of the history which shaped our two realities. The dramatization was a little stylized perhaps, but the events are basically true. I'm about to tell you a great deal more about that history, though at this juncture you probably won't believe me.'

'Why do you say that?'

'Because it's a difficult history to accept.'

'No, I mean why did you say 'probably'?' Alec drank. Then he thought. Then he drank some more. Then he thought and drank at the same time. Then he reached a decision. 'Right, you talk, I'll drink. If I'm still sober when you've finished then I'll tell you what I think. I'll tell you even if I'm not sober, but I'd be less likely to believe me then.'

Pongo balled up the empty peanut packet and tossed it into his sack. 'I can live with those terms.'

Alec got to his feet. 'I'll get some more drinks in then, and if I'm going to be drinking then I'm going to need to eat. I'm sure Jack can rustle me up a sandwich or something.' A sandwich was unlikely. If Jack went rustling in the kitchen then the result would be an 'or something'.

'Good idea, and some more peanuts, if you would be so kind.' Pongo watched as Alec weaved through the maze of tables and plastic foliage en route to the bar. 'There is something about this one' he muttered to himself. 'Something a bit special.'

'I would suggest that I make the next attempt alone, John Bostwicke. Your left leg is broken in several places, your right shoulder is dislocated, and I suspect that you have at least one broken rib.' The unicorn paused, trying to remember some of the human niceties that Pongo had taught him. 'Does it hurt?'

John laughed. Then he groaned. 'Only when I laugh, apparently. It would appear that Draknoor is not in the mood for conversation this day.'

'I cannot recall a day when he was in such a mood. Though we did awaken him, and his kind can be of an ill temper when roused from their slumber.'

'Merely an ill temper? Then I would not like to see him when he was truly angry. I feel I would not like him when he was angry.'

'A wise observation, John Bostwicke. Seeing him angry would likely be the last sight you ever beheld.' John nodded. That much he could do without grimacing. He reached into his tunic pocket, which he couldn't do without grimacing, and produced the last three vials of liquid that Pongo had given him. Two had been smashed and the third was only half-full. John had been regularly sipping his supply of kribble in order to keep Garthang within his range of perception. Now he was using what he had left to dull the pain.

Garthang saw the broken vials in John's hand. 'Use what you have left as sparingly as the pain will allow, John. Once it is gone, I will be unable to communicate with you. Draknoor can see and hear me as a matter of nature, you cannot.'

'I understand. Now be off with you, you overgrown pony. I have things to do and you are distracting me.'

Garthang shook his mane and snorted. He was never happy to be reminded of his equine heritage, even in jest. Nor had his infrequent dealings with humankind given him any great appreciation of their humour. But he did know a brave man when he saw one. 'Then I shall go. Hopefully Draknoor will be more open to my approach if I am alone.'

John Bostwicke watched as the unicorn disappeared back into the cave that John had recently bounced out of. A few moments later there was a deafening roar and John felt a wave of heat roll over him. Apparently Draknoor's mood hadn't improved any.

We're going to leave John at this point because Alec's sandwich has arrived.

It was a perfectly edible sausage and fried egg sandwich, bearing more than a passing resemblance to the sausage and fried egg sandwiches that Sid did in the café. In fact, the 'Sid's Café' napkin that Jack had forgotten to take off the plate made this sandwich identical to a Sid sandwich in every respect. It just cost twice as much.

With his second pint of beer well in hand and his sandwich a devourment in progress, Alec was feeling considerably better.

Pongo chose that moment to make him feel considerably worse again. 'I think it's time I started talking. We had an agreement, after all.'

'No, really-' Alec negotiated the words out past a mouthful of sausage 'don't go to any trouble on my account.'

Pongo thought he should, so he did. 'What you witnessed earlier, and I'm using a certain amount of conjecture here as mind seeding is not an exact art, is an event that some refer to as The Grand Separation. You saw the precise moment when The Single Age came to an end and the two Earths were born.'

'The two Earths? So you're talking about another planet then, or maybe a different dimension?' Alec wanted to pin Pongo's delusion down a bit so he could blow holes in it with his giant intellect. Alec was a clever guy. If he'd also been an observant guy he might have spotted a sausage fall out of his sandwich.

'No, not at all,' continued Pongo, who was both clever and observant. And tactful. 'We all coexist on the same planet in the same dimension, but our worlds are out of phase with each other. Something to do with universal harmonics, I believe. Quantum mechanics isn't one of my specialties, but as I understand it the two Earths occupy the same space but at different times. When your world phases out, mine phases in, and vice versa, but it happens so quickly that nobody on either world could ever notice it.'

'You just made all of that up to avoid talking about 'magic', didn't you?' Alec made quotation marks with his fingers as he said the word 'magic', confirming that he could be as annoying as everybody else when the occasion demanded.

'Actually, no, I believe my grasp of the science is sound. But you're right about my preferring not to mention magic just yet.'

'So when and why did all of this happen?' Alec was feeling smug. His giant intellect had won through and made Pongo admit that magic played a part in his delusion. As everybody knew there was no such thing as magic, then it followed that the rest of Pongo's story was a big steaming pile of poo as well.

'The when would be 500 AD, give or take a few decades. The why is a little more complex.' Pongo gazed somewhat dejectedly at the bright yellow star on his packet of peanuts proclaiming that they were 'new and improved', thus making all previous peanuts he had enjoyed old and inferior.

'Thought it might be.' Alec had progressed from feeling smug to sounding smug.

'Put in its simplest form, a certain individual became concerned about the way that the world was changing. Science and technological advancement were beginning to displace the old ways, and rather than embrace progress and accept the consequences he took it upon himself to create somewhere else for that progress to take place. One world for the old, one world for the new.'

Alec frowned. That was the *simplest* form? 'That was very magnanimous of him. So who was this certain individual?'

'His name was Myrddin, but in your world I believe he is more commonly known as Merlin.' Pongo smiled again, but he managed to do it without looking happy.

'I see. I'm really not getting a warm fuzzy feeling about this you know.'

Pongo shrugged. 'What I've told you is the truth. How you react to it is your own problem.'

Alec's problem was that he didn't know how to react to the truth, because it *was* the truth. Pongo's truth. Technically Pongo wasn't lying to him because there was no doubt that the strange little man believed every word of what he'd just said. Nor was Pongo mad. He drank beer, appreciated women in lingerie and didn't feel the need to wear a hat, which made him sane in every way that was important to Alec. He was clearly intelligent too, having conversed with another man in a pub for ten minutes without once mentioning sport or breasts. Being Pongo's friend until the authorities recaptured him seemed to Alec to be the humane thing to do. 'So we're talking about *the* Merlin then? King Arthur and Camelot and all that stuff?'

'All that stuff, yes,' said Pongo, who hadn't spotted the humanity and was wondering if Alec was trying to humour him or humiliate him. Either way, it hummed.

'This Grand Separation thingy isn't in any Arthurian legend I've ever read.' Not that Alec had read many. Or any. But he was sure it hadn't been in any of the films he'd seen.

'Well that's the thing about a secret, isn't it? People tend not to know about it. This isn't the story of Arthur you are familiar with. It all took place earlier than the legends that persist in your world would have you believe. The players and the stage are much the same, but the backdrop is different. Few people know the truth of it.'

'Few sane people anyway. So is there anything else you feel you should be telling me at this point?'

Pongo nodded. 'Yes. You have a sausage in your beer.'

Thelonius Wisp was no coward. He wasn't stupid either. Lady Gaynor Elfam undoubtedly had power. More power than Wisp had anticipated, less than she would have him believe, but it should have been a simple task for The Guild to send her scurrying back into whatever hellhole had spawned her. Simple once perhaps, but Wisp knew that it was beyond their ability now. Now The Guild was weak, and growing weaker. As Grand Master he was best placed to see the decline, but others were beginning to suspect. If things kept going like this, Wisp could see a time when all of their Magicks would begin with 'pick a card, any card.'

'My dear Thelonius, what *are* you thinking?' Lady Gaynor Elfam sat upon her newly installed black onyx gargoyle-embellished throne, her robes a cloak of darkness that greedily devoured any light that strayed close to her.

'Nothing, milady. Just wool-gathering.' It comforted Wisp to know that Gaynor couldn't yet force her way into his mind. He'd felt her scratching at the door though.

'Wool-gathering? Then perhaps you could weave me a rug, this floor is *so* cold.'

'Most amusing, milady.'

'Please don't toady Thelonius, it doesn't suit you, and I'm not in the mood to kill you today.'

'Oh good.' Wisp tried to sound flippant, but he really was very pleased.

'But then again, now that I know where Excalibur lies, why should I allow you to leave this room alive? What use are you?' Wisp felt some involuntary scrotum tightening as Gaynor stood and stepped towards him.

'Please, no more empty threats milady. We both know that you still need us. You haven't stolen enough energy to be able to leave this place.' Wisp was guessing, but it seemed the most logical explanation for Gaynor's increasing strength and The Guild's growing infirmity.

'How very astute of you, Thelonius. Perhaps I do still have need of your precious Guild. But what use are *you*?' Lady Gaynor's eyes were burning yellow under her cowl.

Oops! Wisp hadn't given that enough thought. By calling Gaynor's bluff, he had angered her into proving that she wasn't bluffing. She still needed The Guild, but she didn't specifically need *him*. He felt the sting of his own perspiration in his eyes and a thumping in his chest as his heart made the most of its last few beats. This was not the way that Thelonius Wisp had envisaged his end. Usually he envisaged a painless coronary whilst having energetic sex on his one-hundred-and-sixty-fourth birthday.

'You are a clever man, Thelonius Wisp. Much too clever by half. And that makes you a threat.' Gaynor took another step forward. The yellow eyes paled for a moment and then blazed red. Blood red. Long, elegant fingers slid out from her floppy sleeves, and Lady Gaynor threw off her robe with all of the melodrama that such a moment called for. Wisp gasped. This was no withered crone standing before him. This was not the aged hag-witch that he had imagined behind that cloak of darkness. She was young. Barely free of her teen years, Wisp guessed, and she was elegant. Lady Gaynor was every bit the lady. Curls of long raven hair tumbled over a gold-trimmed green velvet dress, pinched in all the right places over a figure that had all the right places to be pinched. Around her waist she wore a tan leather apron embellished with runic devices that even Wisp couldn't identify. At her side hung a length of animal fur, the pelt of some exotic cat species. Possibly ocelot. Around her neck she wore an ornate golden amulet that Wisp recognized, though he'd only ever seen it in old paintings and even older etchings.

Wisp was aghast. Wisp was speechless. Wisp was screwed. He tried to take a step back but bumped into something solidly muscular. 'Did you not say that you weren't in the mood to kill me today?'

Lady Gaynor nodded. 'I did say that, didn't I?'

'You lied?' There was no panic in Wisp's voice now, only resignation tinged with sadness.

'Indeed I did.'

There was the 'swoosh', and Wisp saw the tip of a blade pass from right to left in front of him. There was surprisingly little pain.

'So did I.' Wisp had used all of his abilities to mould the torn shreds of his aura around the fatal wound, keeping himself alive for the few extra seconds he'd needed to twist his mouth into a smile and force out the words. Close behind the words came a liquid gurgle from his throat and a grating exhale that could only have been a death rattle. It was over. Moving his jaw had upset the fragile equilibrium, and Brother Thelonius Wisp's head tumbled from his shoulders, making assorted sickening thudding noises as it rolled away from his still upright body and came to rest at Lady Gaynor's feet. She stared down at it. Wisp's lifeless but still smiling face stared back at her (or possibly up her dress, it was difficult to tell). 'So did you? So did you what? Lie? You *lied* to me?' Gaynor stamped her foot and did pouty things, directing her very best doe-eyed look at her sentinel, who was sniffing at Wisp's gaping neck hole. 'He lied to me, Caleb. Can you believe that?'

Wisp's decapitated head rose into the air, though not in a supernatural or magical way, it was just following its nose, which Gaynor had hold of. 'But what did you lie to me about? Not the sword? Tell me it wasn't the sword. It *was* the sword wasn't it? You lied to me about where the sword is, didn't you? It's not in Gallowtree at all, is it? Where is it, Thelonius? *Where is it?'*

Brother Thelonius Wisp declined to reply.

Another petulant foot stamp shook the cavern, bringing a massive stalactite crashing down onto a statue of two nymphs being wholly indecent with a centaur. Lady Gaynor disappeared in a great cloud of dust and a potentially lethal volley of stone nipples. When the dust settled her eyes had lost their fire. 'Now look what you did, Thelonius. You made me all cross and I broke my favourite statue.' Gaynor hooked two fingers into Wisp's nostrils and tossed his head against the wall of the cavern, and then she slumped down onto her throne and sulked.

Lady Gaynor Elfam was having a bad day. It's fair to say that Thelonius Wisp was having a worse one.

The only one having fun was Caleb, who'd found some body to play with.

'Ladies and gentlemen, I give you Anubis, Egyptian god of the dead!'

'Jesus, Mia, why do we put up with this crap?' Chuck Starvinger cringed as a large man in a small loincloth and crude fibreglass jackal's head stumbled onto the stage

Mia Stern looked up from watching a dung beetle roll its burden into one of Chuck's post-show loafers, and for the ninety-seventh time that evening Chuck's long-suffering agent had to remind herself of how much she got paid before she could smile. Mia was screwing Chuck for twenty-six percent, though strictly speaking twenty-two percent of it was for being his agent; only the last four percent was for screwing him. 'Chuck, darling, we put up with this crap because the network is paying a small fortune for exclusive coverage of you making The Sphinx disappear and they wanted a frickin' pre-show, so a frickin' pre-show they're frickin' getting.'

'I'm a great artiste, not some two-bit showman, godammit,' grumbled Chuck as he brushed at the shoulders of his tailored gold lamé suit, showering Mia in sand and sequins.

'Of course you are, Chuck darling, you're pure class.'

'And now,' continued the announcer 'joining Anubis on stage we have his loyal minions, the Nefertiti Dancers.'

Two score and ten overpaid and underdressed nubiles bounded onto the stage, prancing around to a tune that the musical director had considered to be both meaningful and reverential. It was the first time that either of those terms had been applied to The Bangles' *Walk like an Egyptian*.

Chuck's jaw dropped. 'You know that the cultural affairs minister from Cairo is in the audience, don't you? We'll be lucky to get of this country alive.'

'Don't panic, Chuck darling. Everything's fine. You just concentrate on your trick and everybody'll love you and go home happy, like they always do.'

Chuck's grimace got grimmer. He hated his work being called '*tricks*'. He was an illusionist. Perhaps the greatest illusionist the world had ever seen. Chuck thought so anyway, though he generally omitted the 'perhaps.'

'Shooowtime!' boomed the announcer. Chuck took a deep breath and strode onto the stage with all of the flamboyance required of his chosen profession. He did a few simple and heavily embellished sleight of hand tricks whilst the enormous curtains behind him drew closed, and then it was time for the main event. Chuck threw his arms wide, smoke-pots exploded along the edges of the stage and the curtains opened. There were gasps and major 'oohs,' and of course long and thunderous applause. The Sphinx was gone. Chuck allowed the curtains to stay open for as long as he felt that his illusion could stand up to scrutiny, and then he waved his arms and the curtains drew shut. With another wave of his arms and a smile that could be seen from space the curtains opened again.

There were no gasps. No 'oohs.' And definitely no thunderous applause. Just some nervous coughing and a lot of dignitaries shuffling their dignified behinds in their seats. Chuck, still grinning like a loon, craned a look over his shoulder at the empty space that shouldn't have been there. The mirrors were definitely down, Chuck could see them lying flat on the sandy ground, but of The Sphinx there was no sign. For at least five millennia, The Great Sphinx had sat impassively on the sands of Giza. Now Chuck Starvinger had gone and lost it.

'Wow! Great trick, Chuck,' hissed Mia from the wings 'now put the frickin' thing back before we get lynched.'

In all of the ensuing confusion, nobody paid much attention to the immense footprints that led away into the desert.

Morrison stood alone on Falston Bridge. He hadn't planned it that way, it had just sort of happened. Why did nobody understand that if he'd gone to the trouble of making a plan then it really was *de rigueur* that they stick to it? He'd told them as much at the first and only meeting of The Falston-on-Wold Action Committee, and once he'd explained what 'de rigueur' meant they'd wholeheartedly agreed with him. Then they ignored him anyway. This time the plan being ignored was the one where Taff and Thermos met him on the bridge after morning surgery. Morning surgery was done and Morrison had been on the bridge for twenty-three and one half minutes, but of the bickering brace there was no sign. Instead, there were two stern looking gentlemen standing guard at the causeway. A peculiar looking pair, what with one of them wearing the obligatory black suit and the other in a toga fashioned from two lengths of deckchair fabric.

'Pssst!'

That was strange.

'Pssst!' came the strangeness again.

Morrison felt it safe to assume that the psssting was for his benefit, as the security guards didn't look to be the sort of blokes you psssted. He followed the sound to the other side of the bridge and leant over the wall to investigate the down-belowness. A long finger was pressed to his lips, and several more long fingers took hold of his tie and led him off the bridge and down the bank, out of sight of any prying eyes that might happen by.

'Phillip, I need you,' whispered Sara Hagget.

'I feel stupid,' said Ben.

'You look stupid,' said Bill.

'Thanks mate, that was really helpful.' Ben could do sarcasm. It was a useful tool for demonstrating mental superiority over an opponent, apparently. A few more weeks of sarcasm and he'd be ready to tackle irony.

'Well it's your own stupid fault, you randy bugger. You'd still be starkers if I hadn't ripped up the deckchairs. I've got nowhere to sit now, and my corns are killing ... hold up, who's this?'

Ben looked where Bill was looking to see what Bill was seeing. 'I don't know who it is, but he's wearing my suit!'

'Don't be daft. He's at least six inches taller than you.'

'Fair comment.' Ben could see the sense of it, but it really *did* look like his suit.

Morrison was striding down the causeway, trying to exude authority trimmed with menace. His height helped, and the limp lent him an air of danger and mystery, or so he'd always liked to think. Everybody else thought it lent him an air of a man with a gammy knee.

Bill stepped forward and went into polite but assertive mode. 'Sorry sir, this area is currently out of bounds to the public.'

'Which is as it should be, but I'm not the public.' Morrison extended a hand. 'Beresford. Donald Beresford. Down from Warwick.'

Bill stepped back as though Morrison were waving a cattle prod at him. Then he collected himself and stepped forward again, smiling somewhat sheepishly.

Morrison smiled back, somewhat wolfishly. 'Is there a problem?'

'Mr. Beresford? We weren't expecting you until later this afternoon.' It was Ben's turn to step forward, hoping to make a better first impression than his colleague had. As he was the one dressed in a deckchair it was a slim hope.

'So I see. It seems that the rules regarding acceptable on-duty attire have been relaxed recently. I must have missed the memo.'

'Ah, yes, sorry sir. My suit had an accident.' Ben hastened on before Beresford, known throughout the company as 'The Don', could delve further into the nature of his 'accident'. 'May I see some identification please, Mr. Beresford?'

'Excellent. Glad to see one of you is on the ball.' Morrison's calm exterior belied his inner turmoil.

'Thank you, sir.' Ben flashed Bill a nana-nana-naa-na look. 'Can I see it then?'

'See what?' Morrison was stalling. Badly.

'Your ID, sir.' Bill closed ranks with his skimpily clad colleague.

Morrison reached into his pocket and produced the identification that Sara had told him was in there. She had also told him not to look at it or remove it unless he absolutely had to.

Bill and Ben leant in closer and stared. Wiggly, the pink squid bean bag toy, stared back at them, eight dangling polyester legs twitching in response to the nervous shake of Morrison's hand. If Wiggly could have felt the tension in that moment he would have inked himself. Phillip Morrison wasn't the right species and *he* was close to inking himself.

'That all appears to be in order, sir,' said Bill.

'Sorry we had to insist, but you can't be too careful these days, sir,' said Ben.

'Of course.' Morrison wiped the sweat from his brow with Wiggly before returning the hand-stitched cephalopod to his pocket. Sara was going to have some explaining to do, but for the moment Morrison was just happy that nobody wanted to attach anything to his testicles.

Bill and Ben watched in slightly bemused fashion as Donald 'The Don' Beresford limped on down to the tent, went in, came out, walked slowly back down the causeway, trotted over to Falston Bridge, cantered across it, and positively galloped away into the village.

'Moves well for a man with a wooden leg, doesn't he?' said Bill.

'I didn't know The Don had a wooden leg.'

'Yeah, I heard he lost it in Nham.'

'Wow! He was in Vietnam?' Ben was impressed. He'd seen films.

'No, Cheltenham.' Bill's pronunciation was a tad unconventional, but then it needed to be. 'I wonder where he parked his car.'

'His car?'

'Yeah. I've heard that he goes everywhere in a huge Mercedes limo with blacked-out windows.'

'What, like that one?'

Bill did some nodding. 'Yep, that's the sort of thing. One just like that I would expect.'

They watched as a huge Mercedes limo with blacked-out windows drifted slowly and virtually silently onto Falston Bridge. A very wide man in a very black suit and very dark sunglasses got out and stared at them.

The very wide man didn't look happy.

Anatomy wasn't Professor James Stephenson's strongest subject but he thought the thing he was gnawing on was possibly a spleen.

'What's a spleen?'

'Don't know. Doesn't taste of much, does it?'

'I liked the brain. The brains are the best bit.'

Stephenson had to agree. Dowdeswell's brain had been most palatable. Difficult to get at though, requiring much hammering at the skull with an antique-effect bronze elephant paperweight.

'Made a bit of a mess, didn't he?'

Stephenson caught sight of himself in the mirror behind the drinks cabinet. The reflection staring back at him was a deranged circus clown, sunken eyes peering out from orbits of dark shadow, lips circled by a bloody smile, hair red and matted with drying ooze, claret skin stretched drum-tight over his bloated muscles. He'd looked better.

'He looks like shit.'

'I'm thirsty.'

'Me too.'

'We'll get something from the vending machine in reception.' James Stephenson had stopped referring to himself as 'I'.

The lift pinged its arrival on the ground floor and Stephenson stepped out into the foyer.

'Ah, Professor Stephenson, I need to ask you if-' The receptionist stopped talking so abruptly that she sprained a tonsil.

Stephenson stared at the terrified receptionist, and the look in his eyes did nothing to calm her.

'Do we have time?'

'No we don't.'

'Spoilsport.'

After a last lascivious leer, Stephenson bounded over to the vending machine and slammed his fist through the glass panel.

'Now make your selection,' said the machine's tinkling mechanical voice, completely unconcerned that it was being violated.

Stephenson made his selection.

The receptionist watched as her employer exited the building via a window and shambled off towards the main security gate. When she was sure he wasn't coming back she picked up the phone and tried to decide which would be the most appropriate authority to call first.

Alec Gardener and Pongo Smythe were sitting in silence on the wooden bench outside The Queen's Arms when Phillip Morrison galloped by. Neither of them said anything, although Alec had wondered how a vet with a gammy knee could run that fast in a suit tailored for a man at least six inches shorter than he.

After another ten minutes of silence, Alec asked the big question. 'Can you prove any of this?'

Pongo nodded. 'Yes. I can prove all of it.'

Damn. 'How?' Having asked the big question Alec now had lots of little ones that would need answering.

'I think the simplest way would be for me to show you my world,' said Pongo.

'When?' said Alec.

'Now,' said Pongo

'Where?' said Alec

'Up there,' said Pongo, pointing at Falston Wood.

Alec lit a cigarette and got to his feet. 'Right, I'll get the car.'

'Car? We don't need a car, it's not far to walk.'

Alec smiled thinly. 'I have a car so I don't have to walk at all. See you in a few minutes.'

Pongo watched Alec walk away, trailing little puffs of smoke like a steam engine, and wondered if perhaps he should have mentioned that he'd never been in a car before.

'Are our clothes dry yet, Taff?'

'Hold on, I'll check.'

Taff checked. They nearly were. 'They nearly are.'

'Good,' said Thermos 'I've had enough of sitting around here in my underwear.'

'And I've had enough of seeing you sat around here in your underwear.' Taff threw a selection of semi-moist clothing in Thermos' general direction. 'Where the hell *is* here, anyway?'

'I think the right question would be *when* the hell is here.'

'You what?' Taff grimaced; Thermos was about to have one of those moments, the Welshman could feel it in his water.

'Well take a look down there Taff. That's Falston, that is.'

Taff couldn't argue, much as he wanted to. The village nestling in the valley below them *was* Falston-on-Wold. The buildings were different, but they were more or less in the right places. There was a bridge where a bridge should be, crossing a river where a river should be, as they'd discovered when they nearly drowned in it. There had been much coughing and spluttering and smacking of Thermos about the head. Taff hadn't really wanted to, but there had been nobody else there to smack.

'So you see ...' Thermos was still making sounds, and Taff thought that perhaps he should be listening to them '... we must have fallen through a temporary rift in the space-time continuum. We didn't move in space, but we did move backwards through time. Couple of hundred years, I would say.'

Taff gave Thermos' theory due consideration. 'That's bollocks, that is.'

Thermos looked indignant. Not an easy look to pull off when you're only wearing a damp leather posing pouch.

'Likely it's some sort of TV prank. One of those reality show jobbies,' said Taff.

'What, you mean like *I'm a Fat Welsh Git, Get Me Out Of Here*?

That had ended their shortest truce to date.

'Stop!' shouted Pongo.

'Why?' shouted Alec, missing the point completely by not stopping.

'Stop the vehicle now!'

Alec jammed his foot on the brake and the car came to a juddering halt. Pongo's knuckles were white on the dashboard and his face was similarly pale, with perhaps a subtle hint of green.

'What is it?' Alec could see no sign of what had made the small man do the big panic.

'I'm not sure. I sense something; a presence I've not felt since ...' Pongo let his sentence tail off in the appropriate manner as the something he'd sensed floated above the treetops and drifted out over the road ahead of them. A glowing sphere, five feet across, that pulsed and flashed with internal lightning, like one of those futuristic plasma balls that look great in the shop window but look less great shoved in the back of a cupboard when the novelty wears off. The sphere grew larger, the lightning became more violent until it spread over the width of the road and the blinding intensity of it made it painful to look at. Then the ball of light began to spin. Faster and faster it went, churning the air, the edges of the sphere stretching and distorting, throwing out liquid pseudopodia that prismed the sunlight into myriad small rainbows, beautiful to behold and at least doubling the special effects budget.

'It's going to pop,' shouted Pongo over the noise of the wind.

'It's going to what?' shouted Alec over the noise of the wind.

'POP,' shouted the ball, and there was no more wind.

The light was gone, and in its place hung a huge sphere of water. For a second it remained suspended above the road, then it crashed down onto the tarmac as a wave powerful enough to lift Alec's car and deposit it ten feet further down the hill.

'What the hell is that?' said Alec, once he was confident that he was still alive and likely to remain that way for the next few minutes.

Pongo did some serious frowning. 'That was a transfer sphere. A big one.'

'No, not what the hell *was* that, what the hell *is* that.'

'Oh, that,' said Pongo when he saw the thing that was thrashing around on the road in a mightily distressed way. 'Looks like a shark from here.'

'That's too big to be a shark,' hoped Alec. He had a thing about sharks, and it wasn't a good thing.

'Then I stand corrected. It looks like a *big* shark from here.'

It looked like a big shark from everywhere else as well. When the thrashing had died down to just an occasional twitch, Pongo and Alec got out of the car and walked slowly up the road. Carcharodon carcharias was dead. It had died when it hit the road, but it had taken a while for its brain to cotton on. As an interesting aside for the statisticians amongst you, this isn't the great white shark that we met earlier. That one materialized over a remote part of Argyllshire, where it greatly surprised and greatly flattened to death the Laird Don MacDuff. He'd been in his kitchen making toast at the time.

'I think it's dead,' said Pongo as he prodded at the fallen fish with his walking stick.

'You *think* it's dead?' said Alec from quite a long way away.

Pongo sighed. There were times when communication via the spoken word was more trouble than it was worth, but he tried again anyway. 'It is my considered opinion that this creature is now deceased, yes.'

'Oh,' said Alec, from not quite such a long way away. 'How did it get here?'

'You saw for yourself how it got here.'

'Well, yes, but *what* did I see?' said Alec who was now alongside Pongo, so not a long way away at all.

'You saw a transfer sphere.'

'You said that already, but it really didn't help much.'

'A transfer sphere is a method of rapid movement or transportation of matter by the relocation and substitution of two areas of space.' Pongo had kept the explanation simple and he was pleased that he'd been able to avoid the word 'teleportation', a concept that was unknown in this world.

'You mean teleportation?' Alec sat down. He was still standing in the road so the landing was a tad firm. 'Teleportation is physically impossible.' A brave assertion for a man so ignorant in the ways of particle physics that he still believed in the existence of the preon, which was so crazy that the science editor at *Mystic* threw pencils at him every time he went into his office.

'*Physically* impossible, yes, but certain Magicks allow for a degree of manipulation of the physical laws, thus making it possible. Now will you please remove yourself from the centre of the highway?'

'Never mind me, what about *that*?' Alec nodded in the direction of the shark as he struggled to his feet.

Pongo nodded. 'Good point, we had best move it. Can you put it in the rear of your vehicle?'

Alec looked at the shark. He looked at his car. He looked back at the shark. 'We're going to need a bigger boot,' he said.

'Such a tragedy,' said Pongo sadly.

'What is?'

'That such a magnificent creature had to die for the sake of that joke.'

Through a combination of pushing and pulling, a little rocking and rolling, and a whole lot of swearing, Alec and Pongo eventually managed to move the very big fish not an inch, so they left it where it was and covered it with leaves and branches. When they were done they stood back and admired their work.

'What does it look like to you?' said Pongo.

'It looks like a dead shark under a pile of sticks,' said Alec.

'Thought it did,' said Pongo.

'Let's go,' said Alec.

'Agreed,' said Pongo.

Edna Peevey enjoyed having houseguests, but it was a rare pleasure these days as most of the utility, insurance, and double glazing companies had issued their sales forces with instructions to bypass Rose Bungalow. Modern selling was all about shared databases, market analysis and preferential customer demographics and as such Edna Peevey had become the world's oldest computer virus. To combat this hi-tech antisocial behaviour, Edna had taken to returning all of her unsolicited mail with requests for home demonstrations and free no-obligation trials of everything from carpet cleaners to industrial ditch digging equipment. She was always very specific about the dates and times of these visits, ensuring a steady stream of nice young gentlemen washed up at her front door around teatime.

'More tea, Mr. Cooper?'

'No, thank you, Mrs. Peevey. Six is my limit when I'm driving.'

'Lovely. I'll just go put the kettle on. Have another custard cream.'

'No thank you, I really must think about going, I have to be-'

'Or perhaps another of those nice seafood sandwiches. I get them ready-made from the delicatessen, so I'm not really sure what's in them.'

'Fish sticks.'

'Yes it does. Contemporary bun?'

'No honestly, I really must-'

'Just the tea then.'

Dave Cooper watched with dismay as Edna Peevey struggled to her feet and set off for the kitchen. From the moment he'd entered Rose Bungalow he'd know that he was on a loser with this one. If she'd been an animated character, and none had ever accused Edna Peevey of being that, the words 'No Sale' would have rung up in her eyes as Dave shook her hand. Edna Peevey didn't want a Zuz-Zuz water softener. She didn't need a Zuz-Zuz water softener, though that wouldn't have stopped Dave selling her one. She actually had no idea what a Zuz-Zuz water softener *was* (a positive boon when it came to selling her one), but Dave had gone through all of the brochures, fully explaining the workings of the product whilst his customer had feigned interest and plied him with cups of tea and stale custard creams. Dave's professional duty not to be rude to the customer was now in serious conflict with his need to be as far away as possible from this doddery old bat. Hell, this wasn't even meant to be his call. Rose Bungalow had been on Mike Carter's list for today, but Mr. Smarmy Super-Salesman hadn't shown for work, so it had been dumped on Dave on his day off. A day off when he'd had other plans, most of which had centred on his being at the '*Booty4U*' lap dance club over an hour ago.

'Oh my! Are these yours, Mr. Cooper?' The ancient one sounded troubled.

'Are what mine, Mrs. Peevey?' Dave hauled himself out of the armchair that had been trying to assimilate him and made his way to the entrance hall, where he found a perplexed Edna Peevey standing at the bottom of the staircase.

'Is everything all right, Mrs. Peevey?'

'Well, I really don't know, Mr. Cooper. These weren't here earlier, so I was just wondering if they were yours.'

Dave Cooper followed Mrs. Peevey's gaze. There was nothing on the stairs. Nothing on the stairs at all. They were perfectly ordinary stairs. Nope, nothing odd about those there stairs. Dave Cooper walked slowly out of Rose Bungalow's front door and down the cobbled driveway. He turned around and gave the building a long, hard looking at. Then he walked slowly back up the driveway and through the front door. There was that perfectly ordinary staircase again, and like most other perfectly ordinary staircases it had stairs that went up. Very up. Up beyond the ceiling and into a space that was theoretically outside of the building, where they were swallowed up by darkness.

'Well, up you go then, Mr. Cooper,' said Edna, cheerfully.

'Me?' said Dave, confusedly.

'I can't, now can I? The tea won't make itself.'

Before Dave could argue Edna set off for the kitchen at a velocity that fully tested the friction tolerances of her artificial hip. Until she was provided with evidence to the contrary, Edna Peevey was working on the assumption that her home improvement was Satan's work, and The Lord of the Flies wasn't going to dupe her with something as obvious as quality carpentry. Great and various are the temptations of evil when the Devil's been down to *Homebase*. On the other hand, if this wasn't a cunning ploy by Lucifer to entrap her immortal soul then it was a pity that she'd let the stair lift go so cheaply.

'Erm ... Mrs. Peevey? Are you there? Hello?' The only response from the kitchen was the tinkling rattle of bone china cups. Dave had two options; he could run out the front door and drive away like a pathetic wimp, or he could ascend these perfectly ordinary but highly improbable stairs and see what was lurking up there in the dark. Dave felt good about the first option. His natural inclination definitely tended towards pathetic wimpyness. But faintheartedness wasn't the Zuz-Zuz way. They didn't send their sales force on regular team-building weekends and paintballing skirmishes for nothing. As a matter of fact, Dave had no idea why they did that because it never seemed to achieve anything other than give Mike Carter something else to brag about back at the office, but he was sure it wasn't to produce salesmen who couldn't cope when the going got tough. When things get hard, soften them up with a Zuz-Zuz. Up would be what a winner would do. Up would be Dave Cooper being all that Dave Cooper could be. So up Dave went. Once at the top he discovered that the blackness was a very black blackness indeed. Positively thick it was. Dave stepped into it. Nothing very much happened so he took another step, and then another, and then he bumped into a table. An inanimate and harmless glass-topped table, tinted a pleasing shade of rose pink and surrounded by a gaudily upholstered circular sofa. Dave tried to take a step back and found that the staircase had been replaced by something big and solid, which is the way of things with brick walls. As Dave's eyes did that thing that eyes do to make them work better in the dark, he discovered that he was in a familiar private booth, separated from the world beyond by a red velvet curtain. The curtain was drawn back by a 'Booty4U' hostess whose costume barely concealed her embarrassment at having to wear it, and Dave decided that he really didn't care how he came to be there.

Alec had been getting a lot of falling down practice since Pongo had led him into the forest, and he was really getting the hang of it now. So far he'd enriched Falston Wood in the amount of eleven pence in change, a pack of cigarettes, his wallet (real leather, quality stitching), and a Mars bar wrapper.

Alec kicked out at the root cause of his downfall, that being the root that had caused him to fall down, and was surprised to discover that it was wearing trousers.

'Oh, Pongo,' shouted Alec. Quietly. The small but magically endowed one either hadn't seen, or had chosen to ignore, Alec's most recent tumble and was already some way off.

'Yes?' Pongo turned and started back, not looking terribly impressed that his companion's ham-fisted feet had struck again.

'I seem to have found a dead person.' Alec couldn't quite remember where finding dead people slotted into his list of things not to do, but it had just been promoted and now ranked higher than getting any of his frenula pierced.

'Ah yes, sorry, I'd forgotten that I'd left him there,' said Pongo, much too matter-of-factly for Alec's liking.

'*You* left him here?' Alec wasn't sure which part of that bothered him more; the fact that Pongo had left a dead body in Falston Wood, or the fact that it had slipped his mind.

Pongo could guess what Alec was thinking. 'I can guess what you're thinking, and no, I didn't kill him. Somebody else did me that service, and had they not then it would be my lifeless body lying there.'

'Who is he?' Alec thought it would be best to know the type of people Pongo felt deserved to die.

'He has no name. His kind prefers not to use them, and when they do they never use the names they were given at birth.'

'His kind?' Alec was asking a lot of monosyllabic questions these days, and even those were usually just a couple of words repeated from whatever Pongo had just said.

'A hired killer, Alec. An assassin.'

'An assassin?' At least that was four syllables, though Alec would have preferred a different four. 'So he's from your world?'

'He is.' Pongo sat down on a convenient tree stump as it didn't seem likely they'd be going anywhere for a while.

'And the man who killed him?'

'John Bostwicke. A good man, and also of my world.'

'I know I'm new to all of this, but as barriers go this one doesn't sound like much of an obstruction to travel.'

'You are not wrong. Until recently, movement between the two worlds was no easy task, but it would appear that the temporary portals used for such movement have become more permanent of late. Both this assassin and John Bostwicke seem to have travelled into this world inadvertently, and normally such an accident would be impossible. Garthang's presence here was no accident though; I have little doubt that he was sent here to prevent him from reaching Draknoor.' That last part had been Pongo thinking aloud and hadn't been intended for Alec's ears. It hadn't been intended for any other parts of Alec either.

'Who or what is Garthang, and who or where is Draknoor?' As all Alec did these days was ask questions he might as well speed things up a bit and present them in groups.

Pongo paused, pondered, and then prevaricated. 'Perhaps it would be best to take things slowly. You may not be ready to absorb so many new ideas so quickly.'

'Try me,' said Alec, and even he wondered why.

'Garthang is a forest unicorn, and Draknoor is one of the few remaining black dragons. Many believe him to be the last of them.'

'You were right. I wasn't ready for that. So why was the unicorn going to see the dragon?' asked Alec, immediately going into denial about it.

'Garthang is a Messenger, and Draknoor a Defender.' Pongo didn't need to see the blank look on Alec's face to know that it was there. 'Only a select few ever knew where the sword *really* was, and nobody knew who knew because everybody maintained the pretence that nobody knew. It was all very complicated, and even some of those who did know became convinced that they didn't. So as not to draw attention to Falston, a thousand possible locations were allocated a Monitor, a Messenger, and a Defender. Should any Monitor feel that his region were under threat then it was his duty to send the Messenger to inform the Defender of it.'

'But why use a Messenger? Why not go directly to the Defender yourself?' Alec's questions were sounding more intelligent, but that was probably luck.

'Partly tradition, but mostly for safety reasons. Dragons do not play well with others, though even they would not dare harm a unicorn.'

'Why not?' Alec vaguely remembered something about it from a Tom Cruise film, but he couldn't drag up any specifics. He was sure the film wasn't '*Top Gun*' though.

'Unicorns are one of the last inherently magical creatures. To harm one is to risk natural vengeance. Imagine if every animal on God's green planet that could bite or claw or peck or sting saw you as their enemy, and attacked you on sight. If every creature that walked, crawled, swam or flew wanted to do you harm. Every cat would try and claw your eyes out; every dog would try and rip your throat out. Then there are sheep, cows, horses and deer to consider. Even this walk in the woods could be lethal; a swarm of enraged midges can strip a man to the bone in seconds.'

Alec decided to change the subject before Pongo's eyebrows did his forehead permanent harm. 'Going back to this monitor and defender business, it all makes some sort of sense, I think, and unicorns and dragons and the like are all well and good in your world, apparently, but what about here in this one?'

'To be honest, it was never envisaged that there would be a problem on this side of the barrier. After all, nobody here really believes that the sword exists. In this world, Excalibur is the stuff of myth and fable. Even my infrequent visits here were considered by many to be unnecessary, but now that you have raised the issue I feel I should mention that there are Defenders here in your world also.'

'There are?'

'Indeed. The task fell to a cult of assassins known as The Servants of Maurisamern. To do it they chose to leave our world completely, which by all accounts was no great loss. Even today The Guild is tainted by the shame of having dealt with them.'

'So where are they? If the sword is here and it's being threatened, why aren't they here?'

'They no longer exist. Over the centuries they have become integrated into your world and have forgotten their true nature. The Servants of Maurisamern were cold-blooded and lethal assassins, but they were also extraordinarily arrogant. Whilst most of their peers dressed in black, they wore white to prove that their stealth didn't depend on costume. To prove that they could move silently at all times they wore bells on their legs and arms. And to prove they could kill without blade or point, their weapons of choice were simple sticks and inflated pig's bladders.' Pongo saw Alec's expression and shrugged. 'As I said, they lost their way somewhat.

'You're not joking,' was all Alec could think to say.

Detective Inspector George Guv had been a busy little beaver since the meeting with his superior and his superior's superior. He had his command headquarters arranged to his liking, though not to the liking of Mrs. Guv, who had loudly voiced her displeasure when George had stacked the new three-piece suite up against the wall. With nowhere comfy to sit, both Mrs. Guv and the television had retired to the bedroom to watch that flash Yank magician bloke make the Sphinx disappear.

The reason for the disruption to Mrs. Guv's cosy tranquillity had been George's big and impressive map. He'd had the big and impressive map for years, waiting in readiness for the inevitable day when George Guv would need a twelve-foot by nine-foot cork-backed relief map of the British Isles. That day was finally here, and George Guv had not been found wanting.

Around the perimeter of his very big map George had carefully laid out the contents of the manila folder that had been wedged under his arm when he'd left the meeting with his superiors. There were internal memos, newspaper clippings, magazine articles and one-page reports from just about every police force in the country, all documenting strange and often inexplicable events that had been deemed unworthy of further investigation.

Officially, these reports had been shelved because there wasn't the manpower available to deal with them. Unofficially it was because they were all rather silly. These were The Unexplained Phenomena Files, and the powers that be (the powers that be mad, presumably) had seen fit to give George his own task force to investigate them. So far that force totalled one, including George, but that wasn't a problem. George liked working alone. There was less sniggering. The Unexplained-Phenomena Rapid Action Team even had its own ID badge, composed of George's laminated mug shot with the task force's acronym printed next to it in Day-Glo orange letters.

'Ow, bugger!' George pulled a coloured marker pin out of a bloody fingertip. Again. He'd purchased several boxes of coloured pins that very afternoon, and he'd managed to impale his thigh with a green one before leaving the shop. George thought his colour coding scheme was quite ingenious: green pins in the map for the reports that could be dismissed as drunken ramblings, attention seeking loonies or other general bollocks; yellow pins for those that might have some element of truth to them, but were *probably* bollocks; red pins for those stories that George considered the most likely to be factual and not bollocks at all. To each pin he attached a numbered sticky label, and as he planted the pin in the map he pencilled the same number onto the associated report. So proud was George of this innovation that he ran upstairs to tell Mrs. Guv about it. Mrs. Guv had nodded appreciatively, as she always did when her husband excitedly told her that he'd reinvented the wheel. George did that a lot. His insistence on working out his own methodology for even the simplest tasks meant that once in a while he developed an approach that was superior to the ingrained and outmoded techniques his colleagues adhered to.

This wasn't one of those times.

Eventually the folder was empty, and George stood back to see what he could see. What he could see was a cheap old cork-backed map with loads of pins stuck in it, and an expensive new shagpile carpet with loads of fresh bloodstains on it.

After a swift cuppa and the urgent application of salve and sticking plasters, it was on to stage two of Operation Bigmap. Thirty minutes and one surreptitious raid on Mrs. Guv's sewing supplies later, George had joined all of the red pins together with thread, and when he stood back to admire his work it was clear to him that he was on to something. It was also clear to him that if he was going to walk around in just his socks then he should put the unused pins back in their boxes. As he applied plasters to his feet, George pondered on his creation and decided that something wasn't right. Stretching the length of his map was the outline of a pointy thing—a sword or dagger or something of that ilk. George would have preferred a pentacle or hexagram, but you work with what you've got. His problem was that his pointy thing lacked a point. Where the business end of the weapon should have been there was a blunt squared off bit. George wasn't going to allow his efforts to be pointless, even in metaphor, so he did something that by his own modest standards was truly inspired. George extended the outline down and discovered that green pin number 18 was located at precisely where the point of his pointy thing should be. Document 18 was a newspaper clipping stapled to a police report, both relating to one Barry Ogleby and his supposed sighting, and subsequent conversation with, a unicorn. George had allocated it a green pin because the newspaper article had described Mr. Ogleby as a 'local character'. The associated police report had eschewed diplomacy and gone with 'legendary pisshead'. George made a momentous decision and replaced the green pin with a red one. After all, just because somebody was stewed as a prune it didn't necessarily follow that they *hadn't* seen a unicorn.

Now the sword had a point. A point that was pointing somewhere, which is, after all, the point of a point.

'Game on,' said George. It wasn't terribly deep or enigmatic of him, but he never did his best work indoors—Mrs. Guv didn't let him smoke in the house.

George gave a satisfied nod before fetching the road atlas so he could plan his route to the point on the map where the pointy thing was pointing.

Falston Wood was dappled with flittering shadows as the sun slipped inexorably towards the horizon, yellow and orange streamers of light kaleidoscoping through the gently swaying branches, the breeze carrying with it the sounds of woodland creatures being smug and self-satisfied.

'So when will we reach this portal of yours?' Alec hadn't fallen over for a while and was feeling confident enough to operate his feet and his mouth at the same time.

'We did, five minutes ago. You are already walking in the Falston Wood of my world, Alec Gardener.'

'I am?' Alec was disappointed. He'd been hoping for something a bit more dramatic, like swirling vortices of colour, tunnels of light, surreal floating blobs of translucent plasma, or at least a spinning cardboard disc with a spiral painted on it.

'You are. From this point on I would strongly recommend that we do not become separated. Without me you may never be able to return to your own world, so stay close.'

Alec got the point, and took steps accordingly. Two steps, a big stride, and a small jump.

'Perhaps not *that* close,' said Pongo as Alec trod in his sack. 'We're here, by the way.'

'Here where?' Alec hadn't been expecting a 'here'. Pongo hadn't said they were heading for a 'here', but now there was a 'here' and they were already 'there'.

'Falston,' said Pongo.

Alec looked around and was surprised to find that they had indeed reached the boundary of Falston Wood, and he could see the whole of the Wold Valley laid out below. He was even more surprised by what he saw down there. It was a three-dimensional virtual-reality Constable painting. Without the virtual. So just your basic reality.

It was all true. It was real, this other Falston.

This other world.

And that meant that the rest was probably true. Unicorns and dragons were real. Magic was real. Proper magic too, not the stuff that American bloke, Chuck something-or-other, did. It was a sobering discovery, and one that had Alec wishing he'd been drunk. Those parts of his mind that had held out against accepting Pongo's story now had no choice but to capitulate. It was a strange sensation, akin to having his brain nibbled by hungry chinchillas. Alec stared in silence for a long time, and if Pongo spoke at all during that long time then Alec either didn't hear him or chose to ignore him. The long time ended with a short question. 'Pongo, what's that big building with the stable and the two chimneys?'

Pongo answered without looking; there was only one structure in Falston that fitted the description. 'That would be The King's Arms, a very fine coaching inn. 'Tis a pity that our enforced haste prevents us from partaking of a flagon or two, but we must away.'

'Pardon?'

'Sorry, force of habit. I mean if we didn't have to get a move on we could stop off for a couple of pints.'

'Is there anything unusual about the place? Anything *modern*?' It was a leading question, and if Pongo had bothered to look he would have seen where it was leading.

'If by that you mean modern by your standards, then no. You have to understand that technology as you know it simply does not exist here.'

Alec frowned. 'Then why does it have a television aerial?'

Phillip Morrison was back in Mad Ned's caravan, and for the second time in an hour he was wearing nothing but his underwear in the presence of Miss Sara Hagget. He tossed Ben's black suit over a chair, and as there were no indications that Sara would be joining him in his disrobedness he stepped back into his own threadbare but comfortably familiar trousers. 'There is something I have to ask.'

Sara knew. 'I know.'

'How did you know that stuff about Donald thingy from Warwick, and what was that business with the toy squid, and how come that suit fitted me for a while when it's clearly too small for me, and-'

Sara took a step forward and put a finger to Phillip's lips. 'Hush, all in good time. I will give you your answers, I owe you that after today, but not just yet.'

Phillip nodded. 'Then just answer me this. You know what's in that tent, don't you?'

'Why do you say that?' A smile played across Sara's lips, so enigmatic that it made the Mona Lisa's effort look like a cheesy grin.

'Because you haven't asked me what I saw in there.'

Sara's smile broadened. 'Yes, I knew about the sword. I need you to trust me Phillip, and I'll tell you as much as I dare as we go.'

'Go? Go where?' Morrison didn't like going. Going was not one of his favourite things.

'To find Ieuan and Kevin. I saw them go into the tent and they didn't come out, but I think I know where they are and I'm going to get them.' Sara got to her feet, which were still at the ends of her long and beautifully sculpted legs, and she brushed past Phillip as he tried to manoeuvre himself into his shirt. 'And you're coming with me.'

'*I'm* coming?' Morrison stopped smiling.

Sara leant back on the caravan's foldaway table and gently slid forward, her skirt riding up her thighs to reveal the ace up her sleeve. Obviously she knew nothing about Morrison's steely resolve if she thought that a flash of garter and stocking top would sway him.

'I'm coming' swayed Morrison as his steely resolve melted and dribbled down his leg.

16

While he nodded, nearly napping, suddenly there came a tapping, as of some one gently rapping, rapping at his chamber door. Well, knocking on the outside of his oblong box anyway.

'Wakey-wakey, Thelonius. I have something that you'll want to see.' That was unlikely. Lady Gaynor sounded happy, and Thelonius Wisp couldn't imagine wanting to see anything that made her happy.

'Let me pass over or leave me in peace. I shall never tell you what you wish to know.'

'Leave you in peace? My dear Thelonius, I've left you in peace for four months, and there is nothing you could tell me now that I don't already know.

Four months? Could it really be so long? Wisp knew that it was entirely possible. He also knew, mostly because of the smell, that his severed head was sitting in a rectangular oak box stuffed with sphagnum moss, thirteen foxglove blossoms, two dead bats, and a newt. Those were the ingredients for the refusion spell that Gaynor must have cooked up to keep his brain alive. Time was a meaningless concept for a man in his condition. Four seconds or four years might have passed since his death. As long as the moss was kept damp and a fresh newt was inserted regularly there was no limit to how long she could keep him like this, and no way of his telling how long she already had.

'And how has milady been spending her time these four months? Is she still behaving like a petulant child that cannot find its favourite toy?' Baiting Gaynor held no fears for Wisp now; after all, what more could she do to him? He thought about it and quickly came up with a dozen really nasty things she could still do to him.

'Ah, yes, your precious Excalibur. By a pleasant coincidence, that's what I wanted you to see.' There was a gloaty quality in Gaynor's voice that didn't bode well for anybody or anything.

The lid of Wisp's box was removed and a huge hand reached down for him, completely encircling his head. He was lifted free of his mossy bed, though some lumps of greenery did remain attached to the gory dangly bits hanging from his tatty neck. For a moment there was relief as he was able to sniff air that didn't smell of decomposing bat or fresh newt droppings, then as his eyes remembered how to process daylight the relief drained away and the scene resolved itself one of utter devastation. Wisp's head was being held aloft in the central courtyard of Malecot, facing in the direction of the killing jar that had once been Tulston. Every building was ablaze and the cobbled streets ran red with the blood of the mutilated corpses that littered them. The courtyard itself was strewn with robed bodies, with more hanging by their necks beneath the stone arch that separated Malecot from the world beyond. 'Dear God, what have you done?'

Gaynor smiled. 'Oh, I can't take all of the credit. Caleb was feeling a little frisky this morning, so I let him off the leash. He does so like to play. And, of course, I had this.' From beneath her cape she produced a bloody sword.

The bloody sword.

All of Wisp's scheming had been for nothing; here was Excalibur, clutched in the hand that he had sacrificed all to keep it from. 'But how? How could this happen? The sword was safe. Who betrayed it? Who told you where it could be found?'

'Who betrayed it? Why you did of course.'

'I did not! I couldn't have!' Wisp didn't have the bits he needed to make him go purple with rage so he went sort of greenish.

'Oh, but you did. Though under the circumstances it doesn't surprise me that you don't remember.'

'This is a lie! Gallowtree! I only ever told you the sword was in Gallowtree. When did I ever speak of Falston in your presence? Never!'

'I'm afraid you did.'

'When?'

'Just then.' A wicked grin of ear-to-ear proportions cleft The Lady Gaynor's face in two.

'What?' Realisation of what had just happened hit poor Thelonius Wisp like a felled tree.

'Gotcha!' Lady Gaynor squealed in triumph. Positively girlish glee it was.

The scene of devastation around them shimmered and faded. In its place appeared the stark reality of Gaynor's cavern. Only the great hand clamped over Wisp's head and The Lady Gaynor remained, for only they had been real.

Wisp could say nothing. He was beaten; he was distraught; and let's be honest, he was an idiot.

'Oh now don't take it personally, Thelonius. Sooner or later I was going to find out, if not from you then from one of your pathetic sycophants.' She moved in close to Wisp's hovering head. 'Did that sound smug? I hope it did.'

Wisp put on a brave face because he had nothing else left to be brave with. 'You may know where the sword lies, but that's still some way away from being able to wield it.'

'Don't you think it's time for a new catchphrase, Thelonius? That one's getting boring.'

'Perhaps so, but you know as well as I that the sword can only be drawn from the ground by-'

'One of the ancient bloodline, and yadda yadda yadda. Believe me, old man, I shall find a way. You know who I am, and you know who my teacher was.'

'Yes, I know who taught you, but he is long gone, and I doubt that the teacher taught his student all that he knew.' Wisp was confident about that; the teacher in question was far too arrogant to allow himself to be surpassed by one of his own students.

Gaynor frowned. 'That's very true, Thelonius, which is why I'm going to keep you around. You may yet be even more helpful than you already have been. Caleb, put our guest back in his box.'

'So when shall I be allowed to rest in peace, witch?' Quoth the Lady, 'Nevermore.'

'Quiet,' said Pongo.

Alec hadn't been making any sound that he was aware of so he wasn't sure what to do next.

Pongo did some listening.

'I don't hear anything,' said Alec after he'd done some listening of his own.

Pongo nodded, though his eyebrows remained stationary as his forehead went up and down behind them. 'Precisely my point. Falston is never this quiet.'

'Perhaps they're all in the pub watching television.' Alec hadn't planned on sounding so facetious, but he really couldn't help it.

Pongo glared and tapped the end of his walking stick on the bridge, mainly to remind Alec that he was carrying something he could hit him with. 'There are moments when I don't think you're taking all of this as seriously as perhaps you should. Would you prefer to wait here whilst I investigate the current situation in the village? I wouldn't want to expose you to undue peril.'

Under normal circumstances, Alec would have enjoyed not being exposed to peril, but circumstances were as far from normal as circumstances got. 'It might help if you could quantify the peril for me. Will there be entrails?'

'I have no idea, hence the need to investigate. If you'd rather wait here I can go alone, and if I'm not back in one hour, wait longer.'

'Actually I think I'll come with you then. Safety in numbers, and all that.' The number that most concerned Alec was 'one', which was how many people there would be left here on the bridge if he let Pongo go on his own.

'As you wish, Alec Gardener. Then let us away whilst our resolve holds firm, for it serves us poorly to pass our time here and thus make that which hastens us all the more pressing.'

'Stop doing that.'

'Sorry, forgot again.' Pongo turned and strode towards the village. A dejected looking Alec flopped along behind, the sole of one of his Taiwanese knock-off trainers having failed in its primary task of keeping his sock hidden from view. The camouflage pattern on his footwear might come in handy though. It was always good in life-or-death situations to know that your enemies would have difficulty seeing your feet.

The streets of Falston-on-Wold were deserted and eerily quiet, the only sounds being Alec's errant sole slapping against the cobbles, and the gentle sighing of the wind that was making the tumbleweeds dance along the thoroughfare. There weren't actually tumbleweeds, but Alec felt that there *should* have been tumbleweeds, or perhaps an oddly unsettling child sitting on a porch with a banjo resting on the knee of his jeans and inbreeding in the genes of his knee. Curtains twitched, shutters shut and bolts were thrown—the residents of Falston-on-Wold were still in residence, but they were keeping themselves very much to themselves.

'I don't understand this. The good folk hereabouts are normally most welcoming, even to strangers. Even if they were not, I am well known in these parts, and well thought of, if I do say so myself,' said Pongo, saying it himself.

'I think I understand it,' said Alec.

'You do?' Pongo had every right to be surprised, and he made full use of that right. What insight into these strange goings-on had he missed?

The insight that Pongo had missed was the large paper proclamation insight nailed to a post outside The King's Arms.

By special order of The Guild of Magi
Court Advisers to
His Most Holy Majesty King Aethelred XII
The good citizens of Falston-on-Wold are hereby advised: -
To remain indoors between the hours of three in the noon and dawn.
That all sightings of the heinous criminal commonly known as Pongo Smythe are to be immediately reported to The Sheriff of Tulston Town or one of his officers.
The Aforementioned Pongo Smythe should not be approached or spoken to as he is not of sound mind.

Those not abiding by the recommendations as laid out in this Royal decree do so at their own risk.

And under pain of death.

(See Local Press for details. Terms and conditions apply. The value of a life may fall as well as rise and past performance is not necessarily a guide to future longevity.)

God Save The King.

Alec found himself oddly comforted by the absence of a telephone number or any suggestion that he should visit *www.feudalsystem.gov.uk*.

'You're right, that does explain it rather.' Pongo was taking it very well.

'You're taking it very well,' said Alec, who didn't miss a thing.

'In truth I may have gone into a mental foetal position, and am now aghast beyond the point where there is any hope of rational thought.' Pongo's eyebrows had gone into a deep slump, and if their progress wasn't checked soon they would collide with his sideburns and create a new category of facial hair.

'I think one of those flagons of ale you mentioned might be in order then.' Alec had a new personal maxim: when the going gets tough, the tough get going, waved off cheerily by the slightly less tough who then go down the pub and get pissed.

With an effort, Pongo was able to make his head go up and down.

Alec found the interior of The King's Arms to be unexpectedly familiar. The same low-key lighting. The same peculiar collection of mismatched furniture. The same excess of plastic foliage surrounding the corner snug. The same two patrons sitting in that snug.

'Helloooo,' hailed Taff, spraying Thermos with warm beer.

Thermos looked up from his drink, grinned inanely, pointed at Pongo and went 'Phrrrp'. In case nobody had noticed, he did it again, this time sliding sideways off his chair for emphasis.

'Don't worry about him, he's pissed,' explained Taff, redundantly. The rotund Welshman was equally inebriated but, as Jack had observed on manifold occasions, the drunker Taff got the more coherent his English became. Nor was Taff likely to fall off his chair— they'd only just met, but the two of them had become inseparable.

'How the how hell the did hell you did two you get two here get here?' Taff might have stood a chance if Alec and Pongo had asked the question in synch, but the two-word delay was more than his beer filter could compensate for.

'?' went Taff's expression.

'How the hell did you two get here?' repeated Alec with a hand clamped over Pongo's mouth, followed by 'ow!' when Pongo bit him.

'Long story,' said Taff in a tone that suggested he had no great urge to tell it.

'Give us the short version,' said Alec as he examined the bite mark on his finger.

'Me him tent sword fall wet woods dry here drink,' explained Taff.

'Give us the medium length version,' said Pongo.

'You might want to get us all some drinks in first. I'm buying,' said Taff from behind his broad grin.

Pongo glanced over to the deserted bar. 'There doesn't appear to be anybody selling.'

'I know. It's another one of those nifty self-service deals. There was a bloke there when we came in, but he took one look at us and scarpered.'

Thermos was slipping into a coma on the floor, so deep that it might have been a semicolon.

'Pity the telly doesn't work though,' continued Taff 'there was a cracking rugby match on this afternoon.'

'It cannot work here,' explained Pongo 'it's an aberration.'

'You're not a rugby fan then?' misunderstood Taff.

'No, I mean it's an anomaly that slipped through a localized breach in the barrier that separates the worlds.'

Taff blinked. 'Oh, righto. Somebody going to get the drinks then?'

Alec sidled over to the bar and did the honours, then he and Pongo sat themselves down at the same table they had been sitting at earlier, only then that same table had been a different table in a different world, and the glasses had been cleaner.

Taff took a moment to admire his fresh pint for the thing of beauty that it was, and then he opened his address in the manner he thought most appropriate. 'Are you sitting comfortably? Then I'll begin ...'

The medium length version of The Tale of Taff and Thermos ran a little longer than was necessary, what with Thermos being in no state to contradict any of the extra heroic scenes Taff had felt obliged to add.

'A most intriguing tale,' said Pongo when Taff was done 'and one that deserves a toast, I think.' He reached into his sack and handed Taff a vial of clear liquid. 'Here, try this.'

'Oh, right, don't mind if I do. What is it, really strong schnapps or some such?'

'Yes, some such,' said Pongo, noncommittally.

Taff took a small sip. 'Phoarr blimey, this stuff will put hairs on your chest! All this for me?'

'Yes, please finish it. I have more.'

'Marvellous.' Taff drained the vial and his face arranged itself into an expression unlike any that had ever appeared there before.

'How long will he be out?' inquired Alec as he propped Taff back up in his chair.

'It varies, but six or seven hours is about the norm for a single vial.' Pongo recalled that John Bostwicke had only slept for three, but amply proportioned though Taff was he didn't look to have John's constitution. 'I suggest we move ourselves to a table nearer the window while our friends ... rest.' Without waiting for a response, Pongo got to his feet and relocated. Alec followed, making only a small detour via the bar for supplies.

When Alec re-joined Pongo he discovered a round thing on the table. He sat and waited for Pongo to explain, which he did.

'It's a glyphweave.' It wasn't much of an explanation, but then Pongo had been doing that a lot lately. Thankfully there was more. 'A glyphweave is a holding spell given physical form. They are very ancient devices, and the ability to create them has long been lost.'

'Is it valuable?' The world may have been in dire peril but that was no reason for Alec to lose sight of the priorities.

'Invaluable. There is a problem with this one though. It was manufactured for a very specific purpose and its contents have been safely contained within for centuries.'

Alec studied the round thing more closely. 'What contents?'

'That's the problem. If memory serves, inside this glyphweave there should be a large gemstone; an emerald I believe. Gemstones can be used to hold magical energy for short periods, and by placing the gem within a glyphweave that energy is trapped inside the stone on a more permanent basis. This one was created many centuries ago to trap and hold beings that are referred to in the ancient texts as The Mischiefs.'

Alec felt a joke coming on, but he resisted. He'd already made the mistake of not taking Pongo seriously, and Alec was a man who learnt from his mistakes. Except when it came to women. Or bargain-basement hi-fi systems. Or kebabs.

Especially kebabs.

'Little is known about the exact nature of The Mischiefs,' continued Pongo, 'but in your world I believe they are usually referred to as The Seven Deadly Sins.'

'The Seven Deadly Sins? You mean lust, greed, anger and ... and ... the other ones?'

Pongo drained his glass and nodded.

'But how can that be right? Surely those are emotions, or states of mind, or something. And ...' Alec should have known better that to add an 'and'; all he ever did with his ands was dig holes '...if these Mischiefs have been locked away there wouldn't have been any sin going on, and I'm pretty sure there's been truckloads of it.'

'The Mischiefs aren't the sin itself, but a concentrated distillation made *from* the sin. Some two hundred years before The Grand Separation, a skilled Druid by the name of Alban made a name for himself by 'curing' the sinful. Most historians believe that he was extracting negative energies and storing them in a device not dissimilar to this glyphweave. It made him rather popular, and there are suggestions that people were going out and committing some of the more enjoyable sins in the knowledge that they could visit Alban and the taint of those sins could be removed.'

'Imagine that,' said Alec 'a system that allows you to sin as much as you want and then have those sins forgiven by asking nicely. I can see how that might catch on.'

Pongo ignored the glib remark, which was probably the best thing to do with it. 'He did this for many years, and in that time he must have collected a vast amount of concentrated sin. Eventually the intense compression of all that negativity created something sentient, and The Mischiefs were born, although it might be more appropriate to say that they were shat.'

Alec finished his pint, picked up the glyphweave and did some closer scrutinising. It was beautifully constructed, and it felt surprisingly warm for metal. 'So where are these Mischiefs now?'

'I don't know. But I know where they've been. The glyphweave reacts to the presence of whatever it was created to detain. It did so this morning in the caravan, which means that The Mischiefs had been there, and for some considerable time to have left such a powerful residue. That, plus the information you gave me about Robin Madden's apparent obsession with television commercials, is enough to convince me that the poor fellow was host to those vile creatures.'

Alec frowned. 'Television commercials? What connection is there between pure evil and television commercials? Apart from the obvious one.'

'Voices,' said Pongo.

'Voices?' repeated Alec.

'Voices,' explained Pongo. 'Voices that manifest themselves in the brain. Voices telling the host to do their bidding and to satisfy their every need. Telling him what he should *want*.'

'Are we talking about The Mischiefs or television commercials?'

'Both, and that's my point. I suspect Robin discovered that by constantly bombarding himself with advertising he could cause aspiration interference patterns within his own mind, keeping The Mischiefs in check.'

'No wonder they called him Mad Ned.'

'Indeed, though I would guess that was a name of his own choosing, what with it being an anagram of his surname.' Pongo was surprised that he needed to point that out as he'd assumed Alec had spotted it right away.

'Oh yeah, so it is,' said Alec, who hadn't spotted it right away, though I have no idea why not.

'This business with The Mischiefs also suggests that whatever plan it is we have stumbled upon has been in motion for some time.'

'How do you work that out?'

'Because it is believed that infection by The Mischiefs slows the ageing process, and if this man is indeed The Magpie then he is over two hundred years old. If he still looks young then he was infected a long time ago. What I do not understand is why The Guild had John Bostwicke bring me the glyphweave at all. I can see no sense to it, unless it was simply to distract me from seeing their true intentions. I'm certain the proclamation outside is an insurance policy against their hired killer failing in his appointed task. Still, for all of that my greatest concern at the moment is where The Mischiefs went after they left Robin Madden.'

'Are you sure they left him?' Alec had to raise his voice to be heard over the snores coming from the snug.

'Certain. If The Mischiefs had still been present within his mind he would never have been able to leave that note, and I suspect it was he that initiated the runecall I received. That would explain why the address on it was so out of date.'

'But surely if it was these things that were stopping him from aging, once they left him wouldn't he suddenly grow old and die?' Alec was sure that was how it worked; he'd seen films. If you stay young then at some point you will suddenly and rapidly grow old. It was an important axiom, along with 'invisibility drives you mad' and 'building a person out of bits of other people is a really bad idea'.

'Why would he suddenly age? Isn't it far more logical for his ageing process to just continue again normally from where it left off?'

'I suppose so.' Alec sounded disappointed. 'So who is the poor sod that Mad Ned infected?'

'Who indeed. Only Robin Madden can tell us that, and unfortunately The Magpie has already flown.'

The flight of The Magpie had been more of a short hop. Robin Madden's plan had been to make a runecall to The Guild and then wait until The Monitor arrived. As Robin's vardo afforded some magical protection, it seemed best that The Monitor stay there, and Robin had left a note to that effect. After that he had no clear idea of what he was going to do, other than get as far away from Falston and its troubles as possible. It didn't really matter where. Location wasn't a major consideration for a man of Robin's talents, though it was always nice to be close to big houses filled with pretty baubles. After all the years of torment, didn't he deserve some peace? Didn't he deserve some sanity? Didn't he deserve sacksful of cash to buy all of those life-enhancing products that important people told him he couldn't do without? Well perhaps, but whether he deserved them or not, The Magpie could have them. Because he was worth it.

Then a man who might have been The Monitor had appeared. He'd turned out to be the spitting image of Pete, the lingerie salesman, though it couldn't be him. Pete was a jovial type and this new arrival didn't look very happy. Nor could Robin see any reason why a seller of lady's undergarments would have an assassin stalking him. After the assassin came an assassin of assassins, and there might possibly have been a unicorn, but it was tricky to tell when those beasts were around. Then everybody, and possibly a unicorn, had left. Then the man who might have been The Monitor had reappeared with a stranger. Then there had been a glowing ball with a big fish in it. Then everybody had left again. It was getting very complex, and if it kept going on like this Robin was going to have to start taking notes. Frankly he wasn't entirely sure whose side he was on any more, or even how many sides there were. Now, with the golden light of evening filtering through the trees, *this* creature had appeared. Professor James Stephenson was not yet a beast, but he was no longer a man, barely recognisable now as the timid creature that The Magpie had touched that morning by the river. *There but for the grace of God go I*, thought Robin, and with the thought came an understanding of what had to be done. This pitiful creature existed because of him, and it was up to him to put things right. For a thief Robin Madden had a hugely overdeveloped social conscience. He melted back into the thickening shadows, sank down onto his haunches, and waited to see what the creature was going to do next. It wasn't to be a long wait. The thing turned, and for a moment Robin thought that it had heard him. Then, with jaw-dropping speed and power, the overpopulated James Stephenson leapt into the air, possibly high enough to clear a tall building in a single bound, though anything over four storeys might have involved splattage. He sailed over Robin's hiding place and crashed off into the gloom of Falston Wood. Robin breathed again as he stood up, and from a branch somewhere above his head came the clear and flute-like song of a lone thrush. The Magpie improvised some lyrics to go with the thrush's tune. 'A single, fast acting capsule, tum-ti-tum, taken orally, tum-ti-tum, combined with a cream to provide immediate, la-la-la, soothing relief from the external feminine itching. Tum-titty-tum-tum.' With that catchy little number going around in his head and the sun setting at his back, Robin Madden set off in tepid pursuit of Professor James Stephenson.

Robin's improved mood is likely to suffer a setback when he discovers that something fell out of his pocket when he crouched down.

It wasn't the string or the sugar cubes.

Staying the night at The King's Arms had been Pongo's idea, which on the face of it had been a good one, but Alec had reconsidered when the time came to manhandle Taff and Thermos up the stairs. He'd wanted to leave them where they were—they seemed happy enough on the floor—but Pongo had been quite insistent. Thermos hadn't posed any particular problems, but Taff had been as tricky to manhandle as a great white shark. That Alec was able to make that informed comparison was a measure of the sort of day he'd had. Eventually they had managed to roll the wasted Welshman onto the bed beside Thermos, and then they had retired to their own rooms to sleep, perchance to dream. Not a cat in hell's perchance as it turned out. Alec sat on the end of his bed and wondered if Pongo was having the same trouble sleeping.

Pongo was lying awake on his bed, looking troubled. The situation was worse than he'd feared, and he'd feared it was pretty bad. It didn't make for a cheery start to his night's ruminations. Over the centuries there had been numerous amendments, additions, addenda, alterations, and abridgments to the rules governing Monitors, but there was nothing to cover this set of circumstances. Protection of the sword was The Guild's sacred duty, so it wasn't surprising that they had never provided guidelines to be followed in the event that they themselves put their charge in peril. Pongo was going to have to improvise, and with time running short he was going to have to work with the tools already at his disposal. He didn't know much about Taff or Thermos, so the value of those two tools was unclear. John Bostwicke, with Garthang and Draknoor, should have been there by now, and their absence meant that Pongo couldn't yet add them into the plus column of his equation. That left Alec to make up the numbers, and he was definitely a one. There was more to this Alec Gardener than met the eye, or at least Pongo hoped there was. As a rule Pongo didn't hold the inhabitants of the other world in high esteem. The experiences of Pete the undies vendor suggested that the majority of the people spent their time in the pursuit of things that they thought would make them happy, without ever realising that it was the constant pursuit of those things that made them unhappy in the first place. Everybody seemed to have a lifelong goal that they had to achieve, and it was invariably something that was going to be impossible to attain. Wouldn't it be simpler all around if a man's lifelong goal was to own a really nice pair of socks? But no: it was always curing some disease or other, or kayaking naked down the Limpopo. Pongo thought that was a real pity, because if they stopped all this mucking about at living they might discover what it was to be alive. Pongo was aware that people sometimes faked their own deaths, but he hadn't known that they sometimes faked their own lives. In every practical sense these people were already dead, they just struggled more when you tried to bury them.

Two hours later Pongo had the beginnings of a new plan, all previous plans having been made null and void by The Guild's naughtiness in trying to have him killed. Pongo wasn't one to bear a grudge, but he still felt a tad miffed. His new plan was a bold one, and quite possibly downright suicidal. In the morning he would leave for Tulston; if The Guild was so intent on killing him then he was going to walk under Malecot's stone arch and defy them to do it with their hands rather than with their purse. Getting away with the rest of the plan would take luck, but he was due some luck. With that sorted in his mind, Pongo rolled over to get some sleep and fell out of bed, landing heavily on his sack, which was really unlucky.

Jack was not a happy barman. Three of his regulars had chosen not to visit his establishment on this evening, reducing his takings by nearly half, and somebody had nicked the telly from the wall behind the bar. Thanks to some custom security welding by Jack's brother-in-law, the only way to remove said television from the wall was to take the wall with it, which is what the thieves had done. Now that was determined thievery. Tidy too—the missing section of masonry had been replaced by an area of wood panelling, complete with brass candelabra and three lit candles. It looked very pretty, but it wasn't going to cut the mustard come Saturday when everybody came in expecting to see Arsenal play Liverpool.

Jack was ruminating on how this combination of robbery and interior decorating had taken place whilst he had been standing barely three feet from the scene of the crime, when there came a resounding thud at the front door that scared the bejesus out of him. The proprietor of The Queen's Arms responded to the after-hours knock in the legally prescribed manner. 'Sod off, we're closed.'

'Open up, it's the police,' came the voice of the police.

That was fast, thought Jack, *I haven't even called them yet*. After a quick search to ensure that Bladder hadn't secreted himself under a table, Jack began the nontrivial task of unbolting the front door.

'Open up, it's the police,' repeated the impatient voice of the police.

''Old your 'orses, nearly with you,' said Jack as he flustered at a group of titanium-reinforced bolts.

When at last the formidable portal was breached, Jack found himself squinting at a most enigmatic silhouette. The figure in the gloom drew on his cigarette, briefly illuminating his deeply chiselled features in best film noir tradition. 'Is there any room at the inn, landlord?' said he as he flicked his cigarette away. It struck the doorframe and bounced back, hitting the silhouette in the chest and showering it with smouldering embers. 'Sod it!' exclaimed George Guv, swatting at the front of his shirt as it became riddled with pinhole burns.

Jack could do nothing but nod and stand aside as the enkindled officer of the law entered the premises, dragging one of those posh suitcases on wheels. George

Guv waited patiently as the landlord locked locks, slipped bolts back into place, reattached security chains and kicked wooden wedges into the gap at the bottom of the door. As a man experienced in such matters, George felt confident that no thief was going to get past that door. Any self-respecting burglar would come in through the open bathroom window.

'You want a room then?' Jack dispensed with the regional accent of the day. This new arrival was no tourist, and deception may not have been the best opening gambit. A pity, as today was to have been Cornwall and Jack was partial to a Cornish pastiche.

'If you have one.' A strange statement that puzzled George even as he said it. He wanted a room, and he'd still want one even if there were none available.

Jack was tempted to say no. The thought of having a specialist in law enforcement staying under his roof gave him the willies, as no doubt it would for many of his regulars. Not that Jack had anything to hide. Nothing that wasn't already hidden in the shed, that is, and the shed door was a bugger to open if you didn't have the knack of it. Sadly Jack didn't, and it caused him no end of frustration. 'Yes, we have a vacancy. We're never full out of season.'

'Excellent.' Our curious George had to wonder when people *did* come to this backwater, if the middle of summer classed as out of season. Christmas perhaps? George could see that this place might look picturesque under a few feet of snow. George didn't do picturesque. Picturesque didn't fit with the gritty realism of the dark path he had chosen to walk. Nothing colourful grew in the concrete jungle. It was a soulless collection of towering grey edifices pushing up into an ashen sky, where the only escape from the heights of despair was the depths of the gutter. Though none of that was going to stop Mrs. Guv from nagging him to cut the lawn on Sunday.

'You want something to eat?' It occurred to Jack that the chip shop had only been closed for ten minutes, and they probably hadn't thrown out the excess yet. Falston's premier, and only, fish and chip emporium, The Breaded Place, was run by Sid's sister Megan and 'The Suet Siblings' had made the top ten on the British Heart Foundation's hit list nine years running. A few minutes under the grill and the liberal application of condiments did an adequate job of turning fish and chips with mushy peas into *poissons frits avec les pommes de terre ébréchées et les pois détrempés*, with an associated price hike to reflect the cultural acceptability of French italics.

'No, but thank you.' George smiled a knowing smile. Doubtless the barman had been intending to visit the local chippy and then overcharge him for their unsold fare. George was good at his job, and if he ever stopped trying to live up to his 'hard man of crime prevention' persona he'd be a bugger of a lot better at it. 'Do you need me to register or anything?'

'We can sort all that palaver in the morning,' said Jack, who still had no idea where the guest book was. Nor could he recall the last time that particular tome had been called into service twice in the same week. It constituted a rush of hitherto unheard of proportions.

'Fine with me. And the name's Guv. George Guv.' George showed admirable restraint and didn't do a Sean Connery as he offered Jack his hand.

'Will you be wanting breakfast, Mr. Guv?' In a break with tradition Jack shook the hand that was being thrust at him. Until he knew why there was a big city plod in the village it made sense to play nice.

'No, thanks again. I'll go to the cafe myself and save you the trouble.'

Jack saved his discontented mutterings about that remark until after he'd deposited George Guv in his room.

'Oh Caleb, isn't it a joy to be alive? Oops, forgot, you're not, are you? Sorry.' Lady Gaynor Elfam slowly ran her fingers over the sculpted torso of her conjured companion and wished that the woodcut images she'd based him on had been more anatomically detailed, but sadly those woodcuts had cut out the wood. Never mind, there would be plenty of time for that when she was ruler of the world. 'What about you, Thelonius? Are you filled with joi de vivre? Oops, I did it again. You don't have any vivre left to be joi about, do you? I really am going to have to start meeting some new people, preferably living. I can, you know. After all these years I can leave this place and go bathe in the light once more. No prison could hold me, not even death! My body may have been crushed and burned, but it is *I* who will walk away from the battlefield with the pennant of victory! Before this week is out I shall wield Excalibur, and the pain and suffering you could barely bring yourself to contemplate will be delivered tenfold. There will be rivers of blood and towers of flame, flesh will be rent and ripped from bone, and I shall crush the skulls of their greatest generals between my own two hands, and still they will adore me. None shall ... what are you smiling at?'

Thelonius Wisp's head was perched on top of its box, and it was grinning broadly at Lady Gaynor. Thelonius wasn't happy as such, but he wanted to irritate Gaynor and facial expressions were all he had left to work with. 'Nothing, milady.'

'Oh shut up, Thelonius. If you don't start being an amusing companion soon I can make things all the worse for you.' Gaynor lost interest in her conjured muscles and gracefully swept across the cavern to her onyx throne. Rather less gracefully she stuffed herself and her dress bustle down into the seat.

'Worse, milady? Do you truly believe that I fear you now? As you so often remind me, I'm dead.'

'Yes, you are. But you will still be at my right hand to witness the ruination of ... well, everything, really.'

Wisp continued to grin, but it was getting harder. 'You mean to start a war then?'

'If need be. I'm sure they will realize soon enough that the easiest way for them to end such a war is to lose it.'

'You may take control of this earth, but what of the other? There you will face an enemy armed with weapons such as you have never imagined. Their magic may be different, but it is no less powerful for that. They can destroy worlds with their science.'

'Really? That sounds interesting. I may have to get some of those weapons for myself. You see Caleb, that's why I keep my good friend Thelonius around. He has such marvellous ideas.' Gaynor sprang to her feet and there was the sound of tearing fabric as her dress snagged on a gargoyle. 'Oh fiddlesticks!' She kicked out at her throne and there was a loud snap as the heel came away from her boot. 'Damn! You know, Thelonius, this may not be the most appropriate outfit for going to war. Shall I try something different?'

Thelonius Wisp tried a perfunctory shrug but nothing happened.

Gaynor twirled on her remaining heel and there was a thunderous boom and a blinding flash of light. Neither the twirling nor the flashing were required to perform her transformation spell, but she did so love the effect. Wisp may have found her technique to be excessively showy, but he had to confess that she was capable of impressive results. A silver helm with golden wings now sat atop her raven curls. Beneath that she wore a silver breastplate with a red cape attached at the shoulders with golden clasps. Around her waist was a short chain mail skirt reinforced with gleaming silver strips, and her legs were slotted into long silver boots with gold embellishments. Her right forearm was clad in a silver bracer, and on her left hung a golden buckler bearing a silver wolf's head motif.

The Lady Gaynor turned and drew her cape away from her rear whilst trying to crane her neck to look back over her shoulder.

'Does my bum look big in this?'

18

'Good morrow, Alec Gardener, art thou rested?'
Pongo was standing at the bar of The King's Arms and
nodding.

'You're doing it again.' Alec descended the last
couple of steps and rubbed his itching scalp. For once he
didn't have a hangover, which was nice, but now he
really needed a bath; he'd seen bedbugs up in his room
that should have been chasing wildebeest across the
Serengeti. 'You really should get a grip on this Olde
English thing, it's wearing a bit thin.'

'Ha, ha, indeed. Most amusing.' Pongo nodded
faster, and sort of in the direction of the bar.

'What's up with you? Bedbugs get to you as well?'

'Bedbugs! We ain't got no stinking bedbugs!' said
the person that Alec had completely failed to notice,
despite all of Pongo's attempts to draw attention to her.

'Oh. Good morning. I mean morrow. I think.'

Pongo decided it might be best to intervene before
Alec made more sounds come out of his mouth. 'Alec
Gardener, this is Mary Copper. She and her husband
Albert run this fine establishment.'

''Owdo,' said a rotund and cheerful looking cliché
in a blue dress.

'Whilst speaking of Albert,' Pongo continued 'where is he hiding himself on this beautiful morn?'

''E didn't want to come 'ere today, the lazy bugger. Said 'e wasn't going to associate with no wrongdoers and wanted to go fishin' instead, so I dropped 'im off down at the lake on me way in this mornin'.'

'When are you expecting him to return?'

'Never, unless the bricks slip out of 'is pockets.'

Pongo and Mary both laughed, so Alec joined in for appearances' sake.

'Come and sit down and I'll tell you the plan,' said Pongo when the laughing was done and Mary had excused herself and disappeared into the kitchen.

'We have a plan? Since when have we had a plan?' Alec thought it a good thing that they had a plan, especially if it was one where he stayed completely safe and had a jolly nice time.

Pongo ushered Alec over to what was becoming their usual table in both worlds, and they sat. 'Indeed we have a plan. Or rather *I* have a plan; your part in it is optional. I mean to leave for Tulston to confront The Guild; Mary is preparing some food for the journey, and I'm leaving written instructions for Garthang, which Mary will pass on to John Bostwicke on his return. I've also given her a message for Taff and Thermos when they awake. As for you, you may accompany me to Tulston if you choose, or you may remain here with the others.'

'I'll come with you.' Meeting people who might want him dead held more appeal for Alec than spending the day with Taff and Thermos.

Pongo smiled. 'Excellent. Then let's make haste and go and check on the condition of the stealth vehicle.'

'Did you just say *stealth* vehicle?'

'I certainly did. A conveyance of my own design, and a most appropriate vehicle for our journey to Tulston. Mary tends the horses for me, and she's already been kind enough to hitch them up. I knew I could rely on her to ignore The Guild's hollow threats, but we must assume that our presence here has already been reported to them.'

'A stealth vehicle. Now that I must see.'

'And so you shall. Follow me.'

So follow him Alec did.

The barn was at the top end of Falston-on-Wold. This Falston, not that Falston, meaning the Falston he was in now rather than the one he had been in yesterday. Alec tried not to think about that because it made his ears bleed.

'What is it?' inquired Alec, inquisitively.

'It's a barn,' replied Pongo, unhelpfully.

'I can see it's a barn. I mean why are we standing here looking at it?'

'If that's what you meant,' said Pongo as he scrabbled about on the ground looking for something 'why isn't it what you said? Ah, here we are.' Pongo straightened up and handed Alec a length of rope.

'What am I supposed to do with this?' Alec thought it a fair question.

'Pull it.' Pongo though it a fair answer to the fair question, and about the only answer there could be.

'Pull it?'

'Pull it. Hard.' Pongo made a sharp tugging motion, though the mime was unnecessary as Alec was all growed-up and had learning of how to pull things.

Alec pulled the rope. Hard. It was buried about an inch under the earth, and as he pulled it snaked over to the barn, where it disappeared through a small hole at ground level. Alec pulled harder as he felt some resistance, and then the rope went slack. From inside the barn came the solid thump of some sort of counterweight doing some sort of falling. With much creaking and grinding the roof of the barn split in the middle, the two halves folding down flat against the barn walls, and then the walls themselves collapsed to the ground to reveal ... a cart. A very ordinary looking cart, hitched to two unremarkable looking horses. It didn't look in any way stealthy, but then if he could see it well enough for it to look stealthy then clearly it couldn't be stealthy at all. Thinking about that would have made Alec's ears bleed too.

'I know it doesn't look like much now, but it's not in stealth mode yet.' Pongo strode off in the direction of their proposed transportation, and Alec flapped along sulkily behind.

Closer inspection of the vehicle did nothing to change Alec's first impression of it. It was a cart. A big wooden box on wheels attached to two big horses on legs. How could that have a *stealth* mode? How could the word 'mode' be applied to it at all, apart from 'moving' mode and 'not moving' mode?

'You climb up in the back, and I'll run through the special features with you,' said Pongo.

Alec hauled himself up into the cart and discovered that it was already rather cluttered back there. The only space not occupied by cargo was given over to a small stool bolted to the cart floor. As there was nowhere else to sit, Alec sat on it. Springs sprung, pulleys pulled, levers leved, and two banks of large handles slid into place on either side of the chair, three foot-pedals sprung up at Alec's feet, and two wooden panels fell away to reveal hidden storage spaces crammed with weaponry. There were longbows, crossbows, maces, swords, daggers, axes, halberds, and morning stars. Not being an expert in weapon identification, Alec grouped them into shooty things, pointy things and hitty things, with a sub-group to cover the many hitty and shooty things that were also quite pointy.

'So what do you think?' Pongo was leaning over from the front bench seat and making no effort to disguise his pride in his creation. 'I call her The Calamity Cart.'

'I thought it was called the stealth cart?'

'Stealth is what she can do; Calamity is what she is called.'

'Very impressive, I think. What do all of these contraptions do?'

Pongo grinned; he'd never had the opportunity to demonstrate his modifications to anybody who might appreciate their intricate subtleties. Even John Bostwicke, who had assisted Pongo in the building of The Calamity Cart, had shied away from a full demonstration of its capabilities. John was a superstitious man who felt much safer with magic than he did with mechanics.

'The foot pedals,' began Pongo with great enthusiasm 'control the anti-pursuit devices. The one on the far right tips the box of apples, the one next to it deposits straw from a container under the cart. The third pedal raises the iron plate at the rear to deflect arrows and thrown weapons.'

'What about all these levers?'

'Ah yes, the levers. The ones on your right control the weapons systems; the furthest from you fires the two forward facing crossbows, the one next to it the two rear facing crossbows; the next two deploy left and right waist-high sword blades, and the last one springs daggers out from the wheel-hubs. The levers on your left control the stealth attachments. I'll explain those as and when we need them.'

'You know, all of this seems terribly familiar.'

'Really? I can't imagine why,' lied Pongo. Pete the lingerie salesman had seen films, but Pongo saw no need to go into that.

'What are the horses' names?' asked Alec, introducing the need.

'Goldfinger and Thunderball,' mumbled Pongo, with only the faintest hint of embarrassment.

'Good morning, Phillip. Did you sleep well?' Sara Hagget stepped into caravan, which was a fair indication that she'd stepped out of it sometime after Morrison fell asleep. She was wearing a white dress that was possibly the most conservative outfit Morrison had ever seen her wear. Even in the depths of winter she bared more flesh than she had on display today.

'Yes, I did.' And he had. He felt refreshed; he felt content; he did a quick check on his heart, and there was indeed a song lurking in there. *Oh!* thought the besotted vet, *I'm in love.* And he was.

'Good, we have a long trip ahead of us. I have some supplies to keep us going.' Sara deposited one of Sid's brown paper bags on the table, leaving a stain on the tablecloth that would never come out.

'So where are we going?' Morrison threw back the covers and leapt out of bed, caring not a jot that his dangly bits were on full display. He was definitely in love. He didn't have the urge to write excruciating poetry yet, but no doubt that time would come.

'Falston,' replied Sara as she smoothed at the sides of her dress. She'd put it on to look nice—proper nice, rather than sexy—for Phillip Morrison. Just him.

Falston? That didn't strike Morrison as a particularly long trip. Technically it was no trip at all as Ned's caravan was well within the village boundary.

Sara looked at the tall man, and there may well have been a hint of admiration on her face. 'I can guess what you're thinking, but I don't mean *this* Falston. I'll explain as we go. Now get some clothes on, we can't have you running around in the buff now, can we?' Sara smiled her smile. She was getting a feeling when she looked at the naked Morrison, and it was the first feeling of its type that Sara Hagget had experienced in her very long life.

'Aaaaaaaarrrgggggghhhhhhhhhhh no!'

'What was that?' Pongo Smythe had a look of low-to-medium alarm on his face. The scream had been quiet, but then it had also been a long way off; it would have been deafening up close.

Alec grinned. 'Hold on, there should be another one in a sec.'

'Aaaaaaaarrrgggggghhhhhhhhhhh no!'

Pongo's expression went from alarm to puzzlement so quickly that his eyebrows shed a few hairs in the transition. 'So what were *they*?'

'That was Taff and Thermos waking up in the same bed.'

'Oh,' was all Pongo could think to say as he geed up Goldfinger and Thunderball, and with a jerk that nearly spilled Alec over the side, The Calamity Cart bounced off towards Tulston. Apparently Pongo's modifications hadn't extended to the suspension system, or addressed the total lack thereof. If Alec didn't find some seat padding his bum was going to end up as a hump on his back.

'So why exactly are we here?' If Alec was going to be risking his life anytime soon then it only seemed reasonable to find out why. He didn't like thinking about death. Death was something that happened to other people. Whenever thoughts of his own mortality crept into his head he imagined himself in the video for Britney Spears' *Baby One More Time* until they went away.

'To ensure that the sword doesn't fall into the wrong hands, or any hands at all really. If Excalibur is removed from its current location then the barrier will collapse and the two worlds will fold into each other.'

'You mean they'll combine into one big world, with double the population and all that sort of thing?'

'An interesting question, and scholars on the subject are divided between two possible answers. The first, and the one which I choose to believe, is that a recombination will take place. Where there is duplication between worlds then there will be a merging to create a single entity, keeping elements from both originals. Whilst genetic duplication between the worlds is highly unlikely, life-energy duplication is a very different kettle of metaphysics. It's all very theoretical and abstract, based on the replication of souls.'

'So what's the other theory?'

'That the two worlds will disrupt each other on a subatomic level, causing a cataclysmic implosion that will wipe out all existence.'

'And who believes that?'

Pongo shrugged. 'Pretty much everybody who isn't me. Anyway, enough of this morbid talk; we fear the worst before we even start, and that's no way to begin a journey.

Alec agreed. The way to begin a journey was to work out where the danger was, and then to begin journeying in the opposite direction. Instead they had worked out where the danger was, and they were beginning to journey towards it. Frankly Alec couldn't see how that was a sensible thing to do.

'Bloody darft, that's what it is,' announced Jack as he browsed the morning tabloid. The troubled landlord wasn't in the best of humours, and finding his scandal sheet contaminated by frivolous reports of bizarre and surreal events from around the globe was doing nothing to improve matters. Worst of all, he had an agent of most despised officialdom under his roof. Whilst the police may have had no great interest in Jack, there were other connected agencies that might well make dissatisfied tutting noises in his direction. Those fiendish operatives of Her Majesty's Customs and Excise, for instance. He would never have deliberately deceived the appointed emissaries of the dark lord of taxation, but it was his misplaced spouse that had always dealt with the sacrifices to that heinous god, and since her departure Jack had been somewhat lapse in his worship.

'Good morning, landlord.' George Guv appeared on the stairs, and Jack found the pleasant demeanour and cheery greeting most unbecoming for an officer of the constabulary.

George was feeling decidedly more chipper than usual on this glorious morning because today would see his first official action as the big (and only) cheese of the Unexplained-Phenomena Rapid Action Team; the interviewing of one Barry Ogleby vis-à-vis his alleged rendezvous with that fabled creature commonly referred to as a unicorn. If George's suspicions were correct, Falston-on-Wold was the epicentre for all of the weirdness that was bulging out of his manila folder, and this Barry Ogleby knew exactly what was going on. George had already deduced that Ogleby's drunken report was just a cover story to throw the bloodhounds off the scent, making him a very clever and very devious new adversary. 'Would you happen to know a gentleman who goes by the name of Barry Ogleby?'

'I don't know anybody that goes by that name.' Jack wasn't going to do any sticking out of the neck for Bladder, but he wasn't going to make it too easy for this plod either.

'Then you don't know anybody called Barry Ogleby?' George knew that wasn't true; Jack the landlord's name had featured numerous times in the official report on 'the unicorn incident'.

Jack nodded. 'Yes I do.'

'But you just said that you didn't.'

Jack shook his head. 'Oh no I didn't.'

'Oh yes you did.'

Jack thought it best to clarify, as it was too early in the day to get stuck in a panto loop. 'I said I didn't know anybody who went by the name of Barry Ogleby.'

'That's the same thing.'

'No it isn't'

'Yes it is.'

'No it isn't. I do know somebody called Barry Ogleby, but 'e doesn't go by that name. Folks in these parts call 'im Bladder.'

'I see.' George frowned; this landlord was a tricky one, with an intellect close to being on a par with his own. 'And do you know where I might find this Bladder?'

Jack glanced up at the bar clock and corrected for the twelve minute discrepancy between Greenwich Mean Time and Queen's Arms Time. 'As we're open in sixty-three minutes, I would guess that you'd be finding 'im standing outside the front door.'

'Then be so good as to let him in, I'd like to have a chat with him.'

'Is that one of them official requests, 'cos I'll need to see some identification or sum'it?'

George reached into his pocket and produced his new ID card in its faux leather holder, and Jack took his good time over squinting at it and comparing the photo to the face. 'Yep, there's no denying that's a photo of you with 'u-prat' written by it. I'll be opening the doors then, sur. That I will.' On a subconscious level Jack must have been feeling more at ease as he was lapsing into an Irish brogue.

The spry landlord developed both a limp and a stoop en route to the door, and his hands were suddenly crippled with arthritis as he fumbled at the bolts. 'More than 'appy to cooperate, officer,' he announced loudly to the door, 'as I'm sure ol' Bladder will be when you speak to 'im. Yes, I'm sure Bladder will be more than 'appy to talk to the police.'

'There's no need to shout, I'm right behind you,' said George.

'Oh, sorry.' *Still, job done*, thought Jack. Bladder would have to be a right dopey git not to have heard that warning. Jack swung open one half of the double-doors, confident that George Guv's quarry would have turned on his well-worn heels and made with the fleeing. 'Top o' the mornin' Bladder, you eejit.'

'Mornin' Jack. That time already, is it?' Bladder knew full well it wasn't that time at all, but the door had been opened and one scuffed toe had already found its way over the threshold, so there was no turning back now.

Jack stood aside as Bladder barged in, then he hastily shut and re-bolted the door against possible stampedes.

Bladder's knowledge of the interior of The Queen's Arms was intimate down to micrometer precision, so within a second of his hurried entrance he had two questions, both of which he felt the need to voice forthwith. 'Who's this one then?' was immediately followed by 'and where's the telly gone?'

Jack dealt with the queries in reverse order. 'The telly's been nicked, and this is Detective Inspector George Guv of u-prat.'

George grimaced, though in truth he'd gotten off lightly; his superiors had been pushing to have the unit called the Combined United Nations Taskforce.

Being in such close proximity to an officer of the law made Bladder blanch alliteratively. He'd assumed that Jack's warning had been just another ploy to stop him from darkening The Queen's Arms' doorstep in advance of opening time. Less inventive than the large 'X' on the door and the claims of virulent plague that Jack had used last time, but eminently subtler than the pitchfork he'd used the time before that. Bladder's initial panic subsided when it occurred to him that he hadn't done anything wrong that he knew of, unless transposing all of Motorhead's greatest hits onto the trombone was a crime.

'Might I buy you a pint, Mr. Ogleby?' George wasn't given to overt displays of generosity before breakfast, but loosening the purse strings often helped to loosen tongues.

Bladder smiled. Jack didn't. 'We're not open,' he announced in his best barman's voice. No slick city plod was going to catch him out that easily.

'Yes, you are,' said George, flashing his ID again. He had absolutely no authority to alter the licensing laws on a whim, but this backwater pump-puller wasn't to know that.

'No, we're not,' said Jack, resolutely. This backwater pump-puller knew exactly how far George Guv's authority went, and right now it was going nowhere.

'Oh yes you are,' said the irresistible force.

'Oh no we're not,' said the immovable object.

Bladder looked from one to the other and back again. 'Is it panto season already?'

Jeremiah Tauper was a troubled acolyte. Grand Master Thelonius Wisp was missing, and without him The Guild was making like a headless chicken. Actually, thanks to the disparate factions that had formed under the respective leaderships of Brothers Droop, Litmus, and Flange, The Guild was behaving like a super-sized family bucket of headless chickens. Without guidance The Guild was falling apart. Tauper wasn't given to profanity, but there was no denying that things had gotten a tad shitty.

As the morning assembly had yet again degenerated into a juvenile mudslinging contest, Tauper had excused himself; he had important business to attend to. The important business of sitting in the middle of Malecot's courtyard, counting the cobblestones and completely failing to notice the big black cloud that was drifting lazily over Tulston. Had he seen it he might have noticed that is was moving, somewhat atypically for a cloud, against the breeze. Had he seen it he would have been more than a little alarmed; it was one of *those* sorts of clouds, full of menace and foreboding in a way that only big black clouds can be. Had he seen it he might have done something impressive and changed the outcome of The Battle of Malecot, but as he didn't see it we shall never know.

In an uncharacteristic display of frustration, Acolyte Tauper thumped his fist down on the cold cobbles and the ground shook violently. He gave his fist a puzzled look and thumped it down again, cautiously this time, just in case. The ground beneath him lurched and buckled, tipping him sideways and sending cobbles exploding through the air like so much bone-breaking popcorn. The alarmed acolyte scuttled away from the centre of the courtyard, still on all fours as the ground heaved and bulged and did a lot of other things that weren't good at all when the ground did them. Tauper put his arms over his head to protect his skull from the rain of cobblestones, watching through trembling elbows as the courtyard inflated to bursting point, and then went straight past it without so much as a by-your-leave. The straining bulge exploded as four massive stone columns crashed through, one neatly placed in each corner of the courtyard. Tauper would have been crushed by the rubble and debris had he not been cowering in one of those corners. He was still cowering, but now he was doing it thirty feet up atop a black stone column. The air was filled with swirling dust that initially obscured the other columns from Tauper's squinting gaze, but as it cleared he could make out the shapes carved in the stone, and he was aghast. There were all manner of carnal goings-on: men with women; women with women; men with men; and many involving men and women with multiple partners not of the same species, or even of identifiable species.

As Tauper began to hunt for a way down from his precarious perch, the ground below began to undulate once more. Something else was pushing through. Tauper hadn't seen one for some time, but there was no mistaking the fluid surface and translucent blue glow of a transfer sphere. It broke the surface and hovered in the air a few feet above the crater it had made, humming gently as it spun, then it gave off a pulse of energy that rippled across the courtyard and bounced back off the building walls. The floor of the courtyard un-exploded, the crater filling back up with dirt, the cobbles rolling across the ground to neatly slot themselves back into place. There was a tug at his side, and Tauper realized that a cobble had found its way into his pocket and was now struggling to get back to its place of origin. He fumbled at his robe and extracted the stone before it dragged him from his column, watching in awe as it flew from his hand and scuttled along the ground to its allotted place in the courtyard. When the resurfacing was done the sphere sank down and popped open.

Tauper could make out two figures, one seated and one standing. The standing figure was a big one. Big, and a bit oiled. The seated figure was all burnished armour and bare flesh, and Tauper would have found her attractive but for all of the evil megalomania he was sensing from her. When she got to her feet and removed her helm, Tauper decided that a teensy character flaw like evil megalomania was something he could live with. He could sense something else too. It was very faint, but there was no mistaking it; Brother Wisp was down in that courtyard somewhere. Tauper grasped the edge of the column and carefully peered over, but of Wisp there was no sign.

'Well hello up there,' said the Lady Gaynor, who was standing at the base of Tauper's column, staring up at him.

'Greetings,' said Tauper, who was crouched on top of his column, staring down the front of Lady Gaynor's breastplate. It was one of those moments when he really missed having depth perception.

'Enjoying the view, are we?'

'Oh, yes. I mean no. I mean ...'

Gaynor smiled. It was going to be fun having people to play with. 'So who might you be, little man? No, let me guess. Acolyte Tauper, is it?'

'You have me at a disadvantage, milady.' There was no doubting that, given that he was unarmed and thirty feet up in the air. 'Apparently you know me, but I do not know you.'

'But I think you do. Take another look.'

Tauper took another look.

Gaynor frowned. 'At my *face*.'

'Oh, sorry.' Tauper took another look at her face. It *was* familiar. He had to dredge around in his memory to make all of the relevant connections, but when he found them his eyes opened so wide that the false one dropped out. 'Oh dear God, it's *you*!' His voice came out as a croak, his mouth having gone dry with fear.

'Yes, it is me,' Gaynor concurred matter-of-factly as she fished a glass eye out of her cleavage. 'But as not everybody is going to recognize me, I think I shall maintain the pretence a little longer, so call me Lady Gaynor.' The lady paused, and when she continued her voice had acquired a deep and booming quality that she was so very fond of. 'And from this point forward *I* am your god.'

Some of you may be wondering what became of flight 2202 inbound from Madrid to Luton. Well whether you're wondering or not, I'm going to tell you.

The moment flight 2202 had stopped being a blip on the sophisticated equipment designed to monitor blips, a whole barrage of different but equally sophisticated equipment designed to find missing blips began to search for it.

They didn't find it.

Nor did the sophisticated helicopters full of sophisticated men wearing sophisticated Civil Aviation Authority ties.

Even so, flight 2202 inbound from Madrid to Luton was found.

Two men in a cart found it, and neither of them was particularly sophisticated.

'So how the hell did it get here?' Alec didn't sound happy; he was still having difficulty with the 'going towards the danger' thing.

Pongo didn't sound happy either. He sounded confused. 'I really don't know. I've never before heard of anything this large breaching the barrier.'

Large it certainly was, and judging by the trench gouged into the fields it had skidded some distance before coming to rest across the only wide thoroughfare between Falston and Tulston woods. With their path blocked, Pongo had decided that it would be a good time for them to stretch their legs and let Goldfinger and Thunderball graze.

Alec looked at the plane, and then at Pongo. 'Now that we're in this magical world of yours, isn't there some magic you can use to move it?'

'That depends,' said Pongo.

'On what?'

'On whether or not you want to see my brain leak out of my nose and my head collapse like a soufflé.'

Alec frowned. Yoda would have been able to move the plane, and balance a small rock on top of a bigger rock at the same time. 'I guess we're going around then.'

Pongo nodded. 'That would be my guess also, and I think I should mention at this juncture that we're being watched from the trees off to our left.'

'You can sense that sort of thing?' Alec was impressed. Perhaps there was a touch of the Yodas to Pongo Smythe after all.

'No, it's just that they're not very good at sneaking and I can see them moving around.'

'Oh. So what do we do?'

'I suggest we either get back into the cart or get into the plane, where we'll be safe.'

'Safe from what?'

Pongo didn't reply, so Alec assumed he meant they'd be safe from the angry mob that came charging out of the woods, yelling and whooping and generally making like a bunch of savages. They didn't look terribly savage though. There were several Rambo types, stripped to the waist, neckties tied around their foreheads and beer bellies wobbling over the tops of their jeans. There were Tarzans wearing spectacles, Conans in brogues, and Red Sonjas with layered highlights. It looked like a fancy dress party where everybody had improvised a barbarian costume from what they were already wearing. Those without much imagination had gone *au naturel* instead. The only thing this ragtag bunch had in common was that each of them was armed in some way. Most had crudely fashioned spears or clubs. Some of those clubs might once have been maracas. A few had unimpressive looking bows. Unimpressive looking but bizarrely functional, as demonstrated by the banana shaped arrow that spun past Pongo's ear like a boomerang.

'Shall we run, then?' inquired Alec with no great sense of urgency. Their attackers might well have been dangerous, but they looked too ludicrous to take *that* seriously.

'I think that might be best,' replied Pongo as a spear that still had leaves attached landed between his feet.

'Cart or plane?'

'Cart,' said Pongo. He had to say it quite loudly as he'd already gone.

Unfortunately, all of this hullabaloo had unnerved Goldfinger and Thunderball, who chose that moment to depart at speed for calmer pastures. Alec didn't notice that his destination was now a cart shaped empty space until Pongo passed him in the opposite direction yelling '*plane!*'

Pongo got there first and hurdled in through the open door. He didn't have to jump that high, the nearside of the aircraft having dug itself into the ground far enough for the door to be at ground level. As Alec bounded through the entrance the pressure door swung back into place and sealed, just as a hail of misshapen arrows and branches with pointy ends bounced off it. Alec struggled to his feet and joined Pongo at a window to watch a group of semi-naked accountants, software engineers, insurance brokers, postmen and other assorted international travellers, including one minor celebrity, make grunting noises and bang on the outside of the great white bird with big sticks.

With the newest and most immediate danger over, Alec and Pongo surveyed their aerodynamic fortification. The interior of the aircraft had been gutted, with all of the seats piled up in a large pyramid at the rear, and not one of them had their tray table in the upright position. The inner walls were daubed with primitive artwork, coloured with all of the absurdly named shades of red, green and blue that only exist in make-up form. The drawings were simplistic and childlike, but all were eminently recognisable: The Eiffel Tower; The Statue of Liberty; Big Ben; The Colosseum; and other assorted national landmarks. In the middle of the floor was a pile of charred clothing that might once have been the cabin crew's uniforms, and even at this moment of great stress Alec's mind still felt the need to create an image of three naked stewardesses for him to enjoy.

Alec's moment of contentment was spoiled by a small plastic matador bouncing off the window behind him.

'I think we should move away from the windows,' announced Pongo as he grabbed Alec's arm and dragged him to the nearest convenient place of privacy, which was the privy. Not the most spacious of locations for an emergency meeting, but handy if either of them felt the need to use soap.

Alec sat himself down in the obvious place and said 'I don't get it.' And he really didn't. 'What's this thing doing here, and who are that lot?'

'The most likely explanation is that this aircraft collided with a transfer sphere and created a tear in the barrier. From their attire I would say that those are the passengers and crew out there, and the violent and uncontrolled shifting between worlds has driven them all half-crazy.'

'I'd say that was a conservative estimate.'

'Indeed, and their condition will probably deteriorate. What we have here is a bad case of devolution.'

'You mean the delegation of authority, especially from a central to a regional government?' Alec couldn't quite see the relevance.

'No, I mean evolution in reverse. These people are rapidly de-evolving. I would suggest that we move on as soon as possible before our new friends out there find a way in and make mischief with our innards. Or possibly soup.'

'And how are we going to go anywhere now? That lot are still outside and the cart has legged it.' Alec really needed a bright side to look on.

'Leaving should be straightforward enough. There are emergency exits on both sides of the aircraft, and all the banging and grunting seems to be on one side only. As for the cart, I'm sure it will turn up.'

'Really?' Alec's tone suggested that Pongo's optimism wasn't contagious. He got to his feet and flushed out of force of habit.

Once out of the convenient convenience they located the most appropriate emergency exit. The plane was tipped over onto its port wing and the starboard wing had buckled, forming a ramp down to the ground. The exit over that wing was selected as the most likely escape route, and Pongo hunted around and located some door related instructions. He read them aloud, giving Alec the feeling that he was expected to do things. 'This aircraft is equipped with eight emergency exits. You have shown in an interest in the type three over-wing exit, which is located here, over the erm ... wing. To operate, remove the cover plate, depress the toggle, and pull both hand levers inward and downward.

Alec opened, depressed, and pulled as instructed. Then he improvised some kicking and swearing at the stuck door. It suddenly occurred to Pongo that if the wing and fuselage were damaged then the hatch itself might not have survived unscathed.

'Be careful, Alec, that door might-'

Pongo's opinion on the door became irrelevant as the emergency hatch popped out. The buckled metal of the airframe gave the popping a more spring-loaded quality than its designer had intended, and Alec, still clinging to the door, went sliding down the broken wing in best luge fashion.

'Never mind,' shouted Pongo after the disappearing Alec, though it was unlikely Alec heard him over all the screaming.

Skip and jump went Pongo as he hopped through the emergency exit.

Thud and 'Ow!' went Alec as he ran out of wing.

Pongo negotiated his way down the wing to the ground. 'Are you all right?' he inquired of the prone figure spread-eagled on the grass at his feet.

'Fine, thanks for asking,' replied Alec, who didn't sound thankful and wasn't looking fine at all. 'Shouldn't take too long for the bones to knit, though perhaps you could help me look for my testicles?'

'Now may not be an appropriate moment for levity. I really think we should resume our journey as rapidly as possible, all that noise may have alerted the mob to the fact that this aircraft has two sides.'

Alec struggled up to his knees. Levity? Somebody was finding this funny? He held an arm out to Pongo in the hope of getting some assistance with the rest of his upward journey, but Pongo wasn't looking in his direction. Pongo was gazing skyward, so Alec did the same, and he too saw the glowing blue spheres passing overhead. Six of them, all converging on the far side of Tulston Wood.

Taff was staring intensely at Thermos, who was staring equally intensely back at Taff. Then they both turned and stared intensely at Mary, who smiled and stared back, though without any great intensity.

'We're supposed to do *what?*' Thermos knew he'd heard what he'd heard, but the hearing of it made him want to hear it again.

'Mister Pongo told me to tell you gents that you are to ...' Mary paused as she organized the message in her mind, wary of the fact that the vocabulary was not her own '... stay put and not set a foot outside this inn until such time as either he or John Bostwicke comes to get you. If he doesn't return before tomorrow evening then you are to assume that he is dead and that evil has been triumphant, and you will need to make your way through the terrible new world of darkness and despair as best you can, unless the universe has been destroyed by a giant paradox, in which case not to worry.' As Mary's cheery expression was unwavering, it's safe to assume that she wasn't listening to a word of what she was saying.

Phillip Morrison had babbled on for twenty yards before noticing that he was babbling to none but himself. As one of Falston's intelligentsia, Morrison wasn't usually given to solitary babbling, and for the majority of the journey the conversation had been less one-sided, Sara Hagget seemingly hanging on his every word, swerving with him as he skidded off down each new exuberant digression, soaring with him as he took to the skies on silken-winged flights of fancy. All of that does put a rather romantic slant on a conversation that primarily dealt with the difficulties of locating sarcoptic mange mite in canine skin scrapings, but when Morrison babbled he preferred sticking to what he knew, and he knew mites. Mites, ticks, fleas, lice, tapeworms, roundworms, hookworms; none were strangers to him, on a personal as well as a professional level. Such are the risks of being a vet on the edge. Sara didn't mind the parasites; it was just pleasant to talk to a man who didn't need to be staring at her chest to make words come out of his mouth. Phillip was different. True, at the beginning he'd been just like the rest of them, but that phase had passed and he was talking to her as though she had a mind to call her very own. She liked it. She liked him. She liked him rather a lot.

So Phillip Morrison had babbled and Sara had listened attentively. At least she had been listening. Now she was gone, though technically as she had stopped walking and Phillip hadn't, *he* was gone. He walked back the twenty yards he had just walked alone, thus making himself ungone. Sara was standing at the end of Edna Peevey's garden, staring at Rose Bungalow in the manner of a small child seeing their first giraffe. Morrison positioned himself beside her and tried not to be so tall.

'What do you see, Phillip?' Sara sounded troubled.

Morrison frowned. That was the sort of question people asked when there was something out of the ordinary to be seen. He studied Rose Bungalow and its gardens in minute detail, but he saw nothing unusual. Though the gardens did look that little bit more beautiful than they had done on any other morning, and today the bungalow itself looked quaint and cosy rather than small and pokey. 'I just see Edna's bungalow. Why, what do you see?'

'That's all I can see as well, but I can *feel* a great deal more than that. Would you mind if I did a little magic?'

Morrison wasn't sure how to respond, so he stalled for time with a noncommittal answer. 'If you feel the need to.'

Sara felt the need to, and made with the magical mumbo-jumbo. She moved her hands slowly and gracefully in front of her face and spoke softly in a language that Morrison didn't recognize, though Taff might have taken a crack at the odd word or two. As her chanting grew louder Morrison saw something emanate from her fingertips; he decided to call them as ripples, which wasn't right but it was the only description that came close. Circles of force pulsed from Sara's palms, travelling up Edna Peevey's garden path and striking the front door of the bungalow, where they spread out and enveloped the building. As Morrison watched, the roof of the bungalow shimmered, twisting and distorting in ways that it shouldn't have been able to, and then suddenly there was a thing where there hadn't been a thing before. It was a big thing. Morrison's surprise, fear, horror and revulsion at the sight of the creature sitting on Rose Bungalow were distilled down to a single sound, that sound being 'urk!'

'How did you know that?' Sara looked puzzled.

'Know what?'

'How did you know that it was an urk?'

'Lucky guess.'

The lucky guess was sort of maggot-ish, but with overtones of spideryness. Spindly white legs hung from a blubbery mass of whiteness that had an opening at one end, sort of a big gaping maw affair, and Phillip made the reasonable assumption that there was an opening at the other end as well, though he didn't dwell on it. There didn't appear to be any other recognisable features—apparently urks had no use for eyes, ears or nose—but it was difficult to be sure because of the ooze. The urk's body and legs were coated in a thick white mucus, elevating its appearance from simply disgusting to genuinely vile.

The big maggoty beastie shifted its position on the roof of Rose Bungalow. Eight spindly legs tightened their grip on the bungalow walls, and another pint of steaming mucus glooped out of the bottom of the struggling drainpipe. If the urk was aware of its audience, it chose to treat them with slimy indifference.

'Does it know we're here?' Morrison tried to sound interested in a matter-of-fact way rather than a terrified way, but he didn't succeed.

'I don't think so. Urks can only sense their prey at very close range, and even then they're grazers more than hunters.' Sara was doing matter-of-fact much more convincingly, and her apparent lack of fear was compensating for Morrison's apparent lots of fear.

'Grazers? What do they gra ... actually, don't answer that.'

'Don't worry, it really isn't that bad.'

'Now you're lying to make me feel better.'

'Would you prefer it if I didn't?'

'Certainly not; bullshit away by all means.'

'Well actually the end result of what they do isn't very nice, but the way they do it isn't so bad.'

'It eats you in a *nice* way?'

'I'm not even sure I'd call it eating, exactly. It's quite unique. You see the first urks were created accidentally many centuries ago when some maggots fed on the brain of a powerful but decomposing druid and ... and that was altogether too much information, wasn't it? Sorry. Anyway, the urk is basically sentient, though it has very little mental capacity. The mucus it secretes is a powerful hallucinogen that produces the illusion of an enticing pathway that leads directly into its mouth, and once inside that illusion continues. First-hand accounts are difficult to come by for obvious reasons, but most experts agree that the victim sees whatever they need to see to keep them happy, and mentally that's where they remain as the urk slowly digests them.'

'And that's nice, is it?'

'Now that I come to describe it aloud, it really isn't, is it? If it helps any, I can sense that this one's tiny mind is wracked with self-loathing.'

'Personally I think that's only fair. So why is it here?'

'That I don't know. Urk farms were outlawed many years ago, and even when they were legal the urks were destroyed long before they could reach this level of maturity.'

'Urks were farmed?' Morrison had difficulty with the concept; farms were nice places that had sheep and cows and pigs and other endearing creatures that made lovely roast dinners.

'For the mucus. There are still illegal farms, of course, and urk mucus lines the pockets well for those unscrupulous enough to trade in it.'

Morrison tried not to think about pockets full of mucus but it was too late; the image was in there and it wasn't going away anytime soon. 'So this thing is from this other world of yours?'

'It is.' Sara frowned, and Phillip guessed what she was going to say next. He guessed wrong. 'Help me find a bucket,' she said. 'We need to collect some of that mucus before the glamour repairs itself.'

'I see.' Try as he might, even the new man in Morrison couldn't find anything romantic about collecting maggot mucus in a bucket. 'And we need to do this because?'

'Because at some point we might need a bucket of urk mucus, and if we don't have any we're going to feel pretty silly for not taking this opportunity to get some.'

There was no arguing with logic like that, so Phillip Morrison allowed Sara to lead him up Edna Peevey's non-metaphorical garden path.

Even with Morrison keeping his eyes firmly fixed on the oozing urk it didn't take them long to locate Edna's gardening implements—the rustic wooden shed with 'Garden Implements' written on the door had been a big clue—but alas, there was no bucket. There was, however, a small stainless steel watering can that Sara examined and nodded at in a satisfied way. 'This will do us. I'll fill it up, you cover me.'

Morrison manfully took up Edna's pitchfork and pointed it at the nearest urk leg with as much menace as he could muster. He knew that Sara was allowing him to feel all masculine and protective and he appreciated the gesture, even if it were disparagingly obvious that attacking an urk with a garden implement was likely to be as effective as shooting a whale with a water pistol.

'So where is it we're going, exactly?' Phillip had been waiting for the right moment to ask, and for some reason the moment when Sara was filling a watering can with steaming maggot drool was the right one.

'To The Venerable Guild of Magi in Malecot. They usually know who's up to what when it comes to things magical.'

'And this Malecot, it's in a different world? Your world? The world where that ...' Morrison prodded the pitchfork in the direction of the urk, which was already becoming translucent as the glamour that had hidden it from view repaired itself '... comes from?'

'Yes.'

'It's going to be dangerous there, isn't it?'

'Quite probably.' Sara bit her lower lip in her concerned way.

'Right, we'd best get moving then. Can't stand around here all day.'

'And the danger?'

'I laugh in the face of danger. Then I run away very fast and hope the danger doesn't chase me.' Phillip smiled, and for the first time he noticed that there were thin strands of silver and gold woven into the fabric of Sara's dress that caught the sunlight and sparkled as tiny highlights over her body. It was beautiful. Ethereal, almost.

Now that was a man in love.

Rose Bungalow was a hundred yards behind them before Morrison spoke again. 'Malecot? That's an anagram of-'

'Yes, I know. I've always found that a bit corny, but I wouldn't say anything to The Guild, they can be very touchy about their heritage. Last I heard, Thelonius Wisp was in charge. Bit of an old fuddy-duddy, but he's got a good head on his shoulders.'

Thelonius Wisp's good head was sitting in its box beside Lady Gaynor's dark throne, and it was feeling thoroughly sorry for itself. Tauper could sense Wisp's despondency, but he had no clue where it was coming from. The one-eyed Acolyte was still atop his porno post. He could have gotten down if he'd wanted to, but all things considered he didn't want to. From the day he had entered the hallowed grounds of Malecot, Jeremiah Tauper had never doubted The Guild Of Magi's ability to defend themselves in times of crises, yet to describe this pitiful display of ineptitude as a battle would be bigging it up somewhat. The massed ranks of robes had burst out of the great hall, all of them going at it with the major chanting and wavy-armed overconfidence. The full frontal assault looked to be a dubious choice when Caleb cleaved Brother Droop lengthwise into two equally surprised halves. As a statement of intent it was completely unsullied by ambiguity. The halving of Droop sent a shock wave through the bowels of the marauding magicians, but their resolve held and they launched their counteroffensive. A joining of sweaty hands coupled with some particularly rhythmic chanting ignited the very air in front of the chanters, sending a wall of dancing flame speeding towards Lady Gaynor. It was the best trick that The Guild still had up its oversized sleeves, and they charged forward in its wake, confident to a man that the remainder of the day would be spent cleaning their assailants ashes off their sandals. Sadly for them this significant magical display only served to cook the remains of the late Brothers Droop, putting pay to any lingering suggestion that being sliced in twain had left him merely stunned. As the fire raced towards her, Lady Gaynor made a barely perceptible movement of the fingers of her right hand and the flames exploded into a million delicate pink and white rose petals that rained down on the courtyard. Pretty, but basically non-lethal unless you have really bad allergies. Another finger twitch, and each of those petals was transformed into a glorious multi-hued and iridescent butterfly that fluttered away as fast as multi-hued and iridescent wings could carry them, causing a not insubstantial breeze to blow through the courtyard and, thanks to the edicts of chaos theory, twelve feet of snow to fall on Easter Island.

All who witnessed it were amazed beyond words by the appearance of a million butterflies over Malecot, not least Lady Gaynor who'd been expecting a million angry wasps. The Guild had Acolyte Tauper to thank for that. Whilst no great adept himself when it came to the larger Magicks, he did have an uncanny ability to screw-up other people's spells.

The Guild had seen proof enough that this beauty in the bulging breastplate was more foe than they could face, and much nervous glancing around whilst trying to look small and insignificant ensued. The only exceptions of any note were Acolyte Felcher and Brother Litmus. Poor Felcher had been overcome by an attack of youthful zeal and had continued his forward charge, wearing his best battle face and screaming his best battle cry. Lady Gaynor was sufficiently impressed by this lone acolyte's heroic efforts to spare his life. Technically. He slumped to the ground in a most unnatural way, having had his skeletal structure completely and irreversibly liquefied. Brother Litmus' assault had consisted of throwing a rock, but as he'd only managed to hit Brother Kreb who was standing in front of him it doesn't really count. It hadn't even been a big rock. Not much of a rock at all, but bigger than some gravel and a lot more substantial than grit. Sort of a small-to-medium sized pebble type affair. But I digress; the point is that the Guild's hastily conceived 'battle' plan had undergone rapid metamorphosis and was now the 'unconditional surrender' plan.

'Right, can we now assume that you are *quite* finished, gentlemen?' Lady Gaynor was sounding a tad uppity as she glared down at those of The Guild who remained uncleft and non-gelatinous.

A bout of speed-nodding confirmed that they were indeed quite finished. 'Yes, we're quite finished' added Brother Kreb, who had a particularly well-developed sense of self-preservation. Unfortunately for those standing near him he also had a particularly well-developed nervous bladder disorder, and being hit in the back by Brother Litmus' rock had given him rather a fright.

'Good, I'm so glad.' Gaynor smiled. 'I'd hate for there to be any more silly unpleasantness when I so much want us to be friends'.

There was more vigorous nodding from a group of men who had come to appreciate the multitudinous advantages of friendship over silly unpleasantness.

The Battle of Malecot was over. The Battle of Falston was about to begin.

Alec and Pongo were standing in a field, about two miles away from a stricken Boeing 737-700, watching a lot of butterflies.

'That's a lot of butterflies.' Alec's statement was wholly accurate but largely redundant as Pongo was quite aware of how many butterflies constituted a lot. They stood and watched in awe as the air was filled with dancing iridescent grandeur, and even Alec couldn't help but be moved by the exquisite joy and poetry of it.

Perhaps things weren't so bad after all. How could they be, if even in these darkest of hours the world could create a spectacle such as this? This was a message of hope. A shining beacon to...

'Oh bugger!' said Alec as a million dead butterflies fell from the sky and carpeted the field with their lifeless bodies. 'Why did that happen?'

'Don't touch them!' shouted Pongo as Alec stooped to pick up a dead insect.

Alec picked one up anyway. 'Why not, it's just a butterfly. Oh, now it's a rose petal. No, now it's a tiny little flame. Ow!' With a small 'phhttt' the magic dissipated, leaving just the memory of its beauty and a scorch mark in Alec's palm.

There were another nine hundred and ninety nine thousand nine hundred and ninety nine small 'phhttts' that made for one really big 'PHHTTT' and quite a bad smell.

'Conjured,' said Pongo, in the infuriating way he did when things like that happened.

'What?' said Alec, in the baffled way he did when things like that happened.

'They were conjured creatures, created from flame. They can only exist for a short time once they are any distance from their creator.'

'Oh,' said Alec as he patted out the small fire in his hair.

'Excellent,' said Pongo, who had no hair to worry about and was grinning at something over Alec's shoulder.

Alec turned and saw Goldfinger and Thunderball, Calamity Cart still in tow, trotting across the singed grass towards them.

'Told you it would turn up,' said Pongo.

'Smartarse,' said Alec.

As Alec and Pongo were moving inexorably closer to almost certain death, other travellers were congregating in their wake. Taff and Thermos were outside The King's Arms, congregated as newts and bugger all use to man or beast. Potentially a problem, as shortly there would be both a man and a beast that would need to make use of them. Taff gazed down at the plate of breakfast precariously balanced on his knees, prodding at the last of his six sausages with his knife. Losing interest in the sausage, he turned his attention to a slab of bacon that he could have used to re-sole his boots.

The two men had been engaged in serious conversation for over an hour, and Taff was waiting on Thermos' answer to one of the most genuine and heartfelt questions that Taff had ever asked anybody. It had been a long wait, Thermos clearly giving his response the depth of consideration it deserved.

'Nice here, isn't it,' said Thermos, who'd forgotten what they'd been talking about.

Taff gazed lovingly into his pint and then down at his breakfast plate. 'Very. Would be a real pity if it all got destroyed by a huge brace of mallards.'

'You what?'

'That's what her in there' Taff stabbed his knife in the direction of the pub's front door, 'said, wasn't it? The universe might be destroyed by a huge brace of mallards? Or was it a giant pair of ducks?'

Thermos shrugged. 'Dunno. So how much of this stuff about other worlds and magic and all that rubbish do you believe?'

'All of it,' announced Taff. 'I believe every word of it.'

'Bloody hell, you've changed your tune. Last I heard you thought it was all a load of bollocks.'

'That was before.'

'Before what?'

'Before that big bloke over there came riding up the road on a unicorn.'

Thermos looked in the wrong direction and squinted with his whole face. 'You mean that funny looking bloke over there with the bucket?'

'Is he riding a unicorn?'

'No. But he has got a shovel.'

'What's a shovel got to do with anything?'

'Nothing, but it I thought it might be what you meant.'

'Why would I have said unicorn if I meant shovel?' It was a valid question, and Thermos came back with an equally valid answer.

'You're pissed.'

'And you're English, but I'd still expect you to be able to tell the difference between a unicorn and a shovel.'

'Well I can only see a man over there with a bucket, and if that's what I see then that's what I say. I was just calling a spade a spade.'

'No you weren't, you were calling it a shovel.'

Thermos frowned. 'That's just semantics.'

'What have the Jews got to do with it? Anyway, the bloke I'm talking about is over there.' Taff stuck out an arm and pointed down the street with his knife, nearly removing Thermos' nose and sending a sausage on a graceful arc down into his companion's pint.

'Oh, you mean *that* bloke. The one riding the unicorn with the really big dragon following him.'

'That would be the fellow.'

A bell rang in Sid's café. A bell of the 'hanging above the door and singing out with a friendly tinkle when a potential customer entered the premises' variety, though these days the best it could do was belch out a less-than-welcoming rusty thunk. The thunker on this occasion was a troubled looking landlord.

'Problem, Jack?' Sid was no great student of the human condition, but even he could tell that Jack was less than happy with his lot.

'I must confess to you, Sidney, that there have been a number of bewildering developments in this vicinity of late that have me perplexed unto this point of tangible distress in which you now find me'.

Sid frowned. This must be serious; there was no hint of any of Jack's patented accents, and he was making full use of a vocabulary developed over many years of reading actual books when nobody was looking. 'Is that so, my perturbed publican pal? Can you perhaps employ your most erudite locution to elucidate on the precise nature of the episodes that have conspired to create in you such a state of conspicuous agitation?'

Let battle commence. Jack steadied himself, took a deep breath and picked up the gauntlet that Sid had tossed at his feet. 'I will endeavour to do the very same, my paunchy trader of porcine flesh. Let us retire to a bench hereabouts and I shall make account of my afflictions that you may better comprehend the aberrant hap which incites my wretched demeanour'.

Sid staggered back, unable to parry the full weight of Jack's onslaught, but with a counter-thrust of his own already prepared. 'A most apposite suggestion my bombastic barkeep, let us adjourn to ... hold up, did you just call me fat?' Too late Sid realized his mistake; he'd been trapped by the cunning bar steward's risky use of the Prussian Insult Gambit. The correct response should have been the Czech Indignation Defence, though some analysts still vaunt the strategic benefits of the Bavarian Smack-In-The-Mouth Sacrifice.

The line of Jack's smile curled into a smirk at the ease of the victory, though it only stayed in that rare configuration for a few seconds, so as to avoid doing his facial muscles serious mischief. 'Now if we're done with the pratting about I think we 'ad best sit down.'

Sid nodded his agreement that sitting would be best, so sit they did.

'So what's all this about then, Jack? Have you, perhaps, finally finished your grand experiment and proved beyond any doubt that guilty feet *do* have rhythm?'

Jack shook his head. 'Sadly, no. Invaluable as that research could be, I've been somewhat distracted of late.' Jack's 'invaluable research' has been ongoing since his startling discovery that at the *Club Tropicana* drinks are actually quite expensive. Further investigations into song lyrics of the 1980s had revealed that many of the so-called 'classics' of that era were not the incisive or informative messages that we had all been duped into believing they were, and that most had been written for no more noble a reason than 'making a few bob'. There were, of course, shining exceptions; War *was* stupid, and if Culture Club hadn't told us that in 1984, who would have known?

'Distracted, Jack?' Sid would have feigned surprise, but as he was genuinely surprised, he didn't need to. Jack's singular quest for coin of the realm rarely allowed for any manner of distraction, other than perhaps a spot of gardening, or the occasional faux uxoricide.

Jack nodded a nod. 'Distracted, Sidney. Things are not as they should be.'

'Oh? And which things would they be then?' Sid didn't like the direction the conversation was heading, and began to devise a plan to steer it towards a topic he felt more comfortable with. The relative merits of lard were always a good standby at times like these.

'All of them, I'd say. You must 'ave noticed.'

'Can't say that I 'ave.' Sid was still swimming in denial.

Jack knew all about denial, he saw it on Bladder's face every night when he called time. Sid would no doubt be changing the subject next. Jack was anticipating lard, and haven't we all at some point?

Both men were steeling themselves for another bout of verbal parrying, so neither of them noticed that such a hush had fallen over the café you could have heard an 'H' drop.

Jack abandoned his discontented slump, sitting bolt upright so violently that from that moment he would be afflicted with serious lumbago, as opposed to the laughable variety that he cited every time there was any heavy lifting to be done around the pub. 'Well believe me, things are most definitely wrong around 'ere, but it's just come to me how to put 'em right again. Sidney Aluitious Poe, tis time we got our river back.'

Sid sighed. It was too much to hope that Jack had taken to using the royal 'we'. 'The river? How?'

Jack grinned the grin of a man with a plan. 'Let us retire to my place of business, and I shall explain the finer points over a pint or two of best.'

'Excellent as that suggestion is, I'm afraid my lint is tending towards being a touch boracic at the moment.' Not strictly true, but if he was about to become an integral part of a Jack scheme Sid saw no reason to be putting his hard-earned in the man's till as well.

'Fear not, the ale is on the house today, and not the taplash neither.' Once more Jack was offering his foaming lifeblood and asking for naught in return, yet he was still smiling broadly.

Sid suddenly felt very scared.

Bill and Ben the unemployed security men were not happy chappies. It may even have been true to say that the two chappies sitting on Falston Bridge, staring down between their feet at the oozing quag beneath them, were the two unhappiest chappies to be found anywhere on the planet. A few minutes earlier it may not have been true, as there was a snake wrangler chappy in Nepal who'd been particularly unhappy, but he'd just cheered up a bit, so Bill and Ben were back in pole position.

Their dismissal had been inevitable once the real Donald 'The Don' Beresford had arrived on Falston Bridge, and they had both known that no amount of undignified pleading would change that. Didn't stop them trying though. They didn't keep their jobs, but at least The Don had supplied Ben with another suit so that he could remain on duty until his replacement arrived.

'It's a conspiracy, that's what it is,' announced Ben.

'What is?'

'The conspiracy is. First that sneaky bint makes me leave me post and hops it with me clobber, and then that bloke turns up pretending to be The Don.'

'Could be one at that. Not much we can do about it now though.' The statement was drenched in rivers of pathos as Bill struggled to come to terms with the fact that he was no longer contractually obliged to act menacingly.

'Yes there bloody well is.' Ben was acting menacingly on his own time. 'To start with we can find those two conspiratators and try out a few interrogation techniques.' There was a glint in Ben's eye as he spoke, and he began to finger the butt of his inexpertly modified toy gun through the fabric of his expertly tailored black suit.

Bill thought for a moment, and then he began caressing his own bulge, clearly unconcerned by the homoerotic overtones that had crept into the proceedings. 'I'm with you, partner' he declared with more exuberance than was entirely necessary. They were a team, and Bill would have followed old Ben on any damn fool idealistic crusade, even if he did use words like conspiratators.

'Payback,' said Ben.

The two exed security guards leapt to their feet and exuberantly high-fived each other off Falston Bridge.

Bobs looked up from his sniffing and considered the sound that had just rolled into Falston Wood. Having correctly identified it as the noise made when two idiots fall fifteen feet into thick mud, he returned to his sniffing. Bobs had been doing a lot of sniffing recently. Sniffing and leg cocking. Most of the leg cocking had been to emphasize that he could now pee with impunity in either direction, though I guess you have to be a quadruped to fully appreciate how good that feels. The sniffing was an integral part of Bobs' efforts to track down his creature. There had been no scent to follow down in the village, but now that Bobs was in the woods he was having better luck. His creature had been here, and recently too. Much as Bobs disliked being away from the village, he'd noticed that his popularity there had waned recently, and it wasn't just because he was peeing on everything. On some instinctive level Bobs knew that his happy event in the shank department made the villagers uneasy, but he couldn't understand why.

As he sniffed at the undergrowth, Bobs' nose bumped against something solid. A rock. A rock that was strong with the scent he'd been following. It was his creature's rock. Bobs tipped his head to one side as innate behaviour patterns did whatever they had to do to become a course of action. If his creature had lost his rock, then what better way for Bobs to show his affection than to return it? After a brief display of bouncy, barky, tail-waggy canine exuberance, Bobs snapped the rock up in his mouth and resumed his serious sniffing.

George Guv sniffed at the air, though heaven knows why. 'So this is the place then?'

Bladder nodded but kept schtum. He hadn't said anything much on the trek from The Queen's Arms, fully aware that anything he did say may have been taken down and used in evidence against him, or some such.

George Guv hadn't said much either, his silence being an indication that the long arm of the law had much on its short-of-a-picnic mind. Much of that muchness had to do with George's growing suspicion that he knew this Barry Ogleby, aka The Bladder, and it was frustrating him no end that he couldn't remember why. Now he was going to have to live with the frustration a little longer; there was serious official business to be done, so George did that business, seriously and officiously. 'So then, Mr. Ogleby, where exactly were you standing on the evening in question?'

Bladder made with the pointing.

'And the creature you allegedly saw was ...?'

More pointing and a mumbled 'O'er there'.

George got the feeling that his reticent companion wasn't fond of authority figures. The truth was that Bladder had no problem with authority figures per se, he just couldn't understand why they so often believed that authority somehow implied superiority, which in his experience was rarely the case.

There followed some close scrutiny of the two areas that Bladder had digitally indicated. George Guv perused, paced, squatted, and prodded, in best crime scene investigation fashion. George loved this sort of thing, though he was finding it a less rewarding experience without his sergeant there to be condescending to. When he was done with the scrutinizing thing, he moved on to the analysis thing. At this point the scene should fade to black for a few seconds, after which George would be standing in a glass-walled laboratory full of electro-analyser doobries and spectra-thingamajigs, all being expertly operated by an attractive and unfeasibly blonde forensic scientist who would develop into George's love interest in a strangely episodic fashion. Unfortunately as none of these things existed (anywhere), George was going to have to rely on his mental agility and his trusty notebook and pen. His trusty notebook was still sitting on his trusty bedside table back at The Queen's Arms, leaving him with just his mental agility and his pen. It was corroded, badly cracked and only functioned intermittently, so that just left his pen. A very fine pen it was too. Gold fountain jobby with his initials inscribed on it in one of those whirly gothic fonts. His mum had bought it as a gift for when he made Chief Inspector, but eventually she had given up waiting and it had done nicely for George's last birthday.

'We done then?' Bladder wanted away. He had people to see, things to do, bars to prop up.

'Not quite, Mr. Ogleby. Perhaps you could tell me again why you were in this particular spot when the occurrence ... occurred.'

Bladder was confident that he couldn't tell George again as he hadn't told him before. 'I was out for a walk'.

'A walk?'

'A walk.'

'I see. Just taking the air. Stretching your legs. Having a brisk promenade before retiring for the night. Something like that, yes?' George was getting a nice rhythm going as he paced the clearing, using his pen as a baton to conduct himself.

'Aye, sum'it like that.' Bladder was getting one of those uncomfortable feelings that can easily be mistaken for the beginnings of a bowel movement.

'Aha! Well I put it to you, Mr. Ogleby ...' George spun around and made a dramatic pointing gesture that sent a finely honed precision made Swiss writing implement arrowing across the clearing to embed itself nib-first in a tree. George slipped the now redundant pen top into his pocket and started again, though in less dramatic fashion and with almost no pointing at all. 'I put it to you, Mr. Ogleby, that your so-called 'stroll' didn't bring you to this particular place by chance. Not by chance at all. It is my belief, Mr. Ogleby, that you came to this spot on the evening in question with a very specific purpose, namely to make a token gesture of defiance in regard to the new water bottling plant not two miles downstream of us. You came here specifically to urinate into the river, didn't you, Mr. Ogleby?'

Did I mention that when he wasn't pratting around, George Guv was actually good at his job?

Bladder decided his best course of action was to come clean, but somewhere between his brain and his mouth that decision was vetoed. 'Don't know what you mean.'

'Of course you don't. Tell me, Mr. Ogleby, had you been drinking that day?'

'Might have had a jar or two.'

'Drugs?'

'No thanks.'

'Had you been taking drugs, Mr. Ogleby?'

'Like what?'

'Weed, Mr. Ogleby. Or charlie, crack, coke, snuff, snot, racoon, goop, wiffle, luge or perhaps blow?' There was a possibility that George hadn't been paying full attention at his last Prohibited Substances seminar.

'Blow?' repeated Bladder, who had never attended a Prohibited Substances seminar, but still knew that George Guv was mostly talking bollocks.

'Blow,' said George yet again. The word seemed to have gotten stuck, but before Bladder could pry it loose George used it to scratch the itch that had been bothering him all morning. 'Blow!' exclaimed the officer of Her Majesty's constabulary. 'That's it! You're Barry the Blow aren't you? Didn't you used to play trombone with

Satan's Motherfuckers? I saw you guys play Dartford Apollo once. Man, you were real cool cats.' George was having a 'Summer of Love' flashback, which I really can't explain; he'd been six at the time, and for him it had been the 'summer in Hove' with his Aunty Beryl. 'I've got all of your records.'

'We only did one.'

'I know, and I've got all of it. Well I never! Barry the Blow. You know you were really ...'

The rest of George's sentence will have to remain a mystery, probably even to George. Bobs enters stage right, pauses briefly, and then exits stage left. It was little more than a cameo appearance, but its effect on the other players was dramatic.

'Was he carrying ...?' Bladder let the question tail off because he couldn't think of any way of finishing it without sounding ridiculous.

'Yes he was.' George fumbled around in his jacket pocket to find his cigarettes. He could feel an enigmatic one-liner coming on and he wanted to be ready for it. This was more like it! George's film noir sensibilities were being sensually massaged by the thought that this case might turn out to be about something other than trolls and unicorns. Drunken jazz musicians and international jewel thieves were the stuff of *Spade* and *Marlowe*, and exactly the sorts of things George had been waiting for his whole career. All thoughts of mellow trombone breaks were cast aside as George again found himself rueing the absence of his singed sergeant. He needed somebody to follow that dog, as according to Guv logic it would lead him to a naughty wrongdoer. He also needed somebody to make sure that Barry the Blow didn't blow. That was more somebodys than were available.

'You goin' to follow him then?' Bladder had also spotted the somebody shortfall, though he saw it as an opportunity rather than a problem.

'Yes I am.' George manoeuvred a cigarette into his mouth and lit it. Bladder's spirit soared as thoughts of The Queen's Arms loomed large, but the flight was cut short by George's flak guns. 'And you're coming with me, so let's go, I have to see a dog about a man.' George was satisfied with that one, so his barely started cigarette sailed away.

'Oi!' said Bladder as he hastily extracted the smouldering missile from the bottom of his trousers. As our two players exit stage left, a great tit flies down into the clearing, coming to rest on a finely honed precision made Swiss perch, until recently the property of a much greater tit.

Down in the village there were two happy men. There may well have been more than two happy men, but we're going to concentrate on this pair. They were happy because a brief interrogation of the locals had yielded the possible whereabouts of 'the tall bloke with the limp' and 'the redhead with the legs', collectively referred to as 'the marks'. The 'interrogation' of Falston-on-Wold residents Monty and Brenda Pumice had involved stopping them on the high street and asking them very nicely if they had seen anybody matching Phillip and Sara's descriptions. The incessant pressure had been too much for Brenda, who had capitulated and admitted that she had seen the pair heading in the direction of Rose Bungalow. When

Ben had apologized for being really ignorant of local geography and had requested further clarification, Monty had cracked and pointed in the relevant direction. Ben had politely thanked the Pumices, and Bill had called them a pair of no-good tossers, as it was his turn to be 'bad cop'.

With the intelligence gathering phase of 'Operation Get the Bastards' complete, the deployment phase began.

'We going to this Rose Bungalow then?'

'Yep.'

Deployment phase complete.

'We're here,' announced Pongo, pulling back on the reins to bring Thunderball and Goldfinger to a halt, which was a surprise for them as they hadn't been moving.

'Here?' Alec looked around. 'Here' looked the same as the 'there' they'd be travelling through for the last hour. 'Here where?'

'Tulston.'

Alec took another look around. 'Looks to me like Tulston is a one-horse town, and somebody shot the horse.'

Pongo clambered down from the cart and shook his head. 'I find myself intensely irritated'

'Oh? Why?'

'Because I find you intensely irritating. I know all of the sarcasm and humour is simply your way of dealing with the situation, but I would be greatly impressed if you bloody well stopped doing it. Tulston is down in the valley, the other side of those trees. Now if you would be so good as to place the cart into stealth mode we can go and see what we can see. Find the lever marked 'Tulston 2', unhook the safety rope from it and pull it up sharply.'

Stealth mode! Alec had been waiting all day to see this. When he had found, unhooked and pulled as directed, he got his wish. There was clinking. There was clanking. There was also jiggling, thudding, grinding and sliding, as the cart's elegant mechanical devices did elegant mechanical things. The sides of the cart elevated and two long rods telescoped out, extending from the rear of the cart to a point just in front of Thunderball and Goldfinger. Lengths of canvas unrolled down to the ground, then two smaller rods sprung out from grooves in the larger rods, and more canvas dropped into place. The cart and horses were now completely surrounded by heavy canvas, which created a problem.

'There's an escape hatch in the floor. Drop down and crawl out under the canvas on this side,' said Pongo, solving the problem before Alec could whine about it.

Once outside Alec was able to see the full extent of the cart's transformation. The canvas box around the cart and horses had trees painted on it; Alec assumed that the intended effect was one of blending in with the background. The achieved effect was that of mediocre artist having left a painting of some trees in front of some completely different trees. Alec felt it worthy of comment. 'You're kidding.'

Pongo frowned. 'Just give it a second to compensate, and then you'll see.'

A second later, Alec saw. The canvas shimmered; painted branches repositioned; hues darkened; different hues lightened; some hues probably stayed the same. Impressionistic daubs became sharp detail and dark splatters became the subtle interplay of light and shade. The process took less than a minute, and when it was done the cart and its equine power plant had all but vanished.

'The paintings were done using the same dyes as are in my clothing.' Pongo tried not to sound smug, but he didn't try that hard. 'I haven't quite perfected it yet, as you can still see the outline when you're up close like this, but from a distance it works rather well. You can tell me just how impressed you are on the move, as we'd best make haste to Malecot. The horses get restless after a while, and the stealth effect is rather compromised when the cart wanders off in search of better grazing.' Pongo walked as he spoke, heading in the direction of the trees. That was a problem for Alec, who had recently developed an aversion to woodland. Individually trees were fine, but they shouldn't be allowed to hang around in gangs like that. 'Do we have to go that way?'

Pongo stopped and considered Alec's question. 'Technically no, but as we're in a hurry and the alternative is to circumnavigate the globe, I personally favour this route.'

'I thought you said you'd had enough sarcasm.'

'*Your* sarcasm, yes.' With that, Pongo bounded off into the woods. Alec didn't feel much like bounding, so he opted for dejected trudging to the beat of the flappy-soled trainer.

They walked in silence for ten minutes, then Pongo went 'shush!', which struck Alec as an odd way to break a silence. He was about to ask Pongo why he had shushed, and in so doing completely miss the point of the shush, when there was vigorous hand waving. Pongo lowered himself down onto his haunches and disappeared in much the same way as the cart had. Alec followed suit, though when he did it he was just as visible, only shorter.

Acolyte Tauper felt sick. The slop bucket that swung heavily in his right hand was making him feel sick. The smell from the wooden box clamped under his left arm was making him feel sick. The agonizing pain of bone grinding against bone in his ankle was making him feel sick. The fly that was investigating the rim of his empty eye socket was making him feel sick. All in all a lot of sick. But the real truth of it was that Acolyte Tauper felt sick because he was a coward. He had been weighed; he had been measured; he had been found scarpering. With the battle lost, The Guild had ushered their new mistress and her guard into the main hall, presumably to reiterate their unconditional surrender in more comfortable surroundings, giving Tauper the opportunity to clamber down his lofty collection of carved erotica. Unfortunately, the breast he chose as his first handhold was a little too sensually rounded and Tauper lost his grip. Somewhere on the downward journey his ankle struck against an impressive carved penis. Even in that moment of great pain he'd been thankful that it hadn't been his penis striking an impressive carved ankle. His landing was of the heavy thudding variety, and again he was thankful, this time for the excellent impact cushioning properties of his robes. With a supreme effort of will he blocked out the pain from his shattered ankle and struggled over to the far corner of the courtyard to retrieve a rusty slop bucket. Then, trying his best not to look down as he did it, Tauper scooped the gelatinous mass of flesh that was Acolyte Felcher into the bucket.

'Ffaaanksssss,' said the amorphous blob, though Felcher would have been considerably more grateful if Tauper had thought to empty the bucket first.

With his rescue mission complete, Tauper was about to get back to the more serious business of running away when he noticed the wooden box sitting beside Lady Gaynor's throne. He thought for a moment and then went over to the box and bundled it under his arm. Now he calculated he had just fifty-nine seconds to get out of the courtyard and into hiding before the pain from his ankle became unmanageable. It took him thirty-four seconds to get out of the courtyard, through the gates of Malecot and over to the nearest of Tulston's private gardens—an overgrown affair belonging to one Hogard Denby. Another twelve seconds were taken up by Tauper negotiating his bucket, his box, and his person, over the garden wall. Nine more were used secreting himself in a large and bushy fuchsia. Four seconds later he passed out.

When he passed back in there was significantly less pain in his ankle, but it was still going to be difficult to walk on it. It was going to be all but impossible to run on it, and Tauper suspected there was going to be quite a lot of running in his immediate future. Fortunately, he had been trained to identify the blossoms, roots and herbs he needed to speed the healing process. Even more fortunately, they all appeared to be close at hand in the wilds of Hogard Denby's garden. Less fortunately, Tauper had skipped several of the more advanced 'Natural Remedies' lectures because the classroom smelt like poo. He knew that he was supposed to grind the ingredients into a paste, but he had no idea if he was supposed to eat it, apply it to his ankle as a poultice, or stick it up his bottom. Given those choices, Tauper opted for the poultice. Several of the plants were toxic, so eating them didn't seem like such a great idea, and as far as he was concerned his alimentary canal was a one way street and no good could come of anything going up it the wrong way, no matter what Brother Litmus said. He was about to start gathering the ingredients he needed when he noticed an army of reasons why he should stay exactly where he was.

Lady Gaynor's army.

A crowd had gathered in Malecot's courtyard. It may even have been a throng, but Tauper was unclear if a throng was a function of quantity or density so he went with crowd. There was the mandatory angry mob of local villagers, armed, as custom dictated, with pitchforks and all manner of gardening implements, with the possible exception of dibbers. Tauper could make out several shapes that were either large badly dressed thugs or small well-dressed trolls, carrying strange cylindrical metal tubes of a type that Tauper had never seen before. Behind them were the detestable cowards who called themselves The Guild of Magi, and behind them was a group of creatures that were the stuff of nightmares. Either they had once been human and had been reduced to these grotesque bestial forms, or they had once been beasts and had been transformed into vile parodies of humanity. Tauper prayed it was the latter, as the thought that these things might once have been human was truly repulsive. There were maggot-men, rat-men, slug-men, toad-men, and several other thing-men whose origins Tauper couldn't even guess at. Some were able to maintain an upright stance, whilst others scuttled, crawled and slimed their way around the courtyard, making everybody else shuffle about nervously in an effort to keep their distance from them.

As Tauper mused on how these creatures had been gathered here so quickly, two balls of blue lightning drifted into view over Malecot's rooftops, hovering above the courtyard for a few seconds before sinking to the ground just outside the gates. As they landed, they popped open in customary fashion, depositing another of those tube-wielding troll things and a group of angry-looking men dressed in black uniforms with black peaked hats. Angry-looking men who had clearly been dead for some time.

So it was for the next two hours. Tauper watched from his hiding place as the transfer spheres arrived, each bringing a new horror to add to the throng. Tauper was comfortable calling it a throng now as it was spilling out of the courtyard and into the streets. Then there had been a change to the routine. Three more spheres appeared, larger than the others, and Lady Gaynor was concentrating hard to control their descent into Tulston. Even from a distance Tauper could see the sweat glistening as it rolled from her face and down her long, elegant neck before meandering into the valley of ... concentrate, Jeremiah! The spheres touched down a few short feet away from Hogard Denby's garden wall, and through hissing blue lightning Tauper saw Lady Gaynor slump for a moment. She quickly regained her composure, glancing around to make sure that nobody had noticed. Now was not the time for signs of weakness.

The three new spheres cracked like thunder, spitting bolts of blue lightning in all directions. One of them shot over Tauper's head and struck the roof of Hogard Denby's house, shattering the chimney and setting the thatch alight.

'Oi!' came a voice from somewhere deep in the throng, but if Hogard Denby had any other comment about his house burning down he kept it to himself.

Close enough for Tauper to reach out and touch they were: three huge constructs of metal in greens and greys, painted with strange and unfamiliar markings, as well as more recognisable numbers and letters. They were presumably vehicles of some kind, the largest of the three having bands of metal draped over and around its many small wheels. That one also had a long metal tube that protruded horizontally from its domed top. Tauper had no idea what that tube was for, but it was definitely not for hanging washing on. With a deafening roar, the metal monsters burst into life. Belching black, acrid-smelling smoke, and without apparent recourse to man or beast, *they began to move!* The two smaller machines rolled forward, one either side of the conflagration that had been Hogard Denby's house, the disparate elements of Lady Gaynor's army forming into ranks behind them. The larger vehicle lurched backwards into Malecot's courtyard, tearing up the cobbles with its great metal tracks, and sending one of the heavy stone gateposts crashing to the ground as though it had been as insubstantial as smoke. With a growl of pleasure, Lady Gaynor's bodyguard climbed up onto the device, sitting astride it as it trundled forwards again. Lady Gaynor followed on behind the great machine, some fifteen feet in the air, the partially developed transfer sphere she was using to accomplish the feat creating a faint blue aura around her. Tauper froze in panic. As she drifted by, Lady Gaynor looked directly at his hiding place, but apparently, for all of her powers, she didn't have the ability to see into the fuchsia.

Tauper waited until he was sure that he was alone in Tulston. Then he waited some more, just to be certain. After that, he waited a bit. When the waiting was done, he did some gathering, grinding and poultice application before picking up his bucket and box and making for the trees. Lady Gaynor and her army looked to be heading directly for Falston, though soon they would have to turn toward the winding valley road, as it was unlikely that the more sodden ground of the direct route would support those demonic vehicles. By taking a more direct route through the woods, Tauper could get there ahead of them. He wasn't sure what he would do when he got there, he just knew he had to get there to see his magnificent and malevolent mistress do whatever it was she was planning to do. Perhaps on the way he would realize that he was under the influence of some kind of Magicks D'amour, but probably not.

Fifteen minutes into his journey, Tauper spied a figure crouching in the woods. He sensed no danger from this stranger, but then his senses may not have been at their best as he'd completely failed to sense the second person crouching beside him.

'Good day, Acolyte Tauper,' said Pongo cheerily as he stood up.

'And a good day to you, Pongo Smythe,' came the automatic reply.

Alec waved and tipped over.

Tauper took a moment to process this new information. An eventful day it had been, and one full of these little surprises. 'Pongo Smythe? But aren't you-'

'Evidently not, I'm extremely happy to say,' said Pongo, extremely happily.

'Thank the Lord,' said the box.

Phillip Morrison was having an eventful day, full of little surprises. There had been a few huge ones as well, but focusing on the little ones made the big ones easier to deal with. The current surprise was of medium size and involved consensual nudity.

'Are you sure?' Morrison was sure that *he* was sure, but it was important to him to know that she was sure as well.

'I'm sure.' Sara had never been surer of anything.

'Here?'

'Here.'

'Now?'

'Now.'

'And you're sure?'

Sara laughed and slid her arms up around Morrison's neck, drawing his face to hers for a kiss that said she was sure.

'Perhaps we should get naked then?' said Morrison.

Sara laughed again. 'I think we've done that bit already.'

Morrison looked down and grinned. 'Oh yes, so we have.'

And so they had. Falston's lofty gammy-legged physician to the furry, and its lithe, shapely-legged virgin of easy virtue, were together in the altogether. This time Morrison was certain that they were about to do that thing that people often did at times of concurrent nakedness.

Phillip Morrison's transformation into the 'new man' was complete. Standing there with Sara he now understood the distinction between the transcendent intimacy of making love, and the purely physical act of having sex, though never having experienced the former he hoped that the basic mechanics of it were the same. He was sure that the same bits went in the same places, but was he still allowed to grunt?

Sara Hagget was naked. She was as naked as she had ever allowed herself to be, and it was a condition that went far beyond having no clothes on. It was a supremely intimate moment, but there was no reason why it shouldn't be great sex as well.

How great the sex actually was is nobody's business but theirs, and when it was over Phillip and Sara lay naked and silent in each other's arms.

Morrison was the first to disengage from the perspiration-soaked embrace. 'Would it be too crude of me to say that your name is a very apt anagram?' said he as he flicked a woodlouse out of his pubic hair.

Sara smiled and kissed Phillip's cheek. 'Yes, I suppose that would be crude. But not *too* crude.'

'Looks like they're finished. The plan still to follow them?'

Ben didn't reply. Nor was he watching the marks any more. Bill was compelled to turn around and look as well. What could possibly be more worthy of Ben's attention than naked woman bits?

Bobs stared at Bill and Ben. Bill and Ben stared at Bobs. Bobs wagged his tail a bit. Bill and Ben ignored Bobs' tail and stared at the thing in Bobs' mouth. A thing that was causing some unsightly drooling.

'You're drooling,' said Bill.

'Sorry.' Ben wiped his chin with the back of his hand and then went back to staring.

Bill had no idea what it was he was staring at, so he selected a question that wouldn't require him to admit that. 'Is that what I think it is?'

'If you think that it's a manky looking dog carrying an emerald the size of my fist then yes, I think that it is what you think it is. Look at the size of the bloody thing!' A very particular gleam had appeared in Ben's eye.

Bobs spotted the very particular gleam and took a step back.

'Good doggy. Nice doggy. Come and see your Uncle Ben.' Ben crouched down and extended a muddy hand towards Bobs.

'Careful Ben, he might not be a nice doggy.'

'Oh, I'm sure he is. You are, aren't you? You are a nice doggy. Yes you are.'

Yes he was. Bobs was a nice doggy. He was also a clever doggy, so he turned and legged it.

Bill looked at Ben. Ben looked at Bill. 'Shit,' they said.

'Who we following?' Bill was voicing a most serious dilemma; to split up would break every rule in the book, assuming that the only rule in that book was one about not splitting up.

Ben had the answer, and he had reached it with such logical clarity that it would have brought a tear to the eye of Donald 'The Don' Beresford. 'We stay with the original marks. That dog's on to us, and we'll never keep up with him or out-think him now, but in the end he's just the courier. We're after bigger fish than a dog.'

'A fine plan partner, but there's a small problem with it.' Bill was being generous; there was a very *big* problem with it. 'They've buggered off.'

'They can't have.' Ben's incredulity was justified. Bobs had distracted them for no more than a few seconds, barely long enough for their quarry to get dressed, and certainly not long enough for them to clamber up the far side of the hollow. Yet of the redhead and the tall bloke there was no sign. Off, they had indeed, buggered.

'Looks like they've left some stuff behind though,' said Bill.

'Aha!' announced Ben, more triumphantly than was warranted. 'Their first mistake.'

Bill nodded his approval. It was only fair that the opposition should make a mistake, as he and Ben had made at least a dozen in the last two minutes. 'Let's take a closer look.'

'Let's.'

The closer look was eventually looked, Bill and Ben's descent into the hollow requiring a lot of 'making use of the natural cover' and 'watching each other's backs'. The looking revealed the stuff to be: one pair of men's denim jeans; one pair blue paisley socks; one pair gents black leather shoes; one pair ladies sensible white shoes; one knee-length white dress; one pair white stockings; one white lace trimmed garter belt; one pair white lace trimmed panties; one elasticated knee support; one small stainless steel watering can full of something really nasty.

'A Dragon. A real bloody dragon.' Thermos sounded greatly troubled. 'And a unicorn. A real bloody unicorn.'

'Yes, one of those too,' confirmed Taff 'though I haven't seen it for a while, wonder where it went.'

'Went? It hasn't gone anywhere; it's still standing right there.'

'Oh no it isn't,' said Taff.

'Oh yes it is,' said Thermos.

'Ah,' said John Bostwicke, who was unaware of the existence of pantos. 'Perhaps I may assist?'

'Assist? I think introducing me to dragons and unicorns is about as much assistance as I want for one day, thank you very much,' announced Thermos, huffily.

John frowned. 'I understand this has been a great shock for you, much as seeing a machine flying through the heavens was a great shock for me. I also have no doubt that you know many things about your world that I do not, but I also know much about my world that *you* do not, so mayhap you would be wise not to dismiss my council with such haste.'

Taff nodded. So did Thermos, who also added a self-conscious 'sorry.'

John signified his acceptance of the apology by not breaking Thermos' face. 'One thing is certain; our meeting here on this day is most fortuitous.'

'Is it?' queried Thermos.

'It is?' transposed Taff.

'Indeed. You,' John nodded towards Taff, 'are of Celtic origin, and as such will be seen with greater favour by Draknoor. His kind have long had a debt to repay to the Celts. That may be of use to us, as will the fact that your friend is an innocent. He is still able to see the unicorn when we cannot, and as it is not through ale or fasting then it can only be because he is yet to lie with a woman.'

'Well you're wrong then, 'cos I've lied to lots of women,' said Thermos, missing the point spectacularly.

Taff could barely contain his joy, but then he wasn't trying very hard. 'He said *with* a woman. John reckons that you can still see the unicorn because you're a virg-'

'Unicorn? What unicorn?' As Thermos wasn't keen on it becoming public knowledge that he had yet to lie with a woman he thought it best to lie to two blokes. 'I don't see it around anymore. Did it go somewhere?'

Draknoor looked up to see what the fuss was about, giving the sheep that was to be the dragon's lunch the opportunity to defy its ovine stereotyping and burrow to safety. John gave the dragon a troubled look. There was no time for all of this silliness; Draknoor was becoming restless, and a restless dragon was a very dangerous thing. As was a not-so-restless dragon. Even dead dragons could be a bit hazardous.

'I have a thought.' Thankfully it was John speaking. 'Let us suppose that young Kevin here is, of this triumvirate, most able to think in the manner of a unicorn.

Now it was Taff's turn to frown. 'So?'

'So then we may speak as though we were conversing directly with Garthang, and Kevin will be able to relate to us how he *believes* a unicorn would respond, if it were able.'

There was a long silence as everybody thought about it.

'Ah!' said Thermos, getting it.

'Oh!' said Taff, sorely disappointed that Thermos was to be spared many hours of brutally unsympathetic mocking.

'Terallt moen,' boomed Draknoor, and everybody nearly soiled themselves. Though no longer in his prime, Draknoor was still a sight to inspire both awe and terror. The once blue-black metallic sheen of his scales had faded to a deep grey, but they could still deflect all but the most determined of arrows. His great leathery wings were torn and scarred from battles he could no longer recall, but they could still carry him easily over the tallest of towers. He was missing close to half of the teeth and talons of his youth, but those he had lost were deeply embedded in the rotting remains of his enemies, not strung around their victorious necks as trophies. Such was Draknoor, last of the black dragons. Possibly. Nobody had seen another greater black dragon for a very long time, so it was deemed that Draknoor was the last of his kind. No serious scientific study has been undertaken to confirm that assertion. Counting them, for instance.

As the 'local' of the group, John was doing his best to remain nonchalant, but even he was finding it impossible to conceal his wonderment. He'd been little more than a child when he'd encountered his first pyrotile, and frankly John hadn't been that impressed. His father had discovered a lesser sand dragon caught in a snare. It had been a large specimen for its kind, but still barely a foot long, and John had found it difficult to feel threatened by anything so beige. With John's help, his father had tended to the creature's damaged leg before releasing it. To show its appreciation it had incinerated their barn.

'What troubles our winged malcontent now?' John's question was meant for Garthang, so he directed it at the nearest clump of weeds.

Garthang finished chewing before replying. 'He grows impatient. We promised him a great battle and he wearies of waiting for it to begin'.

There was a long silence before Thermos noticed that everybody was looking at him. 'Why are you ... oh, yeah. Well, erm, if I were a unicorn I'd probably be thinking that maybe the dragon was getting sort of bored. Perhaps. A bit.'

John nodded. 'The beast will have his battle soon enough, and if Pongo's darkest fears are realized then few will live to see to its end.'

'Pardon?' Taff suspected that he might have overlooked something important. He understood that the universe might soon come to an end, but it hadn't registered with him that Armageddon might be *personally* disagreeable.

With Taff concentrating on his own demise, John concentrating on his concerns about Draknoor, Garthang concentrating on his weeds, and Draknoor concentrating on only killing the things that he was allowed to kill, it was left to Thermos to say the first useful thing that anybody had said in hours.

'So, what's the plan then?'

Standing in exactly the same spot as Taff, but not at exactly the same time, there was a thing. A pinkish-grey thing. A pinkish-grey thing encrusted with dirt, blood, and excrement that had formerly been known as Professor James Stephenson. The pink thing, that is, not the excrement. The excrement had formerly been known as the Right Hon. Edward Dowdeswell, Member of Parliament for Skipthorpe East. There was nothing left of the good Professor. There was nothing left of the bad Professor either. There was nothing human left at all. Having discovered just how easily they could manipulate Stephenson's body, The Mischiefs had decided to see just how far they could push things before they started to break. Some things had been pushed a long way. Some things had broken. His gait had become hunched and lopsided, one unfeasible long arm hanging limply at his side, the shoulder joint ripped apart by the excess of muscle that had formed around it. Other muscles sat as impotent lumps below his skin, the tendons torn free of impossibly twisted, misshapen bones. For reasons they couldn't even begin to explain, they had also decided that his left leg would be more efficient if it were twisted right around at the knee, so that his left foot now pointed backwards. For other more complicated reasons they were right; Stephenson covered the ground with impressive speed and agility. On the down side, when he wasn't moving he fell over. The solution had been to equip him with sex organs that would have looked impressive dangling below a mature bull elephant. That's not as much fun as it might sound, as a really huge penis limits potential sexual partners, assuming you wanted them to survive the experience. By now Stephenson really

257

didn't care if any chosen sexual partner was still alive after he'd finished with them. Frankly he wasn't that bothered if they were alive at the start. The Mischiefs hadn't given it any thought either; they'd just given Stephenson a huge dong because it made a nifty kickstand.

'My point is that ... erm ... was I making a point?'

'I don't think so.'

'What about the sword?'

'The sword? Somebody is bound to come for the sword. There might even be a chance that she *will come.'*

'You really think she's *still alive?'*

'Of course she is.'

'But the battle. We were there. We saw her fall.'

'Yes, we saw her fall. And then we saw her body consumed by fire, but she wasn't in it. I saw her leave.'

'You did? Well that's got to be good for us, though I have to wonder why it's taken you fifteen centuries to mention it.'

'I say we head for the river. We should stay close to the sword from now on, and if we run into anybody in the meantime, we'll move house. I think we've broken this one.'

'Sounds like a plan to me. Whose turn is it to drive?'

Robin Madden lowered himself out of a tree and dropped silently to the ground. Following The Mischiefs was proving to be a simple task now that he was keeping them in sight. He'd have preferred to keep his distance and follow tracks, but since his quarry's feet now pointed in opposite directions those tracks gave no indication of which direction they were going. Robin had nearly given up, but his newly discovered conscience had reminded him that if he hadn't broken into Malecot's secret library then none of his troubles would have started in the first place. Once he'd found those secret documents in the secret places he could have slipped away into the night, and nobody would have been any the wiser. But no, not our Magpie. First he had to find a trinket worthy of his talents. Something like the pretty green bauble in the intricate brass ball with the runes on it. But the device had confounded him. He'd never encountered its like, and it stubbornly refused to accede to his best efforts at opening it. He could just have stolen the ball and worked on it at his leisure, but that wasn't The Magpie way. To open that ball before he was discovered was a *challenge,* and he could never refuse a challenge.

The coming dawn was a faint glow through the windows of Malecot's great hall, and the first stirrings of the new day could be heard in the corridors beyond the great oak doors when, out of frustration at his impending failure, Robin had tried to crush the sphere between his hands, and with a tiny mechanical 'click' the device had sprung open and the gem had dropped into his palm.

Seven new sets of thoughts vying for attention had greatly complicated Robin's flight from Malecot, and he found that he could only silence them by constantly repeating some really filthy limericks. Robin had read those secret documents that he'd found secreted secretly in the secret library, so he knew about The Grand Separation now. He didn't understand it all, but he understood enough to know that there was a place to hide where nobody would ever look for him. He also knew the location of a portal to travel between the two worlds. Most importantly, he knew where Excalibur was. The snag was that he could only know these things *instinctively*; his higher thought processes had to be kept busy continually rhyming things with 'Bude' and 'punt.'

So it was that Robin Madden came to Falston. The other Falston, from his point of view. As luck would have it there were vacancies for both a village idiot and a three-legged dog. It would be many years before the latter position was filled, but the inhabitants of Falston-on-Wold took great pride in the fact that they had a cracking new idiot. The job even came with a caravan, left vacant when the previous idiot had tried to comb his hair with a plough.

Most of his mind was taken up with fighting The Mischiefs, so it had been left to Robin's subconscious to play a few magical tricks and keep people from noticing that he wasn't growing old, though for the villagers the constant stream of dirty limericks did grow old very quickly. They were mightily pleased when some clever chap invented television commercials and Mad Ned finally shut up. They were so pleased that they thoughtfully purchased a television and video recorder for their idiot, though nobody had thought about it enough to notice that the caravan didn't have an electricity supply.

For what seemed a thousand lifetimes, Robin had kept all that he was and all that he knew buried in the deepest recesses of his mind, where even The Mischiefs would not find them. Now he'd rediscovered much of what he'd been forced to hide. With those memories came the understanding that fleeing to Falston and putting the sword in jeopardy may have sealed the fate of two worlds. All things considered, Robin thought it politic to follow the pinkish-grey thing and try to atone for the damage he had done.

So he did.

Important events were unfolding in Jack's shed. They were Sid and Jack shaped events, and they were unfolding a large tablecloth and draping it carefully over a dozen crates of best six-month-old Korean malt whisky, an acquired taste that none of Jack's regulars had been fool enough to acquire. With the cloth relocated, Sid got his first look at the boxes secreted beneath it. Two small olive drab metal boxes they were, with yellow lettering stencilled on the side. Sid read the yellow lettering. Then he read it again, very slowly. It said 'M112 Composition C4 Block Demolition Charges'. They were also marked 'Handle with Extreme Care', which struck Sid as a tad redundant. 'Bloody 'ell, you weren't kidding!'

'Course I wasn't kidding. Plan wouldn't be much cop if I had been, now would it?' said Jack.

Sid nodded. 'Where the bloomin' 'ell did you get 'em?'

'Long story. Just wanted to be ready if the moles came back. Now we put these on,' Jack lofted a supermarket carrier bag that he'd retrieved from the pub 'and then we grab a box each and head down to the river.'

'Now? We not waitin' 'til tonight then?'

'Nope.'

'Why not?'

'You tellin' me you'd rather handle this stuff in the dark?'

'Good point.' Sid felt as dejected as he looked. He'd rather not be handling the stuff at all, but given the choice it seemed wiser to do it under the cover of daylight.

There was the familiar rustling of petroleum-based polymers as Jack retrieved certain items from the bag and thrust them in the downtrodden café owner's direction.

Sid groaned. Stumbling around in the dark carrying boxes of high explosive was a more appealing prospect than wearing the stuff Jack was holding.

24

The Calamity Cart wasn't in 'stealth mode'. Nor was it in 'silent running' mode, 'evasion mode', 'battle' mode, or even 'à la' mode. Pongo hadn't specifically named the cart's latest disposition, but 'shit off a shovel' mode sounded about right. Many of the elaborate modifications had been discarded in favour of a lighter and more agile set-up. Alec had made the required alterations. With a big axe. Pongo had stood some distance away and whimpered.

Acolyte Tauper sat at the reins, happy at not having to stand on his damaged ankle, and even happier to be heading apace in the direction of his true love.

'This is nice,' said Alec, yelling over the noise of hooves and wheels.

'What?' went Pongo.

'Ffffhhhhhhkk,' went Acolyte Felcher as the cart bounced over a tree root and nearly spilled him out of his bucket.

'Hold on,' yelled Pongo. The little man concentrated and did a bit of hand waving and incomprehensible muttering. A small ball of green light formed in the air in front of him and then expanded rapidly to encompass the cart, before loudly popping out of existence. The horses were still galloping and the cartwheels were still turning so fast that there was smoke coming off the axles, but in the back of the cart there was only a serene silence. Pongo smiled. 'It's called The Eye of the Storm. Very useful for getting served in crowded inns.'

Alec smiled broadly. It was more of a grin really. 'This is nice,' he said.

Thelonius Wisp cleared his throat and a ball of moss fell out of his neck. Pongo glared at him in a manner that suggested he was not best pleased with the head of the head of The Guild of Magi.

'Why the hostility Pongo?' said Wisp. 'I could understand your attitude if you didn't get my message but ... you did get my message, didn't you?'

'Message? You mean that absurd drivel you made John Bostwicke memorize? That message?'

'No, not *that* one, the *other* one.'

'Other one?' Pongo's sails went all flappy as the wind was snatched out of them. 'What other one?'

Wisp glared. 'The one that's inside the glyphweave.'

'There isn't anything in the glyphweave.'

'Oh yes there is,' said Wisp.

'Oh no there isn't,' said Pongo.

'Behind you!' said Alec, getting into the spirit of things.

'Well I couldn't see anything in there,' said Pongo, starting to get the uncomfortable feeling that he'd overlooked something obvious.

'Of course you couldn't see it, I cast a glamour on it, you idiot!'

'Don't you take that tone with me! How was I supposed to know? I'm not psychic.'

'Yes you are.'

'Alright, I am. But only a bit. Why place a glamour around the message and then stick it in a glyphweave? What was the point?'

'To maintain the illusion that I was trying to kill you! I had to make sure that nobody could find out about the message, and for all I knew she had other spies lurking in The Guild.'

'She who?' Pongo really needed to read the message.

'Read the message.' Wisp really needed Pongo to read the message.

Pongo reached into his underused and long-forgotten sack and produced the glyphweave.

Wisp sighed a long sigh. 'Ah. I see that you chose not to open it. Well, that explains a great deal.'

'I didn't *choose* not to open it. I *failed* to open it.' Pongo suddenly wondered why he'd been so eager to make that distinction.

'I do not understand. There is nothing perplexing about opening Albansbane. You merely twist the two hemispheres to align the runes and-'

'Twist? I thought it was just hinged, it didn't occur to me that the hemispheres might rotate.' Pongo emphasized his failure again, just in case anybody had missed it the first time. He tried to twist the two halves of the sphere.

'But they don't turn,' said Pongo.

'Yes, they do,' said Wisp

'No, they don't,' said Pongo.

'Behind you!' said Alec, still grinning happily.

'See?' Pongo held the glyphweave up to Wisp's nose and demonstrated his inability to twist the two halves. 'They don't move.'

Thelonius Wisp squinted to focus; he was beginning to realize just how much he'd taken certain things for granted. Like being able to move his head away from things that were very close. Or move things that were very close away from his head. 'Might I suggest that your problem is the dent?'

'There's a dent?'

'There's a dent. There, just below the locking mechanism.'

Pongo removed the glyphweave from in front of Wisp's nose and held it in front of his own, completely taking for granted his ability to move his head away from things that were very close. 'So there is. I don't remember that being there. It must have happened when I fell on my sack last night.'

I told you that was unlucky.

Wisp sighed another very resigned sigh. 'Pongo, I don't know which causes me the greater vexation; the fact that you have damaged one of the great magical artefacts, or that you didn't try twisting the hemispheres until today, now that your clumsiness has made it impossible to do so.'

'Difficult, but not impossible.' Pongo gripped the brass ball firmly with both hands and twisted. At first nothing happened, but eventually the glyphweave's refusal to budge succumbed to Pongo's refusal to be sensible about it. There was a grinding noise as the two halves of the sphere rotated against each other, after which Pongo waited a moment to allow blood to circulate back to places that weren't his face. Then he held the glyphweave aloft to examine his handiwork. 'Ah yes, when you line the runes up they're easy to read. I'm surprised I didn't spot that.'

'So am I,' said Wisp.

'It says ... actually you know what it says, don't you?'

'Yes, I do. But I would be grateful if you would read it to me anyway.'

'Why?'

'Humour me,' said Wisp. It was gratuitously uncharitable of him, but he was in that sort of mood.

Pongo sighed and humoured him. 'It says 'press down hard and twist to open'.' He cast an embarrassed look towards Alec, who was still in a happy mental place that was nowhere near his body. Pongo was glad of that; the rest of the day was going to be difficult enough without Alec knowing that Pongo Smythe, sworn protector of the greatest power on this, or any other, earth, had been utterly defeated by a childproof cap.

Pongo pressed down hard and twisted. There was more grinding from the glyphweave and more cringing by Wisp, then the magical ball did that quaint mechanical clicking thing and sprung open. The glamour that had been cast on the inside of the sphere stretched to breaking point and beyond, so it broke, and suddenly everybody could see the folded parchment that Pongo had been hoping wasn't there.

'This would be the other message then.' Pongo removed the parchment and began to read it. There were a lot of words; when he'd read about half of them he said

'Dear God man, how could you have been so stupid? You ... you ... berk!'

Thelonius Wisp was simultaneously taken aback and greatly affronted by Pongo's gratuitous use of the forbidden 'b' word. Such a thing was unheard of, and if you're one of those people who use 'berk' to avoid being *really* rude then you might want to investigate its etymology sometime.

'Behind you!' said Alec, and everybody looked at him because they hadn't set him up for a panto gag this time.

Wisp was about to say something when an arrow that had been crudely fashioned from a ski pole struck him in the right temple and burst out of the left, coming to a halt with eight inches of pole protruding from either side of his skull. Before anybody could react to this interesting development, a flaming missile that may once have been a plastic flamenco dancer doll landed in Felcher's bucket. As Pongo looked up to see where the incendiary device had originated, he saw Acolyte Tauper, inconveniently positioned outside of the noise suppression spell, waving frantically and yelling silently, his warning's going as unheeded as Alec's had been. The frustrated Acolyte jumped to his feet, grimaced, clutched at his shattered ankle, fell over backwards, and disappeared into the narrow gap between Goldfinger and Thunderball.

'Oh dear,' said Pongo. With the acolyte gone from his field of view he was able to see the cause of Tauper's agitation; it had been an exceptional sort of day, and there were a lot of people who wanted him dead to keep track of, but he really should have remembered about this lot.

A banana shaped arrow embedded itself in the seat an inch below Alec's crotch. 'This is nice,' he said.

'Where are the rest of our clothes?' As he was already wearing his shirt and underpants, we can reasonable assume that Morrison's main concern was his trousers.

'Exactly where we left them, I expect.' Sara had more reason to be concerned as she was still suffering from a bad case of total nakedness.

Phillip looked around the clearing, wondering what it was he was missing. 'I don't think they are.'

'*They* are, but we're not.'

'We're not?' It was going to take him a while to get the hang of this, so it was a pity that he had a lot less than a while left.

'We must have been right by a portal all along.' Sara bit on her lower lip and looked troubled; something had happened that was going to take her a while to get the hang of.

'A portal? So now we're in-'

'We're in the other Falston Wood now, yes. And now that we're here I think we should keep a low profile until I know exactly what's going on.'

'Oh,' said Morrison. Sara had explained it all to him earlier, but he still hadn't been prepared for the reality of it. Nor was he entirely sure he believed it yet. He was sure that *she* believed it, but did that make it true? Actually it did as far as he was concerned.

Sara could see Phillip's confusion. She didn't need any special abilities to do that, which was just as well. 'Where exactly did you leave your trousers?'

Phillip pointed at the spot where he last saw his forty-inch extra longs. 'Exactly there. Ish.'

'That would put the portal about ...' Sara knelt down and reached out an arm, which promptly disappeared into thin air '...here.' When she stood up her arm reappeared, seemingly none the worse for the experience, clutching Phillip's jeans. She handed them to her favourite vet, who was now looking completely smacked of the gob. 'Convinced?'

Morrison nodded and made a small gurgling sound.

'I'm glad.' Sara smiled. 'Now get those on before we get all distracted again. We have somewhere to be, and I have a feeling we need to be there sooner rather than later.'

'What about you? Much as I like seeing you dressed like that, aren't you going to put your clothes on?'

'No.'

'No?'

'No. I don't need them anymore. Not here.' Sara raised her arms above her head, closed her eyes, and whispered something. Something musical and mystical. Something beautiful and powerful. Probably. It was a whisper so Phillip really had no idea what she'd said. She might have been reciting the list of flavour enhancers off the side of a pot noodle for all he knew, but the *way* she'd said it had made it seem important. When the whispering was done (much too quickly for her to have been reciting the list of flavour enhancers off the side of a pot noodle), the new-born whisper moved away from her, radiating out in all directions as if it were the ripple on the water and Sara Hagget the pebble that had landed in the pond.

Sara's whisper disappeared into the trees and hung around in there for a few seconds, doing whatever it is that whispers do when they're in forests and there's no one there to hear them. Then it came back, bringing with it a gentle breeze. It swirled around in distracted fashion, kicking its breezy heels through the leaf litter and being generally windy until it blew into the naked Sara Hagget, at which point it got rather excited. The gentle breeziness strengthened to a bracing gustiness, and from there it moved right on up to an alarming gale-forciness.

Starting at her feet, the gale whirled upwards in an ever-tightening circle around Sara's body until it reached the outstretched fingers of her raised arms. Her hair became an inferno that blazed around her head, sending up flames of brilliant orange-red as it danced to the storm's tune. Sara Hagget stood at the centre of a cyclone that sucked in the debris and leaf-litter at her feet, drawing it upwards as a swirling column of greens and browns, with just a fleck of black and red that might have been a Mars bar wrapper. If Ned had been there he would no doubt have pointed out that being a cyclone there was no loss of suction and no bag to change.

Phillip Morrison watched in transfixed amazement as Sara disappeared into the maelstrom of nature-bits that surrounded her. He felt like he should say something profound, but he had no idea what, and it was unlikely that he would be heard over the noise of the storm anyway. When the wind abated, and a semblance of calm had returned to the clearing, he did say something profound. 'Bugger!'

The woman standing in the glade was still Sara Hagget, but only just. She had changed, and she had changed in ways both dramatic and barely perceptible. She was no longer naked, but neither was she clothed. From her knees to her chest she was clad in a gown of leaves and moss that covered her flesh, yet did not appear to be in contact with it, and as she took a step her costume seemed to lag behind for a moment. Her features had shifted, her face slightly more angular, the lines of her nose and mouth more defined; it was still the same face, but now it was more beautiful and more powerful, and the green ember that always flickered in her eyes was now an intense blaze. The tornado had also given her hair more volume than had been considered fashionable since 1988.

Before Phillip could react to this new glory, it was gone, leaving only the old glory to deal with. The glow in Sara's eyes faded. Her features softened. Her outfit fell away and became a pile of leaves at her feet. Her hair slumped about her face as a tangled mess.

Sara looked over at Phillip and gave him an embarrassed smile. 'Poo. I'll get my clothes then.'

Back in the *other* clearing in the *other* Falston Wood, Bill and Ben formed a perimeter. Ben leapt forward, drawing his loaded weapon and going into a crouch, his back to Sara's clothes. Bill mirrored his partner, the two men slowly swinging their weapons from side to side as menacingly as was possibly with plastic guns not suitable for the under 6s. It was a standard deployment, and one that they had practiced often enough to be confident that even the stealthiest foe would be unable to approach them from the front.

Sara Hagget stepped into existence directly behind them, quietly retrieved her clothes and then stepped back out of existence. 'Oh, boys,' she said as she vanished.

Bill and Ben spun around and fired in unison.

Bladder looked where George Guv was looking and saw what George Guv was seeing, though he didn't crouch like George Guv was crouching until he was grabbed firmly by the waistband and yanked downwards.

The sight that greeted Bladder's gaze was unlike any he had seen before, and that was saying something given that he'd known Jack and Sid for many a year. At a time when the pub and the café should have been open for business, the proprietors of those establishments were skulking around in Falston Wood. Both men were kitted out in workman's overalls and rubber thigh waders, but it was the bright orange comedy wigs with integral orange handlebar moustaches that took the scene to new heights of inexplicability. The small boxes of high explosives, however, were easily explained: Jack and Sid were planning to blow something up.

International jewel thieves *and* anarchists with explosives—possibly terrorists, but more likely anarchists—was more than George could ever have hoped for. It all made sense now. To him. 'We'd best follow them,' said the happy detective.

'S'pose so,' said the unhappy jewel-smuggling anarchist trombone player. If Jack was here in the woods then the pub wasn't likely to be open, so Bladder had nowhere better to be anyway. Sticking with the plod and following Jack and Sid also meant that he would be on hand to assist with whatever it was they were up to. If that assistance took the form of beating George Guv about the head with a big stick, then Bladder wouldn't be found wanting.

George rose from his crouch and moved off slowly to follow the bobbing orange wigs. Bladder followed, scanning the forest floor for just the *right* big stick.

Lady Gaynor's army was making slow progress in the direction of Falston-on-Wold, but no matter, she could be patient. After all, had she not waited for nearly sixteen centuries to discover the whereabouts of the sword?

Actually, she had not.

After her total, and frankly very bothersome, defeat in battle, Gaynor had tried to escape by discarding her flesh and becoming one with the soil on which her dying body lay. She had failed. The earth had rejected her, vomiting out her essence before it could poison the land. Instead, she was forced to scatter herself into all of the scuttling, burrowing and crawling things that were nearby, diluting her spirit to such an extent that no part of it had the strength to control the whole. Lady Gaynor Elfam would likely have dispersed and faded to nothing had two particular woodlice decided not to mate. Thankfully for Lady Gaynor those woodlice did mate, and they had both contained some slight imprint of her. Their offspring contained a deeper imprint, and an instinctive need to locate it in their own mates. Sometimes that search was successful, more often it was not. Those creatures that were tainted by some colour of the late Lady led ordinary enough lives, but when their time came to die, some compulsion drew them to congregate at that place where Gaynor had fallen.

As Gaynor's essence began to accumulate, it attracted larger beasts. Birds that had eaten an infected insect or worm came. Mammals that ate the flesh of the birds came. Each new addition gave its life willingly for the enhancement of the aggregate, positioning itself amidst the growing pile of rotting corpses and waiting for death. At the centre of this fetid mass was a golden amulet on a severed chain, cleft from Gaynor's neck by an axe blow, the rust-coloured stain of Lady Gaynor's blood upon it now the rallying point for the creatures that carried some part of her within them.

The corner of the meadow in which all of this death was happening became known as a cursed place. Soon none would go near there, and not just because of the smell, so the nasty little ball of rot and decay was left undisturbed to grow into a nasty big ball of rot and decay. In time the collected essence within began to think, and when it had thought for a while it began to remember things. It remembered that it had once been something different. Something not composed entirely of death and putridity. Then one day a life had come to the cursed place, and it was unlike any that had come before. Physically larger than any other creature that had chosen this place to die, this life possessed an awareness of self and an understanding of its own mortality. Like the others it had come to die, but unlike the others it didn't choose to starve the life out of its body.

This one bled.

It bled a lot.

The essence understood about blood, but it had never experienced it in such a vibrant way.

Warm.

Pumping.

Gushing.

Alive.

It was liquid life, and it poured into the essence's vague consciousness as a river of pure being. With it came information. The blood and the life had belonged to a woman. Her name had been Anne. She had been seventeen. Her heart had been broken twice; first by a man, and then by the blade that she had thrust into it. As the life drained from Anne Mellor, the essence realized that not all of the memories it was experiencing belonged to the dying girl. Some of them were its own.

Some of them were *her* own.

She remembered being a woman. She remembered a life before she had become this thing made from death. She remembered her name.

As the darkness she craved finally embraced her, Anne Mellor heard an alien voice inside her own head.

'Thank you,' it said.

With Gaynor's mind came her powers. They were weak, but they were there. Given time, and the right environment, she could fashion herself a new body from the raw materials she had at her disposal. She had the time, but the corner of a muddy field was *not* the right environment. The mass of decay became a thick, viscous liquid that flowed over Anne Mellor's bones, encasing them like an insect in amber, and Lady Gaynor began to move. She burrowed down into the earth and moved away from the cursed place, making agonisingly slow progress at first, but with gathering speed as she grew in strength and confidence. She was positively bombing along by the time she crashed through the roof of a vast natural cavern, plummeting past the stalactites and down into the icy lake below. The cave was exactly what Lady Gaynor had been looking for.

Lots of space.

It was time to fashion a new body. It would be a dangerous time for her. Like a pupating insect, she would be inactive and vulnerable, though unlike an insect she would be in that state for two decades or more. With her physical being now dormant, she reached out from her cavern with her mind to see what she could find. She found The Venerable Guild of Magi, and as her new body grew, so did her understanding of all that had gone on in her absence. With each new consciousness she touched she found another piece of the puzzle. There were bits with Myrddin on, bits with Excalibur on, and bits with a second world governed by science. There were also lots of bits with just sky and clouds on, and one with half a beach ball on that belonged to a different puzzle.

She was strong now, and that was dangerous. Soon her luck might run out and The Guild would sense her presence. She needed a protector. An ally within The Guild who would ensure that nobody discovered her whilst she was defenceless. Somebody whose thinking she could influence, and preferably somebody who could influence the rest of The Guild. Eventually she found the one she needed. He was a senior adept with aspirations of becoming Grand Master.

I really shouldn't need to tell you his name.

'Thelonius Wisp!'

Wisp's eyes snapped open. Then they closed. Then they opened. They did it again as he struggled to focus on the face staring down at him. 'Oh, it's you.'

Pongo smiled. 'I know it is. How are you feeling?'

'Like I have a stick through my head. What about the others?'

Pongo's eyebrows slumped down over the bridge of his nose; they were bored and were thinking about spending a few days as nostril hair. 'Well, Alec seems to be back with us after his flirtation with insanity. The noises Felcher is making suggest that he's not happy, but he wasn't seriously hurt as the incendiary device was extinguished by the liquid in his bucket.'

'You mean the horse piss?'

'Oh, you'd noticed.'

'Hard not to. Tauper?'

'Whereabouts unknown, I'm afraid. I saw him struggle to his feet after the cart ran over him, but I didn't observe what happened after that as I was required to take the reins.'

'And our assailants?'

'It would seem that they considered Acolyte Tauper to be reward enough for their efforts, and much easier prey than a speeding cart.' Pongo shook his head sadly. 'He was a brave soul.'

'No he wasn't,' said Wisp, who still wasn't in a generous mood.

'Well what he did was brave.'

'He fell out of the cart. That wasn't brave, it was clumsy.'

Pongo sighed and stared up into the treetops, searching for inspiration. What could he say that would best sum-up Acolyte Tauper's lifesaving contribution to the day's events? 'He was an adequate distraction?'

'That much I'm prepared to concede, though I'd prefer barely adequate.'

Pongo nodded. 'Not much of an epitaph though, is it? Here lies Jeremiah Tauper. He was a barely adequate distraction.'

Somewhere in the distance a lone dog barked, but it was much too far away for them to hear it.

Alec had gone for a short walk in the trees to do a thing that people sometimes need to go for a short walk in the trees to do. By the time he got back Pongo had teed-up Wisp's head and was addressing it with his walking stick in a manner that suggested he was about to attempt a mighty drive over the trees. Wisp sighed with relief and Pongo shouldered his stick as Alec clambered into the cart.

'Alec, perhaps you would be so good as to assist us in resolving a matter of some contention that has arisen. Does the name Gaynor Elfam have any particular meaning for you, perchance?' It sounded like Pongo was trying to make a serious point.

As it was a serious point, Alec gave it serious consideration. 'No,' he said, seriously.

'Precisely as I stated,' announced Wisp in a tone that was immoderately smug for a severed head with a ski pole through it.

'Perhaps if you see the name written down it might help,' said Pongo, thrusting Wisp's 'other' message under Alec's nose and jabbing his finger at the relevant paragraph.

'Gaynor Elfam,' read Alec, slowly. 'Gay-nor Elf-am,' read Alec, phonetically. 'Gaynoooorr Elllfaaaamm,' read Alec, inanely. 'Oh, hang on, I see! It's another one of those anagram things. Gaynor Elfam is Morgan le Fay.'

'Ooohhhh fffhhhhhkk!' said Acolyte Felcher.

'Don't worry; I'm sure it happens to lots of men.'

'I don't care about other men! It doesn't happen to *me*.'

'Perhaps you were just a bit nervous or a bit too eager maybe? I'm sure if you just relax for a while and try again everything will be fine.'

'Fine? *Fine?* How can things ever be fine again after that ... that ... disaster? God, I feel so pathetic. So ... dirty.'

'Now you're being too hard on yourself. It was just one of those things.'

'One of what things?'

'You just shot off a bit too soon, that's all.'

'That's all! Did you see how much I missed by? Ow!' Ben snatched his hand away from his face and winced. The stinging red spot on the bridge of his nose stung even more when he prodded it.

'It wasn't *that* bad.' Bill was being kind; it had been bloody awful.

'Yes it was! Look!' Ben pointed at a rock off to Bill's right that was surrounded by fragments of pink plastic, the remains of the projectile that Ben's weapon had spat out at high velocity. 'I mean, look where you hit me. Ow!'

'It's nothing a few extra hours down at the practice range won't fix,' said Bill, misty-eyed at the thought of returning to that hallowed place. The 'practice range' was a selection of cardboard advertising standees, nicked from outside the local video shop, positioned strategically around Ben's back garden. These targets were attached to a complex series of ropes and pulleys operated by Ben's mum. The two men had spent many a happy afternoon rolling, diving, ducking, and crouching around the petunia borders, firing plastic pellets at the great and the good of Hollywood. Their unique take on the 'buddy system' had one man yelling out targets the likes of 'Paul Newman, left eye' whilst the other took the shot. The best of these shots to date had been by Bill, who on their last visit had risen like Poseidon from the ornamental pond and floored Nicole Kidman as Satine from *Moulin Rouge!* with a direct hit to the clitoris. It's a close call as to which was the more surprising; Ben's knowledge of the existence of the clitoris, or Bill's knowledge of where to find one.

Before Ben could respond there was snappage.

'What was that?' hissed Bill

'It was a twig snapping. Possibly a branch.'

'I know that, it was a rhetorical question.' Most questions that Bill put to Ben were rhetorical, otherwise he got answers or opinions.

'Well it wasn't a rhetorical twig.'

The two recently exed security guards made with the big stealth, creeping up the slope in the general direction of the sound. The final few feet of the journey were done in best commando fashion, flat on their stomachs, pulling themselves forwards with their elbows and making more noise in the leaf litter than a couple of badgers humping. Below them on the other side on the slope was the twig snapper. There were two of them, but presumably one of them wasn't a twig snapper but a twig snapper's friend.

'Holy shit! Is it my imagination or are those blokes carrying M112 composition C4 block demolition charges?' Ben knew his explosives. Went with the territory.

Bill looked at Ben

Ben looked at Bill.

'Terrorists,' they said.

'So who are them two daft buggers?' Bladder had a way with words, and George was beginning to wish it was much further away.

'I have a hunch that they're security guards in the employ of Beresford Security Limited.' George really was good at his job. Bladder was grudgingly impressed, though he might not have been if he'd known that finding Bill's ID badge in the leaves had been key to George's moment of intuition.

Phillip Morrison knew about militaria. It was a hobby of his. He could even tell you that in its standard combat configuration a German World War II vintage Tiger Tank weighed around fifty-seven tons. In fact, he'd *love* to tell you that, if only because he did know these things and never had the chance to show-off about it.

Lady Gaynor didn't know how much a Tiger Tank weighed.

She was floating directly over one, and she still didn't know.

Silly Lady Gaynor. Fancy her not knowing that.

Caleb was sitting inside the tank now, occasionally popping his head up through the hatch, the body of Gaynor's bizarre army following on behind. Slowly. Progress was so slow that the most able-bodied of the marching infantry had to keep checking their stride so as not to overtake the tank. The problem was that so few of Lady Gaynor's troops *were* able-bodied. They all had bodies of a sort, and they were all able to do *something*, but for many of them just maintaining forward motion was a significant challenge. Some of them could manage a few steps and then fell over. Some of them spun around in little circles and were only moving forwards because their comrades were bundling them along. Others were in such an advanced state of decay that they continually had to stop and retrieve bits of themselves. As the whole could only travel at the speed of the slowest part, this shambolic advance was not the lightning strike on Falston that its leader had hoped for. It was of no real consequence; there was nobody to stop her no matter how long it took. Perhaps The Guild might have been able to, but only with Thelonius Wisp at their head. It was a pity that she'd underestimated that Tauper chap and allowed him to make off with her box of Guild leader, but he'd be back. The infatuation spell she'd cast on him guaranteed that. Perhaps it would be fun to give Tauper a position of power in her new order, just to see what he did with it. Nor had it escaped her notice that he wasn't *un*attractive, once you were past that eye thing. Should he be the one? His abilities were certainly a bonus, plus he was already obsessed with her. That would be a real timesaver. It was certainly worth thinking about. In the meantime, she had best make sure that he was safe, in case he did turn out to be the one. With an almost derisory flick of her wrist she conjured up a small orange ball of light that did a rapid circuit of her head before whizzing away towards the trees. Trees that were on the other side of the Wold's flood plain, which was basically one of those squishy, sinky kinds of marshes that had prompted the evolution of palmate feet on wetland birds (see coots). Lady Gaynor could see a lot of coots, and as they all had palmate feet none of them were sinking into the marsh. Her Tiger Tank didn't have palmate feet, or any other evolutionary development to prevent it from sinking, so at that moment it was moving faster than it had done all day. Gaynor took to the air and watched in dismay as her metal chariot was swallowed whole by the soggy ground, Caleb still trapped inside. He'd outlived his usefulness anyway, as with no cognitive abilities of his own he'd be more hindrance than asset in battle. She'd miss him though. Great pecs.

Gaynor turned in the air and surveyed her army as the last of the tank slipped into the marsh, the exhausts spitting mud around and making disgustingly excremental noises. The other two vehicles were having some difficulty but were still mostly above ground, and the infantry didn't appear to be in any particular distress beyond that which they'd been born with. As for The Guild, they were milling around nervously in their soggy robes, wondering how to react to their new leader making such a fundamental error.

'These things are never easy!' the Lady announced huffily as she manoeuvred her sphere high into the air and drifted off towards Falston Wood to locate firmer ground for her army.

Acolyte Jeremiah Tauper could see his love. There she was, gliding through the air, majestic, terrible, and so beautiful that she brought tears to his eyes. Or was that the onion? He was only seeing her in flashes because of the trees, but she was there. He wanted to cry out to her, but he couldn't make a sound. Then he couldn't see her. Then he could see her. Then he couldn't see her. Then he could see her. Then he couldn't see her. It was terribly frustrating. If he didn't have an onion stuffed in his mouth he'd be pleading with his captors to stop turning the spit for a minute. It was unlikely they'd have listened to him anyway, though he had been able to prevail on them the manifold advantages of tying him to the spit rather than shoving it up his bottom. Nor would he want to deprive them of a nourishing hot meal, as indications were that their diet up to now had consisted primarily of dung. As his love moved away, Acolyte Jeremiah Tauper gave up on the tiny possibility that he might be rescued. Nobody was going to arrive 'just in the nick of time'. There was going to be no eleventh hour reprieve. The cavalry wasn't going to come galloping over the hill.

Jeremiah Tauper was roast.

Then his eleventh hour reprieve came galloping over the hill, arriving just in the nick of time to rescue him. The ball of orange light flew into the camp and buzzed around angrily, scattering ravenous sun seekers both hither *and* thither. In his panic one of them shot past hither, rounded thither and ended up in yon, stumbling into the fire and knocking the spitted Tauper off his supports before running around wildly with his loincloth and Hush Puppies ablaze. The confusion gave their undercooked dinner an opportunity to slink away, so it did.

Alec Gardener was still confused. 'I'm still confused. Merlin died creating this barrier thingy, and you burnt his body.'

'Yes,' confirmed Pongo 'it was a big ceremony on the site of the old court of Camelot. There was probably food laid on.'

'And Morgan died in battle, and you burnt her body too.'

'Yes,' said Pongo.

'And now she's made herself a new body.'

'Yes,' said Wisp.

'And from what you two have said about the bloodline thing, it's impossible for Morgan to get hold of the sword.'

'No,' said Pongo.

'No,' said Wisp.

'Oh,' said Alec. 'That's why I'm confused. You both say that only a *male* of the bloodline can pull Excalibur out of the ground, and even though this Morgan is Arthur's half-sister and so has the right blood, she's definitely a woman.'

'Oh, she most certainly is that,' agreed Wisp with just a smidgen too much enthusiasm. Everybody stared at him and he laughed nervously. A laughing head with a ski pole through it was probably the most unnerving thing Alec had seen. That day. So far. But then he hadn't seen Pongo helping Acolyte Felcher to empty his bowels, which was a process not dissimilar to getting the last of the toothpaste out of the tube.

'So,' continued Alec 'if she can't take the sword, and she knows that she can't take the sword, then why the hell is she coming to get it?'

Pongo looked at Wisp. Wisp looked at Pongo. Alec looked at both of them. It's tricky to tell where Acolyte Felcher was looking.

Wisp shuffled his feet, but nobody noticed because they were still in the cavern under Malecot. 'There is *one* way she could do it.'

Alec shook his head in dismay. 'You're going to tell me about some stupid get-out clause, aren't you? Some Deus-ex-machina ending?'

'No Alec, the rules are unbreakable and unyielding, as they have always been.' Pongo was also shuffling his feet, but at least his were where you could see them.

'Right, I'm getting that bit. And one of those rules is that it has to be a *man* who draws the sword from the stone.'

Pongo nodded. 'Exactly. And Morgan is a woman, Alec. A woman.'

There was a pause as everybody waited for Alec to get the point. The pause got very long.

'Yes, a *woman*,' prompted Wisp.

On went the pause.

'Women are different to men,' Pongo added, helpfully.

Alec was well aware that women were different, but in the end there was nothing a woman could do that a man …'Oh! I see. Well yes, there is *that* I suppose.' Alec got it. Morgan was a woman, with a capital womb.

There was a collective sigh of relief and a burbling sound from Felcher's bucket.

'So you're saying that she intends to have a son? How?'

'You need diagrams?' It didn't sound as if Wisp's mood was ever going to improve.

Alec's mood was getting worse as well. 'Well I know how it would work in my world, but this place seems to be pretty ass-about-face. I mean, having children takes time, and this sprog will have to grow up a bit before he'll be allowed to play with swords, so the battle that's coming isn't exactly imminent. And anyway, what if she does get pregnant and has a girl?'

'Valid points all,' agreed Pongo 'but utterly invalid on the grounds of ignorance.' Pongo seemed to be in the worst mood of all, and he was the best equipped to let everybody know about it. 'Morgan's powers are returning, and she will have little difficulty in manipulating the sex of a child in the womb, and even less difficulty in incubating and maturing it at greatly increased speed. Theoretically, she could produce a son with a physical age of seven or eight years in a matter of an hour or two.'

'Then we're fucked,' said Alec. Profanity had seemed like a valid option.

'Not until she is,' said Wisp. 'Her powers may allow her to do much, but she has no jurisdiction over conception. Fertile ground is naught without the seed, and for that the land must be tended, for it cannot sow itself.'

'To get pregnant she still needs a mate,' translated Pongo.

'A *willing* mate,' added Wisp.

'Oh,' said Alec. He was about to make use of his journalistic instincts and ask another 'question' so that he could 'find stuff out', when he got the uneasy feeling that he was being watched from the trees. He turned around on his seat and stared out into the darkening woods. For a few moments he saw nothing unusual, then a slight movement in a branch drew his eye and he located the source of the feeling.

There was a squirrel staring at him.

Alec stared back. Their eyes met. For an instant Alec touched the void and glimpsed something of the diabolical rodentian intelligence that was scrutinizing him. Then the connection was lost as the squirrel exploded. Not *just* the squirrel, of course, that would have been odd. The section of branch that the squirrel had been perched on blew up as well, erupting into a thousand splinters, the remainder of the fur-encrusted limb crashing down to the ground at the base of the tree.

Only it didn't crash.

The exploding and the falling, and the associated sickening death-squeak, had all happened totally silently. If Alec hadn't been looking directly at the event then he would never have known it had happened.

Thelonius Wisp had seen it as well. 'Oh, Pongo ...'

'Yes, Thelonius?'

'What's the duration of your Eye of the Storm charm?'

'About six hours or so, unless I cancel it.' Pongo was puzzled by the question. 'Surely you know that?'

'Yes, I do know that; I was just checking that you did.'

'Oh? Why?'

'Because now that I know that you know, I can *yell at you for not cancelling it, you idiot!*'

'Alright, there's no need to get all hot under the ... skin-flaps.' Pongo closed his eyes, did a bit of that muttering and hand waving, and then he waited for the soft 'pop' of his spell dispersing. He got his soft 'pop'. Then he got a huge 'whoosh', followed by lots of 'whumps', a collection of 'pings', some muffled 'crumps', a few loud 'kerpows', a long whistling 'fzzz', and a deafening 'kerboom'.

Sometime during either the 'pings' or the 'crumps', and definitely before the 'kerpows', Alec and Pongo had dived out of the cart, both men convinced that prostrate was now the right trait. Goldfinger and Thunderball also decided that there were safer places to be, and they bolted into the woods at high speed. The Calamity Cart, however, had not figured in the horses' decamping plans. The vehicle tipped onto its side, and after a short drag was smashed into planking against the trees. Thelonius Wisp catapulted through the air, coming to rest ten feet up an oak, his ski pole embedded in the tree's trunk. Felcher's slop bucket became entangled in the horses' reins and it, and the floppy Acolyte within, clattered away into the woods.

From somewhere beyond the trees came the sounds of frantic yelling and screaming, together with a lot more gunfire and the thunderous reverberation of a dragon's roar.

Alec lifted his face from the dirt as he and Pongo were showered with the debris of another explosion. 'You know, I think they may have started without us.'

'Once the charges have been shaped and placed as required, carefully push detonator rod 'a' into explosive 'b' and uncoil detonator circuit cords 'c' and 'd'.' Jack was sitting on the bank of the Wold, his feet resting atop the 'accident in inverted commas', squinting to read from the instruction sheet that had been neatly folded inside one of the drab olive boxes. He was squinting because he hadn't thought to bring his reading glasses, and he wanted to be sure he was getting it right.

Sid was extra keen that Jack got it right, as he was the one standing up to his knees in the mud playing with detonator rod 'a' and explosive 'b'. As he uncoiled the wires, Sid tried to remember how Jack had persuaded him that he would be the best man for the job. The exact details were eluding him, but he seemed to recall it having something to do with those crates of whisky in Jack's shed.

'Ensure that primary and secondary switching circuits are secured in the 'off' position—that bit must be important 'cos it's in red—attaching the pared ends of detonator circuit cords 'c' and 'd' to detonator receiving box 'e',' read Jack.

And then proceed to run like 'f', thought Sid. Clutching the ends of the wires he struggled back through the sucking mud and slumped down on the bank beside Jack. 'Jobs a good 'un. Reckon we got a couple of hundred feet of this wire coiled up here, Jack.'

'S'right, but we don't need it. Says 'ere that we can use this transmitter thingamabob to make the stuff go up.' Jack held aloft a small black pistol grip affair that had one of those 'flick open with your thumb' protective covers on the top. Jack didn't open the cover to check, but there was probably a little red button under it. Possibly with 'BANG' written on it.

Sid perked up. 'Remote? How remote we talkin' about?'

''Old up, it says 'ere somewhere.' Jack scanned the instructions. 'Says 'effective line-of-sight range for the supplied remote trigger is two 'undred and fifty metres.'

Sid frowned; the remote didn't allow him to be remote enough for his liking. He'd had his heart set on Norway. 'So what now?'

'So now we go into the woods and wait 'til dark.'

'Oh, so now we wait for dark? Why now, when we couldn't earlier?' Sid reached out a hand for Jack to help him up.

'If we'd waited earlier it would 'ave taken much longer to get dark,' said Jack as he hauled Sid back to the vertical.

'We just goin' to wait here, or what?' Bladder was trying to sound indifferent, but there was a new significance to wanting to know George Guv's plans. If Jack and Sid were going to blow up the 'accident in inverted commas' then Bladder was going to do everything he could to ensure their success, up to and including performing actual bodily harm on a duly appointed representative of officialdom.

'Looks like our friends down there have finished wiring up and are going to wait for dark, so we wait too. As soon as they make a move back towards that detonator box then I'll arrest them.' It was a simple plan, but George liked it. He would have liked it less if he'd known about Jack's remote detonator gizmo.

'What about them security blokes? Looks like they've got guns. Shouldn't you be callin' for backup or sum'it?'

George Guv smiled. 'Oh, I think I can handle those two. A bloke at hand is worth two in the bushes,' said he. He really didn't do his best work without a lit cigarette, but he was down to his last one and he was saving it for a moment when he could really take the pith. For George Guv being low on cigarettes amounted to a speech impediment.

'*So how are we doing?*' Alec was in a hole, shouting. Pongo was in a different hole, listening. The holes were only three feet apart, but Alec still had to shout to be heard over the noise of the battle. The battle that was just a few hundred feet away, which is why they were in holes.

'*Hard to tell, I think Draknoor might–*'

We'll never know what Pongo thought Draknoor might do. What he *did* do was let out a deafening roar and swoop low over the densest concentration of enemy troops, all ripping claws and fiery breath, as is a dragon's wont. A fifty-foot tongue of flame seared across the ground like an oxyacetylene torch, incinerating everything in its path. That was the theory anyway. In practice the flame was sending Gaynor's beasties scattering in all directions, looking a tad singed and patting out small fires in their fur or clothing, but basically unharmed. Pongo shook his head. '*Fifth time that's happened. Fireproofing charms. Army well prepared. Dragon tiring badly. Needs to change tactics.*'

Alec gave up shouting and just nodded.

'Change tactics? I shall advise the beast, though I cannot see that there is anything else he can do.'

Pongo spun around, gasping and clutching his chest. 'Dear God, Garthang! Don't sneak up on me like that! You scared the life out of me.'

Garthang surveyed the monstrous creations of Morgan le Fay's army, their mistress hovering above them and looking thoroughly bored with it all. '*I* scared you?'

Pongo regained his composure and gave Garthang a rapid précis of the situation. At least there was no need to shout for Garthang's benefit; the unicorn would have heard Pongo had he been whispering in the middle of the battlefield. The reverse was also true; nothing would dare impede the passage of a unicorn's voice.

Pongo returned to his shouting. '*My apologies for that, Alec; I was talking to an invisible unicorn.*'

'*Oh, righto,*' said Alec. What else could he say?

'*Here, this might help.*' Pongo said something to the knobbly end of his cane, then leant out over and hit Alec on the head with it.

'*Ow! What was that for?*'

'*Hopefully you shall see shortly. Or even better, you shall see Garthang.*' Perhaps not the best time for a joke, but Pongo took what he could get these days.

On hearing his name Garthang stopped sniffing the grass and lifted his head. 'I seem to ... oh, look out, I believe. Is that the correct phrase? Look out? I seem to recall hearing it once in this context, although ...'

Thankfully Pongo got the gist of Garthang's attempt at a warning before the angry soldier with the rusty rifle ran him through with his pointy bayonet. Pongo spun around in his hole, letting his stick slip through his hand until it was at maximum extension, improving both reach and pendulum effect. The wooden knot dealt the charging infantryman a hefty blow to the crotch that sent him spinning towards Garthang.

Alec's brain finished absorbing the hastily improvised reveal spell that Pongo had administered directly to his skull. *'Hey, I can see a uni-argghh that's nasty!'*

Garthang's horn had entered the charging infantryman through his right eye socket, exiting through the jagged and bloody hole in the back of his head. It was one of those really messy holes, with bits of skull and flesh and brain all mushed into hair, and great big flaps of scalp that have been peeled away like the skin of an orange. All sorts of long stringy bits and important-looking blobby bits hung out of it. The term 'exit wound' really didn't do it justice.

Pongo took hold of the infantryman's feet and Garthang backed away slowly, giving them all a whole new range of sensory experiences.

'Aarrghhh!' Alec didn't want to play anymore. *'Pongo, I think we have a problem!'* It was a measure of the kind of day he was having that Alec had found something less to his liking than a man with a unicorn through his face.

The fifty or more troops breaking away from the main bulk of the army and heading in their direction weren't to Pongo's liking either. The nightmarish half-man, half-spider thing that was leading the group couldn't have been to anybody's liking.

Pongo had an idea. *'I think we'd best run.'*

Alec nodded and both men started scrambling out of their holes. Then Alec stopped. There were figures moving in the woods. Lots of figures. They were surrounded. *'We're surrounded!'*

Pongo looked to his right, and then to his left, and as there was nobody to be seen in either direction he wondered how Alec defined 'surrounded'. Then he saw the figures, the lots of figures, moving in the trees.

With their only viable escape route blocked, and a horde of bloodthirsty unpleasantness only seconds away from them, Alec and Pongo's predicament now ran pretty close to the 'hopeless situation.' Pongo turned back to face the most immediate threat, hefting his cane like a baseball bat. If he had to die today then he wasn't going to slip away quietly; there would be songs and poems to mark the passing of Pongo Smythe. He frowned; that hadn't been as comforting a thought as he'd hoped it would be.

A loud battle cry sounded from Falston Wood, and a great wave broke from the edge of the forest and rolled towards Alec and Pongo. A great white wave that stretched for a hundred yards in both directions, carrying with it the sound of jingling bells and clashing sticks. Alec and Pongo ducked back down into their holes as the wave flowed through Garthang and flooded over them, a great human swell of hanky-waving destruction rushing into battle. The new arrivals bore down on the nearest group of beasties, beating them mercilessly with small squares of white cotton and bladders on sticks. Alec and Pongo just watched, both men having been rendered utterly speechless by the charge of the morris men.

Lady Gaynor was a tad surprised as well. Surprised enough to stop concentrating on the transfer sphere that was keeping her hovering over the battlefield, so her hover became more of a plummet. *The Servants of Maurisamern? But how can this be?* thought the Lady as she fired off a spell to make all present instantly forget the sight of her spread-eagled in the mud. All that Gaynor had learnt during her time beneath Malecot suggested that these most black-hearted of mercenaries had long forgotten their diabolical credo, abandoning their sworn duty to dispense agonizing death to all who offended them, preferring instead to do a bit of light frolicking on the weekends. Yet they were here, joined in battle, and in greater numbers than had ever existed in the legends of old. Just one skilled exponent of the loaded hanky would have been enough to devastate her army, but there were so many of them! So many hankies. So many bladders.

'This is all getting rather tiresome.' Lady Gaynor was talking to herself, but then there was nobody else present worthy of her attention. As her new sphere drifted lazily into position above the battlefield, she assessed the situation and was not happy. Two of her three vehicles were gone, her army was facing a foe that it could not hope to defeat, and the fall had made her thong ride up something chronic.

'Morris men.' Alec said it again. Since the power of speech had returned to him he'd tried a few variations. He'd tried them loudly, with an exclamation mark on the end; he'd tried them softly with a question mark on the end, and then he'd tried them with 'bollocking!' on the front. The best way seemed to be just to say them normally and then pretend he hadn't said them at all. Pongo had been equally nonplussed by the appearance of the wicked white warriors, and for a moment his spirits had been lifted. Then as he watched The Servants of Maurisamern in action it became apparent that they weren't strong enough to hold his spirits aloft for long.

'*So these guys are really vicious killers then?*' Alec's shouting suddenly sounded very loud. 'You did that spell thing again, didn't you?'

Pongo nodded. 'Yes, it seemed appropriate.' Indeed it was. So much so that it was a wonder that he hadn't done it earlier.

'Is that a good idea, after what happened last time?' wondered Alec.

'This time we have Garthang. The unicorn's voice will carry through the silence barrier; he can warn us if anything comes this way, if he isn't *too busy eating to keep watch.*' Ten seconds into the spell and Pongo was shouting again.

'Sorry,' said Garthang through a mouthful of clover.

'So these guys are really vicious killers then?' Alec felt the need to ask the question again since everybody had ignored it the first time.

Pongo wanted to ignore it this time as well. 'No, they're the *descendants* of really vicious killers. They seem to have retained some form of collective genetic memory in regard to their ancient oath, but unfortunately that's as deep as their link to the past seems to run.' Pongo saw the blankness of Alec's blank look. A more practical explanation was required, and one soon came along for Pongo to point at. 'There, look.'

Alec looked and saw a Servant of Maurisamern locked in mortal combat with a thing that was mostly teeth. The beast looked powerful but it was cumbersome, and the white-clad combatant was able to use his superior agility and make the first strike. With lightning speed he lunged forward, a handkerchief in each hand, and delivered two devastating wrist-flicks, the tips of the cloth connecting with his opponents' neck and solar plexus. The puzzled creature looked around to see if anything else was going to happen, then it took a stride forward and bit one of the morris man's arms off.

'I see what you mean,' said Alec, who had developed a much more relaxed attitude towards extreme violence of late.

All over the battlefield the scene was being repeated as morris men were gnawed, gored, gutted, scythed, shot, spiked, and generally slit up a treat. Their presence was also hindering Draknoor. Breath attacks were too imprecise to allow him to strike foe and ignore friend, and the morris men were getting slaughtered perfectly well without his assistance.

'The one thing that's bothering me,' said Pongo, who had much more than one thing to be bothered about, 'is the fact that they are here at all. The Servants of Maurisamern were tasked with defending the sword on the *other* side of the barrier. Nothing should have been able to bring them here, except perhaps contact with The Messen ...' Pongo stopped. Then he started again. 'Alec, wait here with Garthang and keep an eye on the battle. I'll be back in a few minutes.'

'Erm ...ok. One thing before you go though; is there any reason, and this is an entirely hypothetical question of course so don't read anything into it, why a man would get really turned on by seeing a lot of morris men? Possibly.'

'Oh, that's not because of the morris men, it's Garthang. Seeing a unicorn has that effect. Back soon.' Pongo climbed out of his hole and shuffled backwards towards the trees.

Alec surveyed the unfolding battle, and more specifically the attrition rate of the morris men. '*Don't be long.*' He had to shout, because the silence spell was centred on Pongo and he'd taken it with him. Not that shouting would make any difference, because the silence spell was centred on Pongo and he'd taken it with him.

Pongo hurried back to the clearing in the woods that he and Alec had hurried away from earlier. The remains of The Calamity Cart were strewn about, any hope of repairing the vehicle having been lost when a stray mortar round from the battle had landed in the wreckage.

'It wasn't you, was it?' Pongo's question got no response. Thelonius Wisp was still alive, and he was still awake. He was also still pinned ten foot up a tree. 'I said it wasn't you, was it?' Still nothing. 'Talk to me, Thelonius.' Pongo stared up, trying to make eye contact, or nose contact; anything rather than look directly up Wisp's neck hole. There was still no response, but Pongo could see that Wisp's lips were moving. He was *trying* to speak. Pongo tried lip-reading; if Wisp was using his last energy on trying to say something, then it had to be important.

'Can sell thesile enssp hell u id yut,' mouthed the head.

Pongo grimaced. 'Oh, sod it!' He cancelled the silence spell.

'Tell me Smythe, how do you get through each day without accidentally hacking one of your limbs off?'

'Shut up! I've had enough of your games, Thelonius. Do you hear that out there? Do you?' Pongo pointed in entirely the wrong direction if he was trying to indicate the battle, but I think we can let him off because he's quite miffed. 'That's the sound of people dying, and you could have prevented it. If you'd acted sooner, and hadn't been so eager to advance the cause of your precious bloody club for worthless wizards, *you could have prevented it!*'

Wisp stayed silent, and it had nothing to do with Pongo's spell this time. There was nothing he could think to say that wouldn't have sounded crass.

'So now tell me this. Garthang and John Bostwicke crossing through the barrier, that was none of your doing, was it?'

'The Messenger crossed to the other world?' The surprise in Wisp's voice was genuine. 'It is true that I seeded John Bostwicke's mind with sufficient knowledge to allow him to pass through a portal in his search for you, but Garthang's transit was none of my doing.'

Pongo's mind was racing. There had been so many little schemes whirring around inside the bigger schemes, like some big scheme based watch mechanism, that Pongo had failed to see the hand of some unknown ally at work. A hand that had indirectly saved Pongo's life at least twice.

'Pongo.'

The voice had been right at Pongo's ear and again Pongo spun around clutching his chest. 'Dear God! Why is everybody sneaking up on me today?'

'Sorry, I wasn't sure if you still had that silence thing on.' Given Pongo's recent oversights with regard to that particular spell it was an understandable thing for Alec to be unsure about.

'Well, what is it?' Pongo's voice was loaded with huff as his eyebrows peaked out nervously from behind his ears. 'You were supposed to be keeping an eye on the battle.'

Alec could do huffy as well. 'I know, and I assumed that if you wanted me to keep an eye on it that meant you'd want to know if something significant happened.'

Pongo had to concede that; he had rather hoped that nothing significant *would* happen in his absence, and it was hardly Alec's fault that something had. 'My apologies, Alec. You are quite right. What has occurred?'

'She's gone.'

'Who's gone?'

'Morgan what's-her-name in her floating thingamabob. She's gone.'

'She's gone?' Pongo sounded concerned.

'She's gone.' Alec sounded frustrated; it wasn't *that* difficult a concept to grasp.

'I think that we've established, beyond all reasonable doubt that she has, in fact, gone.' Wisp sounded exasperated. Pongo's earlier lambasting had taken him down a peg or two, but Wisp's ego was all rubbery and resilient.

'Damn, I was hoping we'd have more time. We must get back.' Pongo turned to leave.

'*Smythe! Get me down from here!* My strength is fading.'

Pongo paused for a moment. Then he continued walking away.

'Pongo! Help me ... please.' Considering his extensive knowledge of spells and charms it had taken Thelonius Wisp a long time to come up with the magic word.

Morgan what's-her-name in her floating thingamabob had watched Pongo Smythe scuttle back into the woods and she had been intrigued. Not by Pongo; he was obviously a Guild lackey, so of moderate intelligence, limited abilities, and an especially narrow head so that it would slide easily up Thelonius Wisp's backside. Nor was Gaynor particularly interested in Garthang: seen one unicorn, you've seen them all. They had some pointless and overtly mawkish abilities: healing, spiritual cleansing, making flowers bloom; stuff like that. There was that annoying business when you killed one, but that could be avoided by taking the relatively simple step of not killing one. Oh, and somebody had once told her that the presence of a unicorn made cowpats taste like honeycomb, but she hadn't fallen for it. Surprising how many people did though. No, it was the other man hiding in a hole at the edge of the battle that had caught Gaynor's attention. Even from a distance, there was *something* about him. Something familiar. He was the memory of a memory of something nearly forgotten. A figure in the mind's peripheral vision that melted away when you tried to look directly at it. A most intriguing sensation, and one that would have warranted further investigation had she not been in the middle of a bloody battle to decide the fate of mankind. No matter, she would have plenty of time to work it out later. She might also investigate this mysterious stranger's magical abilities. When he'd left the safety of his hole, Gaynor had noticed that the man had invisible feet.

'A woman's work is never done,' she announced as she tossed a bolt of intense blue light at the nearest morris man, instantly turning him to ash. The wanton violence sent a tingle down her spine so she did it again, though this time she incinerated one of her own troops. No matter, she could afford to waste a few. The Servants of Maurisamern were clearly not the force they once had been. They weren't any force at all. They were fodder, and her army was gorging on them. It was all going so wonderfully. With every passing minute Excalibur was slipping from their grasp and into hers.

Ah, yes. Excalibur. So near, and yet ... so near. Lady Gaynor smiled and looked towards Falston-on-Wold and the prize that she had been waiting so long to claim. 'Oh, this is just getting better and better!' Protruding from the ground between Lady Gaynor and the northern edge of the village there was a shiny metal pole that had once formed an integral part of a Boeing 737-700's undercarriage hydraulics. Still attached to the shiny metal pole was a shiny naked part-baked acolyte.

'I could just eat you up, you fertile little man.' Gaynor watched as Jeremiah Tauper struggled to free himself, bouncing up and down and gyrating in all manner of interesting ways. I won't go into detail about exactly how Gaynor was feeling at that moment, other than to say that with everything else that was going on she'd completely forgotten about one of the side effects of seeing a unicorn.

This was the moment. The battle was won. It would take some time to run its inevitable course, but there was no need for Gaynor to stay and watch it happen. She drifted down behind the assembled acolytes and adepts of The Guild, and the Lady Gaynor stepped forward, trying to ignore the 'shlurp' noises her boots were making in the mud. 'Gentlemen, I now require you to honour your side of our bargain. Keep this battle raging, and keep the dragon well occupied.

The Guild was collectively not happy. Having their new mistress leave now was a touch disheartening, particularly as the only way they could keep a dragon occupied was to let it eat them. They made with the murmurings and the feet shuffling, which was about as far as most of them were prepared to go when it came to voicing dissatisfaction with their leader.

Brother Flange was as scared as the rest of them, but as he now considered himself brevet leader of The Guild of Magi he felt it was up to him to say something. 'And what if we'd rather *not* stay? What if we wished to leave this place? A bit. Perhaps. Though maybe not. At all. Actually.' He'd started confidently enough, but the look Lady Gaynor had given him had made his ardour go all floppy.

'You are free to do as you wish, though should you decide to go then I shall consider you in breach of our contract. People who don't keep their word make me angry, and you wouldn't like me when I'm angry.' To reinforce the message she momentarily stopped being Lady Gaynor Elfam and allowed them to see her true face. The face of Morgan le Fay.

'We'll stay then.'

'Yes, staying here is a fabulous idea.'

'Wouldn't miss it for the world.'

'Leave? Now? Perish the thought!'

A brief appearance by her true nature had been enough to convince The Guild to do as they were told. It had also been enough to create an empty space around Brother Kreb.

'Good, then I shall depart for my rendezvous with destiny.' That hadn't sounded quite so corny in her head. 'I leave matters here in your culpable hands. The fire resistance charm will protect you, and I also give you *this*.' Gaynor had no idea what the last of her army's vehicles did, but her instincts told her that it was more important than the others. With a flamboyant twirl of her cape, Lady Gaynor Elfam turned and walked away, leaving behind the bloodbath she had drawn but no longer wished to bathe in. When they were sure that she was really going, and probably wasn't going to turn them all into dung beetles, The Guild shuffled over to the vehicle that their mistress had placed such faith in. It was of a simpler design than the others, uniformly coloured in drab green with a strange symbol emblazoned on the door at the front: an ornate crown above what appeared to be a goblet of fire. The Grail itself, perhaps?

There were sounds of movement coming from within, and then suddenly the side of the vehicle began to rise up, opening onto an area of pure whiteness, the silhouette of a figure just visible beyond the hatchway.

The figure spoke.

'Tea up, lads,' it said.

'I could just murder a cuppa.' Sid wiggled his sore toes and counted them, just to make sure, and then scratched at a scalp that was itching furiously now he'd ditched the wig and moustache. Jack had protested greatly and was staunchly refusing to remove his, even suggesting that he might 'go to the next level' and supplement his disguise with the pale red goatee beard that was in his pocket. Sid thought that was most appropriate, as he'd correctly identified that small triangle of hair as a merkin and today Jack was definitely being a right berk.

'Ask, and ye shall receive, Sidney.' Jack reached into one of the boxes of high explosive and produced a flask and a tower of disposable plastic cups. He poured out two measures of steaming brown liquid and handed one to Sid.

Sid laughed. 'Don't s'pose you've got a sarnie in there an' all.'

'You want 'am or cheese'n'pickle?'

The confused café owner leant forward and examined the contents of the box. 'You've got chocky bickies an' crisps! An' pork pies!'

'That I 'ave. Thought we might get a bit peckish.'

'But where are the explosives and detonators and stuff?'

'Back in me shed. Thought I'd best keep one lot in case the moles ever came back.'

'So when did you get time to do a picnic?'

'Put a fresh one out in the shed every mornin'. A man never knows when 'e might 'ave to spend a lot of time in 'is shed.'

Sid nodded. How very true that was.

'Cheese'n'pickle then.' As Jack handed him his sandwich, Sid amused himself by trying to work out which box *he'd* been carrying.

The sandwiches and biscuits were done and both men were munching on their crisps by the time either of them spoke again.

'It'll be dark soon,' said Sid, who as a child of nature knew that when the sun went down it got dark.

'That it will, Sidney.'

'So what is it we're waiting for, exactly?'

'I'm not sure, but I'll know when it gets here,' said Jack as he stuffed a handful of crisps into his mouth. As he munched he pondered on why anybody on God's green earth had felt the need to try and make a potato taste like a prawn.

Alec and Pongo were back in their holes.

'Greetings again, Pongo. Did you achieve that which you wished to achieve?' Garthang's bearing never seemed to change, and having thousands of souls locked in bloodthirsty combat only a few feet away had done nothing to dampen his spirits. It gave him an air of aloofness that was often thought of as arrogance, which was fair because that's what it was.

'I'm not sure, but I believe so.' Pongo stared out over the carnage and frowned. The fighting had broken up into several medium to large pockets, the ground between each of them littered with the bodies of the slain. The morris men's numbers were dwindling fast, so at least Draknoor was once more able to attack some areas of the battlefield with impunity. The rattle of gunfire and the explosions of mortar rounds had died down through lack of ammunition, and most of the fighting was taking place with more basic weaponry: sharp things, heavy blunt things, pointy things and multi-knuckled things. To their credit many of the morris men had abandoned their ineffectual hanky-based attacks and were using whatever arms were to hand, many of which still had hands attached. They were still losing, but they didn't look quite as stupid doing it.

Beyond the last of the skirmishes stood The Guild. They still seemed to be taking no active part in the overall battle, and from where Pongo was watching it looked like several of them were drinking tea, but, as Alec had taken great pains to point out, there was no sign of their leader. The new one, that is. The one that wasn't sulking in a box under Pongo's arm.

'Where did she go, Garthang?' Pongo was confident that he knew the answer to his own question, which had him wondering why he was risking a conversation with the unicorn by asking it.

Garthang had some important chewing to finish before he could answer. 'You mean she that once called herself Morgan le Fay?'

'You recognized her then?'

'Why would I not? Does she not look as she has always looked?'

'That I wouldn't know, not being sixteen hundred years old or anything.'

'Then you shall have to take my word for it. And in response to your question, she departed on foot in the direction of the river.'

'She's going for the sword.' Pongo was thinking aloud.

'That would seem to be a logical assumption, yes.' Garthang was talking aloud.

Alec thought it might be an idea to join the conversation before everybody forgot about him. 'Hold on, haven't we been here before? She can't get the sword until she has a baby, right?'

Pongo nodded. 'That's correct; she needs to have a son.'

'Then we have a bit of time, don't we?'

Pongo switched from nod to shake. 'Not much if she's already pregnant.'

'Morgan is not with child.' Garthang was hanging around on the periphery of the conversation, but he'd just spied a small tuffet of daisies that required his most urgent attention.

'Good, then she still needs to conceive. That should be to our advantage.' Pongo had that look on his face. That look that said he was planning a plan. 'Here, take this.' Pongo handed Wisp's box to Alec. 'Garthang, where did you leave John?'

'He is in the woods above Falston Bridge, together with the innocent and the Celt.'

'The Celt? Nimue is here?' Pongo's eyebrows scurried about his forehead in excitement.

Garthang shook his head, his golden mane doing those unbearably poetic things. 'You misunderstand. Not *The* Celt, *a* Celt. I have seen nothing of Nimue since my period in the world that is not this one.'

'Yes, Taff, of course, I forgot about the fa ... hold on, did you just say that you saw Nimue in the other Falston?'

'Indeed. She was present in the village for the entire period I was there.'

Pongo sat down heavily and disappeared because he was in a hole. 'Why did you not ... never mind.' We'll assume it was Pongo's voice as there wasn't room for anybody else in the hole. 'Nimue. She was there all along. I wonder if she tried to buy knickers from me?' There was a long pause before the hole spoke again, and it sounded angry. 'Right, now I really feel like I want to throttle something, and I think I shall.' Pongo's head reappeared, rapidly followed by the rest of him as he launched himself from his hole with a mighty bound, spinning and twisting in the air and planting both feet solidly as he came back down. 'Garthang, would you be so good as to convey me to The Guild?'

It was a difficult request to misunderstand, but Garthang managed it. 'You wish to return to Malecot?'

'No, not to the place. To the people. Ask Draknoor to clear a path for us.'

'As you wish.' Garthang pointed his horn at the soaring dragon and did a complex interspecies telepathy thing that no doubt came annoyingly easily to him.

Pongo turned to Alec. 'When we distract what remains of Morgan's forces, you make for the village. With a little luck you should get there before Morgan. If my guess is correct then she will need to stop en route to procreate.'

Alec thought it might be nice if *he* could stop en route to procreate, but then he hadn't thought about sex

313

for several minutes so he was due. 'And then what? What am I supposed to do when I get there?'

'Nimue was in Falston. If she is aware of what is happening then she will surely aid you. Morgan is powerful, but she is no match for The Celt.'

'And if she's not there?' Alec asked the question even though he was sure he didn't want to know the answer.

Pongo took hold of Garthang's mane and leapt up onto the unicorn's back. 'Then take the sword.'

'Take the sword? But I thought only ...' Alec stopped, but even if he hadn't nobody would have heard the rest anyway. Draknoor swooped low over the trees behind them and out over the battlefield, scattering friend and foe alike, parting the combatants in a manner deserving of all sorts of Moses and Red Sea analogies. If Pongo had any more to say then the chance had been lost; his path had appeared and he had to follow it. He raised his cane aloft, gave it a flourish and shouted '*Away, Garthang!*' The unicorn reared up and punched at the air with his front legs, holding the pose for as long as he felt was needed for everybody to get a good look at his majesty. Then he charged off at maximum gallop towards the gap that Draknoor had created.

Pongo picked himself off the ground, rubbed his aching tailbone and looked over to Alec. 'You know, that bloody stupid horse is going to be the death of me.'

Before Alec could respond, Pongo gave a final wry smile and sprinted off after the riderless unicorn, covering the ground with remarkable speed, wielding his cane like a club as the path through the throng closed behind him.

Pongo was gone, but as Alec climbed out of his hole and looked over towards Falston-on-Wold he heard a familiar voice inside his head.

'Until we meet again, Alec Gardener.'

'Hey, guys! Come and look at this. And bring the binoculars.' Since Garthang and Draknoor's departure, Kevin Flask had been watching the Battle of Falston from a perch halfway up one of Falston Wood's ancient gnarled oaks. As the only representative of the video game generation present, and therefore the only one sufficiently desensitized to wanton violence, he had been elected to provide the commentary on what was occurring below. It was all very exciting. Big guns; explosions; lots of people dying; and a dragon. Especially the dragon; now he was *really* cool. Seriously impressive pyrotechnics. Then all those morris men had turned up. Wow! It was all rad to the max. Positively extreme. Potentially even bitchin'.

Such had been the eloquence of Thermos' narration that Taff and John had taken to throwing pinecones at him to see if they could knock him out of the tree.

'Look at what? And what binoculars?' Taff had appeared at the foot of the tree. John was a little slower to arrive. Without Garthang present, John's healing was progressing at a more traditional rate, and he'd needed to fashion a crutch from a tree branch to keep his weight off his damaged leg.

'Oh, yeah, sorry. Force of habit. I usually have my bins with me when I'm up here watching ... birds.'

Taff knew all about Thermos' habit, and the bird in question had once let slip that she slept in the nude.

Thinking back on it, Taff wondered how Sara *had* managed to let that slip when the conversation had been about the cracked sump on his bus. 'So what we supposed to be looking at?'

'Look at the roof of the pub, and then line up with the big chimney. Do you see something in the field just the other side?'

Taff looked. Taff squinted and looked. Taff squinted, shielded his eyes from the sun with his hand, and looked. 'What, you mean those small blobs?'

Thermos nodded. 'Yep. But those aren't just blobs. That's a man and a woman, that is.'

'Right, so both genders of small blob. So?'

'Can't you tell? They're shagging, they are.' Even at this distance Thermos knew sex when he saw it. He may not have actually done it, but there had been extensive research.

'Bloody typical! The fight is still going on down there, and you're more interested in a couple at it in a field.' Taff picked up a large rock as the supply of pinecones was dwindling.

John thought now would be a good time to intervene. 'No, the lad may be on to something. 'Tis unlikely that they would be fornicating so near the battle unless they had good reason to do so. I say we find out what that reason may be.'

Thermos didn't understand. You needed a good reason to shag?

Taff did understand, and he didn't like. 'Go back down there, you mean? But Thermos said that a unicorn would have said that we should wait here. It was safe here, he said it would have said.'

'That may be so, but Pongo said if things go badly in the battle there will be no place safe for the likes of us, and I trust Pongo a great deal more than I trust any overblown pony. I reckon 'tis time we stopped sitting on our backsides doing naught and made a stand. We are men, are we not?'

'Well, yes, technically. But can't we make a stand up here?' There was a pleading quality to Taff's question.

Thermos' inverted face appeared between Taff and John as he hung himself upside-down from his perch, his knees hooked over the branch. That sort of thing is very good for the spine, and Thermos had decided to prove that he had one. 'Men making a stand, John? Well Taff is barely a man, and you can barely stand, but I'm game if you are.'

28

From the battlefield to the village was two miles as the crow might have flown if it had taken the most direct route, which is something crows feel the need to do apparently. Alec wasn't feeling at all crowish. The direct route would have taken him across some boggy looking terrain that might not support a man so heavily weighed down by recent events. The insanity of the last forty-eight hours didn't seem any more or less insane than it had done twenty minutes earlier, but twenty minutes earlier Pongo had been with him. That balding short-arse had been irritating, vague, manipulative, arrogant, and in the end possibly the bravest man Alec had ever met. Not that Alec could cite an extensive list of brave men that he'd met, but of the ones who might have been a *bit* brave, Pongo was right up there.

Take the sword, that's what Pongo had said. Take the sword. That could only mean one thing. Alec had tried to make it mean something different, but he kept coming back to that same thing. But surely he would have known, wouldn't he? Wouldn't there have been some clue that his ancestors were the stuff of legend? Wouldn't that heritage have shown itself before now? Wouldn't it make sense for him to stop walking now that he was standing in the river?

Alec had been keeping to the trees, as was required by the ancient art of 'hi ding', and the Wold had sort of snuck up on him. Amazing what you can miss if you're not paying attention. Like a couple having sex in a field — Alec had managed to completely miss that. Walked right past them he did. It had even been noisy sex.

Alec looked down at the water meandering around his knees. 'Shit.' Succinct, but it did the job. He took a step back out of the Wold, skidded on the muddy bank, and then pitched forward as the sole of his flappy trainer gave way. His spreadeagled body hardly broke the surface as he landed with one of those 'splats' that causes parental cringing when fat children do them at swimming pools. Alec briefly disappeared from view as Newton did his thing, and then reappeared as Archimedes did his.

'Shit. Oh, Shit. And shit.' He struggled back to his feet and drained. When the drainage was down to just drippage, Alec hauled himself back over to the bank and clambered out. Now, where had the box with the head in it gone? 'Shit!' There it was, departing at speed in the faster moving current towards the middle of the river. Alec sloshed off after Wisp's disappearing box, though he was unlikely to catch it as he'd given it a significant head start.

The 'accident in inverted commas' had never happened in this world, so here the Wold still flowed under Falston Bridge. This wooden version was in roughly the same place as its larger stone counterpart, and it too had a Taff and Thermos standing on it. There was also a burly looking man with a crutch, but as Taff and Thermos weren't running away from him it was reasonable to assume that he was one of the good guys.

Alec was just raising a hand to wave at those pleasingly familiar faces when two more of them appeared directly opposite on the far riverbank. From out of the trees, hand in hand, came the tall vet bloke and Sara the stunning redhead. Alec didn't know whom to wave at first, but as he already had his hand in the air he felt that he should wave it at somebody. Another figure strode out from behind the cottage nearest the bridge, so Alec waved at her.

Lady Gaynor Elfam didn't wave back.

For what seemed like a very long time not much of anything at all happened. Everybody looked at everybody else, and everybody else looked back at everybody.

Lots of looking, but no doing.

Sara Hagget was the first to interpret all of this inaction. She was also the first person to recognize Lady Gaynor without the need for sarcastic prompting. 'Morgan doesn't know where it is,' she whispered to Phillip. 'All may not be lost.'

Sara was right. Gaynor knew the sword was in the village, but not *where* in the village. She'd been hoping that Thelonius Wisp might tell her that, but she'd sort of mislaid him. When she'd quizzed Tauper about Wisp's whereabouts, it became obvious that she should have asked *before* having her wicked way with him. Apparently her way had been slightly too wicked, and she'd caused a massive pleasure overdose. Afterwards he'd just lain there with a stupid grin on his face, responding to all of her questions by blowing little spit bubbles or pressing his nipples and going 'beep'.

As everybody waited for somebody to do something, the universe decided to have one of those moments of synchronicity from which entire religions are born, but are actually just coincidences with no causal connections whatsoever. Thelonius Wisp's box, with Thelonius Wisp's head still within, had been languishing unnoticed in some nearby reeds. It selected that moment to slip free and, thanks to some aggressive freestyle work by the newt, it made its way back out into the middle of the river. Seven pairs of eyes were instantly drawn to the bobbing box as it drifted into view, gathering speed in the current and heading for the bridge, which it had to because that's where the river went. Then it stopped. It stopped because something had stopped it. Something below the surface of the water that would have remained safely unobserved had the box not drawn attention to it.

Sara didn't bother to whisper this time. 'That's torn it. Forget what I said; all *is* probably lost.'

'Oh, this is just too delicious, Thelonius. After all that has happened, you still couldn't help yourself from showing me exactly where it is, could you? You know, I would probably have flattened this pathetic village to find it, and still not thought to look in the river.' Lady Gaynor threw her head back and laughed one of those really evil laughs that only really evil people can do. She was a happy bunny, and like many other happy bunnies she was pregnant. Since her arrival a bulge had developed in the bottom half of her breastplate, the metal remoulding itself to accommodate her new shape. The top half was enlarging a bit as well, but only Thermos had noticed.

Now that the big secret was out, Gaynor could kill everybody if she wanted to. She really wanted to, but first she needed to gloat. She closed her eyes and her face became a mask of deep concentration as she spoke quietly and waved her hands around, her dancing fingers leaving long golden streaks in the air like sparklers on bonfire night. On the final word of the incantation her eyes snapped open and she thrust out her arms, sending the ribbons of light snaking out over the river to dance around until they faded away.

'Wow, that was nifty,' said Thermos, who hadn't grasped the significance of what was going on.

The river stopped flowing. Then there was gurgling. Then whooshing. Then the river began flowing again. Vertically. From a point just upstream of the sword the Wold began to pour upwards like a waterfall in reverse, Wisp's box still atop the rising column of water. It was an incredible sight to behold, but nobody beheld it for long because there were lots of other interesting things to look at. That part of the Wold not going up was still going along, babbling its merry way to the sea, seemingly unaffected by being been cut off from its source. In its wake it left only mud, dying fish, and, thanks to some random translocation that Sara hadn't considered, a large assortment of condoms filled with wallpaper paste. In the middle of the mud there stood a short stone pillar that had probably been a rock once, but centuries of erosion had worn away those parts not protected by the aura of the thing that was sticking out of it.

That thing being a sword.
Excalibur.

'Excalibur!' Lady Gaynor added some triumphal gusto.

'Excalibur?' Taff and Thermos both opted for puzzled amazement.

'Excalibur.' Sara more sighed it than said it.

'Excalibur.' Alec and John both selected awe as their preferred option.

'Bugger,' said Morrison.

Sara looked up at Phillip Morrison and smiled a sad smile. 'Stay here, Phillip. There's something I have to do now. I love you.' With a final squeeze of his hand, and before he could voice the objection that was written all over his face, she stepped away from him and addressed her old adversary. '*Excuse me, may I ask you a question, Morgan?*'

Lady Gaynor was taken aback. Morgan? Well, well. This one had some knowledge hidden away in that pretty little head. It might be interesting to find out what else was in there, before she crushed it under her boot. Gaynor's heart had skipped a beat when she'd first seen Sara, but the panic had only lasted a moment; the girl looked like Nimue, but there was no sense of the power that should have been hiding behind the visage. Even The Celt couldn't conceal so much innate ability, which meant that this was just a pretty woman. A very pretty woman, in the most pejorative sense of the word pretty, which until now probably hadn't had a pejorative sense. 'Of course you may, my dear. But please, come a little closer; we don't want you to have to shout now, do we?'

Sara didn't move; she was confident that Morgan's compulsion to swagger would produce an exciting alternative to merely crossing a bridge.

A few mumbled words from Gaynor and the mud began to bubble and steam, and within seconds it had dried and solidified to a rock hard surface. Sara strode purposefully out onto the hard mud. She glanced over at the three men on the bridge and gave them a reassuring smile. All three tried their best to smile back, but the resultant expressions lacked gorm. Sara didn't give the sword a second glance as she passed close enough to touch it, but then she'd been there when Excalibur had been forged so she knew what it looked like.

Gaynor was puzzled by this new development. 'You have me at a disadvantage. Apparently you know who I am, but who might you be?'

'Who *might* I be? Well I might be Sara Hagget.'

'Is that Hagget with two 'g's and one 't'?'

'That's right.'

'Nice anagram.'

'Thanks. Nice boots.'

'Thanks. So, what is this question you have for me? And please keep it brief, I have to give birth in a minute.'

'I was just wondering if you knew why the barrier was full of holes? There weren't any to begin with, so why are there so many of them now?'

Gaynor shrugged. 'Should I care?'

'Yes, I think you should care. Consider this: Myrddin's Grand Separation was as perfect as it could be; no magic but his could affect it, and it would never decay. So I ask you again: where are the holes coming from? What is the only force that could possibly be making them?'

Lady Gaynor pondered Sara's question. 'You can't mean ... Seriously? You think that ... no, that's not possible. Is it?'

'Well, let's just see, shall we?' Sara turned on her heels and started walking towards the sword.

'*Stop!*' There wasn't a lot of ambiguity to Gaynor's command, but Sara ignored it anyway. '*I said stop!*' A bolt of energy shot from Gaynor's fingertips and struck the ground at Sara's feet, causing a small explosion that rained down bits of dried mud and smoked salmon.

Sara slowly turned around and looked back at Gaynor. 'Well, would you look at that; I'm still alive. That's not like you. That's not the Morgan le Fay I remember. Come on, Morgan, let's see the *real* you?'

'If you insist.' Gaynor spread her arms wide and let the costume that was Lady Gaynor Elfam fall away. Her face became gaunt, the colour draining from her skin until she was albino white. It was a good tone for her; it accentuated her eyes, which had turned completely black, as had her hair, which had been black to begin with but had somehow just got blacker, billowing out in response to a wind that wasn't there. 'Is this what you wanted?' When she spoke her voice was pure menace, each syllable a rock power chord, heavy on the reverb.

Everybody apart from Sara took an involuntary step back, each of them fighting the urge to take a lot of voluntary steps back in a manoeuvre commonly known as 'running away'.

'That's more like it.' Sara's green eyes locked onto the black orbs in Morgan's face, and without breaking the contact she stepped backwards over the small crater at her feet and stood alongside the sword. 'Do you remember the Battle of Cenarth, Morgan? Does *this* look familiar?' Still without breaking eye contact, Sara reached out a hand and curled her fingers around Excalibur's hilt. 'Though obviously you have to imagine that you're lying in the mud down at the pointy end.'

'*It is you, you bitch!*' Morgan couldn't understand how this child could be Nimue, but there was no doubt in her mind now; this *was* The Celt. Rage took over and Morgan's eyes went from darkest black to a burning red as another bolt of energy shot from her fingers and struck Sara full in the chest. She slumped to the ground, her hand still clutching the sword.

Morgan took a deep breath. That had been surprisingly easy. 'So, anybody else want to play hero?'

Alec didn't feel terribly heroic, unless heroic types spent a lot of time feeling very scared, but it was time for this man to do what this man had to do, even if that cliché was unclear on exactly what happened to the men who went about doing it. It was time to stiffen something or other, summon up something else, imitate the actions of some kind of big cat, and possibly screw something to a sticky place. It had all suddenly become very real for Alec. Death can do that. He held his breath—it was probably going to be his last so he wanted to get the most from it—and started walking towards the sword.

'Going somewhere, little man?' Morgan liked having the echo back in her voice. Lady Gaynor Elfam had served a purpose, but on the whole she'd been a bit of a wuss.

Alec Gardener knew that he was about to die. He didn't know if there was such a thing as a *good* death, but he was sure that he was about to experience a really bad one.

'*I said stop!*'

Alec took another step. Nothing happened.

He took another. Still nothing.

If Morgan didn't do something soon the tension would kill him and save her the bother.

Morgan was having a problem. She wanted to kill Alec, she really did, but something was stopping her. *She* was stopping her. The energy was there, pulsing through her fingertips, ready to melt the man's spine, but it wouldn't leave. Some part of her was refusing to kill this man. What was it about him? *Who was he?*

Morgan's difficulty didn't go unnoticed. Ieuan Williams saw it. Kevin Flask saw it. John Bostwicke saw it. Through eyes wet with tears, Phillip Morrison saw it.

Phillip was kneeling beside Sara's body, cradling her head in his lap, having already unhooked her fingers from the hilt of the sword. Without looking down, Phillip felt around on the ground for something he'd seen at Sara's feet whilst she'd still been alive. As Alec took another step towards him, Phillip Morrison gently laid Sara's head on the ground, got to his feet, and took a step of his own. Then he took another. Then he started to run.

Morgan le Fay was still struggling with her Alec problem when the Phillip problem presented itself. The tall man was running straight towards her, big hatred in his eyes and a big rock in his hand. She was impressed. Such bravery. Such devotion. Such a waste.

Phillip might have gotten close enough to do some damage had his own body not worked against him. His gammy knee turned his valiant charge into a valiant hop, leaving him with no choice but to hurl his rock and hope for the best. Having it sail over Morgan's head and smash a window somewhere behind her probably wasn't the best he was hoping for.

'Bugger!' said Morrison, for the penultimate time.

Jack stared at the lion, and the lion stared back at Jack. It was to be a fight to the death, tooth and claw versus rippling muscle and sharpened stick. Jack flexed his enormous biceps and dropped into a shallow crouch, his thigh muscles bulging like marrows either side of a loincloth cunningly fashioned from a Whitworth's Brewery bar towel. At his side was his mate, in the sense that she was the female that he had sex with on a regular basis, as perfect an example of woman as he was of man, her lithe, glistening body clothed only in three strategically placed beer mats. She and Jack had been together in the jungle for many years, but he still had no idea how she kept those mats in place.

'Jackzan, Sara scared. Sara not like lion. Lion eat Sara.'

'Don't fret love, I'll protect you.' Jack smiled at his mate, still in the sense that she was the female that he had sex with on a regular basis, and tried out the new cheeky boyish wink he'd been working on.

It was the moment the lion had been waiting for. The beast pounced, knocking Jack to the ground and pinning him there. It opened its great mouth and moved in on Jack's face, revealing a set of pointy pearly-whites and a bad case of gazelle breath.

'Oi, wake up, you lazy so-and-so,' said the king of the jungle.

'You what?' said Jack.

'I said wake up, there's a peculiar doodah in the water.' The lion sounded familiar. It also looked familiar. It looked like Sid. So much so that it was Sid, and not a lion at all. Though it still had a bad case of gazelle breath.

'Oh, hello Sid. What are you doing here?' Jack was groggy so his consonant removal filter wasn't operational yet.

'You tell me. I thought we were here to blow sum'it up.'

'Oh, aye. Sorry Sid, must 'ave dozed off. What was that you were sayin'?'

'I said there's a thing movin' in the river.'

Jack sat up and rubbed his eyes. 'Probably just an otter.'

'It's got eyes.'

'Otters got eyes.'

'It's pink.' Sid could tell that this conversation was going to get complicated.

'Otters aren't pink.'

'I think that was my point.'

'A salmon then.'

'Salmon are pink on the inside, not the outside.'

'A flamingo?'

'Don't think this is a bird,' said Sid.

Jack hauled himself to his feet and tried to take the reins on a conversation that was already careening towards disaster. 'Best take a look at this strange sum'it in the river then. Where is it?'

'In the river.'

'Oh, right. Yes. The river.' Jack and Sid were pioneers in the field of verbal communication, and in the last six months alone they had discovered nine hitherto undocumented types of stupid. 'That would be the river over there 'en.'

Sid nodded. 'Last time I looked it was. It's prone to moving about though, so best be quick.'

Jack examined the surface of the Wold. He saw nothing pink, with or without eyes, that may, or may not, have been an otter or a flamingo. 'Can't see it, Sid.'

'That's funny, neither can I now.'

'There's some bubbles comin' up over there by the dam, maybe it went under.'

'Must have. Wonder what it was?'

There was a great 'whoosh' of spray as 'what it was' launched itself from beneath the river with a mighty bound. It landed firmly atop one of the great stone boulders of the levee, and the outlandish remnants of Professor James Stephenson MSc PhD took a moment to catch its breath and survey its surroundings.

'Flippin' 'eck!' Jack had never seen anything like it, and he was glad. As there were no ecks to flip he instead flipped open the cover of the remote detonator to reveal the obligatory red button. It didn't say 'BANG!' on it, but it really looked like it should.

'You doin' it then?' Sid's question was probably rhetorical as he'd already started backing away.

'I am. Told you I'd know what I were waitin' for when I saw it, and I reckon I'm looking at it right now.' Jack held the remote out at arm's length, heaven knows why, that wasn't the bit that blew up, and braced himself against the impending shock wave. 'Cover your ears, Sidney.'

Sid covered his ears. Jack closed his eyes. The deadly digit of destruction pressed down onto the scarlet switch of setting stuff off. There was a devastating silence that didn't send a huge column of water spiralling into the air, not showering the surrounding area with mud and rock, making no sizable breach in the dam through which the Wold didn't flow unhindered. Nothing had happened. It happened again when Jack pressed the button a second time. 'Sid, quick! Find the bloomin' instructions! Sid! Sid?' Jack opened his eyes. Sid was standing with eyes still closed, fingers in ears, oblivious to the significant nothing that had happened. 'Bugger!' Jack dived for the box with the instructions in and started digging down through crumpled tinfoil and uneaten pork pies.

Robin Madden hauled himself out of the river and up onto the muddy bank, slipped out of his sodden trench coat and waited to see what would happen next.

What happened next was that Bobs, the four-legged wonder, came trotting happily out from the trees behind him. With tail-wagging aplenty, Bobs placed his creature's rock on his creature's discarded skin and sat down to await the attention that would no doubt be lavished upon him.

Jack was on his second high speed re-reading of the detonator instruction sheet before he located the reason for the spectacular non-event. *When the detonation circuit is active, the 'armed' indicator will flash red, unless the mode dial is turned to the 'remote' position. If the mode dial is in the 'remote' position then the detonation button on the remote transmitter will flash.* Jack glanced over at the control box, then down at the remote, and then back at the box. 'Bugger, bugger, and more bugger!' Somebody needed to go over to the box and turn the dial. Jack wanted that somebody to be somebody else, but as Sid still had eyes closed and ears bunged the only way to communicate with him was by smell. Jack sighed a resigned sigh and started edging towards the control box as stealthily as was possible in rubber waders.

'*Cyst and decease!*' Ben had been waiting a long time to say something like that, and in the excitement of the moment he didn't notice what a pig's ear he'd made of it. He 'broke cover' and stepped out from the trees, his non-lethal weapon trained on Jack's bewigged head. He was closely followed by Bill, who was swinging his gun around wildly in an attempt to keep everybody in his sights. Everybody except Robin Madden, that is—Bill hadn't spotted The Magpie or what he was up to.

Robin was up to reading something that he'd just found in the grass. Something that had been lurking in his coat for many months and had just been washed out by the Wold water draining from his pocket. He picked up the business card in his right hand as he reached back and felt around for his coat with his left, his fingers nudging against the emerald that Bobs had so helpfully returned. Robin thought it strange that the gem wasn't in his pocket. Must have rolled out when he'd taken his coat off. He was going to have to take more care with that emerald or he was going to lose it one day.

Back on the opposite bank Ben tipped his gun barrel skywards in the prescribed manner, and Jack raised his hands because he'd read somewhere that it was best to humour these people. He wasn't intending to humour them for long though. There was a button in serious need of pressing, and come hell or high water, both of which were already on the way, he was going to press it. Decisively, and somewhat arbitrarily, Jack decided to count to fifteen and then make his move.

He'd reached three when there was a sound behind him.

The sound of a match being struck.

'Evenin' all.' George Guv had calculated that this would be the best moment for him to make his presence known, and the unfolding drama had warranted one of the classic openers. George took a long drag on his cigarette and then let the smoke curl lazily out of his mouth; it had taken years of practice to be able to do that without hacking up a lung.

'How do, Jack?' Bladder's grinning face popped out from behind George. All of this lunacy was clearly tapping at Bladder's funny bone, but then he hadn't yet spied the monstrosity standing on the dam.

'Five. Not bad, thanks for asking Bladder. You? Six.'

'Fair to middlin', but I've got me a terrible thirst.' With the dictates of courtesy satisfied Bladder was free to move on and ask the question that most needed asking. 'You plannin' to open up anytime soon?'

'Eight,' said Jack.

'Eight?' Bladder checked his wrist, which might have been more enlightening if he'd owned a watch. 'Reckon it's sum'it after eight already.'

'If you gentlemen have quite finished, I think you all have some explaining to do.' After his strong entrance George had lost control of the situation, and now he was going to have to work hard to set himself for his one-liner before he ran out of cigarette. It was then he noticed Professor James Stephenson MSc PhD. 'And perhaps we should start by somebody explaining *that*.'

'Allow me.' Robin Madden got to his feet as everybody else's were too far away. 'His name is ...' Robin re-read the business card to make sure that he got it right '...Professor James Stephenson Musk Phud.'

'Now what's he up to?'

'I don't know, but I think it's time we were away.'

'How are your reflexes, Professor James Stephenson Musk Phud?' Robin had something up his sleeve, and as he spoke he let that non-metaphorical something drop out of his sleeve and into his hand.

'Ve-ve-very go-good.''

'Who the hell said that?'

'Fifteen,' announced Jack, but nobody noticed as everybody but Sid was looking to Robin Madden. With arms still held aloft Jack began sidling slowly and ever so nonchalantly towards the detonator box. For good measure he was also discreet, furtive and surreptitious.

Robin Madden was no gambling man, but as he glanced down at the emerald resting in his palm he knew he was about to place a very big bet. 'Catch!' said he. He lobbed the gem out over the river, and whilst he was no gambling man he would have made a cracking left-arm unorthodox spinner.

'He's bowled a wrong 'un,' observed Bladder.

Bobs set off in pursuit of the flying jewel, having fairly reasonably assumed that Robin's command had been meant for him.

'What's that?'

'Can't see.'

'I'll get it.'

'No, leave it!'

'Is that the gem?'

'It might be the gem.'

'It's the gem!'

'I said nobody touch it! Who's moving our arm?'

'Tha-that would be muh-muh-me.'

'Shit! James, is that you?'

'I'm Juh-Juh-James Burn-Burn-Bernard Stee-Stephenson, and I'm your whur-whur-worst nigh-nigh-nigh ... oh st-stuff it.'

'Somebody stop that arm!'

'On it. Got it.'

It took just under three seconds for the emerald to complete its journey. One second into that journey it didn't look like Robin's gamble was going to pay out; his lob was higher than he'd intended, but not so high that Professor James Stephenson Musk Phud couldn't have caught it with his extra-long arm. That arm had started moving, but then it had stopped abruptly. It was going to take a miracle for Robin's plan to work now. There wasn't a miracle on hand, but there was a miracle on four legs, which after all is a fairly miraculous number of legs for a three-legged dog to have. As Bobs raced after the flying rock he realized, in an instinctive canine way, that to get high enough to catch it he was going to need a platform to leap off. There was one of those available, so he leapt off it. It was more yielding than he had anticipated, tilting downwards under his weight and slapping hard against the wet rock of the dam, scuppering Bobs' trajectory so that his snapping jaws closed on empty space. The disappointed doggy came back down the same way he'd gone up, landing on the same unstable platform.

'Shit and ow!'

'What happened?'

'That bloody dog just jumped on our knob. Twice.'

'I told you not to make it so big.'

'Hey! Our arm! It's moving again!'

And so it was, as was the rest of James Stephenson. The puffy pink mass of possessed professordom stumbled backwards, somehow managing to avoid any further complicated entanglements with Bobs, who had bolted off towards Sid.

George's moment had arrived. The dog had clearly been trained as a courier for smuggled jewels, and in times of panic it would no doubt run for the protection of its master. Ipso facto, that person would not only be a master, but a mastermind. Simple really. The man standing with his eyes closed and his fingers in his ears was the criminal mastermind behind everything that was going on. A fabulous theory, flawed only by being a load of twaddle. Bobs was heading for Sid because Sid had spent his entire adult life smelling of bacon. George Guv removed his cigarette from his lips and flicked it away. 'Looks like I have to see a dog about a man,' said he. Damn! He'd already used that one. That had been his last cigarette, and he'd wasted it on an enigmatic repetition. Perhaps he could rescue the situation by picking it up and flicking it again, or would that look a bit strange given the relative urgency of the situation?

The motion of George Guv's flying cigarette registered on the limit of Ben's peripheral vision, and his instincts took over. He dropped to one knee, rolled to his right and came up shooting. All thoughts of Ben's earlier failure were forgotten as his perfect shot struck the middle of the cigarette, sending the lit end and the filter spinning away wildly in opposite directions.

'Fuck me!' said Bill, who had gained a new respect for his partner's sharpshooting abilities. This new respect lasted until Ben winked at him and blew imaginary smoke away from the end of his gun barrel.

Not far away from the scene of Ben's dead-eyed redemption there was an outstretched arm. On the end of that outstretched arm there was a pink pudgy hand. A pink pudgy hand with misshapen claw-like fingers. Misshapen claw-like fingers that were closing around a big green gem that had landed plumb in the middle of the pink pudgy hand on the end of the outstretched arm.

'I don't feel so good.'

'Drop it! Drop the bloody thing!'

'Can't ...do ... it ... don't ... have ... control ... of ... hand.'

'Why are you talking like that?'

'Sorry, just wanted to heighten the sense of drama.'

'This isn't funny.'

'I think it's a bit funny.'

'It's very green in here suddenly.'

'The light ... must get to the light ... so peaceful in the light ...'

'You're going to get a smack in a minute.'

''Ere Jack, did you know your wig was on fire?' Bladder had just spotted where the lit end of George Guv's cigarette had gone.

'You what? Arghh! Shittin' buggery!'

Bladder translated. Jack had obviously *meant* to say 'Why thank you, Bladder. It so happens that I was unaware of the conflagration in my hairpiece, and I am most grateful to you for bringing it to my attention in such a timely manner.' Bladder forgave Jack for not thanking him properly; after all, his wig was on fire. The panicking landlord dislodged the blazing barnet with some impromptu headbanging, followed by an estampie—a vigorous rhythmic Provençal stamping dance—on the wig, before ending with a variation of the Samoan slapping dance performed on his hair.

The greater part of what had once been James Stephenson was lost forever, but there was enough left to understand what had to be done. Not that he'd ever seen M112 composition C4 block demolition charges with a multi-mode detonation control unit, but you didn't get to be a Musk Phud without being able to work these things out. Still clutching the big green jewel, the pink-grey grotesque rolled over onto its stomach, pressing its chest up against one of the lumps of explosive that Sid had so lovingly moulded into the rocks. The only person to see him do it was Jack, as all other persons were still looking *at* Jack. It was only Jack who looked into those eyes and saw the suffering and longing trapped in the depths of the horror. Stephenson looked at Jack, looked at the detonator box, and then looked back at Jack.

'Nah-nah-now,' said the last remnants of humanity in what had once been a human being.

Jack nodded, and before anybody could react, he lifted his foot and pressed it down on the big red button on the small yellow detonator box.

'*Can I open my eyes now, Jack?*' yelled Sid.

It was white. Really white. Everywhere. There was nothing but white. Pure white, without a subtle hint of anything. Except more white. With no reference points there was no way to tell if the whiteness went on forever, or ended just a few feet away, though if you had a burning desire to find out then there was always the option to move and see if you bumped into anything.

'Annoying, isn't it?'

Sara had been concentrating so hard on all the whiteness that the voice at her ear made her spin around too quickly and she lost her footing, landing heavily on her backside on some horizontal white. She rubbed a bruised buttock and stared up at the figure standing over her, or possibly hovering over her, it was hard to tell. Recognition wasn't long in coming.

'Myrddin! It's you!'

'Correct, it is me. You win a life of soul destroying boredom and abject misery.'

'But how? Why? Where is this place?' Sara's mind had flooded with questions, but she hadn't intended to ask them all at once.

'Well, let's see now, shall we? How? Because you put me here. Why? Because you put me here. Where? Just past the inn and then take a left at *you should bloody know, you put me here!'*

The language may have been modern, but the attitude was pure old-school Myrddin. Arrogant, sanctimonious and egocentric to a fault, yet you couldn't help but like the man once you got past the urge to throw rocks at him. That was the theory anyway; as far as Sara knew nobody had ever put up with the annoying old bugger long enough to validate it.

'Oh yes, it's coming back to me now; we're inside Excalibur. The jolt left me a bit fuzzy, didn't realize a lightning bolt to the chest was such an unpleasant experience. Sorry.'

'Sorry? I think it's a bit late for sorry. About a thousand years too late I'd say!'

'Actually it's nearer fifteen hundred years.' That probably wasn't the most helpful thing Sara could have said just then. 'But then that's hardly my fault. I only put you in here so you'd have no choice but to destroy your ridiculous barrier to free yourself. How was I to know you'd play the martyr?'

'Martyr? Me? Certainly not! You really think I stayed in here, listening to the inane babble of millions of pointless people living out their pointless lives, by choice?'

'Listening?'

'Listening. This place seems to be a receptor for every kind of transmission that humankind has created to foul the air. It is from them that I've learned this new language and of the changes in the world, but mostly they sing, have inane competitions, and complain endlessly about their pointless lives.'

'Well if you're not here by choice, why *didn't* you free yourself?' Sara was getting a bad feeling, and it was about to get badder.

'Chance would be a fine thing. The higher abilities count for nothing here.'

Wait for it.

Any second now.

Here it comes.

'Not even mine.'

Ding! That was it! Myrddin had always 'bigged himself up' whenever possible. At first it was to convince those with sizable purses that it would be worth retaining his services. Later he did it because he'd started believing that he was as good as he pretended to be. In the old days Sara had described Myrddin's self-aggrandizing statements as his 'facade to strike riches'. When she'd translated that from Brythonic it came out as 'facial money shot', which according to Thermos' catalogue meant something altogether different.

Sara thought about what Myrddin had just said and reached the same conclusion as the rest of us. 'That really didn't explain anything at all.'

'I haven't finished.'

'Sorry.'

'Watch.' Myrddin tugged his unnecessarily capacious sleeves up to his elbows and did some arm waving. A ball of green light appeared between his hands and sped off into the whiteness. After a short distance it hit something that was as white as everything else, only more vertical. The ball of green spread out into a disc that darkened and bubbled in nauseating ways before it too sped off.

'Oh,' said Sara.

'Oh indeed. It's the barrier. It permeates the fabric of the sword and gets in the way of any Magicks that might damage Excalibur from within.'

'Oh, I didn't think of that when I put you in here.'

'Strangely enough I'd guessed that.'

Myrddin threw another energy ball at the whiteness and watched the bubbling green scar zoom off to wherever it was they went.

Sara Hagget shook her head and sighed; it was as she'd suspected: Myrddin's barrier was full of holes because the man himself had spent fifteen centuries taking random pot shots at it. 'You know, I had to die to get in here, just to see if I could persuade you to leave.'

'Die? You can't die. Why in Methuselah's underpants would you think you were dead?'

'Because I was hit with a raw energy bolt powerful enough to kill a herd of elephants.'

'So? That means nothing, you're Nimue. You're The Celt. You're more resilient than any number of elephants.' Myrddin managed to convey a good deal of confidence for a man who'd never seen an elephant.

'I was,' said Sara, looking sad.

'Was what?' said Myrddin, looking confused.

'Was Nimue.'

'Oh, so who are you now?'

'I'm Sara Hagget,' said Sara Hagget.

'Are you? Good anagram.'

'Thanks.'

'But you can't just stop being Nimue. There's no way you could just ... oh dear!'

'Oh dear what?'

'Oh dear, you had sex, didn't you?'

'Oh dear, yes I did.'

'Oh dear, oh dear. And of course it was explained to you long ago that the loss of innocence associated with physical love would strip you of your powers and render you mortal.'

'Yes it was. I call it the 'fuck and you're finished' clause.'

'Nimue!'

'Sorry. How about 'hump and you're helpless'?'

'Better. So you finally experienced pleasures of the flesh? That's very sad.' Myrddin lowered himself down to a white bit that was probably the ground and sat on it. 'Very sad indeed.'

Sara looked out into the white and thought about Phillip. 'Actually, I think it was worth it.'

'No, I don't mean *that*. I'm sure *that* was very nice. The sad part is that you believed all that rubbish about loss of innocence.'

'Excuse me?'

'Well, we had to tell you something.' Myrddin had known this would be a difficult conversation when it came, and it didn't help that they were having it fifteen hundred years later than he'd intended. 'Try and think of it from our point of view. Even as a young child it was clear to the Druidic Council just how pretty you were and what a beautiful woman you would become. We felt that until you understood who you were it might be best to discourage you from having strong romantic attachments that might have led to ... other things.'

'Other things? So what you're saying is that you and the rest of your new-age hippy loonies lied to me so that I wouldn't have sex before you were ready.'

'No, we lied to you so that you wouldn't have sex before *you* were ready.'

'Oh, really? That was considerate of you. So what, pray tell, were the criteria for judging my own readiness.'

'There was only one. Love.'

'Love?'

'Love. If you loved somebody deeply enough to want them in that way, even knowing what you thought you'd be sacrificing, then you were ready.'

'Oh.' Sara had planned on staying angry for a long time. Pretty much indefinitely, really. She was already finding it tricky. Yes, they had lied to her, but for once their motives had been selfless. As selfless as a bunch of opportunistic old farts like the Druidic Council could manage anyway. 'Hold on, that doesn't make sense. If it was all a lie then why *have* I lost my powers? I tried to use them just after I did ... *it* ... and I felt them ebb away. All I was trying was a simple forest cloaking.'

'That'll be the endorphins.' Myrddin was back to his usual flippant self now that Sara's anger seemed to have subsided.

'The what?'

'Endorphins. Very pleasant things by all accounts, but a temporary magic suppressant. Your abilities would have returned, though exactly how long it takes to recover does vary from person to person. Most adepts combine natural talent with acquired knowledge; they would recover faster than one such as you, whose power comes from your ability to channel the natural forces.

Think of yourself as providing a conduit between man and nature, a passage through which the elemental powers can flow. During sex your passage gets bunged up and ...sorry, that analogy turned rather more literal than I'd intended.'

'Bugger!' said Sara because Morrison wasn't there to do it for her. Her course of action at the bridge had been driven by her assumption that she was powerless to do anything else. Assumptions, especially those based wholly on a load of old bollocks, were dangerous things that Sara had always assumed were best avoided. She was still Nimue after all. That changed everything. Except that it didn't. It would have made a difference out there, but now she was as stuck as Myrddin. 'So we're trapped in here?'

'Whilst the barrier remains intact, yes. We are trapped.'

'And the only way to collapse the barrier is for somebody to draw the sword?'

'Indeed. To draw Excalibur would separate the sword from the intricate web of forces that hold the barrier in place. '

'And then we'd be able to destroy the sword and get out?'

'Destroy the sword? Certainly not. It would be the only way if the sword were to remain in place, but once drawn I would expect Excalibur to simply spit us out. The sword feeds on the enthusiasm of youth, and I would imagine it finds our ancient dyspepsia somewhat unpalatable.'

Sara nodded. 'Nobody but us knows that we're alive in here, do they?'

Before Myrddin could respond, a small black feline trotted happily out of nowhere and wiped its nose on Sara's leg. Given the surroundings, you have to wonder how it got that close without being seen, what with it being a very black thing against a very white background. The high contrast creature paused to wash its head before continuing on its way to wherever the hell it might be going.

'Schrödinger's cat,' said Myrddin.

'Oh,' said Sara.

The hissing bolt of energy struck Phillip Morrison in the midriff, sending him flying backwards like a backpacker on a bungee. Alec Gardener, the most reluctant of players still active in the game, was reaching for the sword, his fingers only an inch away from grasping his destiny and possibly changing the world in ways too huge for him to understand, when an airborne veterinarian struck him between the shoulder blades. I'm not sure how best to describe the resulting amalgam of flailing limbs and crashing torsos, but we can rule out 'elegant' for a start.

When the Alec Morrison Collective hit the ground, its constituent parts rolled off in opposite directions, the mainly Alec part towards the bridge and the mainly Morrison part towards the river. The Alec part fared better, though as he lay face down on the riverbed making an assortment of muffled groaning noises it would have been difficult to convince him of that. The Morrison part came to rest at the base of the vertical Wold, his left arm held aloft, waving as it bobbed against the rising water. Then his sleeve got soggy, his arm slipped beneath the surface and the river took him, carrying him slowly upwards to wherever the Wold now flowed. Taff and John watched him go, and if either of them had been wearing hats they would have removed them. Thermos wasn't wearing a hat either, nor was he watching Morrison's Ahabian departure. He'd seen something else. Or rather, he *hadn't* seen something else. 'Where's it gone?'

Taff and John both looked, and verily they too did see that *it* was gone. Very verily they did see it.

Morgan saw that *it* was gone too, and she got really cross.

It was Excalibur, fabled, magical, mystical sword of kings.

And it was definitely gone.

'Where's it gone?' Morgan repeated Thermos' question, only he hadn't sounded like he was going to start ripping people's organs out if he didn't get an answer. *'Which of you has it?'*

Thinking logically, there was only one place the sword could be. Morgan thought about it logically and worked out where the sword was. She was closely followed by John, Taff, and Thermos, in that coincidentally alphabetical order.

The last person to work out where the sword had gone was Alec Gardener, which was a poor show on his part given that he was on top of it. With another assortment of 'ouch' noises Alec struggled to his knees and looked down. Lying on the hardened mud in front of him was Excalibur. Alec continued his upward journey, and then with oodles of trepidation he bent down slowly and took Excalibur by the hilt. So this was what all the fuss was about? Alec didn't know much about swords, but he understood the basics. You held the handle thing and pushed the other end into something called a gizzard, preferably somebody else's. He gave the blade a few practice swipes, though as a concession to the seriousness of the situation he resisted the urge to make lightsaber noises.

'What the bloody hell is he doing?' Taff's question was probably rhetorical, but Thermos answered it anyway.

'It looks like Luke's training session with Obi-Wan on the *Millennium Falcon* just before-'

'Shut up now Thermos.'

'Okey-dokey.'

''Tis the sword's doing I believe. I have heard tales that it touches the mind as it touches the flesh.' John Bostwicke's answer to Taff's question was mercifully free of pop culture references.

Taff nodded. 'Yep, he's looking pretty touched all right.'

Alec's swordplay became more flamboyant as he tested the limits of a skill that he hadn't known he possessed because until he'd picked up Excalibur he hadn't possessed it. His gentle swipes had developed into dramatic lunges, swinging pirouettes, and vicious two-handed thrusts that would have wreaked havoc on the sturdiest gizzard.

There was an 'Ahem!'

With an impressive flourish, Alec buckled his final swash and brought his impromptu display of swordsmanship to a close, finishing with Excalibur held aloft in both hands, the blade pointing to the heavens, but without the scantily-clad maiden seductively draped around his leg that purists consider mandatory for that pose.

There was another 'Ahem!' A louder one.

Alec looked over towards the bridge, but none of those there assembled had been the ahemer, they were all otherwise engaged staring at a spot somewhere off to Alec's left.

'I said *Ahem!*'

With Excalibur still held high above his head, Alec turned and saw the pretty lady who wanted to kill them all and rule the world in an entirely non-democratic way. He'd somehow managed to forget about her. 'Oops,' said he, which didn't do the oversight justice.

'I wonder if I might trouble you for my sword?' Morgan's voice was as commanding and steady as ever, but she was having difficulties. Her great and perfect plan was no longer going as greatly or perfectly as ... planned. She was supposed to be carrying within her the only male child of the bloodline; the only one who could draw Excalibur and make claim to the throne. Now this pathetic nobody had gone and done it first. Morgan had another go at killing Alec, and again nothing happened.

'Actually Morgan, I'd rather he kept hold of *his* sword for a while longer.'

Everybody looked around for the source of this new voice, but none of them looked in the right place.

Sara Hagget slowly got to her feet and brushed the dried mud off her dress. Stunned amazement levels peaked as the scorched and ragged hole in Sara's chest healed, her flesh returning once more to unblemished perfection. The unsightly hole in her samite dress did much the same.

It would have been an appropriate moment for somebody to say something profound, but as nobody did we have to move right along to the next moment.

Nothing happened in that moment either, nor the one after, but in the one after that the swimmer splashed into view. With long powerful strokes the he swam down the vertically rising Wold, and when he was ten feet from the ground the he did a nifty tucky turny divey thing and flipped out of the river, landing on his feet beside Sara.

'Now this is getting ridiculous, doesn't anybody stay dead anymore?' Morgan's indignation didn't completely disguise the tremble that had found its way into her voice. When she killed somebody she expected them to stay killed.

'Some people do,' said Sara quietly as she looked at Phillip Morrison. 'Did you have to do that?'

'Now is not the time to discuss it Nimue,' whispered Morrison. 'I am powerless in a body that is not my own, and your link to your powers has been shattered and will take time to repair. Your healing is innate, your other abilities are not, so for the moment say nothing.'

Sara wanted to argue, but she knew that she couldn't. She could feel the emptiness inside, and with it the truth in Morrison's words.

'Given that we're all about to die, may I ask a question?' Everybody was surprised by Alec Gardener's calm bravado, nobody more so than Alec Gardener.

'Be my guest.' Morgan still had no idea why she was letting this annoying little man live. Why couldn't she just kill him and be done with it? What *was* it about him?

'Now I'm sure you'll correct me if I've got this wrong, but from what I understand there's this magical barrier thing that keeps the two worlds apart.'

Sara and Phillip Morrison did some nodding.

'And this barrier thing is held in place by a sword.'
More nodding.

'In fact, *this* sword. And if the sword is pulled out of the ground, the barrier collapses and some stuff happens. If *this* sword, this sword I'm holding over here, is pulled out of the ground. That bit of ground over there, for instance.' Alec tried pointing at the sword, then at the stone column that had been its resting place, then back at the sword. If that didn't work he was going to need a screen and an overhead projector.

'Aha! Now I get it!' It was Thermos who'd got it, and he was already wishing he'd got it more quietly.

'Um ...' said Sara.

'Er,' said John.

'Oh,' said Taff.

'Ah,' said Morrison, who was the last to get it, but compensated by being the only one who could explain it. 'It must be stuck. My barrier has been in place for a considerable time, and has likely developed an equilibrium that can be maintained without the need for an anchor. It would take a shock wave of some considerable size to shake it loose now.'

At that exact moment in another world, Jack was using his foot and some M112 composition C4 block demolition charges to create a shock wave of some considerable size.

Morgan looked puzzled. '*Your* barrier? Myrddin? Is that you in there?'

The only response to Morgan's question was a loud tearing noise, and it didn't come from Myrddin. It came from everywhere. And nowhere. It was followed by a rumble. The rumble got louder and the ground began to shake. Morgan thought it appropriate to withdraw, calmly and gracefully drifting up and away from the quaking riverbed. Everybody else just legged it. Thermos, Taff, and John bolted off the bridge and made for the trees as fast as limps, adipose and virginity would allow. Myrddin ran too, though it was a while since he'd had limbs to command so his hasty retreat was interspersed with some hasty falling down and hasty crawling; he was no coward, but being mortal *and* powerless didn't leave him much to work with vis-à-vis bravery.

As for Sara, she stood her ground. Admittedly, the ground in question was behind Alec and the sword, but still a brave thing to do, though unlike Myrddin she was neither mortal nor powerless. Alec had bought Sara time. Time to retreat into her mind and delve deeper into that empty space to find what was lost. Sara's link to Nimue had been shattered, but when something gets shattered there are bits that need to be swept up. Fragments sparkled in the void like shards of glass catching the light and Sara was sweeping them up, gathering them together, combining them into ... *something*. It certainly wasn't a whole Nimue. At best she had an arm, a leg, and a bit that might have been an ear (people were going to point), but it was better than nothing and more than enough for her immediate need.

Alec had lost interest in what everybody else was doing and didn't notice the hasty tactical withdrawals that were going on around him. He didn't see John, Taff, Thermos, and the bloke who used to be Phillip Morrison, disappear into Falston Wood and tactically hide behind some big trees. Nor was he aware that Sara Hagget was still behind him, what with his attention being centred on the shock wave that had just exploded out of the stone pillar that Excalibur used to be stuck in. As we already know, it was a shock wave of some considerable size.

Alec and Sara were thrown high into the air by the pressure of the eruption. They didn't come down again.

Morgan barely had time to conjure a magical shield before the blast reached her. Her hastily erected defence did its job admirably, but the concussion from the impact sent her spinning backwards into the roof of Falston post office. The *other* Falston post office. The one with the illuminated sign and the notice in the window announcing that the annual coach trip to Nimlet had been cancelled due to lack of interest. The one where Thermos collected his plain brown envelope each month. The one with the thatched roof that Morgan was busy crashing through. The physical damage to Morgan was negligible, but the bruise to her ego was one of those really angry looking purple and black ones. Out of sheer annoyance she tossed an energy bolt at the nearest sizable building. It fizzed down Falston High Street and struck the front of The King's Arms. Or was it The Queen's Arms? The sign above the door had become ambiguous, and then it had become matchwood. The pub door exploded inwards taking the doorframe with it, windows shattered, and the whole frontage was left scorched and blackened with soot. Those of you concerned with what happened to the *inside* of Falston's premier watering hole can flip back to the prologue.

As Sara hung in the air she had an idea. She'd badly needed an idea, and now she had one. She hadn't badly needed an Alec Gardener hanging onto her legs, but she had one of those too.

Morgan stopped picking thatch out of her cleavage and watched with amazement as the landscape and buildings around her began to remodel themselves. She was so amazed that she momentarily forgot about the spells that were keeping her army heading for victory and a river heading upwards. With her concentration broken the Magicks dispersed and her army collapsed to the ground, filling the one remaining morris man with a joy too joyous to put into words. Then a river fell out of the sky.

Two worlds becoming one was too gargantuan a concept to deal with all at once, so everybody just tried to cope with the bit that was most directly affecting them at that moment. For our players at Falston bridge, that bit was the arrival of Jack's newly undammed horizontal Wold, which appeared out of nowhere just as Morgan dropped the vertical one. Pongo would have been smugly content to see his theories on recombination verified, as the combination of the two Wolds somehow only contained the same volume of water as a single Wold, but there was still the problem that a lot of that volume was arriving from above. The vertical Wold landed in the horizontal Wold, and a wall of water crashed down through the trees, and lo, there was much drenching and falling down and cursing. A raging torrent swept underneath Sara and Alec, and after a few loud creaks of complaint the wooden bridge succumbed and set off for the seaside. The stone bridge that appeared in its place looked to be faring better. The flood subsided as quickly as it had come, and soon the river was again making its way through the arches of Falston Bridge rather than over them.

Alec was still clutching Excalibur in both hands, and up until this point had been managing to stay aloft with Sara by keeping the top of her right leg clamped firmly between his arms and his chest. It was a complicated manoeuvre that had him pressing one of his cheeks up against one of hers, and only luck had kept Alec from cutting his own head off or inserting the fabled sword of kings right up Sara Hagget's bottom. The manoeuvre became even more complicated when the falling river had soaked them both, and now Alec's face was slowly sliding down between Sara's damp thighs. It was just the sort of thing he'd been imagining doing since he'd first seen Sara Hagget, but try as he might he couldn't enjoy it. The slide ended with Alec's hands, both still locked tight around Excalibur's hilt, hooked over Sara's foot.

There was a brief but welcome interlude in the almost unbearable tension as a grinning man wearing nothing but a pair of gingham underpants backstroked into view.

'Am I right for Finland?' queried the happy stranger as he passed beneath the dangling Alec.

Before anyone could respond to his question—not that anyone was planning to—the current sucked the man under the bridge, presumably to emerge on the other side in best Poohstick fashion, though nobody felt inclined to check.

Sara Hagget and Lady Gaynor Elfam hovered in the air and glared at each other. Both of them looked very angry. Both of them looked very beautiful. One of them looked to be sinking. Sara had found enough power to get airborne, but the extra weight of Alec and Excalibur had drained her reserves; part of the load would have to go. The part she selected was hanging off her foot and trying to look anywhere but up her dress. 'Sorry sire,' she said, and she really was. 'Whatever happens, you can't let go of the sword.'

Alec didn't like the sound of that. Nor did he like the sound of 'splosh' as Sara straightened her foot and he dropped into the river.

Sara's levitation spell got its second wind and she shot up into the air, a screaming bolt of energy passing through the empty space where she had just been and continuing on unhindered to hit the big tree that Myrddin wasn't hiding Phillip Morrison's body behind any more. He wasn't hiding it there because he'd heard Nimue's voice in his head saying '*whatever happens, you can't let go of the sword*', and he'd understood what that meant, which was more than Alec had. The tree became an eighty-foot inferno as Morrison's body limped purposefully down to the water's edge and dove into the river.

Some distance away, a dirty and bloodied man saw the smoke rising from Falston wood and he knew that he needed to be there. It wasn't going to be easy. The landscape around him was in a state of violent transition, with buildings and fences, and even people, suddenly appearing and disappearing as the two worlds struggled to reach equilibrium. Plus he was going to have to get there unseen, which would mean going the long way round and crossing the Wold further upstream. He sighed, and with difficulty he hefted the really useful thing he'd found up onto his shoulder, ignoring as best he could the pains from an assortment of nasty looking wounds. Well if it was a long way and he didn't have much time, he'd best get moving. So move he did.

Morgan had taken her go, now it was Sara's turn. She didn't have enough energy left to go squandering it in missile form, but that had never been the plan anyway. Instead she clapped her hands together hard, sending a massive shock wave through the air in front of her. Temporarily weakened by her last attack, Morgan's only defence was to brace herself and let her shield take the impact. She was sent spinning back wildly, this time going right through the roof of the post office and travelling for another forty yards before she managed to regain control. When she did there was no sign of Nimue. Oh wait, there she was, floating off to the left above the village. Before Morgan could turn, another shock wave slammed into her. Off she span again, this time travelling much further before she was able to steady herself. This was getting ridiculous. Was this really the best the great water witch could do? Force blasts? It was positively embarrassing. Even without her conjured shield to absorb the impacts these assaults would have done Morgan no significant harm. Force blasts were little more than tricks to amuse children, and even a big one only did 1D3+1 damage. If that makes no sense to you then consider yourself lucky. Thermos knew what it meant, and the shame of it kept him awake nights.

Now where had she gone? Morgan was desperate to do some blasting of her own, but her target of choice was refusing to sit still long enough to be killed. Then she caught movement high above her and to her right; The

Celt may not have been much of a fighter these days, but the bitch was certainly nippy.

Actually the bitch wasn't nippy at all. She wasn't even moving. Her second blast had left Nimue completely exhausted, and she'd tumbled from the air, landing heavily in a field upstream of the village. The fall broke things. Bones mostly. Sara wasn't used to physical pain and suddenly there was lots of it, though the bit that really hurt was the knowledge that she had failed. Two more force blasts would probably have done it, but the power just hadn't been there. Now all she could do was wait for Morgan to finish her. She hoped her end would be quick, though she was anticipating gloating.

Morgan liked a good gloat, but as she was spinning backwards through the air again it didn't seem to be the time for one. All thoughts of gloating had vanished in two puffs of smoke, one from each of Draknoor's nostrils, as the last of the black dragons gobbed out a ball of the fiery stuff and then pulled up hard from the steep dive that had allowed him to approach unseen.

Alec Gardener, journalist and monarch, was a strong swimmer, so landing in the Wold shouldn't have been a problem. Yet as Draknoor whirled overhead and dove for another attack, Alec found that he did have a problem. He was drowning. When Sara had dropped him into the river he'd gone under, and then he'd kicked hard with his legs and waited to bob back to the surface. He'd been in deep water before, and he knew that he bobbed. Bobbing was his thing. He was a bobber. When his feet touched the riverbed and he began to sink into the mud, Alec realized that bob wasn't coming. There were two reasons for that, and both of them were Excalibur. The sword was many things, but 'buoyancy aid' wasn't one of them. The weight of the weapon was keeping Alec submerged, and the only way he was going to get back to the surface was to let go of it. The pretty lady had specifically asked him not to do that, and Alec had given the request some consideration. But not much. It was then he discovered that '*you can't let go of the sword*' hadn't been a plea, it had been a statement of fact. Puzzlement had turned to panic as he tried to prise the sword from his grasp, balancing on his left leg and pushing hard between his wrists with his right foot. Still his hands wouldn't budge from Excalibur's hilt, so he gave up and closed his eyes. A passing newt swam up to Alec's head—it had been spending a lot of time around heads recently—to investigate the humming noises, but being a newt it can be forgiven for not recognizing the melody as Britney Spears' *Baby One More Time*.

Death hadn't descended on Sara's muddy field yet, but its flight had only been delayed, not cancelled. Draknoor's arrival had given Sara some hope, but that hope had faded when it became clear how badly injured the dragon was. Sara had established a mental link to the beast in the hope of directing the assault and she'd barely been able to stifle a scream when the dragon's pain had been added to her own. This pain thing was no fun at all.

The dragon was spent; he had nothing more to give. Immune though he was to any magical attacks Morgan may use, the wounds he already had meant that simply remaining in the battle would be enough to kill him. A sigh escaped Sara's lips between the gasps of pain. Just one more of Draknoor's fireballs might have been enough to finish what she'd begun, but his pilot light was flickering out and there was nothing to be gained by sacrificing the last example of such a remarkable species. Sara concentrated hard and forced a message through the pain, and then she watched as Draknoor took her advice and wheeled away, skimming the treetops as he struggled to stay in the air on torn and broken wings.

'Come back here, you overgrown bat!' Morgan was genuinely disappointed at Draknoor's departure; she would have enjoyed killing the last example of such a pathetic species. No matter. For now the priority was to find Nimue and finish her once and for all. Then at last she could ... ow! And more ow! In all of the excitement Morgan had forgotten that she was pregnant. Not that there was any need to be now: the sword had been drawn so she had no use for the child. Might as well have it though, she could figure out what to do with it later. If she was remembering correctly, the 'joy' of childbirth involved lying around with your legs in a most undignified position and then sweating and screaming a lot until the brat dropped out. To use one of those nicely expressive phrases had become popular in Morgan's absence, sod that for a lark! At the appropriate moment a midwife spell would translocate the child out of her and deposit it somewhere on the ground; all Morgan had to do was select a suitable place. That wasn't *too* much of a chore. Just a short float away there was a clearing in the trees that looked like it would suit. Yes, it would have been a most suitable place if a house hadn't just appeared in it. A very picturesque house, if a little squat for Morgan's taste. Nice rose bushes too.

Alec Gardener woke up and found all of his friends looking down at him. He smiled up at them. It was good to be alive. He'd have thought it extra good if he'd remembered that a minute ago he'd been inhaling river, but he didn't. Nor did he remember Myrddin, in a Phillip Morrison submarine, grabbing his shoulders and pulling him to the surface. He also didn't remember that the weight of the sword had pulled them both under again, or that by then Taff, John, and Thermos, had realized what was happening and had waded into the Wold to assist with the rescue. Being hauled ashore on the village side of the river was absent from his memory, as was having four men with no idea how to do it trying to get the water out of his lungs. Best of all he didn't remember being given the kiss of life by Thermos, which was the part of the rescue that had made Alec repress all of his memories of it.

Taff was about say something when he thought he saw movement in the trees on the far bank. It was just a glimpse. Nothing at all probably. Or just possibly a unicorn. 'That's funny. For a sec there I thought I saw the unicorn, but that can't be right. I *can't* see the unicorn. I've done it. A lot. Honest.' That had come out sounding more defensive than he'd intended.

'A unicorn you say?' It was still Phillip Morrison's voice, but as everybody should have grasped the concept by now it's high time to let go of the past and start thinking of him as Myrddin. 'If there is a unicorn near, then certainly you can see it.'

'I can?'

'He can?' Thermos was pleased that he might not have to go through all of that 'if I were thinking like a unicorn' stuff again, as are we all.

'We all can. We are all close to *that*.' Myrddin nodded in the direction of Excalibur. 'The sword gifts those in close proximity to it the ability to see things that would otherwise be hidden.'

Alec joined the conversation, just to let everybody know that he was alive and they could all stop worrying about him so conspicuously. 'Well if Taff did see the unicorn, where is it?'

Garthang had an ability to arrive right on cue that even the rest of his kind wondered at. Before Alec had finished asking his question, the unicorn galloped out of Falston Wood, across the dirt road and onto the bridge. He looked as magnificent as ever, his mane billowing as he ran, no doubt pleased by the picturesque way his clattering hooves were splashing up the water on the causeway. The little rainbow that arced up through the flying droplets, framing his charge, was also very lovely, but was most likely an embellishment of his own creation as it contained several colours that aren't mentioned in the song.

Pongo Smythe wasn't holding up quite as magnificently as his steed. Where Garthang looked like he'd just been doing some genteel grazing on the Elysian Fields, Pongo looked like he'd just played rugby against the Hades First XV. His patented all-occasion suit was torn and bloodied and encrusted with mud, making it impossible to tell which of its numerous style options it had selected for the occasion. There were wounds over most of Pongo's body, the larger ones plugged with moss and leaves, the others still raw and bleeding, and there was blood running down his face from a deep gash in his scalp. For once he wasn't clutching either his cane or his sack as both had been tucked into his belt so that he could grasp Garthang's mane with one hand and use the other to hold the really useful thing he'd found. At that moment the really useful thing was balanced on his left shoulder, and from where Alec was sitting it looked like a rectangular green metal box with four holes at the front. If he'd been anywhere else it would still have looked like a rectangular green metal box with four holes at the front, because that's what it was. If Phillip Morrison had been himself, regardless of where he was, he would have recognized that rectangular green metal box with the four holes at the front as an M202A1 multi-shot rocket launcher.

Pongo and Garthang thundered past Alec without so much as a glance in his direction.

'And I looked, and behold a pale horse: and his name that sat on him was Death, and Hell followed with him.' It was one of the few biblical quotes Alec knew, which was a revelation.

'You what?' said Taff.

Morgan le Fay had found Nimue. In some ways it was sad that it was going to end like this, but none of those ways were sad enough to stop Morgan from ending it. Her normal modus operandi would have included a long drawn-out coupe de grâce, involving lots of pain and suffering for the victim, but today Morgan was going to have to make an exception. She'd picked her spot to give birth and the midwife spell was already into its final phase, so she was just going to have to stay put and kill Nimue from a distance. It was another annoying concession to motherhood that Morgan hadn't anticipated, but there was some consolation in the knowledge that she would soon be able to enslave the world completely unopposed, which was nice.

As she readied herself to unleash scorching death, a second target hove into view (technically hove is a nautical term so only a ship can do it—Garthang and Pongo should have *heaved* into view, but that just sounds unpleasant) tearing along the road that had just appeared between the village and the stubby little house she was hovering over. As Nimue didn't look like she'd be leaving anytime soon, Morgan decided to kill the mounted target first. She took very careful aim—hitting the unicorn would be bad—and prepared to fire.

Pongo had already taken careful aim and had finished preparing to fire, so he fired. There was a loud 'whoosh' and a cough of flame as the last remaining rocket in the launcher set about doing that which it was created to do. The incendiary missile shot forwards and Pongo shot backwards, rolling over Garthang's rump and ending in a sitting position on the road, the now empty launcher tube still perched on his shoulder. To be fair to Pongo Smythe, he'd been given only the most rudimentary instruction on battlefield deployment of the M202A1 multi-shot rocket launcher, and that from a man who knew little more about it than Pongo did, and at full pelt Garthang hardly constituted a stable launch platform, *and* there was blood running into Pongo's eyes from the wound on his head, *and* he was weak from the battle, so it would be entirely forgivable for his shot to

365

miss Morgan by a country mile. Surprisingly, given all of the factors working against it, Pongo's shot didn't miss Morgan at all. It certainly came as a big surprise to Morgan. There was a blinding flash as the missile struck her shield, and then she found herself at the centre of a blazing fireball as the thickened pyrophoric agent in the rocket's warhead spread out over the surface of her protective bubble. It's a pity that nobody present knew enough about modern weaponry to be able to savour the irony in the fact that the substance in the warhead was chemically identical to the stuff that Draknoor's saliva glands produced.

Morgan le Fay went down, quite literally, in a ball of flame. Sadly, it was little more than an inconvenience. Morgan cancelled the shield spell, which disappeared with the obligatory 'pop', taking the sticking flames with it. Then she concentrated hard to wipe the image of those flames from her retinas so that she could see clearly. Then she gave birth. Then she steadied her fall so that she wasn't spinning wildly. Then she crashed into the roof of Rose Bungalow and was yet again required to deal with the unwanted attentions of thatch. She took a moment to compose herself, and then reached a decision. 'Right, that's it! I am now officially *very* angry.' It was a bad idea to make Morgan le Fay angry. People didn't like her when she was angry. People didn't like her the rest of the time either, but they particularly didn't like her when she was angry. When she was angry she had access to her darkest powers. When she was angry her decision making became a little rash, and she'd been known to unleash forces upon the earth that were none too happy about being leashed again when she was done with them.

Morgan drifted back into the air until she was level with the treetops, then she spread her arms wide. Raw magical energy began to seep from her skin, and she became bathed in a green glow. After all of the 'you wouldn't like me when I'm angry' stuff it was about time that somebody turned green. Her hair billowed. Her eyes blackened, becoming windows on a bottomless abyss. A low moan escaped from between her lips and below her in the trees the shadows darkened and began to stir.

'So, do you think you used enough explosive there Jack?' queried a column of mud that was roughly Sid shaped.

'Did the job, didn't it?' replied a roughly Jack shaped column.

'Aye, reckon it did at that.'

That was the closest thing there had been to a conversation since the explosion. As Jack and Sid have a thick coating of mud but are otherwise unharmed, we shall leave them to harden and move on to the fates of the others present when the big bang had banged big.

Starting with the closest to 'ground zero' and working outwards, we begin with Professor James Stephenson Musk Phud. His was a most straightforward and concluding fate: he was blown into many small bits, and what a blessed relief it was for him.

Next we have Robin Madden and Bobs. They both chose to walk a similar path in the aftermath of the explosion, but they started down it at different times. Bobs went first, bolting into the woods before the first of the debris landed. Robin had waited until it stopped raining mud and rock and small bits of Professor James

Stephenson Musk Phud, and then he too had slipped away into the trees. With The Mischiefs destroyed, and the river returned to where it belonged, The Magpie considered his debt to society paid, which to his thinking made it okay to go back to stealing things.

Since exiting their respective mother's wombs, Bill and Ben had spent much of their time doing things that defied rational explanation. If we use that history of personal weirdness as the paradigm, what happened to them wasn't that odd. They were still Bill and Ben-ish in that some of their features were recognisable, but they were bigger, a tad hairier, generally wartier, a touch more grey-green of skin, and a smidgen more completely naked. As Bill picked up a rock and crushed it into dust, just because he could, Ben stared down with vague recognition at something floating in a muddy puddle at his feet. He tried to pick it up, but his new hands were designed for brute strength not dexterity, and his gun was reduced to a mass of plastic shards and bent metal bits in his palm. For a moment he looked sad, then with a shrug Ben threw the smashed toy away and marched off towards the trees. Bill grunted and then followed his partner's muscular grey-green buttocks into Falston Wood. Partners stuck together, even when they had been fundamentally reworked at the genetic level by the violent merging of two disparate lineages. Went with the territory.

George Guv had no inkling that he was the first man to clap eyes on a human-troll hybrid for nearly two millennia, and frankly even if he had known he wouldn't have given a tinker's cuss. George knew big and important facts that he hadn't known a moment ago, and the biggest and most important of them was that there was somewhere he had to be. Detective Inspector George Guv—nonchalant, nonconformist, and now decidedly non-compos mentis—got to his feet, stripped off down to a fetching pair of hand-embroidered gingham underpants, waded out into the river, and with a cheery goodbye wave that appeared to have been directed at Jack's smouldering wig, launched into his most formidable flappy backstroke and set off for Helsinki.

Bladder was far enough away from the detonation to keep his footing and only get a light splattering of mud, rather than rolling about on the ground looking like one of the legendary bog monsters of Nimlet Marshes. Consequently he was upright and not wiping brown goo from his eyes, giving him an unhindered view of what happened to everybody else. He saw the unnatural beastie on the dam get blown to pieces. He saw Bobs and Mad Ned depart, apparently unharmed. He saw Jack and Sid rolling about on the ground looking like the legendary bog monsters of Nimlet Marches. He saw the two blokes in suits turn to dust and then come back again, only when they came back they weren't in suits and they weren't blokes. That transformation had been almost as shocking as the sight of George Guv in his underpants, and as Bladder watched the beaming bobby splash off down the river he reached the inescapable conclusion that this copper was not the full shilling.

Bladder's own precarious mental state wasn't helped any by the arrival of Pete the lingerie salesman. Given the day he was having Bladder didn't find it even slightly odd that Pete was floating five feet off the ground and looking like he'd just been spat out of a threshing machine. The rocket launcher that Pete was clutching under his arm didn't even register on Bladder's peculiarity radar.

'Barry Ogleby, how extraordinarily fortuitous that our paths should have crossed at this moment. You haven't perchance laid eyes on Phillip Morrison of late, have you?'

Bladder shook his head because there was no chance whatsoever that he'd be able to make words come out of his mouth.

'A great pity and an inconvenience that may yet prove to be a source of some significant regret, though mayhap you will be able to assist me in his stead?' Pete manoeuvred the rectangular green metal box with the four holes in the end out from under his arm and pointed the business end at Bladder. 'I don't suppose you have any idea how this bloody thing works?'

The third and final round of the Battle of Falston didn't last long. Her anger at being unable to swat a few troublesome insects had pushed Morgan le Fay into making a decision that would undoubtedly have serious repercussions later, but she could live with that. Nobody else would though. Morgan had used her darkest powers to summon beings that those who dared to name them called the Animus Wraiths. They were inhabitants of the deepest shadows. Distillations of hate and loathing that even death had found unpalatable. There were so many of them now, spreading out from the shadows beneath Morgan like a black wave, gifting swift death on any they touched. Even the flowers and trees withered and died at their passing. When called upon, the Animus served only their own desire to end life in whatever form they found it, but Morgan still commanded enough control over them to steer them away from those prizes that she wanted to keep for herself. Chief amongst those prizes was Nimue, and she would be saved for last. First to go would be that cussed little guild flunkey who'd been dissin her big and then smacked her upside the head with a bad boy cherry bomb. Morgan frowned; without the barrier to restrict the flow of information she was assimilating fifteen centuries of progress so randomly that even *she* didn't know what she was talking about.

Pongo Smythe struggled to his feet and watched in horror as the blackness poured from the shadows of Falston Wood, leaving only death and decay in its wake. Morgan le Fay was insane, everybody knew that, but even she should have baulked at the madness of releasing the Animus Wraiths. They would only be free to roam from this dusk until tomorrow's dawn, but in that time they could lay waste to an entire county or two.

Pongo tensed, which took his eyebrows by surprise as they'd assumed he was already as tense as it was possible to be. A hundred yards down the road, between Pongo and the Stygian wave, stood Garthang. The unicorn had turned and was looking back at him, and Pongo's heart sank into his boots with the realisation that nothing could prevent what was about to happen. Natural Vengeance meant nothing to the Animus, and as the first of them brushed against Garthang's flank the unicorn crumpled to the ground, an ancient if not terribly bright flame extinguished forever. Then he was lost from view as the blackness rolled over him.

The exhausted rocket launcher clattered to the ground at Pongo's feet as the little man discarded it and waited for his own flame to be snuffed, though apparently the Animus were not to be his snuffers. The blackness drew close enough for him to make out the individual forms that writhed within, and then it wheeled away towards the village.

'The beast was your friend?' Morgan was still airborne, the Animus being too unpredictable for her to risk being within reach of them.

Pongo nodded, the blood trickling down his face now thinned with tears.

'Then here, have a token to remember him by.'

Something flashed through the air and Pongo felt a tickling sensation between his shoulder blades. Then he looked down.

'Oh dear.' It was all he could think to say at the sight of the thick end of Garthang's amputated horn protruding from his chest. As last words went they weren't as memorable as Pongo would have liked, but somehow they suited him. With his place in song and story secured, Pongo tumbled down the river bank and slipped into the Wold.

As the lethal wave reached Alec, it broke, parting to pass either side of him, close enough for him to see the hatred and envy in the dead eyes of those murderous, twisted, wretches. He could also see Myrddin, standing in his own small pocket of sanctuary. Whatever their reason for leaving Alec alive, it applied to the wizard as well. Grateful as he was that the Animus weren't attacking them, Alec saw no reason to return the favour. He swung Excalibur high above his head and brought it down on the nearest wraith. The blade connected with something that wasn't exactly corporeal, nor was it entirely without substance. It may have been more mist than man, but apparently a wraith could still die. Again. The creature dropped to the ground as an oily black liquid, steaming like hot tar and smelling like dead cats. If any of the other creatures cared about their fallen comrade, there was no sign of it. Alec swung again. And then again. Two more oily black puddles and still no reaction from any of the others. This was Alec's kind of fight and he went at it with gusto, swinging Excalibur around with gay abandon until he was sliding around in a pool of steaming ooze looking like he'd struck oil. It was utterly futile of course, there were too many of these things for Alec's hackfest to make any significant dent in their numbers, but at least he was doing *something.* He kept doing it until there was nothing left to do it to. As dusk became night, the flow of black shapes ebbed and the last of them crossed Falston Bridge and merged into the shadows of the woods, the direction of their passage marked by a brown streak across the forest canopy as each tree they touched instantly withered.

Five had stood their ground at Falston Bridge and faced the wraiths. Three had fallen.

John Bostwicke was lying beside the river, his grip still tight on Pongo's arm. The wraiths had struck him down as he'd been trying to pull the body of his friend from the waters.

Ieuan Williams was slumped over the side of Falston Bridge. Kevin Flask lay on the ground beside him. Both were still clutching the branches that they'd been using as weapons. Taff and Thermos had gone down fighting, and they'd gone down together.

'There was nothing you could have done to prev-' Myrddin didn't get to finish consoling his new king. Alec watched as the wizard abruptly launched high into the air as if shot from a catapult, disappearing into the night sky all flailing arms and legs, landing somewhere on the far side of the village. It was a long way off, but Alec was sure he heard a faint thud. There was only one logical explanation for Myrddin's ballistic departure, and Alec guessed that she was most likely floating behind him. 'So, you going to kill me now then?'

'May have to go with a yes on that one.' Morgan drifted around until she was hovering in front of Alec, just out of Excalibur range. She was bluffing. She wasn't going to kill him. She couldn't kill him. Whatever it was that had frustrated her attempts before was being equally frustrating now. She'd hoped the Animus would have done the job for her, but she'd known it was a vain hope; they had no power against the one who brandished Excalibur.

This was his first up-close look at Morgan le Fay, and we should all be thoroughly disappointed in Alec that his first thought was 'wow'. All subsequent thoughts about Morgan's body were more to do with sticking a sword into it. But still, was she really *that* bad? True, there was that making humanity subservient to her will thing, but deep down didn't everybody want that? He didn't know why it had taken him so long to see it, but it struck Alec that maybe he was looking at this whole victory and defeat thing in completely the wrong way. As he watched the black vileness of the Animus soak into his skin, Alec Gardener suddenly knew what had to be done to save that skin. Winning was all just a matter of perspective, and perspective could change depending on where you were standing. Perhaps it was time to change his stance and see what the view was like from the other side? He frowned. All the sweet-smelling metaphors in the world couldn't disguise the smell of the really shitty thing he was about to do.

Morgan sensed the change in the sword-wielder. A moment ago he'd wanted naught but to kill her, but now...

Myrddin's landing had made a right mess of Phillip Morrison's body. The list of broken bones included both back and neck, and a few important internal organs were no longer doing what they were supposed to do. Others were still doing what they were supposed to do, but not in the place where they were supposed to do it. He should have been dead. He was alive because Phillip Morrison's body and Myrddin's spirit weren't fully integrated. There was an unnatural gap between the physical and spiritual planes that had cushioned the impact for both, but just to keep the great cosmic joke chuckling along the fall had fixed Morrison's gammy knee.

'So what's the plan now then?' Sara Hagget was a right mess as well, but compared to Myrddin she was the picture of health.

From the sound of her voice, Myrddin guessed that Nimue was only a few feet away, but I think we've adequately covered why he couldn't turn his head to look for her. Luckily his jaw wasn't on the list of broken bones, and most of the bits required to make his mouth go up and down were still in working order. 'Plan? That rather depends on what assets we have at our disposal. Have your powers returned?'

'No, though at a push I might be able to blow bubbles out my bum.' Sara wasn't joking; making multi-coloured translucent spheres appear from her bottom wasn't her most productive talent, but there were times when it was sort of fun. This probably wasn't one of those times.

Myrddin sighed. 'Then you're in better shape than I. Nothing seems to want to move. And there's something hard pushing into my left temple. Can you identify it from where you are?'

'That would be your right shoulder.'

'Excellent. Well as I have absolutely no feeling in anything below the neck, I would just like to make it clear that my face hurts.'

'What about the others?' Sara knew there could only be one answer to that question, but until she had confirmation she wasn't ready to accept it.

'All but the new king are dead, and by now I would hazard that he too must have fallen.'

'Oh I wouldn't go making rash assumptions like that, old man.' Morgan drifted down from the night sky and then circled around a bit until she was happy that the moonlight was illuminating her with just the right balance of beauty and menace.

'Oh bugger!' said Myrddin. There might have been something of Phillip Morrison left in there after all.

'Go to Hell!' said Sara, though her tone was more defeated than defiant. It was over, and the proof of it was right in front of her. The king, Alec whatsisname, was standing beside Morgan, in as much as he could be standing beside somebody that was floating six feet in the air when he wasn't, and seemingly he was now in league with her. Morgan didn't have the sword, but apparently she had the one who did. Sara knew it wasn't his fault though; the taint of The Animus was still visible on his skin and clothes. Those vile creatures may have been unable to harm Alec physically, but their evil rot corrupted all that it touched.

'Perhaps later, but for now I was planning on bringing Hell here.' Morgan smiled. It was gloating time.

'I have only one thing to say to that.' Speaking was causing Myrddin a lot of pain. 'Phrrrrrrrp!' Blowing raspberries hurt even more, but it had been worth it.

'How dare you! I can't ...believe ...that ...' Morgan's angry tirade was cut short by dozens of multi-coloured translucent bubbles drifting past.

Sara started to giggle. She couldn't help it.

Myrddin joined her.

A few seconds later they were both laughing so hard that there were tears rolling down their cheeks.

'*Stop it! Stop it now!*' Morgan was having her fun spoilt. She'd won, hadn't she? She had everything that she'd always wanted, didn't she? Yes she did, and it was really unfair that she wasn't being allowed to be smug about it.

'She's really not going to get it!' Sara managed to gasp the words through the laughter and pain.

Myrddin tried to turn to look at Sara. There was an unpleasant crunching sound and his head spun right around.

The laughter stopped.

'Oh!' said Sara.

'Phrrrrrp!' said Myrddin.

The laughter started again.

'Right, I've had enough of this!' Morgan rose high into the air, and as fat drops of rain began to drain from a starless sky, she unleashed some more of her endless supply of fury. The ground began to churn and gurgle, the mud began to steam, and the raindrops hissed and spat as they met the seething earth. Nothing that walked, crawled, hopped, slithered or burrowed would be allowed to survive in this field. Things that slunk were likely to be in bother as well. For a hundred yards in every direction the ground was aglow, oozing and shifting like molten lava. Morgan was making sure that Myrddin and Nimue would not escape death the way she had.

'Finish it. Finish it now.' Morgan motioned for Alec to come forward, which he duly didn't. Morgan motioned again, and this time Alec got the message.

'Oh, you mean me. Finish? Sorry, not with you, finish what?' Alec was new to this 'doing evil' lark and hadn't got the hang of it yet.

Morgan frowned at her new 'ally'; she really was going to have to work out how to kill him, and sooner rather than later.

Alec still looked puzzled, so Sara explained the intricacies of what was expected of him. 'I think she means for you to kill us now, my liege.'

'Really?' Alec looked to Morgan for confirmation. She nodded slowly and mouthed a 'yes'. 'Oh, righto then,' said Alec. He stepped out onto the cooling earth and stood over Sara and Myrddin. Twice he raised Excalibur, and twice he brought it arcing down.

It was done.

It was Morgan le Fay's turn to laugh, and she took it.

Loudly.
Victoriously.
Maniacally.

'Excuse me? Hello up there?'

Morgan stopped laughing and looked down. The old woman looked back up at her.

'Hello, dear. My name's Edna. What's yours?'

An egg yolk sun had cleared the horizon and the dawn was filtering through the trees around Rose Bungalow, though it wasn't shedding any light on things for Thermos.

'Explain it to me just one more time.' Kevin was being maddeningly slow on the uptake, and after his impressive run of success he was now definitely not getting it. Odd, given that multiple dimensions and whatnot should have been right up his street. Right up his street, parking outside his house, and using its own key to his front door to pop in for tea and biscuits.

'Oh bloody hell, man! It's not *that* difficult to understand.' Taff was exhausted and irritable. He was also extraordinarily glad that he was still alive. He was equally glad that Thermos was still alive, but no force in the universe would have made him admit that.

Sara Hagget sighed. She would never forget the events of the previous evening, mainly because she was going to be spending the rest of eternity explaining them to people. She looked pale and exhausted, and she was leaning on Garthang both for support and for medicinal purposes. Her powers were returning slowly, but the physical damage to her body was more than her own healing ability could handle on its own. The overall dynamic of the situation was greatly assisted by the fact that, for once, everybody could see the unicorn.

'Right, one *last* time then.' Emphasising 'last' wasn't going to help much, she'd tried that twice already. Her first recital had taken four hours; this time she was aiming for ten minutes tops. She could have done it in under five as a PowerPoint presentation. 'If I go too fast raise your hand or something. When the two worlds merged and Rose Bungalow appeared here ...'

Thermos raised his hand.

Taff elbowed Thermos hard in the ribs.

Thermos put his hand down again.

'...it brought with it a magical creature called an urk. When Morgan le Fay crashed into the roof of the bungalow, the urk swallowed her.'

'But it didn't kill her?' Thermos rubbed his side and glared at Taff.

Sara nodded. 'Exactly, and that's the important part. Our one chance was that Morgan wouldn't realize that she was in danger, and that she'd be so wrapped up in trying to kill us that she wouldn't spot the shift from reality to illusion.'

'So she's still alive then?' Taff wasn't completely sure he got it either, but that was no reason not to give Thermos a hard time.

Sara turned and stared at the roof of Rose Bungalow. She still wasn't strong enough to disrupt the glamour that was hiding the urk, but she could reach into it with her mind. 'Yes, she's still alive, and her last hours will be spent believing she's won.'

'The illusion she's experiencing is really that good?' The question was Pongo's. He and Myrddin had strolled over during a respite from their heated discussion about why the universe hadn't ended, and between the two of them they were truly covering the long and the short of it.

'It's perfect. Too perfect, in fact. That's why I did a bit of tweaking myself,' explained Sara. She wasn't sure how much she trusted Pongo Smythe. He seemed a good sort, but he was one of the Guild's stooges and as yet Sara didn't fully understand their part in all of this. On the other hand, but for Pongo's eleventh hour intervention they would all be dead and the world would have been yomping down the road to perdition, so that was a point in his favour.

'You tweaked?' Myrddin sounded surprised. 'That was a big risk, especially considering your weakened condition.'

Sara shrugged. 'I couldn't let Morgan have it all her own way at the end. If everything had gone *exactly* as she would have hoped then she might have become suspicious. And anyway, all I did was take the shine off her gloating.'

'Then it's over. We've won.' Myrddin sounded very smug for a man who'd done nothing to help. He might argue that saving Alec's life had been helpful, but in the context of the battle it had only been helpful to Alec.

'Over?' Pongo wasn't happy. His eyebrows were livid. 'Of course it's not over. The entire world has changed. Is *still* changing. Considering what's happened here, God only knows what's happening elsewhere. Two very different worlds have just crashed into each other, and now it's up to us to make sure that neither of them are write-offs. Everywhere is going to be in a state of total chaos, and there's not going to be anybody out there who knows what's really going on or how to deal with it.'

'True, but will that really be so different from how it always is?' That had come out sounding a lot more cynical than Sara had intended. 'People have a way of adapting to almost anything. Look at those four for a start.' She nodded in the direction of the figures loitering on the periphery of the conversation.

Sid was busy attempting to remove dried mud from places where he didn't want to have dried mud. Jack had already completed that onerous task, and had just announced that The Queen's Arms would not be reopening, what with the place being wrecked anyway and there being a bloke behind the bar who was wider than the pool table. John Bostwicke was sampling, with some gusto, the large pork pies that were the remains of Jack and Sid's unfinished picnic. Bladder was crying. It was an understandable emotional response to the events of the last twenty-four hours, though the tears had only started when Jack had made his announcement about the pub.

Pongo nodded. 'Perhaps. There is one person who's going to have to do considerably more adapting than most, so if you'll excuse me, milady, I think I'd best go speak with him.'

'Of course.' Sara smiled. It had been a very long time since anybody had called her that.

A mile away, on the edge of a field soaked in blood, a one-eyed naked sperm donor tied to a spit looks up as the shadow of a figure falls across his legs. It is a boy child, about nine or ten years old, with raven-black hair and eyes that almost seem to glow.

'Hello father,' the child says.

Alec Gardener watched in silence as Pongo made his way over to Falston Bridge. He made not a sound as the little man hauled himself up onto the wall. There was naught but quietude from Alec as Pongo sat down beside him and joined him in staring down into the now still waters of the Wold.

After ten minutes, Pongo cracked. 'Bloody say something, will you?'

Alec smiled. 'Sorry. I was just thinking about how much those tadpoles down there look like sperm. Not very regal of me, is it?'

'So you spotted that thing about being king then?'

'Couldn't miss it really. I think there's a family in London who are going to be mightily pissed off about it.'

'Perhaps, if they even exist in this new world.' Pongo stopped staring at the water and examined the thing that Alec was clutching in both hands. He'd never seen Excalibur up close. Or at all, for that matter. His whole life had been dedicated to its protection, but all he'd ever known of it were the legends, the vague descriptions, the faded sketches in old scrolls. 'May I hold the sword for a moment?'

'No.'

'Oh.' Pongo tried not to sound hurt. He did a pretty shoddy job of it.

'Nothing personal, I just can't let go of the damn thing.'

'Ah! That would be Nimue's doing no doubt. I'll have a word with her about it when she's feeling better.'

'That would be nice; I might need my hands for something else at some point.'

Both men turned at the sound of a scream to see Megan from the chip shop, resplendent in her industrial strength cotton nightie and pink fluffy bunny slippers, exit the village at high velocity, sprint across the bridge and disappear into Falston Wood. A few seconds later something raced after her, following the trail of curlers she had left in her wake, travelling so fast that it was just a purple blur as it passed the two men sitting on the wall.

Alec watched the blur vanish into the trees. 'What was that?'

'That? That was just the beginning,' said Pongo.

Epilogue

'I think we should tell them, Nimue.' Myrddin was trying to sound convincing, although he wasn't sure who he was trying to convince.

'Not yet, old man. There's going to be enough disruption as it is without stirring the pot further with news like that.'

The two were standing at the upper edge of Falston Wood, looking down into the valley below. Falston-on-Wold was still there, but now it was a village that had never existed before. It was going to take a while for this new world to sort itself out, and longer still for people to figure out how to live in it. But they would.

Eventually.

'I said you know it wasn't just good fortune, don't you?' Myrddin was still speaking, but Sara hadn't been listening. She was still finding it difficult to look at him. Why couldn't he have found another body? Any other body.

'What wasn't good fortune?'

'Any of the things that apparently were. Smythe tells me of at least three events that suggest some unseen hand directing the course of all that has transpired here, steering back against a wind that should have blown us all to our doom. And let us not forget the serendipitous nature of that urk. At that moment and given those circumstances, our only hope of victory was for there to have been an urk of some considerable size located precisely where there was one. You told me yourself that you had no comprehension of how it came to be there, protected by a glamour that was troublesome to dispel, even for you.'

'You're saying somebody put it there? Put it there in the knowledge that our victory depended on it?' Sara found it unlikely that Myrddin really believed that.

Myrddin nodded. 'I really believe that, yes.'

Sara looked troubled. 'Then that's even more reason not to tell them the truth. Until we know more about this business, my council has to be that we hold our tongues.'

'I'm not so sure Nimue. Don't the people deserve to be told that their new king is an impostor?'

'Perhaps, but I want to see how things develop first before making any rash decisions.'

'Then we shall wait, and make rash decisions later. And in the meantime?'

Sara thought for a moment, but only in part about Myrddin's question. In the main, her thoughts were about Phillip Morrison. She couldn't help it when his body was standing beside her. 'I think I'll stay here for now. The king will need guidance and this is as good a place as any to start searching for the missing pieces of this puzzle. You?'

'Me? My course has been set by necessity. Soon this body will heed the natural law and reject my essence. Before that happens I must find my original body and return to it.'

'Your original body? The one that we cremated and scattered to the four winds?'

'Indeed.'

'Good luck with that then.'

Thelonius Wisp heard a sound. By working his jaw, assisted by some vigorous nose twitching, he was able to tip himself over and look out through one of the many new cracks in his box. There was nobody there. Nobody there to see the discarded and forgotten watering can full of goo that was sitting in a clearing in the forest. Nobody there to see the pudgy pink hand that was floating in the goo in the watering can that was sitting in a clearing in the forest. Nobody there to see the big green emerald clasped in the pudgy pink hand that was floating in the goo in the watering can that was sitting in a clearing in the forest.

The sound came again. Footsteps in the leaves?

'Um ... hello? Is there anybody out there? A little help would be appreciated.' Wisp was in need of help, that much was certain. The newt was gone and the spell keeping the last remnant of Thelonius Wisp alive had already become unstable. Suddenly a face appeared at the crack in his box, filling his vision. It was a face Wisp recognized.

'Oh bollocks! Why did it have to be you?' said the head of the head of The Venerable Guild of Magi.

Fin